MOST
ANYTHING
YOU
PLEASE

MOST
Anything
YOU
PLEASE

a novel

Trudy J. Morgan-Cole

BREAKWATER
P.O. Box 2188, St. John's, NL, Canada, A1C 6E6
WWW.BREAKWATERBOOKS.COM

A CIP catalogue record for this book is available from Library and Archives Canada.
Copyright ©2017 Trudy J. Morgan-Cole
ISBN 978-1-55081-684-6

COVER PHOTOGRAPH: *Shopkeepers Bell* (Detail)
Image provided courtesy of Love Vintage Books, Willoughby Sydney.

We acknowledge the support of the Canada Council for the Arts, which last year
invested $153 million to bring the arts to Canadians throughout the country. We
acknowledge the financial support of the Government of Canada and the Government
of Newfoundland and Labrador through the Department of Business, Tourism,
Culture and Rural Development for our publishing activities.

PRINTED AND BOUND IN CANADA.

 Canada Council   Conseil des Arts   Canadä   Newfoundland
for the Arts   du Canada   Labrador

Breakwater Books is committed to choosing papers and materials for our books that
help to protect our environment. To this end, this book is printed on a recycled paper that
is certified by the Forest Stewardship Council®.

FOR CHRIS
Keep Singing

Old Brown sells from off the shelf most anything you please

He's got jews-harps for the little boys, lollipops and cheese.

His daughter minds the store and it's a treat to see her serve

I'd like to run away with her but I don't have the nerve.

prelude

AUDREY

We've been a part of Canada since nineteen-forty-nine
For most of twenty-five years we've been having quite a time...

That jeezly beer commercial again, I'm some sick of it. VOCM must play it every ten minutes. Gets on me nerves enough I almost goes to turn off the radio, although I can't get through the working day without a bit of music in the shop. But just as they're singing, *On the island that belongs to us, with the beer that's yours and mine*, the door opens and two little ones, only Rachel's age, comes up to the counter.

– A loafa Sunnybee, package a Red Rose and a pack a Export A for Nan.

She hands me a creased-up five-dollar bill. She's an Ivany, that one—what's her name? Linda, something like that. The other little one, staring down at the candy under the counter, looks like a Taylor.

– Yes, I s'pose it's for your Nan. I hope the likes of you is

9

not taken up smoking yet. Stubbing out my own smoke in the ashtray before I reaches back to get the baker's bread and the cigarettes from the shelf behind me.

– You get the tea yourself, you knows where that's to.

She crosses the floor to the shelves on her side of the counter, where most of the tinned and boxed stuff is. She's moving her hand back and forth between the seventy-two and the hundred-and-forty-four of Red Rose, and I knows what she's going to ask before the words are out of her mouth.

– If I gets the big one how much do I got left?

– You buys that big box, you got sixty-five cents left. Buy the small box, you got a dollar twenty, but your Nan'll be mad at you.

I wasn't bad at math in school and I done a bookkeeping course since then, but this is the kind of math always came most natural to me, because I learned it when I wasn't much bigger than these youngsters. While I puts the things in the paper bag the two little ones are figuring out how to spend the change. I sees all kinds in here and there's youngsters would make up their mind in no time flat. Sure, Rachel would have a can of Pepsi and a bag of chips and not even mind there was fifteen cents left. But these two are the careful kind. They spends a good ten minutes looking at the candy, talking it over.

– If we got ten Icy Cups, five caramels, and a box of Smarties, would we have enough for a can of drink too? What about if it was an Aero bar instead of Smarties?

These two won't set foot outside the store till every cent is gone and they got value for their money. I can sit back down on me stool and not have to worry about change because there won't be any change to give them. Smart youngsters. Linda's Nan was Ruby Hiscock, she used to go around with my sister Marilyn. Ruby was a sensible girl too, though the Hiscocks had some queer ways. The old man, Ruby's uncle, used to always be drunk and out in the middle of Merrymeeting Road in his undershirt ranting about Jesus and Satan and the great war in heaven.

Ping! There goes the door again and another crowd of youngsters streels in off the street. The day blows in with them, cold for all the sunshine outside. The wind is in and it's chilly enough that the young ones shuts the door without me having to bawl at them. Now they're all hanging over the counter, helping the other two make their choices. No doubt hoping they'll get a share. I wish Rachel was here with the crowd of them, but I knows already she won't be. I drove her out of the house after breakfast but who knows where that one spends her time? Not hanging around with the crowd on the street.

It's not like I wants her hanging out with a tough crowd like Marie Walsh's young ones, or the Cadwells, but there's nice youngsters here, like this little one, Ivany, and her friend I'm sure is a Taylor. Why can't Rachel run around with them instead of keeping to herself? But there's no good looking at a youngster and wishing they're any different from what they are. If there's one lesson I've learned, it's that.

Finally they got their candies picked out and young Linda doles them out among her friends before she picks up the bag of things for her Nan.

– Bye, Mrs. Holloway. And all the other ones echoing like a chorus: *Bye, Mrs. Holloway.*

– Say hello to your Nan for me.

They all calls me Mrs. Holloway, never guessing the name is more than half a lie. I was a Holloway, and I was a Missus, but never the two of it together. But that's what I gone by for more than twenty years now and it makes as much sense as any other name.

I got to go around the counter to close the door behind them and damned if the radio isn't playing that same friggin commercial again. It's one of them songs gets stuck in your head and you can't get it out all day then. *Blue, Blue, Blue Star, the beer that's in demand, you can take a toast to Newfoundland with a Blue Star in your hand.*

Youngsters are always leaving the door open, and the spring that's supposed to close it behind them is bust. I must have told Alf about it forty times but do he get around to fixing it? The shoemaker's children go barefoot and I s'pose the carpenter's sister got to live with a busted door.

No sooner am I back behind the counter, turning the radio dial to CJON in hopes of a bit of decent music, when the door opens again and Lorraine Penney comes sailing in.

– Oh my word, Audrey, I needs something for Ted's supper before he gets home from work and I haven't got a thing in the house. What are the men like, at all at all. Sometimes I think you're better off the way you are, none of that kind of trouble at all, my love.

Hoists myself back up on the stool behind the cash register and settles in, now. Lorraine will only get two cans of pork and beans but picking that up will take the better part of an hour once she's gone over what the men are like at all. Time to light up another smoke.

one

SHE KEEPS A LITTLE GROCERY STORE

1936 – 1946

ELLEN

Wes Holloway ran his hand along the edge of the shelf. Ellen could tell from his half-smile that the edge was smooth, no jagged bits or splinters. Good thing, too; there was no time for him to go hauling out the plane and trying to make it perfect. In five minutes she would flip the sign to OPEN and there would be customers coming through that door. She couldn't have Wes in here fussing around like an old woman. She had already delayed opening the shop twice so he could get everything to his liking.

"Go on now, you got work to do and I'll be busy in here soon enough," she said, and he shrugged and turned to go, out through the back door of the shop where he'd hung a little curtain to block off the stairs that led up to the rest of the house, their kitchen and living room and bedrooms. There was more work to do up there. Everything was only half-finished, but Wes had to go work on someone else's house now. Their own would have to wait.

One little room at the foot of the staircase was hidden from the store by the flowered curtain but well within earshot. It was just wide enough for the cot to fit in, and the baby, Frankie, slept there while Johnny played with a pyramid of tins on the floor behind the counter. If Frankie woke up and bawled, Ellen might have to take him up, but she hoped he would sleep at least till she went in to give him a bottle. Once the older ones got home from school, the girls could watch Johnny and Frankie, and Alf could haul the cart around if there were any deliveries to make.

It would all work out.

Ellen flipped the sign to OPEN.

It was as if she had imagined that as soon as the sign was turned over, the door would burst open and a flood of people would pour in. As if they were all congregated out on the corner of Rankin Street and Calver Avenue, ready to hammer the door down. She flipped the sign, and stood for a minute looking out through the square of glass. There were children playing on the street—the small ones, not in school yet—but no sign of adults. She opened the door, took in the fresh cold breeze, heard the ping so she knew the bell was working. It was too cold to have the door standing open so she closed it again and went to sit on a stool behind the counter. Johnny looked up at her. "Somebody come in?" he said.

"No, my love, that was just me. Nobody's here yet. But they'll come soon."

When Wes first started building the house, Ellen had thought they would live on the ground floor and rent out the upstairs rooms. That seemed like a way of making ends meet, earning a bit of money to pay for the privilege of living under their own roof. Most of the houses out here in this new part of town, as in their old neighbourhood downtown, were filled up

15

with renters. Ellen and Wes and the children had been renters themselves, living in three rooms on Casey Street since they'd moved into town. But when she was expecting Frank, Ellen decided their days of living in rented rooms were at an end. Land was cheap here on the fringes of town. Moving from Casey Street to Rankin Street would surely be less of an upheaval than the move from Bonavista Bay in to St. John's.

It was her father who gave her the idea of opening a shop. A natural idea for him, being a merchant. Ellen had to work Wes up to it, convince him that having a shop on the ground floor would be less trouble than having a parade of down-at-heel folks streeling through their upstairs rooms all the time. She found she still had a prejudice against the kind of people who rented rooms instead of owning a house, despite the fact that she had been a renter for six years. She was Ellen Holloway, daughter of Ki Tuff; she had grown up knowing her father was king of Candle Cove, and that made her a princess.

She knew, now, what a tiny thing it was to be king of a place the size of Candle Cove, what a low rung on the ladder an outport merchant like her father occupied. Still, he saw things with a clear eye, her father did. When he came into town last fall he walked out with them to have a look at the new house—Wes just had it framed in then—and he looked around at the houses nearby. They were cheap two-storey row houses, less than ten years old but already starting to look rundown. Ellen thought he was going to say it was a shame, what a lovely house on a nice piece of land she could have if she and Wes moved back around the bay. But instead he looked beyond, to the open fields out past Rankin Street. There were streets there—Suez and Suvla, Hamel and Monchy—names that echoed the places Newfoundland boys had died in battle twenty years ago. Hardly any houses on those streets yet, only rutted roads and long stretches of fields between them.

"Someday that'll all be built up like this is," Ki Tuff said to his daughter.

When he said it, she could see it too—see the way the town was bursting and straining at its seams, pushing north and west away from the harbour. "You should open a shop, is what you should do," he said.

"A shop?" She thought of the stores already open nearby. "There's a Mrs. Hickey got a candy store in the front room of their house, just down over the road here. I suppose we could give up one room to do that."

Her father snorted. "Sure what good is a candy shop? No, I means a proper grocery store."

"Something like Mr. Butler got down there on Goodridge Street, or Davises up on Merrymeeting?" New as the neighbourhood was, it already had its share of shops. "Both of them are close to here."

"Folks in town, they wants a little shop on every street corner. Nobody in town wants to walk half a mile to the one shop like they do out home. They wants a shop right by the house, so they can send the youngsters out to do a message, or order salt pork and cabbage delivered for their supper. You mark my words, you opens up a grocery store and they'll be beating your door down."

Again, her father's words worked that magic in Ellen's mind: she saw their shop on the first floor of the house as soon as he said it. Saw herself behind the counter, her son pulling a handcart of goods to deliver to the neighbours. Saw her family living in the upstairs rooms, the children growing up to work behind the counter, the neighbourhood flourishing around them.

But still she had misgivings. "Grocery stores like that,

17

that's a big operation. It's the men in the family that run them, and they usually got someone else in the shop to help them. I don't see Wes doing that kind of work. He likes his carpentry. And I got the house and youngsters to look after."

Ki Tuff shoved his hands deep in his pockets, rocked back on his heels. He was still looking over the newly built streets, not meeting his daughter's eyes. "Didn't you grow up working alongside me in the shop? What's there to running a store that you don't know as good as any man? And before long your youngsters will be big enough to help. You was behind the counter by the time you was twelve, sure."

And now here the shop was, real and solid and ready to open. Their house stood on the corner, attached to the neighbours on one side but with its own outside wall. Wes built it on Saturday afternoons and weekday evenings, after his regular work building other people's houses was done. He had been working fourteen-hour days for a year now, every day except Sunday, and Ellen was anxious for customers to start coming through the front door so she would be making some money too, doing her bit to help out.

She waited half an hour for the first customer and when the door finally opened it was Mrs. Hiscock from two doors down. She stepped inside and looked around, taking in the rows of shelves that Ellen and the children had stocked with canned goods yesterday.

"Well, Mrs. Holloway. Nice little shop you got here."

"Well now, Mrs. Hiscock, I hope we got everything you might need."

"I was looking for a tin of beans for the mister's dinner. I made bread but I never had time to put on beans."

Over time this was something Ellen would get used to—the need some women had to apologize when they bought

MOST ANYTHING YOU PLEASE

tinned beans or tinned soup. Buying it in tins meant they didn't make it from scratch, and some women felt that anything less was a bit of a failure. Poor Mrs. Hiscock—and she was poor, most of the neighbours were—had six children, took in washing, and had a husband laid up with bad lungs he got working in the mines up in Nova Scotia. Who would judge her if she didn't have time to put a pot of beans on to soak the night before and stand over the stove cooking them all morning? But she judged herself, of course.

Throughout that first morning, the women came in ones and twos to pick up a few items, but mostly to look around and chat. In the months since she moved her family into the half-finished rooms upstairs, Ellen hadn't gotten to know the neighbourhood women very well; she knew some of their names and recognized their children, but she had never been one to stand a long time talking over the back fence. She realized it was a strange choice for such a private person, to put herself behind the counter and invite the whole neighbourhood into a shop that was an extension of her home.

She learned more about her neighbours in those first days of shopkeeping than she had in six months of living on the street. She learned that Myrtle Hiscock was frustrated with her sickly husband and would give anything to go back out home to Spaniard's Bay where she came from, but there was nothing to do out there but fish and her husband was too weak to go out in boat ever again. She learned the police had been called in to break up yet another fight between the two men who owned land down on Liverpool Avenue, and that one man had beaten the other with his own wooden leg in an argument over the property line. She learned that Mrs. Hynes was worried sick that her oldest daughter was only being led along by that young Ivany fellow, that he would get her in trouble and leave

19

her. She learned that Mrs. Kelly's daughter really did get in trouble, with Leo Nolan, but they were getting married and nobody was asking questions.

Every house's door hid a dozen stories behind it, and the families criss-crossed each other like links in a chain, related by blood or marriage. Ellen learned which families were which: Mrs. Hynes was the wife of Hynes-from-the-butcher-shop; they bought their handcart from Nolan-the-blacksmith; Mrs. Hiscock's husband was Poor Mr. Hiscock because of his ill health. Downstairs from Mrs. Hiscock lived That Crowd of Cadwells. Louise Cadwell had a husband who was in and out of jail and a crew of youngsters always in trouble.

What took Ellen longer to figure out was where she herself fit into this pattern of neighbourhood that she saw around her. The fact that she and Wes owned a house and shop meant they were better off than most of their neighbours, and that knowledge hung in the background of all her conversations with the neighbour women. They didn't see her as an equal, exactly, but it wasn't the same as her father's or mother's position behind the counter of the store back in Candle Cove, either. A merchant was someone important in a place like Candle Cove; everyone knew his role, deferred to him that little bit.

But the neighbours here in Rabbittown were merciless to anyone they thought was "getting above themselves." All the while Mrs. Hynes's daughter was running around with Thomas Ivany, the oldest Hiscock girl, who was the same age, was still in school, studying hard and getting top marks on her CHE exams. Her mother bragged to the other women in the shop about her Ella's good grades.

"Wants to be a teacher, she do," Mrs. Hynes sniffed one day after Mrs. Hiscock and Ella left the shop. "Can't she see how

MOST ANYTHING YOU PLEASE

hard her poor mother got it? That young one is fifteen years old, sharp as a tack—she could be working in some shop downtown, making decent money to help them out. I got no time for anyone who thinks they're too good to work."

Ellen had a lot of thoughts about this statement: Did Mrs. Hynes understand that studying in school was hard work? Not to mention teaching youngsters, which young Ella Hiscock would likely end up doing? Mostly, though, Ellen got the message loud and clear: *We don't like folks who think they're better than the rest of us.*

But it wasn't as if she had a lot of time to stew over possible slights. Mrs. Hynes was barely done complaining when another customer came in, and Frankie woke up from his nap and started to cry, and Johnny knocked all the Carnation milk tins off the bottom shelf.

Ellen hadn't realized what long days they would be, here in the shop. She opened the doors at eight and served the trickle of women who came in throughout the morning. She shut it from noon to one o'clock so she could give Wes his dinner, which always had to be something she had prepared the night before. Throughout the morning Frank and Johnny napped and played in the crib in their little room behind the shop; they were usually good babies but she had to pop in and out to tend to them, especially Johnny who was nearly four and wanted to be out of the crib, seeing and doing things.

The schoolchildren got out at three and there was a rush of them into the shop as they bought candy and soda-pop and ran messages for their mothers. Her own oldest ones came straight home from school and the girls took the little boys upstairs to watch them while they got supper ready. Then Ellen would collect up the lists people had dropped off or sent down earlier in the day, things they wanted delivered before

21

supper. She and Alf bagged the orders and put them in the hand cart, and Alf went around the neighbourhood making deliveries. If Johnny had been good all day Ellen would let him ride in the cart on top of the groceries, his little face beaming under his copper curls. "I helping Aff!" he would announce loudly to anyone they passed on the street. Alf hardly ever complained about the extra weight his little brother added to the cart. He was good as gold, Alf was, pulling that cart around all afternoon and then coming home to haul a bucket of coal upstairs for the kitchen stove.

"You needs someone to help you in the shop," Wes said to her at the end of their first month. It was nine in the evening and they were both sitting in the front room, the little ones finally asleep and the older ones in their bedrooms. Alf, Audrey, and Marilyn were supposed to be doing their homework but Ellen didn't have the energy to check that they were doing it. If Frankie woke up and started to cry she didn't know if she'd have the strength to pick him up out of the crib.

"I can't hire anybody," Ellen said. "We're barely making enough to cover the cost of the stock I'm putting on the shelves. If we make any little bit extra, I can't afford to pay out wages to anyone—not yet. Maybe never. The shop was supposed to bring in money, but I got to admit I'm having doubts. Maybe it was a bad idea."

"Now, you can't go thinking like that, girl," Wes said. "A shop's a long-term proposition, like. It's not like my work—I works on building a house and gets a week's pay on Friday, and after so many weeks the job is done. A shop needs time— people got to get used to buying from it, and we got to get used to what sells, and how much of everything to order, and all that. Someday, no doubt, it'll make money. And someday the youngsters will be big enough to do their fair share behind the counter. Alf's a great help already, and Audrey will be in a few years. But for now—well, it's wearing you down, my love."

"The girls are a help around the house, but that's only after school. When Frankie's a bit bigger I can put him and Johnny out in the yard to play, but right now I'm only easy in my mind if they're close by."

"I'm thinking about Susan," Wes said. "She's fifteen now, old enough to be going into service somewhere, and Mother says she's getting right restless out home. What would you say to us taking her in here, to give a hand with the youngsters while you're in the shop? It'd be one more mouth to feed, but she'd be a lot of help till our own girls are older."

It was the obvious solution and Ellen had been thinking of it herself, going through her own family and Wes's family for young girls of a suitable age who might want to move into town. Wes's sister Susan was the perfect age and though she had been only a child when Wes and Ellen left Candle Cove, Ellen had never heard anything but good about her. Taking her in would stretch them in every way—they would have to put a cot up in the already-crowded room where Audrey and Marilyn shared a bed. But Susan would be able to watch the boys while the older children were at school; she could cook meals and help with cleaning, and maybe take the odd turn behind the counter. Feeding her would cost far less than hiring a stranger for wages, and if business started to pick up they could give her a bit of pocket money.

Susan arrived on the *Kyle* a month later. Marilyn latched onto her like a new big sister, which put Audrey's nose a little out of joint until Susan took over the job of curling Audrey's hair into ringlets for church Sunday morning, and suddenly Audrey, too, adored Susan. With Susan upstairs during the day, Ellen was able to leave the two little boys in her care and knew

23

she would come upstairs at dinnertime and suppertime to find a meal on the table.

Still, Ellen missed her own cooking, missed preparing meals for the family in her own kitchen. Once Susan was comfortable behind the shop counter, Ellen made it a habit to give her the afternoon shift once a week so Ellen could cook supper. She usually picked Wednesday: a nice mid-point to break up the week a little. So Ellen was standing over the stove making drawn butter to go with the salt fish, listening to her small children play and her bigger ones do homework, when Alf, who had been out making deliveries, came running up the stairs.

"Mom! Mom! Susan says you gotta come down to the shop now!"

"Oh, my foot," said Ellen—her strongest expletive. "Does it have to be right now?"

"She says right now, yeah. Scabs Cadwell stole a whole bunch of candy and I wanted to run after him and beat him up but Susan said to come up and get you instead. I don't know why she wouldn't let me chase him. He wants a good beating, is what he wants."

"Susan is right—no beating up any of the Cadwells. You stay up here. Audrey, get over here. Just keep stirring this, don't let it catch on the bottom of the pan."

Downstairs, she found Susan halfway between fuming and crying. "Oh, Nell, I could just wring his neck—I never saw him do it, but when he was halfway out the door I saw he had the gobstoppers in his hand and called him back, but he just took off, and when he was out on the sidewalk he looked back in at me, just brazen as brass, like he was darin' me to come after him. And there was four or five other youngsters in here, and they all knew he done it, and I thought if I took off after him they might steal more stuff. I didn't know what to do, and then Alf came in, and…oh, I'm some sorry I let it happen. I gets that miz-mazed when the store is full of youngsters."

"It's all right, Susan, it's not your fault." The words were automatic, even while Ellen thought, I should have stayed down here and let Susan cook supper. He wouldn't have had the nerve to do it if I was here. All the Cadwells were loud, unruly, and disrespectful to adults. And what could you expect, with their father in jail for stealing? One time she caught the oldest one—Warren, was it?—out on the sidewalk with a rock in his hand, right in front of the big shop window where she'd painted the specials and prices up in whitewash. Ellen gave him a hard look and he scampered off. She had been afraid since the shop opened that sooner or later some youngster would swipe something. Most everything was back behind the counter but she always had a few small things laid out in bins on the counter, squares and dandy-cakes and hard candies. Odds were good if any child was going to take advantage, it would have been one of the Cadwells.

"Which one was it?" Scabs, Alf had said, but Scabs and Butch and Flea-Bag weren't their actual names. There was a tangle of boys and one girl—Soose—but she was a tiny thing, only Johnny's age. Could the thief have been the same boy she scared away when he was about to bazz a rock at the window?

Susan sniffled. "Not the biggest one and not the little fellow—the one in between. Ricky? I think? The young ones all calls him Scabs."

"Richard." Ellen tried to get a picture of him in her mind's eye, to pull tow-headed Richard—scabs and all—from the snarl of little Cadwells. It wasn't their mother's fault. She was doing her best, no doubt. "And you're sure you saw him with the candy in his hand. You couldn't have made any mistake?"

TRUDY J. MORGAN-COLE

"No, not a chance, I told you, his fist was full of it and he looked back at me brazen as brass. Like he was darin' me to do anything. Should I have let Alf go after him? It might have taught him a lesson."

"Not the lesson he needs to learn," Ellen said. She went to the door and turned the sign to CLOSED. "You go upstairs, finish putting supper on the table. Put a plate in the warmer for me—I'll have mine after." She took her coat and hat from the hook behind the counter, untying her apron before she put them on.

At the Cadwells' door, one of the boys—the smallest one—opened after Ellen's third series of sharp knocks. "Mudder ain't home," he said.

"Not home? At suppertime?" Ellen stared him down, the same look that quenched his older brother with the rock. "Mrs. Cadwell!" she called, over the little boy's head. She heard the racket of the other youngsters inside, and another boy's voice yelled, "Flea-Bag! Get in outa that!"

"Missus from the store is at the door and she wants Mudder!"

"Get back in here!" Little Flea-Bag was yanked back and a taller boy appeared. Was this the culprit? "Sorry Missus, me mudder's gone out."

"Where is she gone to, supper hour?"

"Gone over to Nan's."

"Fine, I'll go to your grandmother's and talk to her there." Ellen was bluffing, of course, but she was sure someone in the neighbourhood could tell her where Mrs. Cadwell's mother lived, if it came to that. She pitched her voice loud, to carry past the roomful of children.

"Mrs. Holloway! Is that you, ma'am?" Louise Cadwell, thin, red-headed, with a face that always looked like she'd just been slapped, came out wiping her hands on her apron. "Warren, you little bugger—sorry, ma'am—did you tell Mrs. Holloway I was gone out?"

"But you told me to say—*owww!*" One of the Cadwells pinched the other, and the protest subsided. Ellen stood as tall and dignified as she could in their dirty front room, sweeping the assembled Cadwells with her eyes as their mother murmured apologies—for her children's behaviour, for the state of the house, for not coming to the door.

Ellen didn't want Louise Cadwell's apologies. She didn't want to be here at all, in this dingy room with the bare wood floor and a mattress and blankets in the corner to show that at least some of the children slept here. A line of clothes hung drying in one corner, and more clothes were thrown into piles in wooden crates on the floor. A barrel in the corner reminded her that while the Holloways' house and store was hooked up to the city water line, people on these little side streets still had to lug water in buckets from a pump on the corner. The Cadwells' house looked like a place where people were camping out, not living, and she was sorry to have brought this poor woman any more trouble. But there was no room here for compromise: other children saw him steal, and other children would hear what Ellen did about it, as would their parents.

It wasn't hard, standing there in her good coat and hat, to elicit a confession from the middle boy, though it was harder to watch Mrs. Cadwell smack him across the mouth. "I'd make him give it back if I could, ma'am, but you know he got that eat."

"Not just me! I gave a piece to every one of ye!" the culprit yelled, pointing a finger at his brothers and sister. "Every one of them ate it and if I gets in trouble they all should!"

"I'd make him give you the five cents if we had it," Mrs.

TRUDY J. MORGAN-COLE

Cadwell said, and her teary eyes caught Ellen's.

"That wouldn't be fair to you," Ellen said. "Richard—it is Richard, isn't it?—he's the one that took the candy and he's the one that should pay. I want him over at the shop Saturday morning an hour before we open up. Most Saturdays I gets one of my own youngsters to sweep out the shop and dust off the shelves and wash the window, but if he does the job for me this week, and does it to my satisfaction, we'll say no more about it."

"You hear that, Ricky?" Mrs. Cadwell said. "Mrs. Holloway's going to let you off for what you done, but you got to go clean up the store Saturday morning. And you better do a good job or I'll give you another lickin' to go with the one you're gettin' tonight."

Richard, or Scabs, shot Ellen a look of pure hatred, blue eyes burning at her from underneath long gold lashes and a tangle of curls. He was about the same age as Audrey, and he'd be a pretty child if he wasn't so dirty and sullen. Ellen would have to watch him like the hawk every second he was in the shop, not just Saturday morning but every time he came in from now on. But word would get around.

"She's some crooked!" Ellen heard the words burst out of Richard Cadwell even before she had the door closed. She remembered fishermen back home complaining that her own father drove a hard bargain, or cheated them out of the value of their catch when he gave them credit for their flour or molasses or twine. And her father behind the counter when they were all gone at the end of the day, telling her, "You can't run a business and have everyone like you, Nellie my maid. That's the one thing you cannot do."

She went back to her shop, back upstairs to her dried-out fish and the last scrapings of drawn butter.

ELLEN

"I'll take a pound of ham and a quarter pound of baloney," said Mrs. Ryan. Ellen laid the ham out on a square of brown paper and carefully sliced through it. She gave Mrs. Ryan a discount, both because the ham was going to go bad soon and because Mrs. Ryan needed the discount. Such a tricky thing, buying meat, because there was always a demand for it but usually not as much as you bought, and unlike the canned and boxed goods it would go bad if it didn't sell. Cheese was the same way, though at least there you could slice off the moldy bits and the rest was still good to sell. It would be easier if everything came in tins but she didn't like to imagine what tinned cheese would be like. Ellen sliced the meat, wrapped it in paper and tied the parcel with twine, and wrote down the cost of Mrs. Ryan's items in the book.

In front of the counter, his head about level with his mother's waist, Jimmy Ryan was just at the right level to eye the candy under the counter. That's why the candies were there, of course, right where the children could see them but not get their hands on them, and ask the parents to buy a treat. But it seemed almost unfair in the case of the Ryans as Jimmy set up a howl for something his mother couldn't possibly afford. On the other hand, it was all going on a tab she'd never be able to pay off, so what difference did it make? "Go on, let him have the candy—I'll throw it in for nothing," she told Mrs. Ryan. With a Peppermint Nob stuffed in his big loud gob, Jimmy quieted down long enough for his mother to pick up her parcel and make it to the door.

Funny, Ellen thought, that she would do that for someone else's youngster when she wouldn't dream of doing it for her own. Alf, Audrey, and Marilyn all knew the best way to make sure they never got anything in a shop was to cry and beg for it. Just last week she left Susan to watch the store and took the girls down to Ayre and Sons for winter coats, hats, and boots. Ellen planned to make a little treat out of the day, let the girls try on their new things and then walk up to Wood's Candy Store for an ice cream afterwards. But Marilyn got it into her little head that she wanted the red tartan coat with the fur trim, pretty but not as practical as the one Ellen had picked out. When Marilyn stuck her bottom lip out and stamped her foot and said, "But I wants the pretty red coat!" Ellen was quick to say, "You're getting the coat I picked out for you, and you should be thankful. There's little girls who got no coats and would be glad to have a nice warm one like that. And if you makes any fuss there'll be no treat afterwards."

Marilyn's lip still trembled, but Audrey, two years older and wiser, jabbed her elbow into her sister's ribs. "Hush. I wants me cake and ice cream!" she hissed at Marilyn, and Marilyn subsided. She still didn't look happy about the sensible navy blue coat as the salesgirl packed it away in a box with the other items to be delivered later, but she kept a still tongue in her head, and Ellen decided that was enough of an effort for a nine-year-old. The promised ice cream went ahead as planned. She didn't mind aiding and abetting in the spoiling of little Ryans—the poor mortals had few enough pleasures—but Ellen was bound and determined that none of her lot would grow up spoiled.

The memory made her call out as the Ryans opened the door to the street and a gust of wintry air blew in with a few snowflakes. "Mrs. Ryan! Could any of your crowd use a winter coat? I just got new ones for all the youngsters—they outgrow them so fast, you know. But the old coats are still in good shape."

Mrs. Ryan, grateful for the offer, stayed to pick up an armload of old coats. Each coat had already been worn through a few winters—the dark green coat passed from Audrey to Marilyn and was now too small for either of them, and the brown coat that Audrey wore for two years was frayed at the cuffs. Alf's old coat was far too big for Johnny, there was such a gap in age between the boys. Might as well let Jimmy Ryan get some use out of it.

Enough money for new coats and new boots—in these hard times, when so many families were barely getting by, Ellen knew she had a lot to thank the Lord for. At bedtime, when the day's work was done, she went through the house, looking at them all, saying goodnight. Audrey and Marilyn snuggled together in the big bed, already both asleep in a tangle of long, skinny arms and legs. In the boys' room, Frankie snored in the crib. Johnny was asleep on the bottom bunk while up on top Alf was reading a Hardy Boys book by the light of his flashlight.

"Put that light out and go to sleep, you'll ruin your eyes,"

TRUDY J. MORGAN-COLE

she said to the glow under the quilt, and closed the door behind her.

It was a grand feeling, at the end of the day, to sit down in the living room with Wes while he read the *Evening Telegram*. Susan sat up with them for a half-hour after the dishes were done, paging through a *Ladies' Home Journal*, to mark her status as a grown-up. Ellen knitted, using the quiet evening hours to churn out mitten after mitten. When Susan said goodnight and slipped off to the girls' room, Wes folded up his paper and said, "Well, Nell girl, another day done. How was things in the shop today?"

"Oh, I can't complain. I don't know if I should have ordered in so much ham as I did from Shortall's, though. I thought people would want more of it, with Christmas coming on."

"It's a worry all right," Wes said. "Folks will want more candy and the like with Christmas coming on too, won't they?"

"I'm getting extra Peppermint Nobs and Kisses from Purity Factories, along with the syrup. They should be delivered Friday."

"I passed Alf on my way home from work today, hauling that cart up from old Mrs. Fifield's place, all the way up Rankin Street. He's turning into a grand little worker. In a few years I'll be taking him out on jobs with me."

"Was Johnny riding up with him? He loves going around on that cart. I 'low by the time Alf's ready to start working with you, Johnny will be big enough to do the deliveries himself. He can't wait." It was hard to imagine four or five years into the future. Alf would be a young man and the little boys half-grown. Audrey and Marilyn would be young girls, working behind the counter—oh, how grand it would be to have more help in the shop—and flirting with boys when they thought their mother wasn't looking. The image of it, of all the years to come, made her brain swim.

"It'll get easier, girl, never fret," Wes said.

"Will it?"

"It will. Times are hard all over, but this Depression can't last forever, that's what the men in the know all say."

He generally looked on the bright side, Wes did, while Ellen herself was more likely to scan the skies for the dark clouds that might bring rain. It was good she was that way: someone had to remember to batten down the hatches when a storm was coming. But she counted on Wes to keep her spirits up. She knitted one more row, then cast off. Another mitt done: she'd have a pair for each of the youngsters for Christmas, and a pair of socks too.

I will believe it, she told herself as she wound up the ball of wool and stuck her needles crosswise through it. It was almost Christmas, a time of hope and joy. She would choose to believe Wes's happy vision of the future—the shop making money, all their bills paid, the children safe, everyone secure. Just for this week, at least, she would really try to stop worrying about everything that might go wrong, try to be grateful for what they had.

She remembered this resolution a few days later, when she was down in the shop selling two bottles of Purity syrup to Bridie Kelly. "A treat for the youngsters for Christmas Eve— we got something a bit stronger for the rest of us," Mrs. Kelly laughed, then added, "But you Methodists are all temperance, I s'pose—don't approve of a drop even at Christmas?"

"I'm sure it's none of my business, Mrs. Kelly." Ellen rang in the purchase and handed the change across the counter.

"Nell?" Susan's voice, from the doorway, interrupted Mrs. Kelly's wheezy laughter. "Can you—I can watch the shop for a few minutes, could you come up and have a look at the boys?

TRUDY J. MORGAN-COLE

They both woke up coughing, and I think Johnny's running a fever."

What bad luck, sick youngsters at Christmas. Ellen went upstairs to find Johnny's little face was red with fever and Frankie was warm too. The two of them were coughing and when Johnny gasped for a breath in between coughs she heard the telltale *whoop* that made her heart sink. Surely she had imagined that; most likely it was just a bad cold. They were both outside playing in the yard yesterday and if they took their caps off Susan might not have had the sense to put them back on. And then Johnny was riding around on the cart with Alf in all the cold wind.

Ellen let Susan mind the shop for the morning, shooed the older children outside to play in spite of the bitter wind. She spent her morning tending to the two little boys, giving them honey for their coughs and using cool wet towels to try to bring down the fever. Between coughs, Johnny wanted to know if Santa Claus would still come even if they were sick.

"He will, my love, don't mind about that. Santa Claus visits the sick children too."

"He better. He's bringing me a truck." Johnny's eyes widened as he pulled in another wheezing gasp and coughed again.

When everyone came home for dinner she went back down to the shop, leaving instructions for Susan, and spent the afternoon worrying. Neither of the little boys was better the next day, Christmas Eve. Wes, of course, assured her it was only a head cold. Ellen told Susan to keep Frankie and Johnny in their room, and ordered Alf to keep out, just in case it was the whooping cough. She sent a message to Wes's cousin Alice over on Freshwater Road, asking if she could have Aunt Mabel and Uncle Caleb to her house for Christmas dinner instead of them coming to Wes and Ellen as they'd planned. She kept the shop open till the early afternoon, when the man came around selling Christmas trees off a truck. Then Ellen shut up the shop and sent Wes and Alf down to pick out a tree.

Upstairs, she found Susan peeling vegetables. "The boys is both after falling off to sleep," Susan said, and Ellen decided to take that as a good sign. The door to the girls' room was closed and she heard Audrey and Marilyn giggling behind it. "Don't come in, Mama, you can't come in!" Marilyn shrieked when she opened the door a crack, and Audrey said, "But can you bring us the twine and scissors, please?"

"They're in the kitchen drawer," Ellen said, and when Audrey slipped out to get the twine and scissors Ellen felt her forehead, which was still cool. In the boys' room, Frankie was asleep, tangled in sweaty sheets, but Johnny had just woken up and was coughing again. A bottle of cough medicine sat on the nightstand. When did Susan last give him a spoonful, she wondered. Was it too soon for more? Between each cough he gasped, and after the spasm passed, he collapsed into her arms. "Mummy, my chest hurts."

"Be a big boy, now. You got to get better before Santa comes at midnight." But the mention of Santa sparked no light now in his red-rimmed eyes. Ellen wondered if should she mention that Santa really was going to bring him a truck. But no: perhaps tomorrow he would be better and enjoy the surprise.

Ellen hadn't had a doctor in the house since Alf, Audrey, and Marilyn all had the measles together when they lived down on Casey Street. She went to the hospital to have Johnny and had a midwife for Frankie, so she'd never had reason to call a doctor. Would Dr. Andrews even come out on Christmas Eve? He certainly wouldn't come tomorrow unless it was life or death. Should she wait till Boxing Day? Johnny started

TRUDY J. MORGAN-COLE

coughing again, sucking in air like he was drowning, and she told Susan to go out and get the doctor.

He came just as Alf and Wes were setting up the tree in the living room. Frankie was awake and coughing too now, and Ellen was back and forth between him and Johnny with the cool cloths and the cough medicine. "Not a very pleasant way to be spending Christmas Eve, is it?" said Dr. Andrews.

"Nor for you either, sir. But I 'low people get sick every day of the year, don't they?"

"They surely do, Mrs. Holloway. Never a Christmas goes by without a tragedy for some poor family. I just came from an old lady over on Goodridge Street who won't make it to New Year's." He pulled out his stethoscope and listened to each boy's chest, his face grave. "Now this, this is very serious business, Mrs. Holloway, and not the kind of news anyone wants to hear at Christmas, but I'm sure it is the whooping cough. And your other children have been exposed to it too."

Ellen stayed in the boys' room all evening, letting Susan give the other children their supper of salt fish and raisin bread. The girls were sent off to bed, neither of them showing signs of a cough or fever yet, thank the Lord. Wes, Susan, and Alf decorated the tree, wrapped the presents, filled the stockings. Alf was pleased as punch, Ellen knew, to be given this grown-up role when last year he was sent off to bed with the little ones to let the Christmas magic happen while he slept. Now the only Christmas magic Ellen wished for was that both boys would get better, and none of the others would get sick.

Marilyn woke with a fever Christmas morning, and coughed over breakfast. Frankie seemed a little better, but Johnny was worse. The longed-for red fire truck, which Ellen had bought with the other gifts at Bowring's Toyland, made him smile, but he didn't have the energy to play with it. The opening of presents was subdued, and Marilyn went back to bed with her new doll tucked in beside her. The cough worked its way up through the family from youngest to oldest; Audrey was sick by nightfall on Christmas night. Alf was the only one of the children spared. Susan, like Ellen and Wes, had already had the whooping cough when she was younger.

The shop was supposed to re-open on the 27th, the day after Boxing Day, but Ellen had neither time nor heart to be down behind the counter. "And it might not even be safe," she told Wes. "Everyone on the street knows our children got the whooping cough; for all we know we could be spreading it by having the shop open."

On New Year's Day, Frankie seemed a little better at last, and the doctor, making what had become a daily visit, gave his first approving nod. "I think this little fellow is out of the woods," he said. "He'll need a lot of rest, still, but he's on the mend." Ellen hoped he would say the same about Johnny— after all, the two boys got sick at the same time, so shouldn't they get better at about the same time?—but the doctor frowned when he put his stethoscope to Johnny's chest. "I'm afraid this little chap may be developing pneumonia."

The day after New Year's, Wes had to go back to work, and Susan offered to open the shop so Ellen could continue to look after the children. So Susan and Wes went to work, Alf went to school, and Ellen stayed upstairs, making soup and changing sheets and caring for Frankie, who was feeling better and whining about having to stay in bed, and Marilyn and Audrey, who were just now getting into the worst of the coughing spells. Johnny, who did have pneumonia, was getting weaker instead of stronger despite all her care.

Ellen knelt by her bedside at night and prayed for all the

TRUDY J. MORGAN-COLE

children to be spared, but in her heart she knew that was asking a lot, even from the Almighty. She had five healthy children with not a single loss, not even a miscarriage, and she was fairly sure she was expecting another one. The reckoning was due. It was as if she owed one of them, not to God but to Fate, or some such thing. How could any one woman, any couple, be as fortunate as she and Wes had been? But how could she pick, if she were asked to give up one? She wondered if she would trade this unborn baby, curled tight in her womb, in exchange for Johnny. *Dear Lord, if I lose this one I won't complain, I promise not to shed a tear, as long as you spare my Johnny,* she prayed, and then was knocked over by a wave of guilt. Who was she, to juggle life and death like that?

It wasn't a choice she was given. Slowly, as the new year of 1938 took shape around them, the coughs were less harsh and frequent, and three of the children got a little better each day. Audrey and Marilyn had missed a month of school but they were bright girls, they would be able to catch up. Ellen knew for sure now that she was pregnant, but she had no time to think about that. All her worries gathered around Johnny, who was still listless, still coughing and struggling for breath, showing no improvement.

On January 23rd, a month to the day since the whooping cough started, Ellen let Frankie get up and play in the front room. He ran the new toy trucks, his own and Johnny's, over the rug, making "vroom" noises. Johnny wouldn't be playing with his truck. Under an oxygen tent in the Grace Hospital, Johnny struggled for breath. The shop was closed again as Susan came back upstairs to care for the three who were recuperating, and Ellen went to the hospital to sit by Johnny's bedside. She blinked at the cold, harsh air as she stepped outside for the first time since Christmas. The house, the beds of her sick children—this was the only world Ellen had lived in, these past few weeks. She hadn't even been to church.

Johnny lived for three days in the hospital. Ellen sat beside her four-year-old, holding his hand. Sometimes she read out loud, as she had been doing to the children throughout their illness. She was reading *Treasure Island*, which Johnny was probably too young to enjoy anyway, but after he went to the hospital she switched to the Psalms. All those promises of care and protection.

But not all promises were to be fulfilled in this life. Ellen had always understood this, always known that out of a family of five children, soon to be six, she wasn't likely to see them all grow to adulthood. Her own mother had lost three of nine. She thought of Johnny riding around on the top of the delivery cart, Alf hauling him with the sacks of groceries. People would say, "Not long now before he'll be pulling that thing himself," and Johnny would say, "Someday I be big!" But he wouldn't be.

Johnny would be all right, safe in the arms of Jesus. *But will I be all right without him?* Ellen wondered. She held his hand tightly, and imagined that when he struggled for that last breath, Jesus would come and she would let go of Johnny's hand and place it in Jesus's. Knowing who was taking him, and where, she should not have found it as hard as she did to let go.

TRUDY J. MORGAN-COLE

AUDREY

Years from now, Rachel will ask questions like "What do you remember about the war, Nan?" Or Alf's young ones: "What was the store like in the olden days, Aunt Audrey?" By that time Audrey's memories will be tangled like skeins of wool in her mother's knitting bag—Audrey's never been much of a knitter herself. Earliest memories? Olden days? THE WAR, all in capitals like on a child's school project.

By the time she's in her sixties—which is how long it takes, apparently, before the young ones start showing any interest in anything she might have to say—she finds it hard to piece together which memories belong to which events. She remembers some things sharply: the green tartan of a skirt she once had; the scratchy heavy wool tights she and Marilyn used to wear on winter mornings. She remembers songs, of course, what was playing on the radio or the record player at various important moments in her life. But she doesn't always have a memory to hang on a tag. The War, for example—she was eleven when it started, old enough that she should remember, as Alf claims to remember, the king's speech on the radio and the big, bold headlines. But Audrey just remembers the war taking shape around her, forming part of her childhood: blackouts at night and uniforms in the streets gradually becoming part of reality. When you're eleven or twelve, these things are just the way the world is.

She knows, if she stops to think about the dates, that Johnny was dead and June was born before the war started. Her memories of that Christmas are blurred by time; her mother's stories are layered over Audrey's own memories till she can't tell which is which. Ellen used to tell these stories often when Audrey and the others were growing up, reminding them about the little brother whose memory faded with the years. Those visits from the doctor, so rare in Audrey's childhood, blend together with the night the doctor came to her mother's room and, hours later, Audrey and Alf and Marilyn were paraded into the room to see the small, blanket-wrapped bundle that was called June.

Audrey remembers the green velveteen dress she wore as a bridesmaid for her aunt Susan's wedding. Not that she and Marilyn and Alf ever called her Aunt Susan. When Audrey was growing up, any woman your mother's age who was close enough to sit down for a cup of tea at your kitchen table was Aunt Something, regardless of blood relation; any friend of your father's was Uncle just as much as his brothers were. But Susan, who actually was their aunt, was only a few years older than they were. She had always seemed more like a cousin or an older sister. When Susan got married in the minister's study in Gower Street church, Audrey got a brand-new dress, bought at the London, New York and Paris downtown. Knee length, padded shoulders, a tiny waist with—did it have a black velvet

TRUDY J. MORGAN-COLE

ribbon around the waist? That's the way Audrey remembers it anyway—dark green velveteen with black trim, suitable for a winter wedding.

Being a bridesmaid, Audrey got to join the adults for dinner at Stirling's restaurant afterwards, while Alf stayed home to watch Marilyn and the little ones. Audrey at twelve, sitting up straight between her father and her grandmother, eating roast chicken and an ice-cream sundae. She remembers music playing, and when Frank Sinatra sang "I'll Never Smile Again," Susan looked at Marvin and smiled. "They're playing our song."

Once the wedding was over, Susan moved out of their house and stopped working in the shop. Over the Christmas holidays that year, Ellen taught Audrey how to work the cash register, and in the new year she was given a regular turn behind the counter, from the time school let out until suppertime. She didn't earn wages, but she got an increase in her pocket-money because she was helping out. And Audrey liked the work. She liked the way grown-ups had to look her in the eye and talk to her differently because she handled their money and passed them things from the shelves.

Her friends walked home from school with her and stayed at the counter chatting, buying apricot squares and bottles of Pepsi. Audrey told them they had to move down to the end of the counter and shut up when an adult came in, because her mother didn't want the shop to look like a hangout for hard tickets. Valerie Hynes and Lorraine Allen laughed about being labelled hard tickets, though Lorraine was a little bit of a hard case—she wore lipstick if she knew she wouldn't get caught, and told the girls that she had kissed Freddy Ivany out behind Nolan's Garage.

"And now Freddy's going around with that one Cathy

MOST ANYTHING YOU PLEASE

Kelly from Presentation. I hope she knows what she's getting into," Lorraine said, leaning on the counter and cracking her gum. Audrey was glad her mother was upstairs in the kitchen: Ellen hated to see girls chewing gum. She said it looked cheap and that any girl who chewed gum when she was twelve would smoke when she was sixteen. Lorraine said she'd already tried smoking, but Valerie agreed with Audrey that both that and the kissing story were lies. Just Lorraine trying to make herself out tougher than she was.

"Freddy's mother'd skin him alive if she knew he was running around with a Kelly. All them Catholic girls are fast anyway, I don't doubt Cathy's cute enough to look out for herself," said Valerie now. "Sure she was going around with Mike Kavanagh last year, and he was in Grade Nine at St. Bon's then, and her only in Grade Seven."

"She developed early," Audrey said, and they all snickered.

"If you call it developing when you puts socks in your bra," said Lorraine. "And I know for a fact she does it because Joanie went over there one time to play with her little sister Tessa, and they went into the bedroom and caught Cathy stuffing her bra."

There was a hint of envy as well as disapproval in Lorraine's voice. Audrey wondered what it would be like, to be brazen enough to stuff socks into your brassiere and go around with older boys. When she looked at the boys in her class in school and the boys on the street, they looked like they had always looked: round-faced, snot-nosed, loud and angry, and a bit stupid. She couldn't imagine wanting to kiss one of them. When she thought about fellows at all it was the faces of film stars and singers she cut out of magazines and taped on the wall over her bed. If someone who looked like Cary Grant and sang like Frank Sinatra came strolling down Rankin Street and dropped into the store looking for a pack of cigarettes, well, that would be a different story.

"There's no fellows around here worth going to that kind of trouble for," said Audrey.

"There's not now, but there will be soon," Valerie said. "There's a whole boatload of American soldiers comin' in sometime this week." There were already Canadian servicemen in town, but Americans were something different altogether, and the cold January air was filled with anticipation. People talked about their arrival like it was either the Second Coming or the devil himself rising from hell, depending on who you were talking to.

Lorraine laughed. "What, you think American soldiers are going to look at the likes of us?"

"Not now, of course not. I s'pose the war will be over long before Mother ever lets me go on a date with anyone, let alone an American. But it'll be exciting to see them anyway. You think they'll all look like fellows in the movies?"

"We should go down and see the ship come in. I bet there'll be a crowd down to the harbour," Lorraine suggested.

"What day will it be?" Audrey didn't have a lot of free time, between school and the shop, but maybe if the American ship came in on a Saturday afternoon, she might be able to get away and see it.

But it turned out the *Edmund B. Alexander* was arriving in St. John's early the next Wednesday morning. "Maybe they'll close school," Valerie suggested to Audrey. "Then we could go."

"Or if they don't close, we could pip off," Lorraine said.

"We'd get in trouble." Audrey couldn't even imagine how mad her mother would be if Audrey pipped off school to go down to the harbour and watch a ship come in.

There was plenty of talk in the shop that week about the

MOST ANYTHING YOU PLEASE

ship. "Are you going down to see it?" Audrey asked Alf. Alf was fourteen and done with school since his Grade Nine exams; he worked on construction with their father now.

"And get docked for a morning's work? Not a chance. I'll see more than enough Americans once we gets working down on that base they're building in Pleasantville." Alf seemed to see the Americans only as a possible source of work, but it was different for boys, Audrey figured. Valerie and Lorraine were still talking about skipping off school to see the ship come in.

We'll start off walking to school like we always do," Lorraine told her, "and we won't go past the school, we'll turn over by Hanlon's shop and go down towards the harbour. There's going to be hundreds of people down there. Nobody will spot us, and we can go back into school at lunchtime."

"What would we do about the youngsters?" The three girls always walked to school together every morning, trailed by a crowd of their younger brothers and sisters. Marilyn would never forgive Audrey if she took off without her.

"Ah, I'll come up with some story, they can go on ahead of us," Lorraine said. "We'll say we're coming after and we'll just never show up to school."

Audrey lay in bed the night before and wondered would they really go through with it. Her mother had told her time and again that she relied on Audrey, her oldest girl, to be responsible and sensible. "Not like some of them foolish young things," Ellen would sniff, and Audrey knew she was talking about girls like Lorraine, or like Cathy Kelly.

Audrey and Marilyn were dressed for school in their coats, hats, mitts, and gaiters on Wednesday morning. Frankie, who still had a year to go before he started school, played on the floor, and June babbled in her crib as their mother wiped down the counters and got the shop ready for the day. Lorraine and Valerie with their own crowd of younger siblings—two for Lorraine, four for Valerie—stopped by to pick them up.

It was a long walk down to Holloway School on Long's Hill. Audrey always felt a little sense of pride that the school had the same name as her family, though it was named after a far more important Holloway who her father said was no relation. They all sloshed through the sloppy snow as far as the corner where LeMarchant Road turned into Long's Hill when Lorraine said, "I'm going into the store for a pack of gum. Audrey, Val, want to come in with me? You kids go along with Marilyn, now."

Obedient as a row of ducklings, the youngsters trailed along behind Marilyn in the direction of the school while Audrey, Valerie, and Lorraine pretended to turn back, lingering just out of sight. "Now we only got to wait till they're a good piece ahead of us and we'll head downtown."

"No." Audrey surprised even herself when she blurted the word. "I can't. Marilyn will know right away what's on the go when she don't see me in school, and she'll tell Mom."

"So what? I'm sure Joanie'll tell on me, too, but by the time anyone finds out, it'll be over. We'll have been and seen it, and no matter what Mom or Pop does to me I'm not missing out on that." Lorraine, brazen as brass, and Valerie, always willing to follow. Audrey, half-walking, half-running, caught up with Marilyn and the younger ones.

There were more students missing from the Grade Seven class than just Lorraine and Valerie when roll was called, though the other truants were all boys. After dinner the missing reappeared, full of whispered stories about the huge ship, American flags flying, and the crowd waiting for it on the wharf, even bigger than the crowds that came out to see the sealing ships come into port in the spring of the year. "There

MOST ANYTHING YOU PLEASE

was a brass band on board the ship," Valerie told Audrey, "and they played 'Hail, Hail, the Gang's All Here' while they were coming in, and the sailors—oh my, Audrey, you shoulda seen them. Just like fellows in the movies. There was some crowd, but we were close enough to see them wavin' from the deck."

"We'll be seeing them around plenty," Lorraine said. "There's a dance on board the ship tonight and Brenda and her crowd are all going down to try to get into it." Brenda was Lorraine's sister, sixteen and old enough to be going to dances.

"It was all being broadcast on the radio, they had these big loudspeakers set up telling us all what was going on as the ship was coming in, listing off how many men were on her and all that," Valerie said. "They'll probably play it over again tonight, or some bits of it anyway."

Sure enough, when her father turned on the evening news at suppertime, VONF was playing the highlights of the *Edmund B. Alexander*'s arrival. Audrey listened with the others, trying to picture it, cursing her own lack of nerve. The worst blow was to find out that Alf had gone after all—he'd showed up an hour late to work after going with some of the fellows to see the ship, and Dad wasn't even mad at him. Mom didn't say a word about it.

That's a story I could tell, Audrey thinks, years later, when the young ones are after her to tell what she remembers about The War. *The day I never saw the American ship come into the harbour. The day I missed it all. The day I made up my mind I'd never be so timid again, that I'd take my chances and never miss out on any good times that were on the go.*

And then she'll look around at the counter, the cash register, the Coke cooler and the ice-cream freezer, and think to herself, *And how's that going for you, Audrey?*

TRUDY J. MORGAN-COLE

ELLEN

Two American servicemen came into the store just after suppertime, when Ellen was putting tomorrow's delivery of bread from Mammy's Bakery away on the shelf. Strapping young fellows, everything about them looking spit-and-polished, from their huge white teeth to the buttons on their uniforms. The Americans didn't often come into the shop—they had their own shops down on the base. There wasn't much reason for them to buy smokes or candy bars at a corner shop in Rabbittown, and Ellen had to admit that having men in uniform all over town still made her a little nervous.

It wasn't like the Great War, when Ellen was a child. Back then, Newfoundlanders went overseas, and every other family seemed to have a boy at the front or in the navy. In this war the boys still went away—Ellen's cousin and one of her nephews were on board Royal Navy ships somewhere in the Atlantic, and she worried about them whenever she heard of a ship sinking. But there was also the blackout here in St. John's, all the windows blocked up at night so not a seam of light would attract a German plane. Then all those poor people drowned when the *Caribou* was torpedoed by a German submarine—not just sailors, but ordinary passengers only trying to cross over to Canada. And on top of that, men in uniform all over the streets. This war seemed less like a war men left home for, and more like a war on their doorstep.

"Howdy, ma'am," said one of the soldiers, sounding so much like a cowboy from *Red Ryder* or some other Western that Ellen had to stifle a laugh. His companion opened the cooler to pull out two soft drinks and laid them on the counter.

"Anything else for you fellows tonight?"

"No, ma'am, just these here Coca-Colas. Well, and maybe a pack of Camels. I'm down to my last two."

"You boys must be meeting your lady friends around here, are you?" Ellen asked as she passed him the cigarettes and rang in their purchases.

"Yes, ma'am, we're heading up to the roller rink," the soldier said. The rink was only half a block up from the store, and so popular with the American servicemen that Alf had told her the Canadians got beaten up if they tried to go there. The soldiers were no doubt stopping in here for a smoke and a Coke before going to meet their girls.

Which girls, she wondered? Vera Allen had been in here talking about it earlier, how shocking it was, young girls going around with servicemen. "I told Brenda just the other day," Vera had said, "if I ever sees you talking to one of them Yanks, I'll lock you in your bedroom till the war is over. Say what you like about the Americans coming into the war, it don't matter— we all knows what kind of girl goes around with soldiers."

It'd give Ellen a good laugh, to tell the truth, to see one of those soldiers walk past the window with young Brenda Allen on his arm, because Ellen knew Brenda, like most girls, got away with a lot more than her mother ever guessed. But she agreed with Vera, for the most part. The American soldiers and sailors might be useful for beating Hitler, but they were trouble for the mothers of young girls here in town.

The other day Wes had run across Frankie and a couple of other youngsters, the littlest Ivany and the biggest Hussey, hiding under Mrs. Vokey's gallery hollering out to a pair of girls who were walking with soldiers, "If ya can't get a man, get a Yank!" Wes told Ellen that the soldiers didn't pay any mind, though the girls looked annoyed. "But I told Frank and the other youngsters that them Yanks would tear a strip off them, they're soldiers after all and spoiling for a fight. Best to put the fear of God into the youngsters—you don't want 'em making trouble."

"You got a nice little store here, ma'am," one of the soldiers drawled as he took his change, his voice like honey on warm toast. "My folks got a corner store back home, this place kinda reminds me of it."

"Is that so? And where is home?"

"Muncie, Indiana," the boy said, and he really did look like a boy now, a fresh-faced blond boy with a bristling crew cut under his uniform cap, a sprinkle of freckles so pale they were almost blond too, spanning the bridge of his nose. A boy behind the counter of his parents' corner store.

"Did you used to work in the store, growing up?"

"Yes, ma'am I did, from the time I was about twelve, right up till I joined the army last year. What about you, you have any young'uns to help behind the counter? Or yours are not big enough yet, I guess, ma'am."

"I'm big enough," Audrey said, and Ellen turned. She hadn't even heard Audrey come down the stairs, but there she was, fourteen years old, her copper-coloured hair freshly brushed and shining, her new little breasts straining against the white cardigan she wore over her red tartan skirt. *Oh yes, my girl*, Ellen thought, *make no mistake, you're big enough.* And the war could last for years yet.

She reached out an arm, hooked Audrey's shoulder and pulled her closer. "This is my little girl, Audrey. She's a grand help around here, even though she's only in Grade Nine." Audrey looked sixteen, easily, and suddenly the soldier Ellen was talking to shifted back from looking like a wholesome young boy to a menacing man in uniform.

"Come on, buddy, we gotta get going, the girls'll be wondering what happened to us," the other soldier, the dark-haired one said. With a smile and a nod that encompassed both Ellen and Audrey, the young men turned to leave.

"Mom, can I go up to the rink tonight with Maxine and Valerie?" Audrey said, as soon as the boys were out the door.

"No, I got a headache, I'm going to need you to watch the store tonight."

"Oh, Mom! I told the girls I'd go, and I got all ready."

"Well, you shouldn't have done that without asking me, should you?" And now Ellen really did feel a little bit of a headache starting, which was good because it meant she wasn't lying. "If they come by, tell them some people got to work for a living. You just told them soldiers you're big enough to work, now do your fair share."

"That's not fair, you're not being fair!" Audrey said, but Ellen was halfway up the stairs, and another ping of the door cut off Audrey's complaint.

TRUDY J. MORGAN-COLE

AUDREY

"Be quiet, will ya? If Mom catches us, she'll have my guts for garters."

"She won't catch you—Mrs. Hiscock is in the store with her, you know they'll be jawing for half an hour." Lorraine grabbed Audrey's hand and pulled her toward the back fence.

"I'm going to tear me skirt if I goes over that fence!" Audrey warned, but in fact it was Lorraine who snagged her hem and muttered a bad word under her breath as she followed Audrey up the laneway. The only door from the Holloway house onto Rankin Street was the shop door; the back door led into the tiny backyard but there was no gate out of the yard, so the only way to escape the house without passing under Ellen's watchful eye was to slip out the back door and climb the fence. Not an easy prospect when you were wearing a party dress and dancing shoes, but it was worth it for the prospect of going to a dance at the Caribou Hut.

Both girls were giggling as they reeled out between the

houses onto Calver Avenue. Audrey knew her mother would have a thousand objections if she knew where the girls were going: Audrey should be home studying, not out gallivanting; Lorraine was a bad influence. Dances were nothing but trouble, and any big gathering might be dangerous—look at what happened to those poor souls at the K of C. Nearly two years had passed since all those people died in the fire, people who had crowded into the Knights of Columbus Hall to hear the Barn Dance show. Everybody in St. John's knew a family who had lost someone, and the shadow of the tragedy still hung in the air like the heavy gray smoke did for days afterward. And though it had never been proven, folks still said it might have been German spies that started the blaze.

Lorraine had been going to dances for months now but this was the first time Audrey had been able to get away. She would be in trouble later—even if Ellen didn't find out exactly where they went, she would know when she came upstairs from the shop that Audrey was out without permission. But it would be worth it.

The doors of the Caribou Hut were crowded with girls in pink, blue, yellow, and green dresses, and young men in khaki. Uniform after uniform: it was rare to see a boy in civilian clothes at any kind of dance, but the Caribou Hut was especially for entertaining soldiers. Newfoundland boys, when you did see them, always looked underdressed and unpolished next to the Americans. It wasn't just the crisp uniforms: the Americans had bigger, shinier teeth, and the sugary drawl of their accents made the Newfoundland boys' voices sound like the yip of angry crackie dogs nipping at the soldiers' heels.

Audrey hoped she didn't have the same look in her eyes that she saw in the eyes of Lorraine and the other girls around her. The girls looked over the soldiers like they were scanning blueberry bushes on an August afternoon, waiting for the ones ripe enough to fall into their buckets. They looked too eager, although it didn't seem to bother the soldiers, who came over to introduce themselves and ask the girls for dances. Audrey and Lorraine went to stand with their friends, Valerie and Maxine and Cathy. They had each danced once or twice so far, the girls reported. Audrey practiced trying to look cool and bored, as though, at sixteen, she was just *so tired* of going to dances and meeting American soldiers.

Maybe it worked, because here they were, a clutch of boys in uniform who looked at least nineteen or twenty. They introduced themselves: Fred, Harry, William. It was William who took Audrey's hand and led her onto the floor as the band started playing "Don't Fence Me In."

"I love this song!" Audrey said as William swung her around.

"Really? I never thought of this as a song a girl would like."

Audrey wanted to ask *how come?* But you were supposed to ask a fellow about himself, so she said, "And where are you from, William?" That was the good thing about Americans; it was easy to make conversation because you just had to ask where they were from, and the place would be so strange and faraway there would be something to talk about for sure.

"I'm from Ithaca, New York."

"Oh, New York! I got two uncles on my dad's side, and another aunt and uncle on Mom's side, all in New York. In Brooklyn. Is that far from Ithaca?"

William shook his head. "It's a whole other world. Ithaca's upstate. It's only a small place compared to New York City— Brooklyn's in New York City."

"Oh." A city inside another city? Audrey realized that for all the years they had been getting cards and letters and hand-me-down barrels from Brooklyn, she didn't really know anything about the place. She didn't even realize New York City was in a state called New York, too. New York City she knew from movies and magazines; she knew about the towering skyscrapers and beautiful rich people. Brooklyn didn't sound like that, from the way her mother talked about it when she read Aunt Louise's letters.

"So what do people do in Ithaca, New York?"

"Well, my dad worked in a factory his whole life, and I didn't want to do that. My mom cleaned house for a university professor and his wife, and I used to come with her sometimes and look at all the stuff they had, the books and paintings and stuff, and when I was a kid I thought that'd be a pretty nice way to live, don't ya think? But I wasn't all that hot in school as it turned out, so I figured my best chance at seein' the world would be joining the army. So far all I've seen is St. John's, Newfoundland."

He laughed, not the nicest kind of laugh, so Audrey figured he wasn't too impressed with St. John's. And why would he be? He came from New York and he thought he was going to Europe to fight Nazis, and here he was on a rock stuck out in the ocean, a place where nothing ever happened.

It was the time in the conversation when he should have probably said, "So, what about you?" It wasn't as if he could say, "Where do you come from?" If he'd been here a few months and danced with a few other Newfoundland girls he knew everything he needed to know about where Audrey was from. And he could likely tell that she was only sixteen, no matter how hard she tried to look older.

So he didn't ask her anything, and Audrey said, "Well, I hope you get to go someplace more exciting before it's all over."

"So do I." Then he kind of grimaced. "Not too exciting, though. I mean, at least it's pretty safe here."

"That's true." She hadn't meant to sound like she was wishing for him to go overseas and get shot, or be on a ship that got torpedoed. It was hard, this business of talking and saying the right thing, or at least trying not to say the wrong thing. So for a few steps they just danced—he wasn't a bad dancer, but Audrey wasn't sure yet whether she was a good dancer herself. Bing Crosby sang about wanting to straddle his old saddle and be turned loose on his cay-yoose.

"I wonder what a cayuse is?" Audrey said.

"I think it's some kinda horse. You know, it's a cowboy song, so his cayuse must be his horse, right?"

"Is that why you think it's a song girls wouldn't like? Because it's a cowboy song?"

He thought for a moment; the effort made him miss a step and he narrowly avoided treading on her toe. "Yeah, I guess. I mean, it's a manly thing, isn't it? Wanting to get out there, ride under the open skies. 'Don't fence me in.' I just always figure ladies are more inclined to—well, home and hearth, and all that jazz."

"Do you think it's a girl he's singing it to?" Audrey said, suddenly a lot more interested in the song's lyrics than in William from Ithaca. "I mean, maybe he's telling her, don't try to make me settle down, don't fence me in. If she wanted to get married, or something like that."

The song was ending now, and William grinned. "You sure do think hard about things—I don't think I ever paid that much attention to the words of a song before. You always talk this much?"

"I don't know. I do think about songs a lot—I love music. And I like cowboy songs, even though I'm a girl." And it was this statement, the one thing she had said about herself in a three-minute dance with this boy, that turned out to be her exit line. He led her off the dance floor as the song ended, nodded politely and said, "Well, it sure was nice meeting you, Angela. You enjoy those cowboy songs."

"He called me Angela," Audrey said to Valerie, who was back from her dance too, flushed and giggling. Her partner hadn't abandoned her; he went off to get her a drink. Val took cigarettes out of her purse and passed one to Audrey. Another thing Mom would kill her for if she knew, Audrey thought; Ellen didn't approve of women smoking in the first place, much less girls who were still in school. But Audrey knew it made her look older, which was important tonight.

"Oh, don't mind what he called you. They can never remember your name, not after one dance." Valerie sounded like she'd been to a dozen of these things, danced with a hundred soldiers and sailors.

It wasn't that he couldn't remember her name; she could barely remember his. It was the confidence with which he said "Angela," as though he knew more about who she was than she knew herself. Just like he knew that girls didn't like cowboy songs, that men didn't want to be fenced in. Like he knew that he lit out from Ithaca looking for adventure and he was here in St. John's and hadn't gone nearly far enough.

He would go farther, though Audrey would never know about it. Most of the boys in this room would spend their war safe in St. John's, or back stateside, but some of them belonged to units that would be shipped overseas. William's unit would be sent over just in time for D-Day; he would set foot on the soil of Europe for exactly twenty-five minutes before he bled to death on Omaha Beach.

"Now, I take exception to that," said another warm,

TRUDY J. MORGAN-COLE

drawling voice—deeper and the words stretched-out longer than the other boy's had been. Audrey looked up to see a tall, dark-haired soldier handing a glass of punch to Valerie. Dark brown eyes glinted with mischief. "I danced with Val here, and I remember her name, and I'll bet if you and I were to dance together I'd remember yours too. Who was this fella who called you by the wrong name?"

Audrey looked around to see William talking to Cathy Kelly. "That's him over there—I think his name is Walter?"

The soldier laughed, getting the joke right away. "Yup, that Walter, he ain't much of a gentleman. So, wanna put me to the test? Tell me your name and see can I remember it?"

Audrey glanced at Valerie. If you danced with a fellow, and he went to get drinks for both of you, shouldn't you expect that he'd stick around instead of flirting with your friend? And the dark-haired soldier was definitely flirting; she could feel the focus of his attention like he'd shone a torch at her, so different from Walter/William who didn't even seem to see her even while dancing with her.

"Tell you the truth, I'm parched," Audrey said. "Would you be sweet and go get me a drink too? Me and Val'll just sit down here, and you come join us while we finish our drinks."

He went off, and the girls sat down at a table. "You don't mind?" Audrey asked Valerie.

"What, me? No, we had one dance together, it's not like I owns him," Valerie laughed. "Anyway, I got my eye on that redhead over there, the one Eileen Howse is dancin' with."

"What's his name?"

"The redhead? No clue."

"No, the one I was just talking to."

"Oh." Valerie paused to think. "I'm not sure—that's shockin', isn't it, when I just said that about the fellows not remembering names—oh, wait. Harry Something. He's from down South—that's why he got that accent you could cut with a knife."

Harry Something was back at the table then, bringing a drink for Audrey, sitting down with them. He talked to both girls, but even when Valerie was talking, his eyes drifted back to Audrey. He told them his name was Harry Pickens. "Slim pickins around here these days, I know," he said, as if he had to make the joke before anyone else could, "but since it's slim pickins, maybe you'll honour me with a dance, Miss Audrey?"

The band started playing "Besame Mucho," and Audrey burst out, "Oh, I love this song!"

"Then let's dance," said Harry, and she followed him out onto the dance floor.

TRUDY J. MORGAN-COLE

ELLEN

"So I see Audrey is goin' around with a Yank now, is she?" Mrs. Ryan's groceries were paid for and bagged on the counter beside her, but she was in no rush to make for the door.

"I wouldn't say she's going around with him. She's had him into the shop to say hello. He seems like a sensible enough young fellow." Ellen counted through the stack of tickets Mrs. Ryan had given her from her family's ration books before putting them away in the box with the others. Taking ration tickets had come to be as much a part of her routine as taking money or writing purchases down on people's tabs.

"But you never knows with the Yanks, do you?"

"No, I suppose not." It was more of a formula than anything, now, a repeated caution without any real sense of danger behind it. Vera Allen's daughter Brenda had married a Yank; one of the Ivany girls was engaged to one. They were a part of the landscape now, and although everyone said the war was drawing to a close, it was hard to imagine St. John's without American soldiers in uniform. Truth be told, Ellen was far more worried about young Alf going around with Maggie Ryan's niece Theresa, the Ryans being Catholic and all.

Best for everyone to marry their own kind, she used to think. But Ellen had grown up in Candle Cove where everyone pretty much was the same kind: all Protestant—the Catholics lived over in St. Bridget's—and everyone descended from people who'd fished out of Candle Cove for two hundred years. Here in Rabbittown, Catholics and Protestants lived cheek by jowl with each other. The youngsters went to different schools, but they all ran around together on the street. The boys from the Catholic schools might get into rackets with Protestant fellows, but they'd be eyeing their sisters at the same time. Bring in the Canadian and American soldiers on top of it all, and who was to say who your kind was anymore? Even in tiny Candle Cove, her own mother hadn't thought Wes Holloway, a fisherman's son, was good enough for a merchant's daughter. What right did Ellen have to pass judgement?

And here were Alf and Treese, pinging in through the front door, picking up Pepsis on their way out to the roller rink. Treese was a sweet little thing even if she was R.C., Ellen couldn't deny that. She was always polite to her elders, which mattered a lot in a young girl. "Thank you, Mrs. Holloway," she said now, even though it was Alf who'd gotten her drink out of the cooler. Treese was smart enough to know that every free drink or bag of chips the Holloway children took from the store cost their parents a few pennies.

"Did you see Audrey while you were out?" Ellen asked Alf.

"I saw her this afternoon, walking up LeMarchant Road with Harry."

Maggie Ryan nodded. "That's the Yank, isn't it?"

"They're only people you know, no different from us,"

Alf said.

"Oh, I don't know about that, young Alf."

"What, Mrs. Ryan, you think Yanks are not people?"

"Don't get smart, Alf," said Ellen, at the same time Maggie Ryan said, "They may be people but they're different from you and me all right, you mark my words. Them American soldiers only got one thing on their minds."

"Not like us Newfoundland boys—we got all kinds of things on our minds." Alf grinned at Treese, and took her hand as they walked out the door.

"Well. Now. What are we going to do about them two, I wonder, Mrs. Holloway?"

"What, Alf and Treese? Sure it's only puppy love, I s'pose they'll get over it."

"What are they, eighteen? I wouldn't count on them getting over it. I was married at seventeen."

Ellen was twenty-one when she was married, a good respectable age for it, she'd thought at the time, and still thought now. Anyway it wasn't as if she and Maggie Ryan, here over the counter of the store, were going to come up with any kind of magical solution that would stop Protestant boys from going out with Catholic girls. Or stop Newfoundland girls going around with American soldiers for that matter. The US Army itself had tried to ban that and what good had it done? People loved who they loved, and neither church nor state nor parents had that much to say about it in the end. She still had hopes Alf would find a nice United Church girl, and surely Audrey had more sense than to marry some fellow who would streel her off halfway across the world.

All the same, when Audrey got home that night, Ellen asked her to stay down in the shop for a few minutes. She looked almost too pretty, that light green dress showing off red hair that swung down past her shoulder. Audrey wore it long even with the permanent wave in it; she looked a bit like Greer Garson or one of those film stars in the Hollywood magazines she was always reading.

"What is it, Mom?" That eye-rolling voice, that assumption that if Ellen wanted to talk to her she had to be lecturing her about something. *I'm almost seventeen, Mom*, as if seventeen were thirty-five or something. And Ellen had never liked being called "Mom"—she missed the softness of "Mummy" on her children's lips and if they had to graduate past that she'd have preferred the old-fashioned "Mama" or the more dignified "Mother." But they all called her "Mom" now.

"Just about this young fellow. This Harry."

"What about him?"

"Well, tell me about him."

Audrey sighed, draped herself over the counter. "What's there to tell? His name is Harry Pickens, he's been in the army since he was eighteen, he's twenty-one now."

"What do you know about his people, anything? Or the place where he comes from?"

"He's from Louisiana. That's down south. He says it's pretty dull down there. His father's a farmer—hogs, I think. He got two brothers and three sisters. That's really about all I knows about him."

"And are you…is it serious?"

"Oh, Mom. I don't know. What's *serious*? We've been going around together for…what, four months? And his unit might get shipped overseas, he thinks."

"Now? But the war's as good as over."

"Yes, but Harry says the US is going to have troops occupying Germany for a long while after the war, so he figures he might be sent there. It's just a rumour though… the men don't know for sure. They never knows anything…he

TRUDY J. MORGAN-COLE

didn't know he was coming here till the ship docked in St. John's. And he didn't know where Newfoundland was or nothing."

Ellen had only met this boy twice. She ought to have invited him in for Sunday dinner, gotten to know him. But if there was a chance he might be shipped out soon, surely there was no need. This thing with him and Audrey—it couldn't last.

"Are you—I mean, I know you're a good girl, Audrey. I hope you—I hope you'll always be a good girl."

Audrey smiled a slow, lazy smile, a smile Ellen had only seen on her these last months and didn't trust at all. "You don't need to worry, Mom. I'm a good girl, and what matters more, I'm a smart girl."

That didn't give Ellen much comfort. *Smart* was all very well, but how quickly it could desert you when you thought you were in love. "You should be studying for your exams, not going around with soldiers."

"It's not as if I'm going around with a whole platoon of soldiers, just the one. And anyway, I'm going to do fine in them exams. I got good marks."

"Yes, but those exams can make or break—it don't matter how well you've done all year if you don't get a good mark on the exam. And if you don't, you might not get into your commercial course."

"I'll get into the commercial course, Mom. And then I'll get a nice job in an office on Water Street and bring home my pay. You got nothing to worry about."

"Are you sure you want to work in an office?"

Audrey's eyes slipped past her mother's gaze, to the counter, the cash register, the coolers, the shelves of stock. She didn't say *It will be better than this*, but the look on her face was as plain as if she had spoken the words aloud.

MOST ANYTHING YOU PLEASE

AUDREY

Monday to Friday, nine to five, she worked in Johnson's insurance office. Two or three evenings a week, and every Saturday, she was behind the counter in the shop. She made good money at the office but nothing in the shop; she was working nearly as many hours for no pay as she was working for fifteen dollars a week. You couldn't complain about it: that was the whole point of having a family business; everybody pitched in to do their part.

But it didn't stop her from resenting it. She especially hated working Saturdays, the worst day of the week for youngsters from the neighbourhood coming in, buying dozens of four-for-a-penny candies, trying to steal stuff off the shelves when she wasn't looking. She brought down a stick of baloney over Snotty Cadwell's knuckles when she caught him at it one time and told him he couldn't come in the store for two weeks.

A slew of them had just left the shop when a girl about Audrey's own age came through the door and looked around as if she were unsure whether she was in the right place. She was a stranger, dressed in a white dress with green sprigs on it, dark hair in a permanent wave, clutching her handbag like a life preserver. Audrey wasn't one bit surprised when she opened her mouth and a foreign accent—English or Irish or something like that—came out.

"Pardon me, d'you have, er…," she looked down at the list in her hand, "bologna? And bread? And, er, tinned peas?"

"We got it all," Audrey said. "Here, give me your list, I'll get it for you." As the girl handed over the folded piece of paper, Audrey said, "You must be Lester Parsons's wife, are you?" Once she heard the accent, it wasn't hard to place the girl: Audrey had heard months ago that Maxine Parsons's cousin Lester, who had joined up with the Canadian military, had married a girl overseas. Then just last week she heard that Mrs. Noseworthy was renting out two rooms to a soldier who had come back from overseas with a war bride. There couldn't be that many of them, not in this part of town.

The girl blinked. "Yes…yes, I'm Doris Parsons. Do you know my Les?"

"I knows his people," Audrey said. "I went to school with his cousins. Maxine and Jim and Betty."

"I've met Maxine and Betty," Doris said, looking at her groceries as Audrey put each item on the counter. She squinted at the labels. "Les told me St. John's was a city, but it's just like a village, the way everyone knows each other and all each other's business."

"That's just Rabbittown. The neighbourhood," Audrey clarified.

"Why is it called Rabbittown?"

Audrey shrugged. "It's not on no signs or nothing, that's just what everyone calls it. Some people says they used to catch rabbits out here before it was all built up, and others will say it's because the streets are all narrow, and close like a rabbit warren. But I've heard some folks say it's because the place is full of poor people and we all breeds like rabbits." She laughed, and the other girl joined with a hesitant giggle, as if she wasn't sure she was allowed to laugh. "I don't see no eggs on your list, but you'll want a dozen, won't you?"

"Oh, aye, please. I knew I'd forget something."

"Anyway, everyone knows everyone in Rabbittown. I wouldn't know if somebody on the South Side brought home a war bride, but if it's here in the neighbourhood, then you can bet everyone knows about it."

"I suppose that's what I am, isn't it? A war bride. It sounds a bit funny when you say it."

"But that's what you are."

"I know…it's just that it sounds romantic, and I suppose I thought it was, but now it's just— living in a tiny flat, not even a flat really, just rooms to let. And buying food at the corner shop—all the things I'd be doing if we'd stayed back home. Only, doing them here, where everything's so different."

"Where's home?"

"Glasgow. In Scotland. Well, near Glasgow—it's a place called Kirkintilloch, actually, but you'd not have heard of it."

"Oh, so that's a Scottish accent is it? I wouldn't know; we don't get many Scotch people around here. I don't know if I've ever met one before. So, what branch of the forces was Les in?"

"Navy. Canadian navy," Doris said, taking her money out of her purse as Audrey rang in the purchases. "Although…this isn't Canada, is it?"

"No, it's Newfoundland. Another country altogether," said Audrey. "Although there's talks about us joining up with Canada, from what I hear, but who knows if anything will come of it."

TRUDY J. MORGAN-COLE

Doris was in the shop almost every day after that and Audrey enjoyed chatting with the Scotch girl, trying to imagine how St. John's might look to someone coming from so far away. "The weather's not much different," Doris said. "We get the rain and the fog up in Glasgow too. I didn't think if we were living in a big town we'd be doing without running water, though."

"That's just the street you live on. Some places are hooked up and some aren't, though they say everyone should be soon. We got water but the people around the corner from us got to get it from the pump. And there's plenty of well-off people in St. John's—you just didn't happen to marry into one of them families."

"Les told me his family was comfortable. When we were keeping company he showed me a snap of himself standing on the lawn in front of a big white house and said that was where his people lived. But later on he told me that was the Bungalow in Bowring Park and that they really lived in a much smaller house, but he still said it was nice. We go to his parents' house for Sunday dinner every week. It isna what I'd call nice. And I don't think his ma likes me."

"What about your people, did they mind you marrying a fellow from over here and ending up on the other side of the ocean?"

"Mum loves Les," Doris said after a brief hesitation. "And I think Da always liked him too—if he'd settled down in Scotland and stayed wi' us. They didnae want him taking me so far away. They weren't best pleased wi' that at all."

Audrey put the last of Doris's purchases, a tin of loose tea, into her paper sack, and pushed the bag across the counter to her. "It's the same way here," she said. "Girls go around with American and Canadian soldiers and sailors and the parents are always warning us not to, but I think the main reason is they don't want us moving far away."

"So what about you, are you going to move away with an American?"

Audrey shrugged. "I was going around with a fellow, but he got posted overseas just before the end of the war, and his unit's still over there in Germany. He writes to me." Harry wasn't much of a letter writer, it turned out. Everything she liked about him turned on his presence. He was the best-looking of all the soldiers she'd met at dances, and he was a wonderful dancer too. But beautiful dark eyes and light feet didn't mean a lot when all you had was letters.

"Well, if he comes back, you want to think twice about marrying him and running off to America. I love my Les and all, but the truth is I cry myself to sleep every night, I'm that homesick."

"It'll get better, I'm sure," Audrey said, putting on her best smile for the sad Scottish girl as she went out the door. It was too bad, she thought, that British girls who married Newfoundlanders felt that way, but really, could you blame them? They were coming to St. John's, Newfoundland, after all—and they were the lucky ones, the rest were going to some terrible old outport like Candle Cove, where Audrey's grandparents lived, a place where it might as well be 1846 instead of 1946.

But the Newfoundland girls who married Americans—well, that was a whole different story. They were going to a country where people had *more* of everything—more shops, better clothes, everybody had those big gleaming cars driving on lovely blacktop roads, there were skyscrapers and the latest fashions and cute American accents. *If I could get to the States*, Audrey thought, *there'd be no crying into my pillow at night.*

Homesick? Not likely!

It was a funny coincidence, she thought later, that she and Doris had that conversation about war brides on the same day she got Harry's letter. While he wasn't a good letter writer at all, this one leapt to life off the page if only because she could hear him saying the words, hear the tremble of emotion he would fight hard to keep back.

> *We got a big shock today, a real shocker for all of us. One of my buddies, George Crowley from Ohio, he got killed today. Now a few months ago before the war ended we wudnt have thought nothing of saying one of my buddies got killed, sad but true we all got used to it in that time and there was no shock sometime you didnt even realize till after. But now we are at peace and were just here helping Germany get stabilized or whatever you wanna call it, you dont expect anyone to die and thats why we're all in shock over poor Crowley. The jeep he was driving rolled over and it shudnt of happen but it did. Yesterday we were all havin a good time laughing and carrying on with Crowley just like the other fellas and now he is dead.*

> *Made me stop to think and realize that I figured when the fighting ended everyone was safe and I had come thru ok but now it just kinda brings home to me that bad things can happen anywhere, anytime, to soldiers in peacetime or even to pretty girls waiting back home. If anything happend to me or you and we never had our chance to be together it would feel so wrong to me. So I guess in this very roundabout way I started out this letter telling you about poor Crowley and now I'm asking Audrey, will you marry me when I get discharged?*

MOST ANYTHING YOU PLEASE

*I could come back to Newfoundland so we could be
married at your home if that's what you want and then
we could go back to my home and you could meet my folks.
What do you say?*

Audrey read his letter in the front room with the radio
tuned to VOUS, as it always was when Audrey was in control
of the dial. The American station broadcast from down on the
base and they played a lot more music than VONF, always the
best and latest hits. Frank Sinatra was singing "Five Minutes
More." The words about staying together just five minutes
longer made her think of saying goodbye to Harry, that last
night before he shipped out. She had wanted that so much,
then, just to stay wrapped in Harry's arms forever. It was more
than a year since he'd gone away and that desire, just like the
memory of him, had retreated a little bit each day.

Now he wanted to come back and marry her, to take her
back home to the States with him. Why? Because a buddy of
his had died in some freak accident. Harry was right: life was
short and anything could happen.

She had been out with other fellows since he left; they had
made no promises. In fact she was going out this very evening,
to a dance down on the base. She would dance with half a
dozen other young American soldiers, hoping to find—what?
Audrey wasn't even sure anymore. She folded Harry's letter
away, stuck it with the others in the dresser drawer with her
underwear and stockings. Audrey, Marilyn, and June each had
a drawer; Audrey and Marilyn shared the big bed and June slept
on the cot. The one thing you could say for getting married was
that it was a sure way to get out of your parents' house, out of
sharing a room with your sisters.

The upstairs of the house was quiet. Mom took over the
shop at five when Audrey's Saturday afternoon shift was

TRUDY J. MORGAN-COLE

finished; Dad and Alf were still out finishing a job. Marilyn was off at some friend's house, and the youngsters, Frankie and June, were playing outside. In half an hour they'd all be back here wanting supper: Audrey, if she was home, would be expected to fry up a pan of chips to go with the leftover baked beans from dinnertime. Then she and Marilyn would fight over the bathroom mirror as they both got ready to go out, and Alf would push them out of the way so he could shave before his date with his fiancée. Alf and Treese had finally made it official: no date set yet, but land bought and a house started. Treese was proudly flashing around the world's tiniest, cheapest diamond ring and the two of them were doing their best to ignore all the ructions a mixed marriage had stirred up among the older folks in both families.

Audrey put her good stockings and the blue-dotted Swiss dress she bought with her last paycheque into a bag with her best shoes. "I'm going to get supper over to Val's and change over there," she told her mother as she passed through the shop.

"Where are you going tonight? Another dance?" Ellen, good Methodist girl from around the bay, still couldn't keep that little edge of disapproval out of her voice whenever she said the word *dance*. Much like when she had to introduce Alf's girlfriend as Treese *Ryan*, admitting that her son was going out with a Catholic.

"Yes, Mom, down on the base."

"Keep an eye out for Marilyn, she's supposed to be going up to the roller rink with that one Sharon, but I wouldn't put it past her to try to sneak out to a dance. She's no better than you were at her age."

"If Marilyn shows up at Fort Pepperell I'll have her sent home in an armoured car. I promise."

The shop door closed behind Audrey and she stepped out

into a warm, golden summer afternoon. Rankin Street was busy with youngsters; she heard her brother Frankie's voice but couldn't see him as a small crowd ran past playing "Hoist your sails and run." On the corner of Liverpool Avenue, her sister June and three other little girls—two Taylors and the littlest Hiscock girl—were playing hopscotch. Audrey turned there, heading down towards Val's place. Mr. Hynes had built a new house out on Suez Street, a couple of years ago, in a space that had been all open fields when Audrey and Valerie were little. The new house stood alone, not attached to its neighbour, and Val had a bedroom to herself.

A door opened in one of the houses as Audrey passed, and a woman called: "Charlie! Libby! Diane! Five minutes till suppertime! You get yourselves back in here now!"

All down the road, the cry was repeated, women coming out onto the galleries to call in the children. Two boys, kicking a ball across the street, looked up, and one scooped up the ball to run for home.

Five minutes more. The song echoed in Audrey's head. If she wrote back with a Yes, she would have not just five minutes more but a whole lifetime with Harry. She could imagine dancing with him to that song. When they danced together, when they were holding hands or in each other's arms, then she was in love. And if she married him, he would take her away. Away from the streets, from the shop, from this small, narrow life where everyone knew everyone.

In Valerie's kitchen she found Valerie and her parents and also Lorraine Allen, all sitting at the table having a cup of tea. "Staying for supper, Audrey?" Mrs. Hynes asked. "It's only a drop of pea soup."

"That's grand, thanks. I thought I'd come over here to get changed before we go out." Now that the girls were older, out

73

of school and earning their own pocket money, Valerie's parents, like Audrey's, had accepted dances down on the base as something their daughters were going to do whether the old folks liked it or not. They made little fuss as long as the girls kept to a midnight curfew. Lorraine, who had urged Audrey and Valerie to sneak out to dances with American boys when they were sixteen, was now, at eighteen, engaged to Ted Penney from Mayor Avenue. As a result, Lorraine was going to spend her Saturday night playing cards with Ted's brother and his wife instead of dancing with soldiers down at Fort Pepperell. She didn't seem any too thrilled about it, either, though like Treese she was fond of showing off her dinky little ring.

All evening, Audrey thought she would tell Valerie about Harry's letter, his proposal. There was plenty of time; they walked all the way down to the base in the soft evening air. Children were out playing again, young folks heading up to the roller rink, older folks sat out on their galleries enjoying the rare warmth. Everyone called hello. Up on Merrymeeting Road they ran across old Moses Hiscock, who provided a bit of a change from the friendly greetings of most of their neighbours. "Are ye girls goin' off dancing? That's Satan's playground, them dances! You puts your soul in mortal peril! Read the Scriptures, for they was out laughing and dancing and giving in marriage till the Day of the Lord came upon them like a thief in the night! A thief in the night! Stay home and read the Book of Revelation!"

"He's three sheets to the wind already, and what is it, only seven o'clock?" Valerie said.

"Ruby said Uncle Mose has been going to revival meetings—is it the Salvation Army? No, it's the Seven Day Adventists, that's why he's all up on the book of Revelation.

Mind you, they don't drink either, but I don't think he got up to that part yet. Oh look, there's Donna Crocker with Mickey Nolan—are they going out together?"

"First I've heard of it."

The evening slipped away—the walk, the dance, turning around the dance floor in the arms of one crew-cut American boy after another, walking back home through the velvet-dark night with a crowd of girls and soldiers. The songs they danced to lingered in Audrey's mind longer than any of the boys she danced with; she was humming "The Old Lamplighter" and wondering if there was ever a time when real lamplighters lit the streetlights in St. John's. She only pretended to listen to the boy next to her—what was his name? Freddy? Eddie? He had to be twenty, at least, but he seemed younger than Audrey. The lamplighter song somehow twisted into "Five Minutes More" in her head, and there she was in front of Holloway's Grocery and Confectionary, taking her key from her purse and saying good night to everyone.

Upstairs in her room, she undressed in the dark, keeping the bedside lamp off so as not to wake her sisters. Marilyn stirred and mumbled in her sleep; June just kept snoring. Audrey had had some thought of taking Harry's letter out of the drawer to re-read, but she remembered most of it anyway. Tomorrow would be Sunday, with church in the morning, Sunday dinner and then the long afternoon stretching out before them. Elderly relatives would visit; Dad would play hymns on the accordion, the one time in the week he sat down to rest instead of working. The shop would be shuttered and quiet. Plenty of time, tomorrow, to write back.

ELLEN

Ellen came downstairs to the shop at five o'clock, leaving a pot of fresh meat soup on the stove for supper for Wes and the youngsters. Marilyn, who had been working at the counter all afternoon, was talking to a couple of her friends. Ellen stopped for a moment in the door, arrested by the sight of the three of them, full skirts swinging almost to their ankles, hair crisp in permanent waves. They were sixteen: when did they all get to look like young women instead of little girls? Ellen had seen this transformation twice already in her two older children but it still took her by surprise.

"All right, Marilyn, you go on upstairs and set the table. Dad will be home in a few minutes and then ye crowd can all have supper."

"Mom, I got something to tell you first, wait a minute. The mail came while you were upstairs."

Ellen took the handful of envelopes, skimming quickly—a letter from her mother, another from her cousin Louise in

New York, a bill from the electric company. Marilyn held one envelope back, already opened, holding it in front of her chest like something she was showing off, though it was only a plain envelope. "What's in that one?"

"My grades! I got my CHE results—well, we all did today."

"Oh, let me see. Did you pass?" It was the routine question Ellen asked Audrey when she finished Grade Eleven, the question parents always asked, though she knew it was foolish to even wonder in Marilyn's case. She was near the top of her class. Ellen looked down the list of 80s and 90s. English, Mathematics, Civics, Science—excellent marks in everything. "This is wonderful, Marilyn."

"A lot better than mine!" Sharon Hiscock said. "Marilyn's like our Ella, always a great one for the books."

"But you passed everything, did you?" Ellen asked Sharon and the other girl, the Taylor girl she always got mixed up with her sister. Such a slew of girls in that family. Shirley, was it? No, Carolann.

Both girls nodded. "I'm going to do the commercial course in September," said Carolann.

"S'pose I'll just keep working at the Royal Stores," said Sharon. "Till I finds some rich man to sweep me off me feet."

"Don't be talking like that, now. Kind and hard-working is more important than rich any day," Ellen chided, and looked back at her own daughter. Marilyn hadn't said a word all summer about what her plans were now that school was over. She had been working in the shop, hadn't looked around for a more permanent job, but she could certainly do a commercial course and get a job in a good downtown office like Audrey had done.

"So…I've been thinking, Mom…what I really wants to do is take the nursing course at the Grace Hospital. Do you think…is that something we'd ever be able to afford?" Marilyn said now, still holding on to her exam results as if it were a ticket she needed to board the train.

"Nursing! Well, it's the first I've heard of it."

"I didn't want to say anything before my marks came back. I was afraid I'd get my hopes up and then my grades wouldn't be good enough."

Ellen had never thought of her girls doing anything more advanced than a typing course, or going straight to work. But nursing was a wonderful profession for a girl if she was ambitious and willing to work hard, and the Lord knew Marilyn was both those things.

"It's suppertime now, go on and get upstairs. I'm sure the rest of ye got your own suppers to go to. I'll talk to your father about the nursing school business, Marilyn, and we'll see what he has to say."

The other girls scattered, out the door and back to their own homes for supper, and Ellen took her place at the counter. She was tired after a morning in the shop and an afternoon of housework upstairs. If Marilyn went to nursing school, Ellen would most likely have to hire someone to help in the shop. Frank was only twelve; the girls had started working behind the counter at that age but Frank was still only a youngster, Ellen thought. Give him another year or two. Ten years they had managed to keep the shop going with only family working there, but as the youngsters grew up, Ellen knew she'd have to hire someone.

Audrey wouldn't be home till nearly six, by the time she got off work and walked up from Water Street. Alf had most likely gone straight from the job he was working on over to the lot where he was building his own new house; Wes would go help him after supper. The two of them were working full days down on the base and then working on Alf and Treese's house as long as it was light. Alf's piece of land was over on Little Street, just up from Empire Avenue—the Old Track, as Ellen still called it, though the railway hadn't run through there since before she moved to town.

There was a thing to be proud of, now—her son, twenty years old, working since he left school at fourteen, having enough money saved to buy a piece of land and build a house for his bride. The only help Alf would accept was his father's labour. And Wes was more than willing to help with building, though he said he wouldn't go to the wedding. "I just don't know if I can go along with it, Nell," he had told her that very morning. "I mean, I can see they're going to get married no matter what we haves to say about it, and if they had of done it in the judge's office I s'pose I could have been reconciled. But a Catholic church, up in front of a priest? I can't see myself sitting there watching it. I just can't."

Ellen had sighed, glad Alf was already gone out so he didn't have to hear this. Wes was a good man and a good father but he was a stubborn one too, when he dug in his heels. She'd heard enough back and forth about this wedding, now, to last her a lifetime, and whatever feelings of her own she had about Alf marrying a Catholic were long buried under her wish that everyone could just make peace and get along. Treese's father and brothers wouldn't even help with the house; Alf and Wes were doing it all.

The house would be closed in by winter, and the men would continue working inside till spring. When the house was done, there would be time to talk about the wedding, although it was clear enough already there was no solution that would make everyone in both families happy. Unless the youngsters broke off the engagement, and then they'd both be unhappy, for

TRUDY J. MORGAN-COLE

anyone with eyes could see they were crazy about each other.

Ping! She looked up, expecting Audrey, but it was Peter Walsh from a few doors down. Poor man: his wife had died in childbirth in the spring, having their twelfth child. The baby died too, but that still left poor Mr. Walsh with eleven youngsters. The youngest ones were parcelled out among his family: two boys nobody had room for went to Mount Cashel orphanage, but the older three were still with their father, and the eldest couldn't have been more than fifteen. It was easy to trace the hard time the poor man was having by his visits to the shop: he was in to pick something nearly every day, usually baloney or tinned beans. Sometimes it was tomato soup, and there was always a loaf of baker's bread.

"How are you doing today, Mr. Walsh?"

He stood in front of the counter, holding his hat in one hand and scratching his head with the other, looking at the shelves as if looking for inspiration. "Well I'll tell you now, Mrs. Holloway, it's not easy and that's the truth. I'm lookin' for something to give the youngsters for their tea and I haven't got a thing in the house. I s'pose it'll have to be beans again, will it?"

Ellen took two cans of beans from the shelf. "They could do a lot worse than beans and toast. Do you need bread?"

"Oh, you knows I do, I had a loaf last night but when I gets home from work they got that all gone, same as always."

Of course they did, poor little mortals—nothing to eat all day but tea and toast for three growing children. They played out in the street with the rest of the crowd, and when the other youngsters got called in for dinner, the little Walshes went in and ate whatever they could find, which was usually little enough. "Your young one Maureen must be big enough to be some help now, isn't she?"

"Ah, well, she makes sure the boys has something to eat for their dinner and she tries to keep the place clean. She talks about getting some kind of a job to help out, but it's hard enough for a grown man to keep a job now, with men coming back from overseas and so many of the Americans leaving the base. What chance do a young girl her age have to find anything? I s'pose she'll end up going cleaning house for someone, but then I got nobody to watch the boys. I don't want to send them to Mount Cashel as well, bad enough having Paul and Anthony in there. I hate to think what my poor missus would say if she were alive to see it, Mrs. Holloway, I do."

Ellen handed the poor man his beans and bread, another box of tea, and a tin of tobacco, and wrote it all down under his tab. What to do about the tab for her poorer neighbours had been a vexing issue as long as they had had the shop, a faint echo of her father's headaches in the merchant's store in Candle Cove where all the fishermen lived on credit. Some people here in town paid cash; most of the neighbourhood regulars ran a tab but settled it every payday. But there were always the few—the Cadwells, the Walshes, the Ryans, the Hiscocks—who had a running tab that would run till Doomsday. They put a little down on it every payday, but it would never be settled. Still, you couldn't let your neighbours starve.

"You could be a bit stricter with them, though, Mom," Audrey said, coming in from work a few minutes later and lingering long enough to hear her mother's thoughts on the poor Walshes. "You need to at least demand the money off people, let them know it's a business and not a charity. You're too soft. And don't tell me you're thinking about hiring Maureen Walsh to work behind the counter just because you feel sorry for her father."

TRUDY J. MORGAN-COLE

"I'm going to need someone, and if it can't be family it might as well be one of the neighbours. The Walshes are poor but they're not crooked. Well, Maureen isn't anyway. The boys are little Tartars, but who can blame them?"

"I don't think she's right in the head, Maureen, though. I think she's simple."

"You don't know that."

"*You* don't know she'd be any good to work in a shop. Why not hire Treese? She's only got part-time work and she'd be glad to make some extra money before the wedding, I'm sure. Maybe even after—there's no reason she couldn't go on working till they start having babies."

"Glory be, Audrey, don't be talking about babies already. It's enough of a shock, all of you growing up so fast. If anyone comes at me with the thought of grandchildren I don't know if I'll be able to carry on."

Audrey's face changed for a moment, became serious—she had been half fooling so far, giving her mother a hard time about not being tough enough on customers. Ellen saw that serious look, and her breath caught. Her first thought was, *Please Lord, no, don't let her tell me she's expecting a baby*, and her second was, *Who's the frigger that done this to her? I'll tear him apart with my bare hands.*

"Harry's getting discharged from the Army," Audrey said. Ellen's brain scrambled for a moment: Harry? Thoughts of some feckless boy getting her girl pregnant scattered in an attempt to remember who Harry was.

Seeing her mother's face, Audrey repeated, "Harry Pickens? The fellow I was seeing before he went overseas, the one I've been writing to?"

"Oh, Harry, of course." Ellen wished she could go back, erase her first response, make her eyes light up with interest at

Harry's name. "So he's going back to…where was it he was from?"

"Louisiana. But he's coming here first. Mom, he asked me to marry him, and I said yes."

"What?" This was too much, too quickly. First Alf and now Audrey? "Your father would never say yes to that, you're only eighteen."

"Nineteen, by the time Harry gets back here. And you know that if my mind's made up we'll get married anyway, no matter what Dad has to say about it. But we'd rather have your blessing."

"Oh. Oh my goodness, Audrey, I don't know what to say."

But in the end, what was there to say? She talked to Wes in bed that night when their children—not children any longer—were in their rooms asleep. "Bad enough Alf and Treese getting married, but at least they'll be only a few streets away. But if Audrey marries this Harry? He'll take her to the States, and we might never see her again! We could have grandchildren we'd never see!"

"Now, Nell girl, that's the way of the world," Wes said, his sleepy voice settling over her like a quilt. "Youngsters grow up and they go away. Sure it's worse than it used to be, with the war and all these girls going off marrying the Yanks, but when you think about it, how often have your parents or mine seen our young ones? Once every year or two, maybe. And all our crowd down in the States, sure when have the folks ever seen them? Not for years. Young folks got to go away, make their own start."

"But so *far* away! And what are we going to do with this business of Marilyn and nursing school? I don't want to hold her back, she's a bright girl, but how can we afford that?"

"Now, girl, you're gettin' ahead of yourself there. Borrowing

TRUDY J. MORGAN-COLE

trouble, is what it is. Let the good Lord worry about tomorrow, like the Good Book says. 'Sufficient unto the day is the evil thereof.'"

Ellen suspected Wes of quoting Bible verses or hymns when they talked late at night because he knew it was something she couldn't argue back with, and then he could roll over and go to sleep. He was good at leaving things in God's hands, while Ellen, for all her faith, struggled to hold onto things with her own hands. She couldn't help remembering that God's hands were supposed to have kept Johnny safe.

Sufficient unto the day…It wasn't as if this day had brought any real evil. One daughter had good marks in school and wanted to be a nurse. The other was marrying a decent man who had served his country in war. And Alf was marrying Treese, who was a sweet girl. This time, Ellen managed not to add *even if she is R.C.*

"Wes?" He had just started to make the humming noise in the back of his throat that came before the real snoring started.

"What? What is it, maid?"

"Please don't make trouble about the wedding. If they do get married by a Catholic priest, I mean."

Wes's almost-snore turned to a heavy sigh. "I'm not meaning to make trouble, Nell, but I can't change what I think is right and wrong, can I? If he gets married in her church, he got to stand up before a priest and swear they're going to have the youngsters—our grandchildren—baptized Catholic, going to a papist church, muttering confession to some priest. That's not how either of us was brought up, and you know it's not right. Superstition, is all it is. Praying to statues and the like."

That was a long speech for Wes, especially this late in the evening. "I know all that," Ellen replied. "But I had Treese's mother and her aunt down in the shop only a few weeks ago, both of them crying their eyes out, swearing they couldn't go to the wedding if it was in front of a judge. And now you saying you won't go if it's in their church. Sooner or later, somebody got to give an inch, or we could lose Alf altogether. And the children—bad enough if we had grandchildren down in the States we never saw, but what if Alf had children here in town and we weren't allowed to see them?"

There was more she could say, but she stilled her tongue. Alf had been like Wes's little shadow ever since he was old enough to trot around behind his father and hold a hammer, and she knew the thought of their son turning against him would hit Wes harder than anything the Bible or any minister might have to say against Catholics. She'd said her piece and now she would have to leave it at that. Wes could be led, if you know how to lead him, but he was as hard to push as a piece of string.

He said nothing, and after a moment she heard his breathing grow steady and the first snores begin. Pictures of the future chased themselves around in Ellen's mind, but she tried to lay them aside. Her children were growing up. Sufficient unto the day.

TRUDY J. MORGAN-COLE

musical interlude

WES HOLLOWAY

We've no less days to sing God's praise
Than when we'd first begun

The last notes of "Amazing Grace" finished, I settles the accordion on my lap a bit more comfortable.

— Now this is a song I learned from my grandfather, old Zeb Holloway out in Candle Cove.

I doubt any of them are even listening to me, half-asleep as they are from a big dinner of salt pork, cabbage, pease pudding and all the rest. Church in the morning, family to dinner, youngsters off to Sunday School while the women cleans up the dinner dishes. Now, with the shop closed and the young ones back home, it's the one time in the week we gets a bit of a rest. The one time I gets to take down the accordion and play a few tunes.

— Like we never had enough hymns in church.

It's only a mutter, Audrey to Alf, the two of them thinkin they're too big and too smart for this now. But I gives them the look and they says no more, even if Audrey rolls her eyes a bit.

— Anyway this one is not a hymn. It's an old song from out in Bonavista Bay.

— Oh, I remembers poor old Uncle Zeb, he must of known a thousand songs, says Aunt Jemima Tuff. Her and her husband, the one everybody calls Ragged Ralph behind his back, are in town for the week so Aunt Jemima can see the specialist at the Grace Hospital. There's a few more relatives here too, Louise and Cal who are heading down to the Boston States soon for work. And me own youngsters, Audrey and Alf looking bored, Marilyn trying to look bored because she copies everything Audrey does. The little ones, Frank and June, are glad enough to sing along. Them and the old folks belts out all the hymns and folk songs, from "When the Roll is Called up Yonder" to "The Star of Logy Bay."

— Well this is one of grandfather's old songs, and it's about a ship called the *Sallie Ann*. Nothing to do with the Salvation Army, now, this was long before we had any of them people down our way. No, the captain named it for the woman he loved. Who, it so happens, was not his wife. His wife was named Barbara, and was she pleased about the ship being called the *Sallie Ann*? No she was not, and no more was Sallie Ann's husband, which was a shame because he was the first mate.

Audrey ducks her head and whispers something to Alf again, and I knows she's saying that half the time my stories about the songs goes on longer than the songs themselves. I knows the young ones don't have much patience with the songs, but then I never did myself when I was their age. I learned these few songs from grandfather Holloway, but how many more would I have learned if I'd paid attention instead of being in such a hurry to go beating around the cove with me buddies? You can't make young folks listen no matter how much you wish they would. No matter how much they'll wish it themselves, years on when it's too late.

Come all ye good people and gather ye 'round...

Never mind, the first notes and the first lines of the song are here, and I'm singing for them whether they likes it or not. Singing for poor old Jemima who'll likely be dead of that cancer in her stomach before the year is out. Singing for Louise and Cal off to the States, and Cal's brother out on a navy ship in the ocean, and everyone else far from home. A few songs from home to tuck away in memory, take with you on the journey.

Mostly I 'low I'm singing for her, though. My Ellen, my lovely little Nell. She sits there by the coal stove, her back straight as a rod, a couple of grey threads just starting to show in her hair but as pretty and proud as she used to be back behind the counter of her father's shop out home. The hours she puts in now in our shop, the work and the worry on top of looking after the house and the youngsters. She deserves this, her day of rest, a few minutes of music and peace and quiet. She loves a bit of music.

As for the youngsters, the ones paying attention and the ones not—will there be any one of them, or their children, who'll want to pick up the accordion and learn a song? Alf showed a bit of interest in it a year or so back, but now he's older all he thinks about is making money and going out with girls. Still and all, maybe there'll be one of them, someday, or maybe some grandchild who's not even born yet, who'll say, *Now this is a song I learned from my grandfather, old Wes Holloway from Candle Cove, who moved into town and worked as a carpenter, but who was always a bayman at heart.*

There might be. You never knows what the future might hold, do you?

two

SO LONESOME I COULD CRY

1948–1953

AUDREY

Audrey suspected Harry's sister-in-law Ruth had helped him plan their anniversary celebration. Maybe she had even suggested it. Dinner in a restaurant in Shreveport, then the Hayride show at the Municipal Auditorium: Louisiana's own version of the Grand Ole Opry. When they were courting, Audrey had imagined her life would be full of evenings like this—dressing up, going out to eat in restaurants, going dancing or to a show or to the movies. They were going to live in America where people did things like that all the time, where women put on pearl necklaces and matching earrings to greet their husbands when they came home from work. All Audrey's pictures of life in the USA came straight out of the pages of magazines.

She had given the USA a year of her life so far, and nothing in it looked like a movie or a magazine. She had never imagined a town like South Ridge, Louisiana, although when she complained about it in letters to her sister, Marilyn said it sounded no worse than any small town in Newfoundland. But Audrey wouldn't have lived in a place like Candle Cove or Wesleyville or Bonavista. Not for any man she'd ever met would she have streeled herself off to some outport fishing village and lived like it was the last century. She'd made the mistake of assuming that going to America had to mean going to something better.

The Pickens family home was no smaller, in terms of square feet, than the house she'd grown up in. It might have even been a little bigger, though it was all on one level instead of the two storeys she was used to. And where the house at home had had Mom, Dad, four siblings and the shop, it had never felt as crowded as the house with Harry's parents and grandmother felt to her. Their house was a bungalow that looked like it was sinking into the ground, and it always looked sad and run-down. Harry's mother was forever painting windowsills and planting flowerpots, putting up new curtains, so there was no reason for it to look as tatty as it did. The house should have looked smart but it was as if the land was pulling it down, sucking it into the sandy clay, fighting Mrs. Pickens's every effort to make it beautiful.

Harry said it would be better when they had their own place. He had a piece of land near his parents' house and he had a little house framed out and roofed. "We'll want that before any young'uns come along," he said with his slow grin.

Audrey remembered Alf working on the house he was building for himself and Treese. Treese had been off her head with excitement about painting and wallpapering, picking out towels and sheets and collecting hand-me-down furniture from various relatives. Audrey wished she could feel some of that same excitement when Harry talked about their new house, but she would have been a lot happier if he'd said he would get them an apartment—even a little place, even two rooms—over a shop here in Shreveport, or any decent-sized town. Anything bigger than South Ridge, any place with shops and people instead of the endless empty miles of land and sky and those huge gnarled oak trees that looked like something had gotten out of hand and just kept growing, like cancer.

Harry's father was aggressively silent: he could be in the house for hours without uttering a word. Audrey thought she had probably heard him say about a hundred words since she'd met the man. Harry's mother only spoke when she needed to, usually to give Audrey directions about some chore. Some days, when the silence pressed down too hard, Audrey would sit out on the front porch. It was so hot, and a lifetime in Newfoundland had taught her that outdoors was always cooler. This clearly was not true in Louisiana; outside was hotter here, at least in the height of summer. Even under the shade of the porch the sun's heat would hit her like a slap, she who had always thought, like everyone back home did, that heat was a good thing.

A warm sunny day at home was the thing that lifted your spirits, the thing you slogged on towards after a long cold winter. Here in Louisiana, heat was something else altogether. Harry's sister had near to died of heat stroke as a child, his mother said. *Near to died*. Heat was something that could kill you if you stayed out in it, like the cold could at home.

But still she sat out on the porch. Outside, Audrey would look at the empty fields and imagine streets running up and down through them. Then she'd imagine houses, one after another, row upon row. Houses that huddled together and leaned on each other for support. She imagined voices, layering the yells of children and the shouts of their mothers calling them in for dinner over the lonely sound of the birds calling. She built herself a whole Rabbittown out of memories there in the fields in front of the cabin, and then she imagined the ping of the door behind her, people going in and out of the shop.

In letters to her mother and father she put the best face on it, told them about her chores around the house and what a good housekeeper Harry's mother was and how kind she had been, none of which was untrue. In letters to Marilyn and Valerie and Lorraine, she made fun of the things that made her want to cry. She joked about how isolated the farm was, how tiny the nearest town, how backward and slow and silent the people were. She wrote these letters out on the porch, sometimes, or other times she'd be driven by the heat back inside to the table. The rare times that Mrs. Pickens took the old lady and they went to a neighbour's house were the best, because Audrey was alone in the house and she could turn on the radio and listen to music.

The radio wasn't on much, except for news and weather reports. Mrs. Pickens considered it a waste of time to listen to radio serials, and nobody in the house seemed fond of music. The Harry that Audrey had dated back home loved the hit parade and loved to dance, but Audrey had been sentenced to months of near silence in his parents' house, except for hymns at the Baptist church on Sundays.

But tonight they were going to Shreveport. Audrey felt her spirits lift as they drove away from the too-quiet house in South Ridge. When Harry had suggested a night out in Shreveport for their anniversary and asked would she like to go see the Hayride show, Audrey knew Ruth must have given him the idea. But she pretended that it showed how well he knew her, how he understood her unhappiness and knew that music was the only thing that gave her either bit of comfort.

TRUDY J. MORGAN-COLE

The first act was the Tennessee Mountain Boys. The headliner for the evening was Bob Wills, who would come on later; Audrey was excited about that because she had seen him in the movies as well as hearing him on the radio. She snuggled up against Harry, wishing he would be a bit more affectionate. He had his arm over the back of the seat but it wasn't really around her, just lying there. She remembered how he used to hold her hand when they went to movies and concerts back home. Of course couples weren't so affectionate after they'd been married awhile, but only a year? They were going to a hotel, and that had to be a bit more romantic than their bed in the room next to Harry's parents' room, with the walls that seemed paper-thin. She'd expected that over dinner, or during the show, he'd start acting more affectionate, saying romantic things like he used to say to her. Then later, when they had relations in the hotel room, it would be different from the hurried, almost shameful business it was in his parents' house.

But Harry just sat there, tapping his toe to the music, his free hand beating out time on his knee rather than seeking her hand. A new singer came out, a tall dark-haired young man with a guitar, and Audrey hoped he'd sing something romantic, something that might put Harry in the right kind of a mood.

The singer talked a little bit before he sang, telling the crowd this was a new song he was just trying out and they were going to be the first people ever to hear it. His voice had that same southern drawl that everyone's did around here. It sounded so exotic when she used to hear Harry talk back home, but accents like that were a dime a dozen all around her now. Audrey knew that deep drawl was like a round-the-bay accent back home: to some city folks, it marked a person as being from the backwoods, poor and uneducated. But when this man with the guitar opened his mouth, even though it was pure hillbilly, it gave Audrey a shiver. His voice was so slow and rich, it was like something poured over her.

Then he began plucking the strings of the guitar and the song rolled out, and though she had been listening to music all evening it was like this was the first song tonight, maybe the first song ever.

Hear that lonesome whippoorwill
He sounds too blue to fly
That midnight train is whining low
I'm so lonesome I could cry

Audrey wasn't sure what a whippoorwill was—there were so many strange birds down here, all with their different calls, and the only birdsong she could remember from St. John's was the harsh squawk of seagulls. But she did know the whine of that midnight train, and she knew the aching longing in the singer's voice.

Sudden tears welled up in her eyes. What would Harry think? But he didn't notice, didn't look her way at all as Audrey, who never cried, let the tears roll down her cheeks.

The singer performed another song or two after that one, his voice as lovely, but neither one cutting to her heart the way the lonesome song did. It was his face that Audrey couldn't keep her eyes off of, that long mobile face and those haunting dark eyes. When he stepped back from the microphone and the emcee repeated his name, she etched it on her memory. Hank, Hank Williams. She felt the way she did the night she met Harry at the dance at the Caribou Hut—like she had fallen in love, though only with a man who stood behind a guitar and a microphone half an auditorium away from her.

She wished she could buy that song on a record, to listen to it over and over, but of course they didn't have a record player and she couldn't see any way they could get such a luxury anytime soon. When Hank Williams left the stage Audrey scrubbed her face with her handkerchief to make sure no trace of tears remained.

Their hotel room looked like a palace compared to the narrow room with the sagging bed they had slept on all those long months. Audrey's eyes roamed the room, taking in the firm, high white bed, the crisp bedspread, the polished wood of the bedside table with its lamp throwing a circle of warm light. Then Harry did that throat-clearing thing she hated and said, "Don't seem like much for five dollars, does it?"

But they lay down together and made love, though not with the hungry passion that used to fuel them when they kissed and necked in a lane off Merrymeeting Road back home. Why was it so much less exciting once you were allowed to do it every night? In the dark, Audrey closed her eyes and pictured the singer's face, heard his voice. Her mother would probably say that was a sin—picturing some other man while she was in bed with her husband. But Audrey was so lonesome, so lonesome she could cry.

AUDREY

Audrey waited till she was three months along before she told Harry. It wasn't like she ever made a decision to keep it from him; every day she woke up and thought, *Today I have to tell him,* and then somehow the day would unwind and she never got to the point of saying the words. It seemed too personal a thing to share with someone who, she thought more and more often, was almost a stranger to her. But of course that was foolish.

She justified it by telling herself she couldn't be completely certain till she'd missed her monthlies three times and she felt her breasts swell a little and get tender. Even her stomach began to round out a tiny bit, not so anyone would notice when she was dressed, but she could see it herself. It wasn't like she could go to a doctor; she didn't even know where the doctor's office was except that it was in town somewhere, and when they needed to go to town Harry's father drove there in the truck. She could just see herself asking Mr. Pickens to drive her to the doctor's office and having to make up some kind of reason why.

Audrey cooked roast beef for supper on the night she knew she couldn't put it off any longer. A roast was a treat; lots of nights she made corned beef hash or beans. Pork and chicken came from the Pickens family's own hogs and hens; she didn't often buy meat. Now that they were in their own little house she had to cook every night, but she stuck to cooking things that were familiar to her, not Southern things like the rice and gumbo Harry's mother cooked. When Mrs. Pickens put a stew on the table one night and told her it was squirrel, Audrey thought she'd pass out and slide under the table. Harry complained that Audrey didn't make the things his mother made, but Audrey, who knew she herself was no great shakes as a cook, had no intention of trying any of Mrs. Pickens's recipes.

Harry looked at the roast as she slid two slices onto his plate and said, "Well, this looks nice."

"I hope it is nice."

"Beef's a little pricey though, ain't it?"

Audrey brought the gravy boat to the table. When she and Harry first got married she was used to the way her mother did things at home, with everything set out on the table and the family all sitting down together. At home, Dad said grace and everyone served themselves from the dishes on the table. But Harry expected things to be done the way his mother did. Mrs. Pickens sat her husband down at the table and brought everything over from the stove, filled his plate for him, even poured his cup of coffee, before she sat down and served herself. So now Audrey did that too.

"I thought I'd cook something special. It's kind of— it's a special occasion. I've got some news, Harry." Though she was seated now and it was okay to dish up her own dinner she didn't reach for the platter. Her hands twisted in her apron. Her heart was pounding so hard she was surprised Harry couldn't hear or see it.

She waited for him to prompt her, to ask what the news was or even give her a knowing kind of look, but he sliced into his meat and chewed a mouthful in a way that felt like a reproach, even though he didn't actually say it was tough or dry. Something about the motion of his jaw—she knew he was thinking it. Finally, into the silence, she made herself say, "It's good news. I think you'll be happy."

"You better tell me then, see if you're right about that."

"It's—I'm expecting. A baby." Still he didn't say anything, didn't even look up from his plate, so she added, "In May, I think, or thereabouts."

Harry finished the mouthful he was chewing, wiped his mouth with the napkin, laid down napkin, fork, and knife and looked up at her. His eyes met hers but she couldn't read his expression. "A baby. You sure?"

"About as sure as I can be without going to a doctor."

"No call for a doctor if all's going well." He nodded. "Well, that is quite a thing. A baby. I don't—I don't know what to say. I mean, it seems a bit sudden, but I know it's not. We been married more'n a year, and Ma keeps asking me if you're in the family way."

"I know. It's just—the idea takes a bit of getting used to, don't it?"

"It does, at that. It does take some getting used to."

"Maybe that's why it takes nine months—so you have some time to get used to thinking about it." Imagine if babies just showed up one morning, without warning, no time to prepare or plan at all. Harry's eyes swept the tiny room and she

TRUDY J. MORGAN-COLE

knew what he was thinking. A baby, in this tiny, half-finished place.

"I can get the old cot down from Ma's attic," he said. "There'd be room for it over there, between the stove and the window."

She smiled at him, and after a moment he smiled back. It broke her heart open, that smile. She'd always thought that the joy of knowing a baby was coming was supposed to unite new parents, bring them together. Instead it seemed Harry and Audrey were drawn together by uncertainty, by the fact that neither of them had any idea what to do with this news.

"In May? You're pretty sure about that?" he asked.

She wanted to tell him that she was sure because she knew when the baby had started—on their anniversary, the night of the Louisiana Hayride. She couldn't be absolutely certain, of course, but it seemed likely, given how seldom they'd had relations around that time, and the fact that was one night she knew for sure they'd done it. She took up her own roast and potatoes, finally, and remembered the hotel room bed, how she had closed her eyes and pictured Hank Williams instead of her husband. It felt almost like she'd cheated on him.

"Sure as I can be," she repeated, and Harry put down his fork a second time and rubbed his face with one hand. She could see there was stuff going on in his head, and she could have bet she knew what it was: the extra money they'd need, how he was going to work longer and earn a bit more, maybe they could build another room on the house.

She wanted him to say it out loud, to talk to her about his plans, his hopes, his fears, but she'd already learned that in Harry's mind, it was a man's job to worry about things like that. Audrey thought of her parents. She had been only eight or nine when they built the house and opened the shop, but she remembered, with a flush of nostalgia she'd never expected to feel, how everything between them was talked about, hashed out. It used to irritate Audrey, the shop and the way their family's life centred on it, the way her mother was always calculating and planning. Now she was hungry for some of what they had had, that sense that a family was an operation everyone had to pitch in on.

They went to bed that night with not another word said about the baby or how they would manage. While Harry snored, Audrey stared up at the low ceiling, rubbed her belly, and thought about home.

AUDREY

The general store in South Ridge was a big place. You could probably fit four or five of Holloway's Grocery in there, but then, it was the only store of its kind in the town. Still Audrey was flooded with homesickness every time she set foot inside, which generally was every Wednesday when Harry's parents did their shopping. His mother was protective of Audrey now—not of Audrey herself, she realized, but of the unborn heir inside, who was making her feel so huge that she waddled instead of walked into the store.

The aisles of the store were lined with big barrels of flour and feed, and dry goods stacked on shelves. Her grandfather Tuff's store out in Candle Cove was like this, a place where people who scraped a living off the land or out of the sea came to get the few provisions they couldn't grow, raise, or make themselves, always in large quantities and always on credit. Her mother's shop, and the other street-corner St. John's shops like it, served a different purpose for a different kind of customer. A few slices of ham and a bag of potatoes: a quick supper thrown onto the stovetop before the mister came home from work. Or a can of soup for the office girl who dropped into the store on her way back to her rented rooms. And always, of course, the endless packs of cigarettes, and the chips and gum and candy for the little ones.

Around here folks were more likely to buy loose tobacco and roll their own, or that nasty chewing tobacco Harry liked. There were shelves of candy here, like in the shop at home—that was universal, the children's desire for something bright and sweet, and the need of mothers to deny it and then hold it out as a bribe. Steering her own strangely broad and heavy body through the aisle she heard a woman drawl, "Y'all ain't gettin' none of that now, the way you two been gettin' on, you just wait till I tell your father 'bout how you been carryin' on. No, Bobby Joe, you put them lollipops down, now, don't even touch that, Betty!" She only needed to shift the accent and switch around a few words and it could be Mrs. Cadwell from two doors down, slapping Soose's hand away from the candy. Mrs. Cadwell might have said "shenanigans." *What are ye like at all, the crowd of ye, oh all right, shut up whining. Quit yer shenanigans and I'll get a box of Smarties. Just the one, between ye, now.*

Sometimes the voices of memory in her head seemed louder and more real than the voices of people around her, which Audrey was pretty sure was a sign she was going crazy. Standing here in the middle of the store, she tasted and smelled a different air, imagined the blast of northeast wind that blew in with every ping of the door instead of this sultry heat that pressed down on her like wet blankets.

There had been a letter from her mother in this morning's mail—for the first time, a letter with a Canadian stamp on it. It wasn't that it looked so much different from the old

TRUDY J. MORGAN-COLE

Newfoundland stamps—the king's face, in silhouette, and "Four Cents" above it—but there was something about the word CANADA right there across the stamp that made it seem like a child's game of make-believe. Like they'd made up a whole new country while she was gone. Audrey knew that if she went home, she'd see the same streets, the same houses, hear the same voices—but she'd be in a different country.

The change didn't bother her mother, who was quite happy with the Confederation. She had never been one to have much interest in politics, but government cheques coming in the mail—now that was something Ellen Holloway could appreciate.

> ...So we are going to be getting a new cheque called the Baby Bonus, so much for every child under 18, can you imagine what a blessing it would have been for us in the days when you crowd were all little? Now we'll only get $15 every month since all we have home is Frank and June but even so every bit will help, and with Alf and Theresa's little one due in the summer they'll be getting a cheque too. And there's another cheque every month called the Old Age Pension, your grandparents will be glad to see that and it's something to put my mind at ease for when your father and I are getting up in years. I must say I can't see why anyone ever campaigned against Confederation: the politicians who didn't want us to join up with Canada are a wicked lot if you ask me, only out to line their own pockets and not thinking of the good of poor folks like us at all. Do they have the likes of that, Baby Bonus, down in the States? I suppose they don't need it though, people being so well off.

Audrey thought of her mother's words now as she looked

around the general store at the ragged assortment of country people come in to do their week's shopping. Two barefoot children, both clad in overalls with no shirt or anything underneath. A Baby Bonus cheque would go a long way to helping those children; for that matter, it would be a great help to herself and Harry once the baby came.

Wiping sweat off her forehead, Audrey remembered shivering in the foggy drizzle back home and dreaming of being someplace warm. She'd never imagined a place as hot, clammy, and dank as Louisiana. Everyone was sweaty, and everything smelled worse the hotter it got. She wrote to Marilyn that by the middle of summer it was like living in someone's armpit. First she'd written "like living up in the crack of someone's arse" but knew she couldn't put that on paper, even to her sister, so she tore up the paper and threw it away. It made her laugh though, and it probably would have made Marilyn laugh if she'd been brazen enough to actually send it. Poor Marilyn, working as a district nurse out in Bonavista Bay, could have used a few laughs and even a bit of Louisiana heat.

Audrey wouldn't have minded being home with a bit of rain, drizzle, and fog now that she was nine months along. She felt big as a barge navigating the aisles of the store, rivers of sweat running down between her shoulder blades, down the backs of her legs. In fact it really did feel like a river down her legs, as if she had peed herself—she'd been running to the bathroom every half hour, it felt like, for these last few months. Was this a thing that happened to pregnant women? Did you start to pee your pants? *Nobody told me this!* Audrey thought, wishing her mother were nearby. She looked around instead for Harry's mother. What would she say to Mrs. Pickens? "I have to get home, I've peed my pants"?

TRUDY J. MORGAN-COLE

It was gushing now, nothing she could do to stop it. Audrey looked down to see herself standing in a puddle of liquid. Her already-flushed cheeks reddened deeper with shame: she was standing in the middle of the general store while everything inside her flooded out onto the floor and she had no idea what to do. Audrey fought to keep back tears as she started to waddle away from the shameful pool at her feet.

"My Lord, Audrey! Has your water broke?"

So that was it. There was a name for it. Mrs. Pickens steered Audrey out of the store, and while everyone stared, just as she'd feared they would, there were smiles on the women's faces and murmured good wishes as they loaded her into the truck. It felt like that, like she was a bale of goods being loaded up for the journey to market, but in fact she sat up on the front seat on top of an empty feed sack Mrs. Pickens had quickly spread out. She leaked all the way home, where they bundled her into bed and waited for the doctor.

AUDREY

"Mama, wanna go down by the creek." Little Hank's voice, sweet as it was, had a whiny note to it sometimes, in the middle of a long, dull winter afternoon.

"I can't take you out, I'm busy now. Maybe if Lee and Bobby come by later you can go out and play with them." She was pretty sure his cousins, Fred and Ruth's boys, wouldn't be over today. It was the highlight of Hank's life when the boys came over to play, and he'd spent most of the summer with them, exploring the fields, woods, and creek behind the house. When they went back to school in September he was lonesome and cranky. It would be another two years before he went off to school himself. Audrey wondered if she'd lose her mind before then.

He was supposed to go down for his nap in half an hour. It was Audrey's one break in the day and she planned for it carefully. Her letters from this morning's mail—one from Mom and one from June—were laid aside along with the *Life* magazine she hid from Harry because it made him angry that she spent his hard-earned nickel on such foolishness. She also saved her mail to read when Harry was at work and Little Hank was asleep, because Harry got annoyed when she sat down to read a letter from home.

She started with June's letter. June was, what, fourteen now? She was growing up fast, and she was a grand hand to write a letter. She described the big snowfall they had had the second week in December:

> *I bet you won't believe it but the snow was way up over the shop window, and Dad and Frank had to dig a tunnel in from the path that was cleared down the street, into the shop door. The walls of the tunnel are higher than our heads. And up in our room—well, just my room now—I can open the window and step right out onto the snow. I can walk right across the street to Shirley's window if I jump over the part where the path is shovelled. I never saw snow so high in my life, did you?*

Audrey wished she could share that with someone, the image of her parents' house and street buried in snow, the dim light of the store with the snow-covered windows, not quite as dark as nighttime but more filtered and blue. She hadn't seen snow that high since that big storm when she was June's age. Nobody here in Louisiana would believe it. But if she told Harry, he'd snort and say, "That's about what I'd expect up on that godforsaken Rock."

So Audrey kept her letters to herself, for this little island of time and quiet after she had cleared away the dinner dishes and put Hank down to nap, and before she started supper. This afternoon she had an extra job because it was New Year's Eve and they were invited to Harry's parents' house for tomorrow.

Audrey was supposed to bring a cake. Every year Mrs. Pickens cooked a turkey for Christmas and a ham for New Year's and invited all three boys and their wives and kids. Harry's sisters were all married and living far from home, but the sons and daughters-in-law and grandchildren made a fair-sized crew. Every year Mrs. Pickens asked Ruthie to bring her chicken gumbo and Adele to bring pecan pies. She had tried Audrey with several different things over the years but nothing ever turned out well.

But the cake could wait for half an hour while Audrey sat down with a cup of tea and a cigarette—this was also when she had her one smoke of the day since Harry, who used to light her cigarettes for her when they were courting, had now decided he didn't like women smoking. Audrey leafed through the magazine, paused on an article about Hank Williams and his new wife. "That'll never last," she said out loud; she was disappointed when Hank broke up with his first wife, and not just because the first wife was named Audrey. Everyone had one perfect match, and if you found that person you better hang on for dear life. If you married someone who wasn't your perfect match, well, you could expect a lot of heartbreak.

With her letters read, the magazine paged through, and the remains of her tea cooling in the bottom of the cup, Audrey took out her recipe book, the one she put together before she left home, writing down Ellen's favourite recipes in hopes that she could take a little slice of home away with her. She hadn't counted on the fact that she would be so unhandy in the kitchen. She had all day at home while Ellen only had the scattered hours she stole away from the store, but Ellen was a born housewife, and Audrey was—something else. *What?* she thought, but had no answer, except the one she had always had: *Not this. Not this.* She sighed and opened the book to her mother's pound-cake recipe, scanning the list of ingredients. She heard little Hank's cranky, snuffly cry as he woke from his nap.

New Year's Eve. Nothing special in the Harry Pickens household, no cause for celebration. Harry got off work at the usual time, ate his supper with the usual lack of conversation. There was a dance down at the community hall in the evening. Just about the time Audrey figured the musicians would be tuning up their instruments, when Hank was settled into bed for the night, she made a half-hearted effort. "You know, if I ran up and got Jenny Desroches to come over and keep an eye on Little Hank for an hour or two, you and me could go over to the dance."

Harry was well settled into his chair by the stove with a chew of tobacco and a stick he was endlessly whittling—two habits that drove Audrey about crazy. "Now, what'd we want to be doin' that for?"

"You used to enjoy a good dance," Audrey said, putting away the last of the dishes. "We met at a dance."

"Sure we did. That's what young fellows do when they're stationed overseas—go dance with the local girls. And young girls hang around dances trying to pick up a soldier."

"Lots of married people goes to the dances. Ruth and Fred are going tonight, she told me. Her sister's watching the boys."

"I don't know why Freddy gives in to that. Them dances are only for young folks and flirting and carrying on."

It wasn't as if she had expected his answer to be any different. Dishes finished, child asleep, pound cake cooling and covered, Audrey sat down across from her husband and picked up her bag of socks and her darning needle. No idle hands here to be tools for the devil.

The first day of the new year dawned cool, by Louisiana standards. Audrey was up early because three-year-olds didn't take holidays. Harry slept in and she didn't begrudge him that. Six working days a week and church on Sundays: let the man sleep till nine on a holiday if he wanted to. Christmas, New Year's, Good Friday, Easter Sunday and the Fourth of July. She couldn't think of many other days that Harry took off. "You can't ask for much more than a man who's a good hard worker," Audrey remembered her mother telling her and Marilyn as their father came home late and work-stained. But then Wes would bend over to kiss Ellen on the cheek, and she'd smile while she squirmed and swatted him away, and Audrey would think, *You can ask for a little more.*

They left at noon for dinner. The elder Pickens's house was the most cheerful that drab little bungalow ever got on a day like this, with all three sons and their wives and children packed in. Little Hank was absorbed by his boy cousins, and while the men settled on the porch Audrey brought her pound cake into the kitchen. There, her sisters-in-law Ruth and Adele, and Adele's fifteen-year-old daughter Janine, worked together to get dinner on the table, ducking and weaving around the elder Mrs. Pickens, polite to her face and laughing slyly behind her back in an elaborate language of shared glances and rolled eyes. Audrey loved that her sisters-in-law were so irreverent about the matriarch, but she knew they were every bit as capable of making fun of Audrey herself when her back was turned. They were polite to her, but she would always be the outsider, with her funny accent and her strange ways.

Still, she let herself be absorbed into the chaos and did her best impression of an agreeable woman, carrying knives and forks out to the table while Ruthie got the giant, gleaming ham

111

out of the oven. A flurry of small boys screeched through the kitchen and out the back door. "Henry sure looks glad to be back with the big boys again," says Adele. The other boys were all Ruth's sons, Adele having been blessed only with well-behaved daughters.

"Oh, he loves it. He's always asking me when they're coming to play with him again. It's hard for him to understand they're at school all day and he can't go for more than a year yet," Audrey said.

"I never did approve of children that young going to school," Mrs. Pickens piped up. "Children should be at home till they're seven. That's what Ruthie should have done with her boys."

"That's old-fashioned, Mother Pickens," said Ruth. "All the children go to kindergarten now, and they're better off for it. Gets them out from underfoot, too," she added in a lower voice meant only for the younger women to hear. Adele snickered.

"Although they do pick up some bad habits," Adele said. "When my Libby went off to kindergarten she came back full of sassy talk, I had to give her a good swat on her little backside to keep her in line."

"All youngsters are like that, saucy as blacks if they can get away with it," Audrey said, and looked up to see both sisters-in-law staring at her.

"Saucy as blacks? Is that what they call it up in New-FOUND-land?" Ruth asked with a smile. "I thought Harry said you didn't have no coloured folks up there?"

"Oh, it's not—I mean, we don't. I don't think it means Black people—it's something to do with Catholics and Protestants." Audrey had a vague memory of a boy from Brother Rice calling Alf a "dirty black Prod" one of the few times her brother got into a fight on the street. She was sorry she'd used the expression now; she hadn't intended to draw any attention to herself and the faraway place she came from

"Well there weren't none of that kindergarten in my day and I can't say any of my boys suffered for not going," Mrs. Pickens said. "And you should keep Henry home till he's older, Audrey."

Another thing: none of them would call Little Hank by his right name. He was christened Henry Charles Pickens the third. The old man was the First, and Harry, though his youngest son, was Henry Charles Pickens Junior. When Harry wanted the same name for his son, Audrey agreed, thinking she could call him Hank after her favourite singer. Hank was a good nickname for Henry, even if Hank Williams's real name was Hiram. But nobody else liked the nickname except Audrey: everyone called him Henry after his grandfather.

Dinner was a repeat of Christmas dinner a week ago: the same jokes, the same conversations, the same arguments flaring up and quickly tamped down by Southern good manners. When the women got up to clear the table, everyone segregated again by age and gender: children outside, men to the parlour where someone turned on the radio hoping to hear scores from one of the big football games. Music drifted in to the kitchen where the women had turned to the work of cleanup: Audrey scraped the last of the rice out of the serving dish to the tune of "Don't Let the Stars Get in Your Eyes."

Then, through the babble of chatter, she heard the DJ mention Hank Williams, and wondered what song was coming up. The men's talk out in the parlour hushed a bit and she heard the sombre tone from the radio, the dreary music behind the announcer's words, and Harry's brother Bert said, "Well that's a damned shame."

"At one a.m. this morning...found dead in his car on his way to..."

"Can't really say it's a big shock, all they been sayin' about his drinking," said Fred.

"Opry let him go because of it. Drank hisself to death, I'd say." Bert again. Then Harry's voice, raised a little, "Come in here, Audrey, you're gonna wanna hear this."

She moved, dreamlike, to stand in the parlour door. The men all looked a little bit sad, the way you were supposed to look when you heard somebody famous was dead, but a little bit smug too, because they could say they knew it was coming, he was headed for trouble. Harry's eyes met hers over the other men's heads, and she didn't like what she saw. He was almost smiling, like there was a kind of triumph there. Surely she had to be imagining that.

The sad news of the young singer's death—only twenty-nine years old, found dead in his car late at night, the circumstances murky—occupied the conversation in both parlour and kitchen for all of ten minutes. Then the second Hank Williams song was followed by the football scores and the men turned to discussing the game, while the women were quickly diverted from the distant spectre of Hank Williams drinking himself to death to the more immediate one of Adele's brother-in-law, Verle, who was doing the very same thing at much closer quarters and made a fool of himself at the dance last night. *Nobody cares*, Audrey thought: that's what singers and movie stars were for, after all. To distract folks for a few minutes with the glamour of their success and the shame of their fall. Frank Sinatra and Ava Gardner had had another big fight on her movie set; Liz Taylor was having a baby with her second husband; poor Hank Williams was dead. On to the next thing.

She wouldn't mention it, wouldn't bring it up again, would pretend that a silly crush on a singer didn't touch her real life at all. Except that Harry brought it up, that night when she was getting ready for bed. "Sure is a damned shame about Hank Williams, ain't it?" he said. "Maybe you wanna stop calling little Henry after him, now? Not much of a model for a young feller to look up to."

"Judge not, lest ye be not judged," said Audrey. "Be glad you never had his troubles."

Harry laughed: not a nice sound. "Oh, you'll always be quick to defend any handsome feller—I know what you're like. Always sniffin' around for someone you think is better than your own husband."

"You be quiet, now! I never did a thing to deserve that! I haven't laid eyes on another man since we've been married...."

"No, you don't get much chance, stuck out here in the country, do you? Don't you think I know why you're always at me to take you off to dances and into town? I remember you back at them dances on the base in Newfoundland, always after the fellows, flashing your tits at anything in a uniform—"

Too late, Audrey realized he'd had more than a few whiskies with Bert and Fred, and while Harry wasn't a frequent drunk or usually a mean one, there was something different in him tonight, a snarl in his voice that made her protest die unspoken in her mouth. He crossed the floor in two quick strides—it was a tiny room—and grabbed her by the wrist, hard enough to hurt. He pushed her down onto the bed, shoved her legs apart with his knee planted between them.

"Harry, stop. You're hurting—"

"You bitch. You'd like to be off at dances, wouldn't you, putting the moves on every sorry-assed fella there, wouldn't

TRUDY J. MORGAN-COLE

you? But not your husband. You got no time for your own husband."

That was hardly fair. It wasn't like he'd even come looking for it much, not since she had lost the second baby. Mostly he just rolled over and went to sleep, and if he did want anything it was a quick fumble in the dark. It was hardly any surprise she hadn't gotten pregnant again—Audrey had begun to feel Harry didn't even want her anymore.

Tonight he wanted something, but it wasn't her, not in any way she recognized. His hands pinned her shoulders to the bed, both his knees were shoved between hers, forcing her legs apart. She wanted to cry out, to kick, to bite, but with every nerve she was aware of her son asleep on the other side of the wall. She closed her eyes as her husband's hands moved from her shoulders, tearing at her clothing, his clothing. She prayed that it would be over quickly.

The next morning, the second day of 1953, she woke up at the same time as always, got little Hank up, cooked breakfast. Harry went off to work with the same goodbye as always. Audrey turned on the radio and heard another Hank Williams song. The announcer said his body was being taken back to Montgomery, Alabama, and the funeral would be held there in two days.

Audrey took her son's little pile of wooden blocks and lured him into her bedroom to sit on the bed while she took out her suitcase and began to pack her clothes.

AUDREY

She took the five o'clock out of town, changed trains in Shreveport, and travelled through the night. "We're taking a little trip!" she had told Hank. She hadn't told Harry anything. Packed and left while he was at work and didn't leave so much as a note. She knew that was wrong. She should have left a note or something. What would she tell him when they came back home? How could she ever explain running off to Alabama for Hank Williams's funeral?

Those were the thoughts that kept her mind churning and her hands trembling throughout that dark night ride. Eventually, when Hank fell asleep across her lap, she dozed off too, waking fitfully every time the train pulled into a station in some tiny town and passengers around her got on and off. They changed again in New Orleans, Hank so sleepy he was almost like a piece of luggage. She had her own big suitcase and a little one for him. She had packed way more than they'd need to go to Alabama for two days. When Harry got home and saw what was missing from the closet, he would think she had taken the boy and run away for good.

By the time the train stopped in Montgomery, her neck and back were all stiff and sore and her eyes felt like they'd been rubbed with sandpaper. Hank woke confused, twisting his head up to look at her and say, "Where are we, Mama?" That little drawl in his voice that made him sound like half a stranger to her. "I'm hungry."

"Me too, honey. We're going to get off this train now and find a place to get some breakfast."

They found it—scrambled eggs and grits—in a diner a little ways from the station, after Audrey had put their two suitcases in a locker. She'd come back for them once she figured out where they were going to stay tonight. The diner was busy, and the waitress, a chatty middle-aged woman with bottle-blonde hair piled high on her head, said, "Looks like half Alabama's come to town for the funeral."

Audrey nodded. "That's what we came for, too."

The waitress's face softened, as if they shared a common loss. "It's a cryin' shame, ain't it? Him so young, and so much talent. Folks 'round here have always been proud of him. Where'd y'all come from?"

"Louisiana, up near Shreveport."

"That's a long way to come, just for today."

"I loved his music a lot. I seen him once, at the Hayride. I just—wanted to be here."

The waitress laid a pitcher of syrup on the table along with their plates. "That's what folks are saying," she said. "They say the hall will be all full with the important folks, but they're settin' up speakers in the park across the way for folks who want to hear the service. If y'all'da been here yesterday you coulda gone past and seen the coffin, they say thousands of folks did." Audrey knew she had to be careful about every penny, but she left the waitress an extra nickel as a tip.

It would be easier to do this if she were on her own, to follow the crowds till she came to the park outside the auditorium, where people were already gathering for the funeral service at one o'clock. She could even have come yesterday, filed past the coffin, seen his face for the second time, closed and peaceful in sleep. But she couldn't do any of it easily today, with a three-year-old in tow, whining about the heat and about being thirsty. "Where are we going, Mama? Can I go play? Play in the park?"

There was no place to play; it wasn't that kind of park. Just a little grassy square across the street from the city hall, and even if it had been a place for children to play, it was too crowded. There was barely space to stand, and all over she saw squirming children held by their parents' firm hands.

A woman nearby gave Audrey a smile of sympathy. "It's hard for a young'un to understand, ain't it?"

"It is," Audrey said. "He's named after Hank Williams, I just wanted him to be here today, so he'd be able to say, later, that he was here."

"Seems like the least we can do," the woman said.

Was that really why she had brought little Hank? "This is the man you were named after," she told him on the way over to the park from the diner this morning. "I called you Hank because of him. He's the one who sang all those songs we like to sing along with on the radio, you know?"

"Like about the whippoorwill," Hank said. "And the jambalaya."

"That's right." Now she tried to quieten Hank down as the crackle and hiss of the speakers announced that the service was about to start. The park, and the streets around it, were packed

TRUDY J. MORGAN-COLE

with more people than Audrey had ever seen in one place in her life. Nobody around her had even tried to get into the municipal auditorium. "I talked to a man who lined up all last night to get in this morning," said someone nearby, "but there's only about twenty-five hundred it can hold, and they do say there's more like twenty-five thousand people come to town just for the funeral."

When she'd thought about coming she'd imagined, of course, that she would be inside the auditorium. Probably all these people crowded around her imagined that too. She'd thought she'd be able to see Hank Williams up front in the casket, that it would be like being at a church service. She hadn't imagined little Hank at her side, wriggling and trying to twist out of her iron grip on his wrist. Yet she'd never even considered leaving him home with his father.

There was a pop in the speakers, and then quite suddenly a man's voice, deep and resonant, flowed out of them.

The Lord is my Shepherd, I shall not want
He maketh me to lie down in green pastures...

The old psalm, recited so often to her by Ellen, memorized in Sunday School, stilled the crowd, line by line, till when it ended they were all hushed as if they really were in church. Surely goodness and mercy had not followed Hank Williams all the days of his life, but perhaps he would dwell in the house of the Lord now, at last.

The preacher finished the psalm and announced a "coloured quartet" whose harmonizing voices came out of the speakers next. Then it was back to the Scripture, with the part from 1 Corinthians—wasn't it?—the bit about the dead being raised incorruptible. Old words, comforting even if you didn't know whether you believed them. *O Death, where is thy sting?*

The crowd in the park stayed quiet, except for a few squalling babies. Folks gave the mothers of the babies dirty looks, and when Little Hank interrupted to whine, "When are we going *home?*" Audrey squatted down to whisper in his ear, "You be quiet now, or I am going to give you a good lickin' on your behind, so just hush up!" Her voice must have been fierce enough to convince him because he folded cross-legged onto the ground at her feet, playing with the toy truck she had had the good sense to put in her purse. For the next little while only the weight of his small body against her feet and ankles reminded her that he was there.

More Scripture, then the minister introduced Roy Acuff, who said a few kind words about Hank ("No finer boy has ever come or gone, as far as we're concerned") before he began singing Hank's own song, "I Saw the Light." All around Audrey, people wept openly, but Audrey was dry-eyed.

It was as if she had come all this way for the funeral thinking she'd see and hear Hank himself, like she did that night at the Hayride, and while that was clearly a crazy thought, she did have that feeling of letdown. As if she'd bought a ticket for a show where he was on the bill, and then found out that he'd cancelled, last minute. Why had she expected that standing with a crowd of people outside his memorial service would make her feel closer to Hank Williams?

Little Hank stood up and started pulling at her skirt. "Can we go now, Mama? Can we go?"

"You hush that youngster up," snapped the man next to Audrey. Everyone was straining to hear the preacher speaking over the public-address system now, and Audrey bent down again to hiss another threat into Little Hank's ear. He should have been home with his daddy, she thought. He wasn't going to remember this day anyhow. The preacher was talking now

121

TRUDY J. MORGAN-COLE

about Hank, but not really about Hank, after the first few minutes. It was all about America and Jesus. America, such a great country, where even a little shoeshine boy could grow up to sing songs that were loved by millions. And Jesus, everyone needed to just put their hand in the hand of Jesus and it would all be all right when God called us home, like he just called Hank. Lots of tribute to how much everyone loved his songs, but not a word about the man's struggles. He wrote "I Saw the Light" but it seemed to Audrey, following the gossip in the papers these last months, that mostly he saw darkness, and tried to sing his way out of it. You wouldn't talk about that at the man's funeral, of course—you wouldn't mention his drinking and divorce and all the nastiness. Don't speak ill of the dead.

The last hymn was another quartet, this one singing "Precious Memories," and around Audrey, the people gathered in the park joined in the singing, first a few thready voices and then more and more until it was a chorus that swept her up. Little Hank was still wriggling and twisting around the hem of her skirt and she gathered him up in her arms, nestling him on her hip. Lulled by the voices around, maybe, he stopped fighting her and snuggled in, drooping his head on her shoulder.

Audrey sang along, all the voices rising together, and in the middle it hit her that she travelled all these miles as if somehow thinking she'd hear Hank Williams sing again, and the truth was, he never would. Not this song nor any other. She'd never see that long, sad face she remembered so vividly from that night at the Hayride, the night she pictured Hank Williams instead of her husband next to her in bed. It was over, all of it—Hank Williams's young life, and her own marriage, and whatever bundle of hopes and dreams she had dragged down south here with her. She no longer wondered why she had hauled her son along to a funeral he was too young to understand, or why she had packed two suitcases. Or what she would say to Harry when she went back.

Tears were rolling down her cheeks at last—what a relief to be able to cry, here with all the other crying people, all this sadness in one place. Little Hank reached up his hand and patted her wet cheeks. "Don't cry, Mama."

When the hearse had gone past and the speakers had hissed to silence and the crowd began to disperse, Audrey sagged onto a bench under a tree while Little Hank ran around and round in circles. She needed someplace to stay for the night—some boarding house where they could get a meal and a decent night's sleep.

Audrey had been thinking for months—years, maybe— that she could go on like this, that things would get better someday. New Year's night had made it clear that she'd been lying to herself. She must have known—packing those suit-cases, buying that one-way ticket—that she wasn't coming back. Coming home. She had never once said that in her mind about South Ridge, Louisiana, about the house she shared with Harry. Never described it as home.

She went back to the train station, dragging a tired Hank. She would get her suitcases back, ask someone there about boarding houses near the station. Fifty cents should get them both a room for the night.

She looked at the big board with train times and destina-tions. A train was leaving in a few hours for Washington, DC. A big city, with connections to other big cities. She asked the man behind the counter what it would cost for a ticket to Washington D.C., and beyond that, one from Washington to New York.

If she could get past Washington, she'd be out of the South. In New York, in Brooklyn, her father and her mother both had people, aunts and uncles who had settled there. She could make a long-distance call home, get an address, turn up on their doorstep, and they would take her in. They were family.

"You'd be lookin' at about forty dollars for the whole trip, ma'am," the ticket agent said. "That'll be for yourself, and a child's ticket for the little boy…and you'd need to change trains…." His voice drawled on but Audrey stopped listening when he said forty dollars. She had taken twenty—she thought of it as stealing, knew Harry would see it as stealing—to come here, and the tickets from South Ridge to Montgomery had cost half of that. She could get back to Harry if she turned around and bought a ticket right now, but that was all she'd be able to do. If she bought a ticket back to South Ridge, she wouldn't have enough left to rent a room or buy a meal.

She thanked the man and went to sit down on a bench. Hank was crying for something to eat. Somehow, in less than forty-eight hours, Audrey had become a woman who had stolen money, run away from her husband and abducted their child, a woman with no home and no place to go. She could still go back, tell Harry about the funeral, apologize for being so reckless and foolish. Take her medicine.

Instead, she went into the nearest snack bar and bought a bag of chips and a Coke for Hank, then went to the pay phone. She hadn't made a long-distance call once in the time since she had left home; Harry would have been horrified at the cost. Long distance was for emergencies. She didn't want to have this emergency, to throw herself at her parents' mercy, but the only other choice was the one thing she could not do.

As the operator connected the call and she listened to the

MOST ANYTHING YOU PLEASE

distant ring on the other end, Audrey thought of the comments she had heard Ellen make about divorces, which were rare in the neighbourhood when Audrey grew up. Putting up with it, making the best of a bad situation—that was the rule. Ellen might well tell Audrey to stiffen her upper lip, buy the next ticket back to South Ridge, and submit herself unto her husband.

"Hello?" It wasn't Ellen; it was June, her voice young and light, crackling over the miles.

"I have a collect call from Audrey," the operator's voice said. "Will you accept the charges?"

TRUDY J. MORGAN-COLE

ELLEN

"Now, I won't be gone that long, and you don't need to worry about anything—your father's right upstairs and I told him to leave the door open. You call out if you need him, all right?" Ellen stood on the unfamiliar side of the store counter, rubbing her index finger over the softened edges of the piece of paper she clutched. June had been working in the shop after school for months now, but Ellen had never left her alone there in the evening, and wouldn't have done it now if Wes hadn't been upstairs.

Not that there was anything to worry about, of course not. None of the neighbours would cause any trouble, but what if some stranger were to come up the street, stop into the store for a pack of cigarettes, and give a hard time to the fourteen-year-old girl behind the counter?

"Everything will be fine," Ellen said.

"I know it will, Mom. I don't know what you're worried about." Fourteen, so sure of herself. Ellen remembered this stage with both Audrey and Marilyn, that sudden shift from little girl into young woman, standing behind the counter, looking like they knew it all. Like they could handle anything life might throw at them. The very fact Ellen had to go to the train station tonight proved how untrue that was.

She looked out at the street, waiting for the headlights of Alf's car. She unfolded the telegram once more—it fell open easily, its creases permanent and deep from the many times she had read it and tucked it away since it had arrived. CROSSING ON *CABOT STRAIT* THURSDAY STOP TRAIN ARRIVES ST JOHNS FRIDAY EVENING STOP CAN YOU MEET US STOP.

A telegram, at least, was a more common thing than a long-distance phone call—Ellen still wasn't fully recovered from the shock of Audrey's collect call a couple of weeks earlier. She couldn't think when she'd ever seen or heard her eldest daughter cry, since Audrey was a little girl. But there she was on the phone, calling from some place in Alabama, telling them she'd left Harry and she had the little fellow with her, and she only had ten dollars to her name.

Alf pulled up in the new Dodge he was so proud of. "You know we're too early," he said as Ellen got in.

"Train comes in at eight." Ellen checked her watch; it was only seven-thirty, but she wanted to be in plenty of time.

"Train's *due* in at eight. You really think the Bullet's going to get here on time for once, just because Audrey's on it?" Alf, like a lot of people, had picked up the habit of calling the train the Newfie Bullet like the American servicemen did during the war. They used to laugh at it because it took forever to get across the island. Ellen knew it was nearly always late, but she couldn't count on that, not with her daughter and grandson arriving.

TRUDY J. MORGAN-COLE

From her purse, during the inevitable wait at the railway station, she took out the other things she carried, like good-luck charms, to prepare her for this meeting. Audrey's last letter from Louisiana, written to tuck into her Christmas card, no hint that she was thinking of running away from her husband. The letter had sounded like Audrey's letters always did: funny, interested in the news from home and family, not exactly happy about her own married life but—what was the word? *Resigned*, maybe. A fair bit short of *contented*, but Ellen had often told her life was no bed of roses. To be married with a small child and living far away from your own people was a hard row to hoe. Audrey, she had thought, was making the best of it.

She looked at the letter again now, as she had done over and over in these last two weeks, re-reading it to see if she could find a hint of what Audrey was about to do. But there were none: it was a card with a poinsettia on it, signed, "Love from Audrey, Harry and Hank," and a breezy two-page letter. And a small photo of her grandson, only the second photo she had ever seen of the boy. Audrey didn't have extra money for going to town and getting a family picture done.

The boy, Henry—named for his father and grandfather; Audrey called him Little Hank in her letters—was a handsome little fellow, with dark brown hair and serious eyes that stared straight at the camera. She couldn't see anything of Audrey in him: he looked just like Harry Pickens. Ellen had one picture with Harry in it: Audrey and Harry on their wedding day, looking happy and hopeful as a young couple should.

"Why do you think she left him?" Ellen said now. The clock said eight-thirty and the man at the counter said the train had left Mackinson's at eight.

"How would I know? You're the one who was talking to her."

"Yes, but—she didn't say much. Well, she wouldn't, on the phone, would she? But she writes to you and Treese. Did she ever give any hint, anything…I mean, I know she wasn't very happy, but I thought she was just homesick."

"Had to've been more to it than that."

Alf, like his father, was a man of few words. Of course, anyone married to Treese didn't need to talk a lot; she'd do all the talking for him, and Ellen had already pulled her daughter-in-law's tongue on the subject of Audrey's marriage and her sudden departure. The one who really could have told her something, Ellen suspected, was Marilyn, up in Toronto. She was the second of Ellen's daughters to marry and move far away, though Marilyn's letters sounded more cheerful than Audrey's did. Perhaps Marilyn and George were really in love, or perhaps Toronto was just a more interesting place to live than a farm in Louisiana. There were lots of other Newfoundlanders around up there, Marilyn said. Of course George was a Newfoundlander himself, from down on Bond Street, not some stranger from a faraway place. And as they hadn't had any children yet, Marilyn was still nursing, so she had work to keep her occupied and out of the apartment all day.

"There must be more to it," Ellen said now. "It don't add up, doing something so drastic like taking off without a word to her husband or a penny in her pocket, just because she's lonely."

Ellen and Wes had wired the money for Audrey to buy a train ticket for herself and the little fellow up to Toronto, where they had stayed with Marilyn and George for two weeks. The second phone call had come from there; a long one where Ellen and Audrey had hashed out the possibilities. Audrey could stay up there in Toronto with Marilyn for a while, though they didn't have much space in their apartment. "That's probably what I'd do if I was on my own," Audrey said.

"But you're not. It'll be hard, finding a job and finding a place, if you're a…a single mother. A child needs to be raised in a family, Audrey, and if you're not going to take him back to his father, then you should bring him home here. There's always a bed here for both of you, and a job in the shop till you gets on your feet."

"I'm not going back to Harry, Mom. That's out of the question." Audrey's voice sounded like it used to be when she was a young girl arguing with Ellen over breaking some rule or sneaking out of the house with her friends. You couldn't turn that girl an inch once her mind was made up. *Hard as nails*, Ellen used to say Audrey was.

But when Audrey stepped off the train into the icy January wind that cut down the platform, she no longer looked hard as nails. The red-haired woman with the sleepy child in her arms looked softened, worn by stress and trouble. Her tired eyes searched the people waiting on the platform without seeing her mother and brother. A porter set two suitcases down beside her as Ellen stepped forward to greet her daughter.

"Oh, Mom. You're here. They told us the train was late so— I didn't know." Audrey hugged her mother, or accepted Ellen's hug, as well as she could with her arms full of Little Hank. Alf picked up the suitcases.

"Is this all you got?"

"That's everything." Audrey met her mother's eyes again and tried to smile. "It's not much. I didn't—well, you know. I didn't plan this very well. Marilyn loaned me a few things, winter clothes. I can't—anyway, you know. I'm going to pay you back, don't worry. I just…," her words stumbled off into a silence Ellen understood. For Audrey, "Help me" and "Thank you" were two of the hardest things to say.

MOST ANYTHING YOU PLEASE

"Now, don't you worry about any of that. Plenty of time to sort it all out when you're settled."

"Oh, this is your car, Alf? Very nice—what year is it?" Audrey's voice was brighter and sharper when she had something practical to talk about, and Alf, who had been pretty much at a loss for words since she got off the train, was almost chatty, talking about his '51 Dodge Wayfarer and what he had paid Tony Nolan for it second-hand.

"There, you get up in front with Alf, now, I'll sit back here with Henry," Ellen said as Audrey laid the sleeping boy on the backseat. Ellen covered him over with the extra coat she had brought along. Poor little mortal was wearing a cloth jacket—he wouldn't have known cold like this ever in his short life. He had stirred and opened his eyes and whimpered a few times while Audrey carried him from the platform to the car, but it was better he was sleeping through this arrival.

"It's all right," she murmured to him as they drove down Water Street. "You're home now. You're home." It wouldn't seem that way to Little Henry, of course, but at three years old his notion of how things were would be shifting all the time anyway, and soon St. John's would be home to him. She stroked his dark hair, ran a finger down his rounded cheek. Thought of Audrey at the same age, sprawled off asleep, long-legged and round-cheeked. "You're home now," Ellen whispered again, though nobody heard her.

AUDREY

"Hank, you little frigger, will you get out of that! Go outside and play, you got me drove up the wall."

"Don't call me that."

"I'll stop calling you a little frigger when you stops acting like one."

"Not that." He stood in front of her with the bag of chips he'd taken from the shelf, his little cowlick down in his eyes. She wanted to hug him and smack him all at once. "Hank."

"It's your name, what else am I supposed to call ya?"

"Nan and Pop calls me Henry. MeeMaw and PawPaw calls me Henry. Daddy calls me Henry."

Four years old, talking plain as you like—and talking back to her like that! Already as stubborn as…as what? Stubborn as the mule, was the expression. Audrey didn't know much about mules, but she did know the truth she saw reflected in her son's face. It was Harry's eyes and Harry's chin she saw, but the expression in those eyes and the tilt of the chin were her own.

Stubborn as me. Mom's old curse: *I hope you haves one just like yourself.* And now it was Mom's words he was flinging back at her: "Nan says" and "Nan does" had become potent weapons in Hank's little arsenal over the months since they had been back home. He was right: her parents, like his Louisiana grandparents, had not taken to calling him Hank. With Harry's parents she had always assumed it was because they wanted him to be called Henry like his grandfather. But Ellen just sniffed and said, "*Hank* sounds like a cowboy in a Western. It don't sound like a serious man's name."

"He's not a serious man; he's a little boy."

"Yes, but he'll be a man someday and he'll want a man's name. I was always careful over that with my boys," Ellen had said, pointing out as usual how she had done everything perfectly. "Alf and Frank, neither of those were names boys would be ashamed of when they grew up. You get in the habit of calling him Hank, and he'll be after you to change it when he's sixteen. Better to start the way you mean to go on."

Now here he was, four years old, already after her to change it. Audrey shook her head. "They can call you what they want, but you'll always be Hank to me."

OK," he conceded, tilting his head like he was thinking it over. "But not out loud. I won't come if you call Hank."

"I'll call you whatever I damn well please and you mark my words, you'll come when I call or I'll swat your backside. Now take them chips and get out of the shop, I don't need you underfoot."

"OK but when you call me for dinner, you better say Henry!"

Audrey opened her mouth to get the last word but the door had already swung shut behind him. She sighed as she lit up a smoke. That youngster loved to win a fight. She couldn't

TRUDY J. MORGAN-COLE

picture how saucy he'd be by the time he was thirteen. Outside the door she heard him hollering at the other little boys playing out in front of the shop. Hank's—Henry's—little voice was a weird mixture of the southern drawl he heard for the first three and a half years of his life, and the St. John's accent he was already picking up. She wondered if someday Louisiana would be erased from his voice altogether, along with memories of MeeMaw, PawPaw, and Daddy.

"You're taking my son away." She could still hear Harry's voice over the telephone line. She had stood in Marilyn's little kitchen in Toronto, one hand gripping the handset of the phone and the other hand knotted into the phone cord, playing with the little loops like Treese's Aunt Maggie playing with her rosary beads. She had waited till she was safe there at Marilyn's, out of the US and into Canada. Only then had she felt able to call Harry, to face his anger.

If he had said, "Come back, Audrey, you know I love you"—what would she have done? All through that endless train journey, from Montgomery to Washington, Washington to New York, New York to Toronto, all those crowded second-class carriages, all those hours of Little Hank complaining and her trying to keep him entertained—the main thing she had felt was relief. Like she had been tied to a chair and someone was snipping away the ropes that held her, one by one as they crossed each state line, crossed the border into Canada.

The door pinged as her brother Frank came in. "Henry and them other little ones was starting to head off down the street but I told them they couldn't go no farther than Mrs. Vokey's gallery," he said. "You wants to watch them—I know they're only little but Butch Cadwell's young one, Eddie, is the ringleader and all the other ones follows him like ducklings."

"I'm sure they won't get into too much trouble, out there

on the street with the neighbours watching," Audrey said. "It's a nice change for him to have other youngsters around to play with."

"Ah, I'm sure he'll be fine. I'm only sayin' watch out for the Cadwells as usual." Frank headed up the steps.

Funny, Audrey thought, how easy it was to slip into old roles when you moved back home. She was like a young girl again, both arguing with and depending on her mother, working in the shop. She was still Little Hank's—Henry's— mother, but most of the time it felt like Henry was one more baby for Ellen to raise, and Audrey was a big sister to him as well as to Frank and June. She didn't feel the burden of being a mother the way she had all those long days in the little house in South Ridge. Here, Henry had other youngsters to play with and she had her family. She missed Marilyn—June wasn't quite old enough to fill the gap, and while she got on all right with Treese, there was always a bit of distance with her brother's wife. She needed her own friends, her own crowd, but the girls she had grown up with were either moved away or married.

But tonight was going to be different. She had run into Valerie Hynes downtown—Valerie Gillard, she was now—a few weeks ago. They hadn't really kept in touch, except for a few letters right after Audrey had moved down South and Christmas cards every year since then. They had squealed, and hugged, and done all the things you did when you saw an old friend after years apart. They traded news, or rather Audrey heard all Valerie's news—two babies and another on the way, a new job for her husband working for CN, as the railway company was called now. "And I heard you moved back home…I've been meaning to drop by the shop and see you, but you know how busy it always is when you have youngsters," Val said. "And you've got just the one? A little boy?"

TRUDY J. MORGAN-COLE

They had ended the visit in the shoe aisle at Bowring's with the promise that they would get together soon. Valerie gave Audrey her phone number and said she would have Audrey over to the house sometime. But she wasn't in the neighbourhood anymore—they had bought one of the new houses in around Churchill Park, so it wasn't as if she and Audrey were going to run into each other on the street or drop over after supper for a cup of tea. If Valerie didn't call, Audrey supposed, that would be the end of it.

But Valerie did call, and tonight she had invited Audrey over to her house for supper. She had also asked Lorraine Penney and her husband Ted. Audrey had seen Lorraine in and out of the shop since she'd been home; these days she was nearly always with Ted's sister Selena, who had married Freddy Ivany. Lorraine had never suggested that she and Audrey might get together, but now she sailed into the front porch of Val's little bungalow, kissed Audrey on the cheek, and shrieked, "We got the old gang back together!"

Not all their old crowd was available to get together, of course. Most of the conversation over dinner was taken up with tracking old friends and classmates, bringing Audrey up to date on who had married whom, who had moved away, how many children everyone had. Eileen Howse was down in the States; Maxine Parsons and her husband were up in Toronto. Donna Crocker was still living over on Summer Street and had two sets of twins.

"And Cathy Kelly—did you hear? Well, you knew that wasn't going to end well, herself and Ricky Ryan—sure he was fifteen years older than her if he was a day," Lorraine said, digging into Valerie's orange Jell-O mold with gusto. "And it's not like Ricky was the kind you'd ever say was steady or reliable. Well, the fights they used to have! They were only next door to my mother, you know, the bottom floor of that house next to her that's all cut up in apartments? She said— well, she said, but I saw it with my own eyes a few times when I was over there—they used to be screaming, yelling, out in the street, throwin' things at each other—making a holy show of theirselves."

"It was shocking," Val said. "We lived over by them too, when we were first married, but I was some glad to get out of there. They weren't the only ones getting on like that."

"No, but they were the worst. Anyway, she took up with Kevin Downey, from the South Side—do you remember any of the Downeys, Audrey? There was a sister used to go round with one of the Crockers for a while, I can't remember her name. Anyway, Cathy Kelly and this one Downey, they took off together for the mainland last summer, not a word said to old Ricky Ryan— she just up and left him."

In the little silence that followed Lorraine's story, Audrey watched both her old friends remember that she, too, had up and left her husband without a word. Lorraine looked down at her plate, and after a moment Valerie said brightly, "Well, now, if anyone's ready for dessert, I tried something new—I hope it turned out all right—it's a no-bake cherry cheesecake. I got the recipe out of *Good Housekeeping*...."

Valerie was trying so hard, like she'd read something— probably also in *Good Housekeeping*, right next to the recipe— about being the perfect hostess, making all these fancy new dishes like the molded salad and the no-bake cherry cheesecake. She got up and went into the kitchen.

"I mean...she probably did the right thing," Lorraine added. "Cathy, I mean, leaving Ricky. He wasn't very good to her. Only it was a big shock to everyone."

"It always is," Audrey said.

After supper, Valerie's husband—a nice fellow, Bryce Gillard from Grand Falls—suggested a game of bridge, which everyone thought was a good idea till they realized there were five of them. Then Bryce said he would sit out and let the other four play, and Ted chimed in and said no he would. The two men got into a competition over who wouldn't have to play. Lorraine suggested another game, 120s or 45s or something. It turned out the only games anyone could think of with five players were kids' games like Go Fish or Crazy Eights, and Audrey thought this might be the reason adults normally went around in couples.

It was a little bit fun, and a little bit awkward, and a little bit sad, all in equal parts. Lorraine and Ted offered her a ride home but Audrey said she'd rather walk. It was a nice fall evening, a few folks still out on the street, mostly young couples twined around each other with no eyes for the lone woman walking up the road.

"Audrey! Is that you, Audrey Holloway?" A voice from the step of one of the houses near the bottom of Cairo Street rang out in the still air, and Audrey turned to see Doris Parsons coming down the steps.

She had seen Doris a few times in the shop since coming home, but there had never really been a chance to talk or catch up—and if Audrey had had any doubt that catching up with old friends was a bad idea, surely tonight had proven that it was. Anyway, she and Doris had never been friends, not like she had been with Val and Lorraine. They hadn't gone to school together, or gone to dances and flirted with the same boys, or hung around at each other's houses. Doris had already been a married woman when she arrived in the neighbourhood, marked as an outsider by her Scottish accent. The accent was blunted a bit now by seven years in St. John's, but was still distinctive enough to draw stares when she spoke.

"It's me—just back from dinner with Valerie and Bryce. You remember Valerie, don't you?"

"Yes—her parents live up on Suez Street, don't they? I remember you and she were great friends," Doris said. She came down from the step and met Audrey at the front gate; both women stood, one on either side of the gate, each with a hand on the gatepost.

"I suppose you must have had girlfriends like that, back home in Scotland, before you married and moved over here?" Audrey asked, suddenly curious.

"Oh, I did! Myself and Winnie Gates, we were great pals from the time we were in grammar school, all the way up. We were both going around with soldiers when the war started, but I married mine, and she split up with hers."

"Did she marry someone else? You keep in touch, do you?"

"Oh aye, we write each other, pretty regular. She's seeing a fellow now, but I don't know how serious it is."

"Do you miss it a lot—home?" How strange that she was asking Doris the kind of personal questions she could no longer imagine asking Val or Lorraine.

"Oh aye, every day I miss it. Miss me mam and da, and the neighbours in the street, and Winnie and the rest of my pals… it wouldn't be so bad if I could ever go back for a wee visit, but they're all away on the other side of the ocean." Doris sighed, then tried to laugh. "I don't know why I'm telling you all this. I try not to talk about home. Les doesn't like for me to be sad."

"I don't think Harry ever knew or cared whether I was sad or not," Audrey said.

"Then you're better off back here, aren't you? It's hard enough to be so far from your own people—if Les wasn't good to me, I'd be on the first plane home even if I had to sell my clothes to buy the ticket and go home in my birthday suit."

Both women laughed, and then Audrey pressed her hand against her mouth to stop the laughter turning to a sob.

"Les works nights now," Doris said. "Some nights, anyway. Once you've got your little fellow put to bed and my girls are asleep, you drop down here some night for a game of cards and a cup of tea. All right? I'd be glad for the company."

"I'll do that," Audrey promised. "I will."

musical interlude

HENRY HOLLOWAY

Lean into the mic, finger that first chord on the neck of the guitar. Clear my throat before I talk.

—Now you might not say it to hear me talk, but I was born in Louisiana. Waayy down south.

Tried a southern accent there, but didn't really pull it off. What do I sound like? A St. John's corner boy, voice roughed up a bit by years in Toronto, trying to fake a Southern accent. But there's songs where it sounds so natural, my voice just slides that way. Singing's not like talking. On with the story.

— I left the South when I was just a little fella, my mom was one of those Newfoundland girls married to Americans, and I guess it didn't work out so well. So she brought me back to the Rock before I was old enough to know much of Louisiana. She didn't ever have much good to say about the place, or any of the people down there, including my old man, from what I remember, but she sure did love the music. She saw Hank Williams, Senior, live at the Louisiana Hayride, and a few years after that she did one thing I'll always be grateful for—she took me to that great man's funeral. 'Course, I don't remember much about it, being only three years old, but we stood in that street while his hearse went by. Old Hank was my mom's favourite, and she loaded me on a train and travelled all through the night from Louisiana to see him laid to rest in Montgomery. And then she took another train north, and kept going, and never went back to my daddy again.

Play the first chord, drag out it. Let 'em guess the song with its lonely whippoorwill. This crowd knows all the standards.

Little burst of applause. I wouldn't say the crowd goes wild exactly. Not really enough of a crowd here in this little bar to go wild, anyway. But them that are here, like this song. Who doesn't?

Not many like it like Audrey does, though. Tell the truth it's almost creepy, the way that woman loves Hank Williams. Whenever I tell that story to intro this song, I never mention the other part. How that show she saw at the Hayride was nine months before I was born, nearly to the day, and I always thought she had the two things tangled up in her mind somehow. She used to call me Hank when I was little, know that? I never liked it, dug in my heels and wouldn't answer to it. When I got older, of course, knew who Hank Williams was, I thought it woulda been cool to be called after him. Too late to change back, then.

I don't remember a damn thing really about Hank Williams's funeral, not like you'd expect me to at that age. Don't even remember much about South Ridge, Louisiana—not from then. A couple of memories from the other two times I was down there later. The first one all full of dry summer dust and boredom, broken up by some good jazz music I learned on the guitar. The second trip—well, no need to talk about that. Or think about it, even.

All I got are these few images of the place, and I stitch them into Audrey's stories about when I was little, and try to pretend it's a memory. But it's not, not really.

And I got this chorus coming, inevitable once you start it, and all you can do is lean in like you own it.

three

LIKE A
ROLLING
STONE

1964–1966

AUDREY

Nine o'clock; time to close the shop. Audrey counted out the money in the cash register and zipped it into her bag to take up to the safe. She was more than ready to go upstairs and rest her feet.

They had a good system worked out now, herself and her mother: Ellen opened the shop and did the morning shift; Audrey worked afternoons and evenings. They had Doris Parsons's young one, Laura, in now and then to work a shift, but most days Audrey put in a solid eight hours.

This had never been her plan. Well. Leaving her husband and moving back to St. John's hadn't always been her plan either. But even after she did that, more than ten years ago now— had it really been that long?—Audrey hadn't imagined that when she was thirty-six she'd still be living with her parents and working in the shop. What had she pictured? Probably that she'd find an office job like she used to have before she was married, and get a little apartment of her own for herself and Henry.

There were times, she wouldn't deny it, when the idea of a quiet little apartment to herself seemed nice. But it would also be lonely, and surely it was better for Henry to grow up in the middle of a family—his grandparents, his Aunt June and Uncle Frank when they were still living at home, Alf and Treese's crowd only a few streets away. Raising a youngster all on her own wouldn't have been easy; it wasn't easy now, with Henry fifteen and up to all kinds of foolishness. But at least she had Mom and Dad to help.

And then there was the shop. It had seemed natural to take her place behind the counter, helping her mother. She had taken a bookkeeping course so she could oversee the financial affairs of the business, which Ellen had said were getting to be too much for her, and then Alf wanted her to do the same for his contracting business, so she did that on the side. The shop, like rising bread dough, had a way of expanding to take up whatever bit of time you had, and once she and Ellen worked out a system to pay Audrey her fair share of whatever the shop earned, she didn't see the point of going out and getting a job in some office. She'd be some boss's secretary, and in the shop she was her own boss.

Henry clattered down the stairs. "I'm goin' out, Mom."

"Where and with who might I ask?"

"Oh, nowhere. Just out around with the b'ys."

"Well don't be gone till all hours."

"Don't worry, Mom."

Now there was some impossible advice to follow. Don't worry. And it wasn't as if Audrey was a world-class worrier like her mother. She'd always thought of herself more as the take-it-easy type. When Henry was a youngster she had never spent much time worrying he'd break a leg or cut his foot open on a rusty nail or run into any other kind of trouble while he

TRUDY J. MORGAN-COLE

was out roaming the neighbourhood for hours at a time with the other youngsters.

But now that he was nearly grown, a year away from finishing school, tall as his grandfather and blessed or cursed with his father's dark-haired good looks, she worried. He hung around with all the young fellows from the street and most of them were decent fellows, but there were a few hard tickets among them. And it was more than time enough to start worrying about girls; there always seemed to be a cloud of those around, pretty little things with the skirts right up to their yin-yang. Girls who just yesterday had been playing hopscotch in the street and now were showing off long legs and teasing their hair up into big shiny bouffants, trying to look like women in the magazines.

She stepped outside into the cool gray May evening. Henry hadn't gone far: he and a crowd of youngsters were hanging out in front of the shop window. There were a couple of Nolans there, and the Hiscock boys, Butch Cadwell's young fellow Eddie, as well as a few girls. Henry was talking to a pretty little blonde thing, skinny as a rail and with long bangs hanging down into her eyes. Audrey was almost sure she was a Nolan, but was she Tony's girl, or Mick's? Whoever her father was he couldn't have been paying much attention, letting her out of the house wearing a skirt that barely covered her bum.

"Oh, come on, please, you got to. Everybody wants to hear it," the little one Nolan was saying, and Henry said, "Hi Mom—I'm just going back up to get my guitar."

The guitar had been a present from Frank when he was home last Christmas. Henry loved listening to the radio and his mother's record collection. He had her love for music, but unlike Audrey he could actually carry a tune—Audrey always thought she'd been given a terrible curse, to love music so much and not be able to sing or play a note of it.

Henry didn't have much time for going to church—not that Audrey expected him to, she didn't go herself—but he loved the old hymns. And unlike his mother, who had no patience with what she called "Newfie music," Henry soaked up his grandfather's old songs on the accordion about shipwrecks and weeping maidens and great catches of fish, though he had never set foot on the deck of a boat.

Wes had tried to teach him the accordion, and Henry, like his Uncle Alf before him, had learned a bit but never got really good at it. Audrey thought that was just a flaw in Henry's character; he didn't have any stick-to-it-iveness. His grades at school were only so-so and he would have dropped out after this year if she wasn't making him go back for his Grade Eleven. He took a turn in the shop now and then, but he wasn't like some of the young fellows, working every job he could find and saving up money for a new bike or motorcycle. Audrey was afraid her son was going to drift through life never settling down to anything.

But the guitar was different. When Frank gave it to him Henry's face lit up like a neon sign. He spent hours teaching himself to play, and then he went off looking for someone to give him lessons so he could learn a bit more. He even paid for the lessons himself out of the pocket money he earned Saturdays in the shop. Audrey was glad to see him giving his attention to something finally, although it would be nice if it was something a bit more useful.

She looked at the girl, who slouched against the wall waiting for Henry to come down. Audrey was never sure what to say to youngsters when she saw them without the store counter between them. "You're one of the Nolans from the

149
TRUDY J. MORGAN-COLE

garage, aren't you?"

"Yes, Mrs. Holloway. My dad's Tony, him and my uncle Mick got the garage."

"That's a good business. You got brothers to go into it?"

"Oh yes, there's five boys in our family and Uncle Mick got six. Pete and Tim and Phonse all loves working on cars—the other ones don't care about it so much." Her face tilted and her smile brightened as Henry came out the door.

"You be careful with that guitar now, that cost your uncle Frank a nice bit of money so don't go bangin' it around anywhere," Audrey warned.

Henry grinned, the guitar strap slung across his shoulder and his free arm draped around the girl. "Now, Mom, you knows I'm going to treat that like it's my baby. Won't I, Stella?"

Don't you go talking about babies, Audrey almost said, but bit back the words—the youngsters would only laugh, and it might go putting ideas in their heads. Stella, then. Stella Nolan. There were always girls around, but she had thought Henry was too young to have any kind of a steady girlfriend. She'd have to keep her eye on this one.

Upstairs, Audrey put the kettle on for her cup of tea and put a record on the stereo. Poor little Patsy Cline, another lovely singer gone too soon. Audrey had convinced her parents to buy the oil heater and the gas range, but her one big purchase just for herself was a floor-model record player with the radio built into it. Some women spent a lot of money on clothes and shoes, some on fancy vacations. Audrey was happy to have a good stereo and a steady supply of records. She had always loved the Top 40 but these last few years she found she wasn't liking the stuff on the radio as much. She couldn't see the point of The Beatles at all, though her sister, June, was gone off the head over them. Most of the records Audrey bought now were country music—the kind of music they'd played on the Grand Ole Opry and the Louisiana Hayride. And of course she had all Hank Williams's albums.

Her mother and father would want the TV on later—they always wanted to watch the evening news—but they didn't mind Audrey putting on Patsy Cline in the living room while she sat down with her tea. She was just settled when the phone rang and Ellen, answering it, said, "Just a moment, please—Audrey?" As Audrey got up she saw her mother mouth the words "Long Distance."

If it had been Marilyn or June, Ellen would have been chatting on the phone herself; both the girls called every month or so and talked to both their mother and Audrey. She couldn't think who else might be calling long distance. "A man," Ellen's lips shaped as Audrey picked up the phone.

"Audrey? That you, Audrey?"

Such a long time since she'd last heard her ex-husband's voice. There had been a couple of phone calls right after she moved back home, including the one where he'd threatened to get a lawyer onto her to get custody of Henry. She had gambled on the fact that he had always been suspicious of lawyers, also on the fact that she didn't think he really wanted Henry back with him. The final business of the divorce had all been carried out by mail.

"It's me. What…how are you?" *What do you want* would have sounded too harsh.

"I'm…I'm good, everything's good down here. Carol had her baby, uh…back in March. Little boy. Two months old now."

I suppose he would be, if he was born in March. Harry had never appreciated her smart mouth. "Congratulations."

"Have you given it any thought, Audrey? What I wrote to you?"

They exchanged cards at Christmas. She had to be civil to him even after the divorce was final. He was Henry's father, after all, and she had promised that someday she would bring Henry down for a visit. She sent Henry's school picture every year, and Harry asked on each year's Christmas card— *Sure would like to see him, when can you bring him down here?* but Audrey never answered back till the following Christmas when she told him what grade Henry was in and how his schoolwork was. She never mentioned the visit.

Three years ago, Harry wrote that he had married again. Then this last Christmas, the news that Carol was pregnant, with a long note saying that at fifteen, Henry was old enough to fly down to Louisiana by himself. *I really want to see my son before he's all grown up.*

"I've thought about it," she said now. "He still seems young, to go all that way on his own."

"I'll send him his ticket, and he'll only have to change planes twice. I'm sure he's old enough to handle that. I'm within my rights, Audrey—I haven't seen the boy in more than ten years."

"That's why I'm not sure it's a good idea. He don't even know you."

"And whose fault is that? I *want* to know him. I want him to get to know his stepmother and his half-brother, to see his grandparents again before they pass on, to see the place he was born. Half his roots are here, and I bet he can't even remember the place."

Later that night she talked to Henry about it. "I suppose you don't remember anything about Louisiana at all, do you?"

"Not really—I think I remember a dog. Did we have a dog?"

"No, that was your Uncle Fred and Aunt Ruth's dog.

You used to play over there with your cousins." He had cousins here in St. John's too, of course, Alf and Treese's kids, but it struck her that by taking him away she had robbed him of knowing half his family. If they had stayed in Louisiana, the Newfoundland relatives would have been strangers to him.

Henry shook his head. "No, I don't remember any of it. How come we never went back, like even for a visit or anything?"

Audrey drew a deep breath. "It wasn't easy for me. Things between me and your dad were—well, I left him, so you know it wasn't too good. But he's not a bad man. He probably would have been a good father—I don't know."

"I wish I knew him."

"That's—he wishes that too. You know how he always says in his Christmas cards that you should come down for a visit."

"So, why didn't we ever? Just because you don't get along with him…that's not fair, is it?"

Nothing got Audrey's back up more than Henry telling her things weren't fair. "Don't give me none of your lip, now. The truth is I just got off the phone with your father and he wants to send you a plane ticket to come down and see him when your exams are over."

"Really?" Henry looked a bit shocked, as if he'd been asking for something just to be difficult and then found out he was going to get it after all. "What would I—do down there?"

"Not much, I imagine—if it's like it was when I lived there, there's not all that much to do. And you'd be away from your friends all summer." This was the part that had made her think it wasn't a bad idea after all, now that she'd seen him with the Nolan girl. "But you'd get to know your father and your other grandparents. You know he's married again, and they have

TRUDY J. MORGAN-COLE

a baby. So you got a half-brother you never seen. It might be a good idea."

"I don't know. Would I have to go on the plane all by myself?"

"Yes, but your father would meet you at the airport. He got it all arranged, where you'd have to change planes and all that."

Henry's lower lip jutted out a bit. "I don't know," he repeated.

"It's not up to you to know or not. Your father and I talked it over and it's time for you to go down there, see the place you were born and get to know your family." She had hung up from the conversation with Harry not fully convinced she would let Henry go, but if that young frigger was going to start digging in his heels and whining about it just because he didn't want to leave his little girlfriend for the summer—well, that was another story. The more Henry stuck his lip out, the more sure Audrey became. It was the right thing to do. And it might keep him out of all kinds of trouble.

AUDREY

"We should have waited till next summer, they say the whole road will be finished then, all the way from here to Port-aux-Basques. Going to be paved and everything." Treese ground out her cigarette in the big ashtray on the counter and Audrey passed her another one. Treese and Alf and the kids had taken the train to Nova Scotia for a week's holiday earlier in the summer. "Maybe we'll do it again in a couple of years, when we can drive all the way. You should do it too, take a couple of weeks and go up and visit Marilyn and June."

"If I got any urge to go to the mainland I'd most likely fly," Audrey said. "It's all right, I s'pose, for people out in them places like Botwood and Grand Falls who'd be hard pressed to get anywhere otherwise, but I don't say I'm going to be spending much time driving on that new road."

"What about you, Mom? When you were young it was all getting around by boat, wasn't it?" Treese turned her gaze and her foghorn voice on Ellen, who was not supposed to be down

155

here now—her shift ended when Audrey's began—but who was looking through the cooler for anything that might have gone off.

"By boat or by train, that was it," Ellen said. "I minds the first time I came into town on the steamer, I was only fourteen and I never seen so many people in one place all at the one time. I thought St. John's was a real big city then, like New York or London."

"Funny how different things look, depending on where you came from," said Doris Parsons. "When the steamer came into St. John's harbour in 1946 and I looked out at it, well, the last place I'd seen was Liverpool, and I thought St. John's looked like a little fishing town compared to what I knew back in England. But if I'd gone, like my mate Lil did, off to Harbour Breton or someplace like that, likely I'd've died of the shock."

Audrey laughed. "Oh, I'd go cracked. I was half-cracked anyway down in the States, sure Harry's place was out in the back of beyond, no neighbours closer than a mile away."

"What did young Henry think of it when he was down there over the summer?" Doris wanted to know. Henry had been back since Labour Day, out with that one Stella Nolan every minute he wasn't in school.

"He never had much to say about it, tell you the truth."

"Must have been strange for him, though, staying with his father after so many years," said Doris.

"I imagine it would be, but he never said. You know what boys are like." She nodded at her mother and Treese, who both knew what boys were like. Doris had four girls.

Henry had phoned her twice while he was down in Louisiana. She'd talked to Harry for a few minutes each time too. It was strange, carrying on a conversation with Harry after all these years. Harry had said Henry was doing all right, although he seemed a bit bored with small-town life and missed his friends. "Harry said he spent a lot of his time playing the guitar," she told her mother, Treese and Doris. "There was an old coloured man down there—some fellow who works for Harry—loaned him a guitar and was teaching him some new stuff. Not like formal music lessons or anything, but just sitting down playing the blues with him, and Henry seemed to like that."

What Harry had actually said was, "Carol doesn't think it's right, him spendin' so much time with a coloured man. But it's not like it's a bunch of boys his own age—Jeb's an old guy, and he's respectful, and I don't think it'll do Henry any harm. I just didn't want you to worry, if he came home talking about it."

"Why would I worry?"

"Well, no reason I guess, only cause of how it looks. I wouldn't want you to think we were exposin' him to anything bad."

"It sounds like all he's being exposed to is a musician who knows a lot of music and can teach him a thing or two—I imagine Henry's over the moon about that, he loves all that jazz and blues and rock 'n' roll stuff. What odds do it make if the man is coloured?"

"You know the way things are down here, Audrey. You know we like people to keep with their own kind."

"And you know it's not like that up here. Henry wasn't raised to worry about the colour of a man's skin." All Henry had said when he came back was that he'd been lucky enough to meet up with an old fellow who once played with Robert Johnson, King of the Delta Blues, when he was young, and the old fellow had taught him a bunch of blues riffs and "really cool stuff." Cool was a word he had picked up down in the States and now he threw it into every conversation.

TRUDY J. MORGAN-COLE

"Who's that young one I sees him around with all the time?" Treese wanted to know.

"She's a Nolan—Stella, her name is."

"Nolan?" Treese wrinkled her brow. Audrey knew what she was thinking: Nolan was as much of a Catholic name as Treese's own maiden name, Ryan. Of course, "keep with your own kind"—the Newfoundland version of it—didn't matter much to the young ones today, if it ever had. If it had mattered to Alf and Treese twenty years ago, then Treese wouldn't be married into the family and wouldn't be here right now taking up space on the counter. Audrey remembered all the fuss back when they got married—Treese's mother refusing to go to the wedding if it wasn't in a Catholic church, and then Dad refusing to go if it was, everybody crying and carrying on. As if it made that much difference what building you got married in! In the end it was at St. Teresa's and everybody went, Dad included, and Treese was as much a part of the family now as the cash register was part of the store counter. She and Alf had moved out to a new house Alf built way out on Cornwall Avenue a year ago, but she still dropped into the shop two or three times a week, planted her elbows on the counter and stayed for a good hour.

"Now would they be the Nolans from down on Empire Avenue? Old Mr. Nolan would have been from Cappahayden," Treese suggested.

"No, they're the ones with the garage on Freshwater Road—her grandfather is Mike Nolan."

"Oh, right, them Nolans. Well that explains the old-fashioned name they got on the young one—she'll have been named for her Aunt Stella, she's a Presentation Sister. Me and Stella went to Presentation together, she's the last girl I ever would have guessed would become a nun. There was four in our class what went into the convent and she was the least likely—wild as the loo, she was, when she was twelve or thirteen."

"I suppose the convent settled her down a bit, did it?" Doris asked.

"It must have, though I haven't laid eyes on her since I left school—well you don't, do you, once somebody becomes a nun."

"I wouldn't know about that," said Ellen, who was now stacking tins of peas on the shelf. There was just enough disapproval in her voice to remind them all that while Treese's Catholic background was acknowledged, it shouldn't be flaunted. Talking about nuns was taking it one step too far.

"Well, I never heard Stella say nothing about an aunt in the convent but it do make some sense of the name," Audrey said.

"Would her father be young Micky, or Brian?"

"I think she's Tony's girl."

"Oh, Tony was a lot older—she must be the youngest of a big crowd, is she?"

They were rapidly reaching the bottom of everything Audrey knew about Stella. She couldn't have picked the girl out of a crowd of youngsters before she saw her with Henry that day back in the spring, the day she decided to send him to his father. But she was in and out of the shop all the time in July and August when he was gone, picking up one thing and another, chatting to Audrey. Stella had told Audrey that her and Henry were real good friends, and she asked for the address down in the States so she could send him a letter. She talked in this soft little voice, and between that and the blonde hair and blue eyes you'd think she was a little angel, but brazen as brass to go asking a fellow's mother for his address like that.

Ellen brought it up that night, when the store was closed—

TRUDY J. MORGAN-COLE

the business of Henry and Stella and her being Catholic. "Do it really matter all that much, really?" Audrey asked.

Henry wasn't home yet; she had told him to be back by ten but here it was nearly eleven and there was no sign of him. Audrey and Ellen were in the kitchen having their cup of tea and toast, Ellen with her feet up and Audrey with hers in a pan of water. Her corns were killing her after standing at the counter all afternoon. She liked to soak her feet while she had her tea in the evening. Wes sat in his chair by the TV, watching the news, occasionally passing a comment but leaving most of the conversation to his wife and daughter.

"That she's R.C., I mean," Audrey added. "I know you and Dad wasn't too pleased at first when Alf married Treese but they're happy enough together."

"Yes, happy enough, but all the youngsters are baptized Catholic," Ellen said.

"What difference do that make? None of them goes to church except Christmas and Easter anyway. Neither do me or Henry, for that matter."

"Don't remind me," Ellen said. "I always feel like if I hadn't been so busy with the store and all, I could have done a better job of bringing all ye crowd up in the church."

"Marilyn goes," Audrey said. She hoped to God that Marilyn never gave up going to the United Church up there in Toronto, because it was the one thing that reassured Ellen she hadn't failed as a parent. "But if I don't go, and Henry doesn't either, what odds do it make if his girlfriend is Catholic or Protestant?"

"It's just better in a family, if you're both of the same faith," Ellen said.

"But if you're of no faith at all, that's what I'm saying."

"Nobody's of *no faith at all*, Audrey, don't be so foolish.

Everybody got a religion, even if they don't practice it. Just because I go to church every week, I'm not foolish enough to think everyone does or everyone got to. But you got to have something to fall back on. When everything else fails you and you turn to God, you got to know where to go. That's all."

"Will your anchor hold, in the storms of life," Audrey quoted.

"Right. That's what I mean."

We have an anchor, that keeps the soul, steadfast and sure while the billows roll. It was a hymn Dad liked to play on the accordion and sing on a Sunday evening. That, Audrey thought, was the bedrock of Ellen's faith—that for her and Wes and all their wandering, disappointing children, there was still an anchor to hold them in place. Good old Protestant Jesus, watching over his flock.

It wasn't something Audrey had ever felt, or felt the need for. The billows rolled, all right—she had had her hard times. None harder than when she was down there in Louisiana, far from home, married to a man she didn't love anymore, if she ever had. Her anchor then was the thought of home, this house and this store and this street, here waiting for her at the end of her train ticket. Steadfast and sure, all right. *Fastened to the Rock* which cannot move. Jesus was supposed to be the Rock, but when Audrey heard that hymn she was reminded of how the American servicemen used to call Newfoundland "the Rock." Her Rock, the one that was here when she needed it.

"You got bigger worries with Henry and that young girl than what church she goes to. If you're going to worry, worry about him being out with her all hours of the night like this," said Wes, standing up and folding the newspaper that had been open on his lap for the last hour. "If he's out late at night he's up to no good—you can count on it."

Before Audrey could reply they all heard the sound of someone at the shop door down below. It must be Henry, coming home, but there was always the fear of a break-in so both Ellen and Audrey sat up a little straighter. No, there was the key in the lock and the sound of the bolt being drawn again. Next came Henry's footsteps up the stairs, and then he was in the kitchen with them. He must have grown three inches while he was away; he looked so much more like a young man now than when he'd left home at the start of the summer. Tall, his hair a little too long, guitar case in his hand.

"What time do you call this?" Audrey said, her voice sharper than it might otherwise have been with her father's rebuke still hanging in the air.

Henry glanced at the clock over the stove. "Sorry, Ma. I lost track of the time."

"Yes, now, I s'pose you did. Were you out with Stella?"

"There was a crowd of us. Stella was there."

"You watch yourself, now mind. Don't do nothing foolish." Henry shifted from one foot to the other, his eyes still on the clock over the stove, not meeting his mother's or his grand-parents' gaze.

"You wants to be careful, now," Wes echoed Audrey's warning, then said goodnight and went back to the bedroom.

"I'm going to bed too," Henry said.

"You don't want a cup of tea or a few cookies?" Ellen offered.

"No thanks, Nan. Me and Stella got a plate of chips at Marty's."

"You're a growing boy, you always got room for a couple of ginger snaps."

Now he did look at Ellen, and smile with the real warmth he sometimes still had for his grandparents, though rarely for Audrey, these days. Henry and Audrey were always rubbing each other the wrong way lately; everything one of them said seemed to irritate the other. That's what it was to have a sixteen year old, Audrey thought. In a few years it might be better. When Audrey was sixteen she and Ellen could hardly be in the same room without sniping at each other, and look at them now, sat off together having their tea like the best of friends.

"Your father's right, you got to be stricter with him," were the first words out of Ellen's mouth when they heard the door of Henry's room close behind him. "You mark my words, if you're not careful he's going to get that little one in the family way and what do you think we're going to do then?"

Audrey sighed. "What do you want me to do, Mom? Chain him up in his bedroom?" It just went to show, she thought, no matter how easy you thought things were with your mother, there was always a piece of advice or criticism she could pull out of her hat. No matter how old you got. Maybe things would never be easy.

TRUDY J. MORGAN-COLE

ELLEN

"What do you want me to do, Mom? Chain him up in his bedroom?"

That was Audrey all over, saucy as the crackie. How many times had she said that when Ellen had suggested she needed to be stricter with Henry? There were times with all her own youngsters when Ellen had wished she could have done that. Keep Alf chained up till he got over Treese and met a nice Protestant girl. Keep Audrey locked in her room till the war was over and all the American soldiers were gone. Keep Marilyn, June, and Frank chained to the counter at the store so they couldn't take off to the mainland. If she could have kept them all safe at home, wouldn't she have done it?

And yet. There were Alf and Treese, four lovely children of their own now, happy as larks as far as Ellen could see. There was Marilyn happily married up in Toronto with two youngsters, and June and Frank both with good jobs up there, making decent money and sending a bit home. Audrey was the one failure if you looked at how things were supposed to work out—divorced, raising young Henry on her own—and yet what would Ellen do now, running the shop and all, if Audrey hadn't left Harry Pickens? Ellen couldn't wish her back down there with him, and if she wished Audrey never gone and married him in the first place, that would be like wishing young Henry had never been born.

Henry had finished school and managed to pass his Grade Eleven, "Magna Cum the Skin of his Teeth," as Audrey put it, shaking her head over his exam marks. Alf had offered him a job but Henry was in no hurry to take him up on it. Neither Alf nor Wes thought Henry had much aptitude for, or interest in, the carpentry business. Frank had been the same way of course, never really took to the work, but then Frank had the initiative to go off and take the plumbing and heating course, and now he had a good trade of his own. Henry didn't take much interest in anything except for the guitar, his noisy rock 'n' roll music, and his girlfriend, Stella.

Ellen worried more about Stella than she did about the music or Henry's lack of interest in work. The girl was a year younger than Henry, still doing her Grade Eleven at Holy Heart of Mary, and stuck to Henry's side every second she wasn't in school. He was out till all hours of the night and saucy to his mother when she questioned him about what he was up to. Ellen had thought she had her hands full with Frank when he was that age, but Frank had nothing on Henry.

So the night Henry came in with Stella in tow, about nine in the evening when the shop was closed and Wes was out working late, Ellen knew even before the two of them sat down. She knew just looking at them, Stella's little head, which she always held up so proud, bent down so her long blonde hair brushed the tabletop, like a curtain she could hide behind.

165

Henry, to give him credit, looked straight at his mother and grandmother when he told them.

"So, I know you guys are going to be mad about this, but, um, I better just say it…. Stella's going to have a baby," he said. "I mean we are, we're going to have a baby. And it's all right, you don't need to worry about nothing, we're going to get married. I got my Grade Eleven now and I'll get a job—I'll probably go work for Uncle Alf. Only we might need to stay here until we got enough to get a place of our own."

He had timed this pretty neatly, cute enough to know this news would go down better with his grandfather if it came filtered through the women of the family. Wes would blame Ellen, as Ellen blamed Audrey, for being too soft on Henry. Just like the Garden of Eden, Ellen thought now: Adam blaming Eve and Eve blaming the serpent. At least Henry didn't blame Stella, didn't try to hint that she'd led him astray. You had to give him some credit for that.

Ellen broke the news to Wes when they were both in bed that night. Wes's anger, the rare times he got mad, was as quiet as his happier moods were. He groused out his anger and disapproval, but ended up saying the youngsters could move into Henry's room once they were married. By the time he fell asleep, with Ellen still lying wide awake on the pillow beside him, Wes seemed to have accepted that this was the way things were. Henry was going to be married at seventeen, working for Alf and tied down with a wife and child. It wasn't what any of them wanted for him, but what could they do?

About a week after Henry and Stella's announcement, Ellen was working in the store after supper while Audrey was gone off somewhere with her friend Doris. It had been quiet in there ever since supper hour but about half-past eight, just as Ellen was thinking she'd close up soon, Mrs. Hynes and Mrs.

Hiscock both came in at the one time, and both of them got to talking while they picked up their groceries. They were there at the counter having a grand chat when the door pinged again and Stella sidled in. On her own, no sign of Henry around. She wasn't her usual brazen self, either—she took a step towards the counter, then backed away, crooking her finger for Ellen to come over to her.

"Are you lookin' for Henry? He's not there, I thought he was out with you."

"No, I know he's not out, he's gone off somewhere with Nick Lahey but I don't know where they're to. Um, can I talk to you, Mrs. Holloway?"

Ellen glanced at her two neighbours with their bags of groceries, already bagged up and paid for, settled on the counter. The two of them were all ears, naturally, not wanting to miss a bit of this.

Ellen sighed and slipped out from behind the counter, leading Stella over to the door that went upstairs. "What is it, my love?"

The girl looked like she was close to bursting into tears. "I'm sorry, I'm sorry to bother you like this but I got nowhere else to go, Dad's after throwing me out of the house."

"What? Go on upstairs, you poor thing. Get Audrey to give you a cup of tea or a mug of cocoa or something, I'll be up in a few minutes."

Of course Mrs. Hiscock and Mrs. Hynes were quick to comment: "That's Tony Nolan's little one isn't it? She goes around with your Henry? I don't know what the young ones are like, at all, at all." It was a few minutes before Ellen, giving nothing away, could shoo them out and put the CLOSED sign up in the window.

"We told them yesterday, together, just like we told you,"

Stella was telling Audrey when Ellen got upstairs. "I knew they weren't pleased but they never said much one way or the other until tonight when they had me to theirselves. Then Dad went off the head, yelling at me. He called me a little w-h-o-r-e, can you believe it?"

"And you can't go to your sister's house, or anything like that? Not that you're not welcome here, it's only I don't know what time Henry's likely to be home," said Audrey, pouring up cocoa. She opened a package of Purity biscuits and laid them on a plate in front of Stella, who was really crying now. "Dad told them they couldn't have me in the house either! I was going to go over to my friend Lois's place, but her mother is some strict, once it came out what it was all about, that I was you-know-what, she wouldn't have let me stay there either. But I can stay here with ye crowd, can't I?"

Wes, in the living room, made a grumbling kind of noise from behind the *Evening Telegram.* "We'll talk it over when Henry gets home," Ellen said quickly, thinking that knowing Henry, he might not be in till all hours.

But for a miracle, he was home early tonight, darting up the stairs about half an hour after Stella. She poured out the whole tale again for Henry, with a good few more details besides.

"He called you what?" Henry stood up from the table when Stella again spelled out what her father had called her. "I'm going over there right now and give him a piece of my mind—I'll beat the living shit out of him!"

"Sit down and shut up," Audrey said. "You're not going nowhere this hour of the night. And keep your voice down; we don't need the neighbours knowing our business."

Stella's parents were not happy with their daughter's plan to marry her boyfriend and become a mother at sixteen. Their plan was for Stella to go out around the bay to stay with her Aunt Kath, have the baby, and have the parish priest down in Witless Bay put it up for adoption. There was a strong suggestion that after the baby was adopted, she might be better off to follow her Aunt Stella's example and dedicate her life to God. If not, she could go down to Boston with another aunt and take a secretarial course. And, of course, she was never to see or speak to Henry Holloway again.

"But I don't want any of that!" Stella wailed. "I don't want to go out around the bay, I don't want to give up my baby, and I certainly don't want to be no frigging nun! And I don't want to go to Boston either! I want to stay here with *you*," she said to Henry, "and have our baby, and get a little apartment, just like we planned. But Dad said if I don't go along with their plan I can't darken their door never again, and he called Mary Louise and Elaine and told them if either of them ever wants to come in the house again, they can't let me stay at their place either. So I got nowhere to go but here."

Stella slept on the couch that night—Wes wouldn't hear of her being up in Henry's room if they weren't married, and Ellen went along with him, though if that wasn't a case of locking the barn door after the horse was stolen she didn't know what was. The next morning when Ellen was behind the counter of the store, the door banged open, its usual welcoming ping lost in the roar of Tony Nolan's voice as he demanded, "Is my daughter here?"

Ellen looked the man up and down. She had never spoken to him, but she recognized him as one of the men she'd seen in coveralls down by Nolan's Garage. "I suppose you must be Stella's father?"

"You knows damn well who I am, missus, and if my daughter is in this house you better bring her down to me or I'll have a policeman in here so fast it'll make your head spin. And I'll have that young fellow of yours hauled up on charges too, for corrupting an innocent girl!"

Ellen was not a tall woman; she was dwarfed by this angry, large, red-faced man. Everyone was out of the house—Wes at work, Audrey at the wholesaler's putting in their orders. Henry and Stella had gone out after breakfast; Ellen had no idea where to, and it was better that way. She hoped they wouldn't come home while Mr. Nolan was here. She pulled herself up to as tall as she could make five foot three look and spoke in her most careful voice, the one she would use for the minister—or for a policeman, if there really was one here. She would not let this man drag her down to his level.

"Mr. Nolan, my understanding is that you turned your daughter out of the house and told her married sisters they were not to take her in either. It's only natural she should come here. I'm sure you're no more happy about this news than we are, but we are not the kind of people to put our own child out into the streets to starve. Of course the children made a foolish mistake—" she was not going to let him put all the blame on Henry; it took two, after all, "but they plan to get married."

"Get married? Sure they're nothing more than children theirselves and they haven't got a pot to piss in! I might have known this would happen when she got tangled up with the likes of ye crowd, you've only got to look at his mother to know what kind of stock that young fellow comes from!"

"He's offered to marry her. As far as I'm concerned he *has* taken responsibility. We'll do all we can to help them, and we'd expect you to do the same."

"That's what we won't, then! Help them? At their age? Help them shack up and try to support a child? My Stella is throwin' her life away on your useless young fella and ye crowd are helpin' 'em all right, ye're helpin' them go to wrack and ruin! And Jesus, Mary, and Joseph, I'll see you in hell before I stand by and watch that happen to my daughter!"

He brought his huge clenched fist down on the counter with the whole weight of his mechanic's arm and a father's rage behind it, and looked almost as surprised as Ellen at the cracking sound. They both looked down to see the spider-web shatter and the long cracks reaching out from it, and for a moment Ellen felt the violation of her store counter almost as strongly as Tony Nolan felt the violation of his Stella.

"I won't have you stand in my shop and insult my family like this, Mr. Nolan. If you don't leave now, I'm the one who's going to be calling the police."

"Police, is it? You'll have plenty to do with the police when I'm finished here. Where's your husband? I know that young frigger of yours got no father but he's got a grandfather who can answer for him. If that man of yours is upstairs hiding out like a coward go haul him down and tell him Tony Nolan got a few words for him!"

If Wes was here this would turn into a fistfight, Ellen thought, though she hadn't seen Wes fight anyone since he was sixteen and got into it with David Vincent down on the wharf in Candle Cove. She could see how frustrated Nolan was at the lack of a man to punch, and she was afraid he might start heaving tins through her front window next.

"Is she upstairs? My Stella, is she upstairs?" He moved toward the swinging door that barred the shop off from the area behind the counter, behind which was the door leading upstairs. Ellen moved quickly to block it, and Nolan reached for her but then let his hand fall.

"She is not upstairs. She's not in the house at all. And if you go through that door, that's trespassing, and I'll have you

171

arrested for that."

"My God, you got some nerve, missus. You with your nose up in the air like you think you're better than the likes of us, and your dirty little bastard got my little girl in trouble!"

It was the ping of the door, again, that saved her—not Wes or a policeman or, thank God, Henry and Stella. It was only two women from up the street, shopping bags over their arms, who came through the door talking to each other and then stopped short at the sight of the angry man towering over the little shopkeeper.

Tony Nolan turned to look at them and deflated like a popped balloon, taking three steps back, away from Ellen and towards the door. "You haven't heard the last of this, missus," he threatened as he left the shop, his voice easily half as loud as it was earlier.

"Is everything all right, Mrs. Holloway?" Mrs. Vokey asked.

"Yes, yes, everything is fine, just a…disagreement," Ellen said. "Now, what can I get for you ladies?" She laid her hands flat on the counter to hide how much they were trembling, and when the women looked down at the counter they could see the cracked and splintered glass.

AUDREY

It wasn't as if Audrey had a lot of illusions about weddings. Her own was nothing special—she had a nice dress, and she still remembered the pale-pink pumps she had dyed to match it, even though you couldn't see them in the one photo of the occasion. She remembered the feel of Harry's arm through his uniform jacket as she gripped it tight going out of the chaplain's office down on the base. There were only the six of them there—the bride and groom, Ellen and Wes, Marilyn as Audrey's bridesmaid and one of Harry's army buddies as his best man. Even so it had felt more like a wedding than today's business in Judge Davis's office.

Stella cried in the car all the way downtown, and Henry was irritated. When she had first moved in with them he used to be so gentle with her crying fits, and Audrey would look at him and think that it might work out after all, that her boy was turning into a kind young man. Then Henry started getting short-tempered, and Audrey thought it was shocking, how he could be so unkind to the poor girl.

Then, sometime around the third week of Stella's stay, Audrey had started to get annoyed herself. Yes, the poor girl had it hard—barely sixteen, and pregnant, forced to choose between a shotgun wedding or being banished off around the bay to give up her baby. And yes, it was hard on her that her father had ordered the whole family to cut her off, so none of them could take her in or even come visit. But even so, you couldn't spend every day sitting down crying, could you? You cried a bit—in private, if you could manage some privacy—and then you wiped away your tears and got on with the business at hand. That was how life worked. If you still had tears to shed you did your crying alone, and never let anyone know you were upset. That was the sensible way: Audrey's way.

But it wasn't Stella's way. Stella's way was to sleep till ten or eleven every morning, fry herself two eggs and some bacon, then sit down and watch the television. Not even a bit of knitting or crochet in her hands to make use of the time, and her with a baby to prepare for. And whenever anyone came through the room, she'd start in about how she called her sister Mary-Louise but Mary-Louise hung up the phone, and oh my, what are they going to do when the baby comes, she don't know nothing about babies?

Stella had cheered up a little the last few days with the thought of getting ready for a wedding. She was almost happy when Audrey hauled her down to the Royal Stores to buy that nice little dress in the black-and-white hound's-tooth check. But now, dressed up and ready to go, she looked at herself and Henry in the mirror and it seemed to strike her, just as it struck Audrey, what a mean, sad little excuse for a wedding this was. Stella's response was to start another flood of tears that lasted all the way to the judge's chambers. Audrey's response was to say, "Let's hurry up now, we haven't got all day."

All the way in the car Stella kept glancing over her shoulder. "What are you looking at?" Henry asked, halfway down Long's Hill.

"Nothing. I only thought…."

"You think your old man is coming after us? Going to try to stop the wedding?"

"Nobody even knows it's today," Stella sniffled.

"So there's no reason to be looking out for him. In half an hour it'll all be legal and you got nothing to worry about. There's nothing he can do to us." Henry didn't sound like he was convincing even himself.

As they waited outside the judge's chambers, Audrey wondered if she should be more worried about her boy making a mistake that was going to change his life, maybe ruin it. Tony Nolan had threatened to have them up on charges for keeping Stella in the house. Bridget came over secretly to talk to Audrey, whispering as if she thought her husband had spies about the place, begging Audrey to change Stella's mind. They had all gone cracked, as if being married young and having a baby was the worst thing that could happen to a girl.

"It's not just because he got her in trouble, it's because we're not Catholic," Ellen told Audrey. "If that was some young Ryan or Malone that got her in the family way, they'd have the two of them bundled off to the priest before you could say Bob's your uncle. It's happened before, in both their families—in fact I wouldn't be surprised if Bridget herself was expecting when she married Tony. You think me and your father are old-fashioned about mixed marriages, but it's the RC's who are the worst about it—they think all Protestants are going to hell. Sure don't you remember what Treese's crowd were like? They came around in time, and I 'low the Nolans will too, once Henry and Stella are settled in together and that youngster is born."

TRUDY J. MORGAN-COLE

Regardless of the difference in religion, a young girl getting pregnant like that was a terrible shame to any family, but Audrey thought that in Henry's case a shotgun wedding might not be the worst fate in the world. Better if it were three or four years later, perhaps, but having a wife and child to provide for would steady him a little. Already he'd settled down to a regular construction job with Alf. The boy had never had any real get-up-and-go about anything except playing his guitar. And while Henry had a bit of talent, from what Audrey could tell, he was no Hank Williams. He would have to work whether he liked it or not, and this might be just the thing to make him grow up.

So she told herself, anyway, papering those thoughts over the scraped-off shreds of doubt underneath. The secretary called their names and the three of them walked in. Stella said her vows in such a tiny, choked voice they could hardly hear her. She started to cry again as they left the office. "I'm sorry," she told Henry. "It's only—I thought Mom might come. Right up to the last minute I thought she'd be here."

"How could she be? We never told anyone!"

Audrey understood the forlorn hope. Bridget probably would have come, if she'd known and if she could have gotten away. Tony Nolan announced to the rest of the family that Stella was as good as dead to them. Anyone who visited her or tried to talk to her would be the same. "I never knew he was such a hard man," Bridget Nolan had whispered to Audrey the last time she visited. "I don't dare come no more, he might put me out on the street too."

Then you'd be out with your daughter, and you could help look after her and the baby, Audrey thought. It wasn't as if life with Tony Nolan could be such a picnic, that this woman would risk losing contact with her own daughter and grandchild just so she could stay with him. But of course she was a woman who'd gone straight from her parents' home to marriage, had no trade or business, no way to keep herself much less help anyone else. A woman like Bridget Nolan was tied to her husband. Not for the first time Audrey felt a rush of gratitude: she wasn't one of those women.

There was no money to spare for giving the youngsters a honeymoon night in a hotel or anything like that—and anyway it seemed indecent, for a young girl who was already five months pregnant, to be thinking of honeymoons. Stella's belly had bloomed overnight, just these past couple of weeks: she looked distinctly pregnant now in the hound's-tooth maternity mini-dress, and not a soul in that judge's office would have the slightest doubt why these two teenagers were in here getting married. *They're judging me more than they're judging Stella and Henry*, Audrey realized as she steered the newlyweds out past the pairs of eyes in the waiting room.

On the way back up from downtown, Sonny James came on the radio singing "Take Good Care of Her." Audrey turned it up: as good a theme song for today as any, she thought. She pulled the car over to the curb on Freshwater Road. "Anyone hungry?"

"No," Stella sniffled, at the same time as Henry said, "I'm starved."

"Let's go get a plate of chips at Marty's. My treat."

"I could eat a few chips I guess," said Stella.

"Go on, then," said Henry. "Thanks, Mom."

So that was their wedding lunch—chips and vinegar in a booth at Marty's. Henry ordered chicken with his, and told Stella about how the apartment they were going to rent upstairs in Donny Vokey's house would be ready by the end of next month, and he was going to get the baby crib that Donny's sister was finished using. "And we'll be out from under yours and Nan's and Pop's feet before the baby comes," he told Audrey.

"It'll be nice to have a place of your own," Audrey said. "Make your own start together, like. Everything will be just grand, you'll see." The trick was to make it sound as if she believed it.

musical interlude

HENRY HOLLOWAY

I play a C, an F, an F major seventh. Glance at the sound guy hoping he'll bump the guitar up a little because I don't think half the room can hear me. Time to talk over the intro.

— Now, everybody laughs when I tell them this song reminds me of my ex-wife, but it's true. Partly because she loved the song and partly because...well, you can figure out the rest.

That's all I need to say on this one. Strum a chord and start to sing, wait for them to laugh after the first word. *Crazy...*

That intro always gets a few laughs, at least if people are paying attention and sober enough to get the joke. It's all lies, of course. I don't remember Stella liking this song. Mom was the one who listened to Patsy Cline, another doomed singer she loved. Not that I'm trying to sound like Patsy. A bit more Willie Nelson maybe. A man's version, and I like the way his voice sounds rough and broke-up with it. Damn hard to do a cover without sounding like you're trying to be someone else, and covers is all I'm any good for.

"Crazy" was on the radio a bit when Stella and me were first going out, and I do remember this one time coming into the kitchen of that crappy little place on Graves Street, the baby screaming in her crib and Stella at the table crying. The radio was on and I'm almost sure it was playing this song. Or maybe I made that up because the song fits so well.

The other lie, of course, is saying ex-wife. But that gets a laugh and the truth wouldn't.

That memory, that shitty little apartment, the screaming baby, all tangled up in my head while I'm singing. Probably shouldn't even sing this one if it's going to make me think about stuff like this. Trying to settle down the baby—wasn't a mother's touch supposed to do it? Because for damn sure the touch of a teenaged father coming in half-cut after stopping for a few beers on the way back from work, that wasn't doing a thing.

That whole year, it was all like something out of a soap opera or a bad sitcom, only with no laugh track. The stressed-out wife, the unhappy baby, the shiftless husband. Holding the screaming little thing and realizing she hadn't been changed in hours, the stink of the diaper, screaming at Stella while she's screaming back at me, both of us wondering what the hell the other was doing all day. All those old clichés.

If it was a soap opera it would have ended with the girl taking the baby and running back to her mother. But she couldn't do that, and didn't she love reminding me that was all my fault, that she had no home to go to.

And then that second verse about wondering what in the world I did, only I know damn well what I did, getting a girl knocked up—the worst sin you could commit, and the punishment sure as hell fit the crime. That night Patsy Cline might or might not have been singing "Crazy," Stella was flying at me like a little tornado, then all of a sudden she was curled up in a ball on the floor and I couldn't get a word out of her. I think that was the night I took my first shot at changing a diaper, and did a piss-poor job of it too, excuse the pun, and left the dirty one in the middle of the floor because I didn't have a clue what to do with it.

Trying to settle Stella down then, telling her things would get better, although how in the sweet frig anything was going to get better, I didn't have a clue.

There's this other memory too—maybe that night, maybe one of those other nights. Maybe it was the night she hit me across the face and I hit her back. Maybe it was the night she had the knife and I thought she was coming for me till I saw the blood on her arms and knew this was way worse than I'd ever imagined. Maybe it was the night I brought the baby up to Mom's and asked if they could keep her till things got better.

I was out of work by then. Uncle Alf told me blood was thicker than water but not thick enough to keep a lazy hangashore on the job. We lost the apartment and moved into one room in a house with some fellows I was playing in a band with. Mom and Nan looked after the baby, blood thicker than water, blood and tears and Stella screeching and screeching. She used to scream at me that she couldn't handle the baby and then when I took her away she blamed me for that too, for taking her baby away.

We were yelling at each other almost all the time by then, and I thought she was screwing Nick, one of the fellows we lived with, because she damn sure wasn't screwing me much by then. Only this one night I remember a crazy, screaming fight, and then the two of us going at it like wild things, like we were still in love and hungry for each other. I thought that was later, when we slept on a mattress on the floor in Nick and Chris's place, but then I have this memory of Stella falling asleep in my arms, and the baby waking me up screaming, and me going out to find the dirty diaper still in the middle of the floor. So I'm not sure when that would have been, or if it ever happened at all.

Anyway it's not like it's a story I'm ever going to tell between songs. That's not one that will warm the crowd up.

I don't tell anyone that story. I don't tell anyone about the night we had the last fight, when I called her a whore, the same thing her father called her, and she grabbed Nick's car keys and ran out into the rain. But those are the pictures that flash in my head when I sing this song. Me standing there frozen, like I was at a fork in the road wondering what would happen if I did or didn't run after her. By the time I ran down to the street she'd taken off in the car. She was only taillights in the rain.

Taillights in the rain. Now that would be a country song, if I were any good to write a song. Like "Blue Eyes Cryin' in the Rain," only sadder. I used to try to write songs but they were all shit, none of them fit to sing. I'm better with other people's words, other people's feelings. Final verse now, Willie's broken words and Patsy's broken heart, and my own story wrapped up so tight inside there nobody will ever hear it.

four

CRAZY

1967

AUDREY

Audrey just had the baby settled from her midnight feeding when she heard someone battering at the shop door downstairs. Just what she needed. The youngster, in her crib, stirred and whimpered. She wasn't a good sleeper. She'd been two months with Audrey and Ellen now and they were finally getting her onto some kind of a schedule. Stella never seemed to keep her to any sort of schedule at all—no surprise there. The poor thing was put down and picked up at all hours and fed whenever her mother took it into her head to feed her. She had come to them with a diaper rash so bad that Ellen couldn't even bear to talk to Stella for a while afterwards, she was so mad that anyone would let a baby get into such a state. "I don't care what the poor girl is going through, she got no right to do that to a baby. I don't think she's a fit mother." Some of the harshest words Audrey had ever heard her mother say about anyone, but then Ellen loved babies.

Audrey did not love babies. She had gotten through Henry's babyhood and expected never to have to do this again.

Ellen would gladly take over all the responsibility, but at sixty-two she didn't always have the energy to be getting up at nights with a crying infant.

"What's that racket?" Wes said, getting slowly out of his chair. He, too, moved more slowly and stiffly these days, and when the baby cried at night Audrey worried about her keeping Wes awake.

"Don't worry, Dad, I'll go. Mom, keep an eye on her, make sure she stays down."

"You watch yourself, Audrey." Wes had eased back into his chair but still looked worried. "There's some hard crowd around here these days."

"It's nothing, Dad. Probably Mike Walsh figuring he can't get through the night without another pack of smokes."

It wouldn't be that, of course—none of the neighbours, even the drunks and the crazy ones, ever tried to come into the store at this hour of night. And a thief would have broken in the window and took what they wanted by this time. *Someone in trouble*, Audrey thought as she went down the stairs, fumbling for the light switch. Someone who would come to the door instead of phoning.

Sure enough, Stella stumbled through the door when Audrey opened it. "Where is she? Get her dressed, I'm taking her!"

Audrey put her hands on Stella's shoulders. The girl was soaking wet, wearing only a thin blouse and a pair of blue jeans, no jacket on a night like this. "What are you, girl, crazy? That child is not going out of this house tonight, middle of the night in the pouring rain. Where's Henry?"

"I don't give a damn where Henry is! I'm leaving and I'm not going back to him, and I'm not leaving my baby with ye crowd either!"

"Oh, is that so?" Audrey pulled her hands from the girl's shoulders, folded her arms over her chest. "And where would you be off to, young miss Stella? You may not be too fond of us at the moment but me and Mother Holloway are looking after your child, which is more than your own family is willing to do. I knows you're not planning to take her home so where else would you be going this time of night?"

"Out. Away. Away from here!" Stella's last words turned into a howl, something garbled and barely even human. She was half-crying, half-yelling, shivering with the cold and wet and with something that might be fear or rage.

Audrey's impulse was to tell the girl to come upstairs, give her a warm robe to put on, make her a cup of tea. How many times, in the years that came afterwards, would she play out that scene, wonder how it might have ended if she had taken Stella upstairs? A thousand times, surely. Ten thousand. And she played out the other scene too—what if she had let Stella take the baby with her?

But she didn't do either of those things. She stayed there in the shop, Stella shaking and crying, Audrey immobile between her and the store counter. Audrey had had enough of it. This was not the first time Stella had come bursting into the place wanting Rachel back, though it was the first time she had come this late at night and in this bad a state. If she came in the daytime and looked half-sensible, and if she had a stroller with her, Audrey would let Stella take her daughter for a little walk, though she had started to wonder if even that much was safe.

The state she was in tonight, there was no way Audrey would let her take the baby. Audrey had been up with Stella's fussy child for an hour after being on her feet in the shop all day, and she had no time for Stella's foolishness.

"You needs to go home to your husband and stop your

shenanigans," she said. "You're a big girl, Stella. You can't be getting on like this no more."

"What do you know about it? What the hell do you know about my life?" Stella tried to push past, but she was a little squirmy thing, no match for Audrey, who grabbed her arms again, this time to hold her back.

"What do I know?" *About being married too young, having a baby without my mother or any of the rest of my family there to help, about wanting to grab my baby and run away from it all?* Audrey didn't say any of that. Stella had no right to Audrey's confidences, and anyway, she was in no place to be thinking about anyone but herself.

Stella spat a word at her—it took Audrey a minute to even pick it apart and understand what she had said, and when she did, it was a word that nobody in Audrey's life had ever called her—at least, not to her face. She tried to grab Stella, to keep her from running away—which made no sense, because she didn't want Stella there in the first place. Certainly not anywhere near the baby. But the thought of the girl running out into the rainy night in this state worried Audrey. Where was Henry? He should be here, dealing with this crazy girl he had himself chained to.

Stella wrenched away and ran, not for the staircase up to the living room, but back out the front door. "Get back in here!" Audrey called—though she still wasn't sure why. She went to the door in time to hear a car engine start and the screech of the tires pulling away. Whose car was Stella driving, and should she be behind the wheel in a state like this?

Audrey went back into the shop and called Henry. The phone rang and rang and rang. That damned house they were living in, a bunch of feckless young fools who between them couldn't tell their arse from a hole in the wall.

187

Back upstairs, Audrey put the kettle on. Ellen was sitting up in the armchair with Rachel in her arms; they were both asleep. Audrey hoped a cup of tea would settle her nerves, but she was so worried about Stella and Henry she was like a cat on hot bricks. She was waiting for another sound from downstairs, and when she heard it about half an hour later—the scrape of Henry's key in the lock—she went down into the store.

"Is she here?"

Henry was like a drowned rat. He was breathing hard, like he'd run all the way up here from downtown.

"Who—your wife or your child?"

"I meant Stella. The baby's here, isn't she?"

"Only because I told Stella she couldn't take her."

"She was here? She wanted to take Rachel?"

"Henry, that girl is in trouble. What are you going to do?"

"I don't know, Mom. I swear to God I got no idea what to do."

"Well I s'pose you got to go find her. Whose car is she driving?"

"Nick's. Can I take your car, Ma?"

"Do you even have a clue where she's gone?"

Henry just stood there, dripping, shaking his head. "I don't know. She can't be gone back home, can she? To her parents?"

"Her father's said a dozen times he won't have her in the house. Don't she have friends? Anyone she'd go to?"

Again he shook his head. "No...I don't think she's seen any of her friends in a while. I called Beth Hussey and what's her name, Lois, but they both said they haven't talked to her in ages."

Audrey went upstairs and got the car keys out of her purse, brought them back down to Henry. Maybe she should go out with him; maybe he was no more fit to be driving than Stella was.

He came back two hours later, when nobody in the house was awake but Audrey. She heard the car pull into the spot by the curb and went down to let him in. "I looked everywhere I could think of—even drove by all of her sisters' houses. There's no sign of her." He looked up, his eyes searching hers, and suddenly he looked ten years old again. "Do you think she could have left town? Would she really take off like that? Should I call the cops?"

"If she haven't shown up by morning, maybe. Come upstairs now and I'll make you a cup of tea."

He came up, drank a cup of tea, went over and over with Audrey all the places Stella could have gone. "Nick says he'll have her up on charges for stealing his car if she don't have it back by morning," he reported after calling back to the house to see if she'd shown up there.

"I'm sure she'll be back by then," said Audrey, who was not at all sure. "Or she'll call. She'll phone and let you know she's all right."

It was two o'clock in the morning by then. The phone didn't ring, and there was no knock on the door. Henry lay down on the couch. Finally Audrey herself lay down to get a few hours' sleep.

The knock on the door didn't come till Audrey went down to open the shop in the morning. Upstairs, Wes was getting ready for work, Ellen was feeding the baby, and Henry was still asleep. Audrey heard the ping of the door and looked up to see a policeman in uniform asking for Henry Holloway.

ELLEN

Nobody knew what to do about the funeral, not even where to have it or what minister or priest would have the service. Poor little Stella's body—what there was left of it, after they pulled her out of the car at the bottom of the cliff—stayed in the morgue at St. Clare's . Audrey and Tony shouted at each other. Ellen tried to hush the baby; Bridget and her daughters cried. Henry should by rights have made all the decisions, being the husband of the deceased, but he was like somebody shell-shocked, sitting there in the chair staring off into space.

Tony Nolan, suddenly willing to claim his daughter now that she was dead, said Stella should be sent to Caul's and they would have Father O'Keefe to do the service. But Father O'Keefe caused more trouble than he was worth. He met them in the Holloway's living room because everything had to be done around Henry, even if Henry never said a word.

"There's a question, though, isn't there?" the priest said. "I hate to bring it up, at a time like this, but from what the police have said—well, the poor girl—isn't it likely that she intended to take her own life?"

Bridget wailed and blew her nose. "How dare you say a thing like that?" Tony Nolan demanded. "As if my wife isn't already upset enough, losing our little girl in a terrible accident, and for you to suggest—to say that she—"

"But that's what everyone will be saying," said Audrey.

"Who gives a damn what everyone says?"

"Well, the state she was in when she came in here that night—"

"What did you let her go out like that for?" Bridget burst out. "You never should have let her go!"

"She wouldn't have come here in the first place if she'd been allowed to go to her own home!" Audrey spat back.

"She came here because she wanted her baby!"

"And a damn good thing I never let her take it, because where would the baby be now?"

"You don't know that!" Tony shouted. Bridget was crying too hard to answer. "If she'd of had her child with her, she never would have been so desperate. She'd of been thinking of the baby, she would of drove more careful. It was an accident, is all it was. She was upset, and she was careless."

"And whose fault was it if she was upset? When her own father—"

"Now, now." Father O'Keefe poured words like honey over the screeching voices of Audrey, Tony, and Bridget. "Now, my dears, it's a terrible tragedy you've all been through, but there's nothing to be gained by turning on each other, by fighting over whose fault it was. Any of you would have prevented it if you could have seen the end from the beginning, but God hasn't given us that power, has He? For His own mysterious purposes."

They were still snapping at each other when he started speaking, but by the end of it they had settled down, like his

TRUDY J. MORGAN-COLE

voice had some magic that could soothe them all. A balm in Gilead, thought Ellen, observing the whole thing from the kitchen door.

"I 'low you're right, Father, but it's some hard," Bridget sniffled.

"Mother's destroyed over it," said Elaine, who sat next to Bridget, rubbing her back. "She haven't slept a wink since Saturday night. No more have I."

"Do you think young Henry's slept?" Audrey said, nodding toward him. Nobody, Henry included, offered an opinion as to whether he had slept or not.

"I understand how difficult it has all been for you, for all of you," Father O'Keefe said. "The only difficulty is, if it was in fact suicide, the church has, as you know, a prohibition against performing a funeral mass for someone who has died by his own hand. Or her. Her own hand."

Stella's hands, gripping the wheel of a car. Ellen hadn't seen Stella that night so she didn't have the pictures in her head that Audrey and Henry had, of how desperate she must have been. What a mercy she didn't have Rachel with her! Of course Audrey would never have let her take the baby.

As if knowing she was the subject of discussion, Rachel whimpered. Ellen went into Henry's old room, which they had made into a sort of nursery for Rachel. Audrey had never wanted to admit the baby was with them permanently, so she had never put any effort into it, but Ellen thought now of painting the walls, maybe a nice soft yellow or pink, something cheery for a baby's room. She was sorry for poor Stella, of course, but she couldn't be sorry that Rachel might stay with them: Ellen loved having a baby in the house again, even if her back twinged in protest when she reached down to pick Rachel up.

"…Enough of this foolishness," Audrey was saying when Ellen went back out, cradling Rachel in her arms. She stayed back in the kitchen, reluctant to let the Nolans see the child. They hadn't asked to see her yet, hadn't acknowledged the existence of the baby who had caused all the trouble. Ellen felt sure that if Bride Nolan once got a look at Rachel, she'd lose all her righteous anger over this little merrybegot and latch onto the living child who was a piece of her Stella. And if the Nolans tried to take Rachel, then Ellen would fight like she had never fought for anything before.

"Enough of this foolishness, and enough of your Holy Mother Church, sitting in judgement on a poor girl who wasn't in her right mind," Audrey told Father O'Keefe. "We'll have poor Stella over to Barrett's and we'll get Reverend Gill to do the service."

"She will not be buried in a Protestant graveyard! That girl was baptized in the Church!" said Tony Nolan.

"Much good that'll do if your precious Church won't bury her in consecrated ground!"

Wes's voice, slow and heavy, had not been heard in this conversation so far. He sat as he always did, listening much and saying little. Now he spoke. "Tell you the truth, Audrey, I've known United Church ministers wouldn't bury someone who took their own life. There was a young fellow out home years ago—sad story, it was, not much older than poor Stella, hung himself in his father's fish store.…"

"I'll never believe poor Stella wanted to end her life, I never will!" wailed Bridget.

"Well, that's the thing," Wes said. "It might well have been an accident, and if it was accidental—"

"Then of course there would be no objection, from the Church's point of view," Father O'Keefe said. "But it seems—"

"Of course she wanted to kill herself!" They all turned towards Henry, as shocked to hear him say anything at all as at what he was saying, at the sudden angry energy in his voice. "She was always at it. She used to cut her wrists with the kitchen knives—you never knew that, did you, none of ye! She used to bawl at me that she wished she was dead, that if she was dead all ye crowd—" his glance raked the room and rested on Tony and Bridget and the sisters, "ye'd all be sorry for how ye treated her. She used to go on and on about being dead, and I'd be there, trying to calm her down and tell her she had to stay alive for me and for the baby, and finally she went off and did it. Stella hardly ever even *drove* a car—what would she of took Nick's car for, that night, if not to go driving it off the cliffs in Outer Cove?"

The meeting with Father O'Keefe fell apart after that, everybody stalking out of the house angry. There was another meeting the next day, this time just Ellen, Wes, Audrey, and Henry with the United Church minister, who also said what a tragedy it was. He didn't come out and say he'd refuse to perform the funeral service for a girl who took her own life, but it was clear he was uncomfortable with the whole situation.

"If her family is Roman Catholic, it might be better—" he said, looking around the room, helpless. He knew Wes and Ellen; they were his parishioners, but Audrey and Henry were Christmas-and-Easter strangers to him. It was a big church.

In the end the Nolans put up another fuss and they went back to Caul's. They found a different RC priest, from St. Patrick's, who agreed with the family that it could easily have been an accident. The dark night, the wet road, a young girl with a husband and baby and everything in the world to live for. Yes, she was upset, and no doubt that made her reckless, but that wasn't the same thing as going out intending to take your

MOST ANYTHING YOU PLEASE

own life. This time Henry made no outburst; he sat slumped in silence as the priest agreed that surely Stella's death was a tragic accident, and under the circumstances the Church could have no objection to him performing the funeral mass, nor to her being buried in the family plot in Belvedere Cemetery.

And so here were Ellen and Wes in the backseat of the car with Audrey and Henry up front, driving to Caul's for the wake. The baby was over at Treese's for the night, being watched and fussed over by her girls, Judy and Nancy. Ellen felt a hard knot of dread along with the sorrow and grief lodged below her breastbone. This was going to be the hardest kind of a wake, the kind where there was nothing comforting or kind anyone could say.

"Ah well, poor girl, she's in a better place now, out of this vale of tears." That was the best effort Nellie Taylor from across the road could make. Ellen smiled and nodded, but Audrey said, "She may be in a better place but she got a husband and child left behind here in this world."

"I know, poor things," Nellie said, and Maggie Ryan leaned into ask, "How is poor Henry taking it? What a shock, at his age!"

Ellen knew that all these women, so friendly and concerned when they came into the shop, had plenty to say when neither herself nor Audrey was around. They had passed comment, no doubt, on the shame of Henry Holloway getting a girl in trouble so young and having to get married. Although could you be surprised really, looking at his mother? Ellen could imagine their words and their tone of voice because she had heard them applied to others so often, at her very own store counter as the women tallied up the sins and misdemeanours of the neighbourhood.

But this had caught them all off guard. A shotgun marriage

and a baby you never expected—that was the rightful price to pay for fooling around, that and the knowledge that neighbours would talk behind your back. But this—this messy death that might or might not have been a suicide, a beautiful unhappy girl who might have been out of her mind—these things were outside the realm of the price you should have to pay for sin.

Most wakes Ellen had been to had soft tears and the quiet condolences punctuated by the odd shaky giggle, sometimes rising to a hearty laugh as people shared stories about the departed. The stories and laughter blunted the edge of grief like a fire in the stove took the worst of the chill out of a winter day. But there was none of that here. Maybe Stella had done cute and funny things they'd like to remember, but nobody felt safe doing so. There was nothing natural about this death, no sense of a life coming full circle.

"He's not taking it very well at all, but what would you expect?" Ellen said. She looked around for Henry and didn't see him, either near her own family or over by the Nolans. In between the two families, ill-at-ease in their Sunday best, were a straggly crowd of young people, Henry's and Stella's friends, who buzzed around the room like bees in a flower garden, lighting here and there before moving on. No laughter even from this crowd; the girls were all crying and the boys looked like they were being strangled with their own neckties, so strained and panicked were their faces.

She expected to see Henry with them, but he wasn't there—maybe he was off having a smoke or a bite to eat in that little room they had for the families to relax in. Only when it was getting close to nine o'clock did she hiss at Audrey to go find Henry, and Audrey reported back that he was nowhere to be found.

"I think he went off with Eddie Cadwell and Tom Walsh

and them," said a stringy girl Ellen identified only as a Hussey, and that was mostly by her nose. "They took off a while ago, I think Henry was with them."

Well, the likes of that. Running away from his own wife's wake, not even telling anyone where he was going. Ellen tried not to judge the boy, though his own mother showed no such restraint. Audrey cursed him roundly all the way home. As for Henry, he didn't come home at all that night, though he rang about midnight to say he was sleeping back at the apartment.

Audrey hung up the phone after taking the call. She and Ellen were having their tea late; a few neighbours had come back to the house for a cup of tea and a slice of cake. It was only when they had gone that she could brew the second cup, the one they could really enjoy with their feet up, if anything was enjoyable in this day.

"He sounded like he'd been drinking," Audrey said with a sigh.

"That's a shame. But it's what you might expect—I mean, if he's in the habit of it anyway, after such a shock."

"He's too young to be in that habit. He only just turned eighteen."

"He's not really eighteen anymore either, though, is he?" Ellen blew on her tea to cool it. "Is there either bit of that cherry cake left? I never had any when they were here, seems like I can't eat these days with anyone watching me. I feels like I might choke."

Audrey got the cake and cut her a slice. "I suppose in a way he's older than eighteen, with all he's been through. Married, a father, and widowed."

"Most men haven't been through that by the time they're fifty."

"Well, I hope it makes him grow up," Audrey said, settling

back to her own cup.

"I'm sure it will. It's a hard way to grow up, but it'll make a man of him." Privately Ellen was not at all sure of this, but she had to put the best face on it for Audrey. Henry had already given his mother enough worry to last a lifetime.

"Will it, though? Going through hardship don't always make a person better. Sure look at Nathan Taylor—his missus and two little ones both died in that fire, and what happened to Nate? Went right off his head and he never had good sense again after. Can't hold a job, can't even carry on a sensible conversation. If Nellie and Bern hadn't taken him in he'd be living on the street."

"Poor Nate. Well, it's true, not everyone takes hardship the same way, and all the Taylors got that melancholy streak. The same sun that hardens the clay melts the butter, like they say."

"So what's Henry—clay or butter?"

"Only time will tell, I 'low," said Ellen. "But our crowd, we've mostly always been clay. You'll see."

AUDREY

The baby was awake at five. Ellen got up with her if she cried in the night so Audrey could get a full night's sleep, and then it was Audrey's turn to see to her in the morning. Audrey got up, changed and fed Rachel, then made breakfast. After breakfast, Ellen went down to open up the shop. These morning hours while Ellen worked, which once used to be Audrey's free time to do her own messages or do a bit of housework, were now consumed with watching Rachel. It took her back to when Henry was this age, not a time Audrey had fond memories of. She wasn't like some women, Treese or Doris, who went on about how they couldn't wait for the grandchildren to come.

"See how much you likes it when you got your grandchild all the time," Audrey muttered. She was washing out a pail of diapers, a task she'd have been happy never to have to do again in her life, while Rachel was in the playpen. Any normal child would be amusing herself with her rattle and bear—the youngster was over a year old now, big enough to play and keep herself occupied. Big enough to train out of those diapers soon, too, Audrey hoped. Rachel loved to throw the rattle out of the playpen. Ellen or Wes would always pick it up and give it back to her; Audrey thought that would only teach Rachel she could rule the roost. She was better off to learn that if you threw something away it was gone and no amount of crying would bring it back.

Audrey finished with the diapers, put a load of wash through the wringer of the machine, and carted Rachel downstairs with her to hang it all out on the line. She wasn't sorry when dinner time came and she heated up and served what was left of the pot of pea soup Ellen had made the evening before. Wes came home for his dinner and Ellen came upstairs to eat hers while Audrey went down to take over the shop. Even with people coming in and out, the shop was more peaceful than being stuck up in that apartment with the baby.

She tried to air her complaints to Doris, although she knew that would be useless. Doris couldn't wait till one of her girls had a baby and she could look after it.

"Looking after it is one thing, I mean the scattered evening, nobody minds that," Audrey said, lighting up a smoke. "But I've had care of that child twenty-four hours a day since the poor youngster was six months old. Yes, Mom's been a grand help, but she's not as spry as she used to be."

"And Henry? Does he take any interest in her at all?"

"He comes by and looks at her. Sometimes he picks her up. But what can you expect from a young fellow like that? I don't recall seeing Dad take much interest in any of the youngsters till they were old enough to walk and talk, and Alf seemed to be the same with his crowd. Just because her poor mother is gone, I don't s'pose it means he's suddenly all interested in the baby."

"What about Stella's family?"

"Not a peep out of any of them for weeks after the funeral, and then out of the blue Mary-Louise waltzes in here last week, large as life." Mary-Louise lived clear over on Campbell Avenue so there was no chance she had just happened into Holloway's store. All the time she was picking up her groceries and talking to Audrey about poor Stella, what a sin, she was peeking around like she expected to see the crib in back behind the counter. Finally she came out and asked how the baby was doing and if she could see her.

"And what did you tell her?"

"I told her the truth. I said, you crowd treated that poor child like a common whore and turned her out of house and home just because she married my son. If you'd offered some help to her and the baby, she might not be where she is today. The time for you Nolans to take an interest in that youngster was long ago, I told her. She's my son's daughter, my grand-daughter, and I'll decide who sees her and who don't."

"How did she take that?"

"She looked like I was after slapping her, and she said, *Well, you got some nerve, missus,* and then she turned and walked out the door, and I haven't heard another word from her or any of the Nolans before or since."

"If you ask me, she's the one has got the nerve. Any of them, really, after how they treated her. I had a cousin, poor girl, whose family was like that when she got in trouble, but her mother had enough backbone to defy the father and keep in touch with her—otherwise I often think poor Morag might have ended up like poor Stella. And Morag wasn't married, either, poor girl—in her case, the man already *had* a wife and children, so of course the shame was even greater."

Audrey sometimes thought she could listen to Doris's voice

TRUDY J. MORGAN-COLE

all day. That Scottish accent, still clipped and precise after twenty years in St. John's, was her favourite thing about her friend. Not that she didn't like the things Doris actually said, it was just that the accent made everything sound better. Audrey got bored with almost everyone else, but never with Doris.

"Oh, I think Bridget sent Mary-Louise here to test out the waters, you might say," Audrey replied. "To see what kind of a reception she'd get. Bridget don't dare show her own face around here; I gave her a piece of my mind after the funeral."

"It's a crying shame, that's what it is," said Doris, picking up her bags. "Well, I must toddle off, Les will be wanting his tea."

Henry came in about an hour later. It had been a good three days since Audrey had seen him—he had gone back to living with his buddies, and he had been working again the last few weeks. There was plenty of construction work on the go with the new apartment buildings being built down on Graves Street and Anderson Avenue, and Wes, Alf, and his crew, including Henry and both of Alf's sons, were all working there. It was good for Henry to have work, she thought, something to take his mind off it all. As if his mind would ever be off Stella.

"Do you want to go up and see Rachel?" Audrey glanced at her watch. "Mom will be just finished giving her a bath now, she's always in a good mood after her bath." That was a bit of a stretch, in Audrey's personal opinion: the baby was *more* likely to be in a good mood after her bath, but that wasn't saying much.

Henry shook his head. "Nah, not right now. I came over to talk to you. I've…I made up my mind about something."

"About what?" Was he going to take Rachel back with him, or hand her off to the Nolans after all?

"I'm going away for a while. Nick and Chris have been real decent to me—they've been letting me stay there without paying the rent and they gave me back the damage deposit I paid them back when St— when we moved in there. And I got paid today, so I got a bit of money. I'm gonna buy a plane ticket and go on down to see Dad and Carol."

The possibility that Henry might go away had not been far from Audrey's mind. They had all kinds of family up in Ontario now, Marilyn and June in Toronto, Frank in Whitby. Alf's oldest, Randy, was talking about going up there; his uncle Frank had assured him he'd find a job in no time. Audrey had heard Henry talking over the plan with Randy and she wouldn't have been surprised if he'd announced they were both moving upalong. It might be the best thing for Henry to be away.

Still and all, Louisiana had never crossed her mind as a possibility. "There's lots of places you could go, lots of family you could stay with up in Toronto or Whitby. Sure we even got people in New York if you wants to go to the States."

"Yeah, I want to go back to Dad's place for a while. I've been talking to him on the phone and he told me I could come anytime. I like it down there, there's a lot of good music and I think I could learn something. And probably Dad could help me find a job or something. I'm not going to stay down there forever or anything, I just thought…well. I just want to go there."

It's as far away as you can get, Audrey thought. It made sense if you looked at it that way. As far removed from the memories of Stella and the daily reminder of baby Rachel as possible. It wasn't like Henry could book a ticket to Timbuktu and have someone waiting at the other end who'd put a roof over his head.

"What about the baby?"

"Will you go on looking after her, Mom? You and Nan and Pop? You're way better at it than I would be. I don't know what to be doing with her."

"I don't either, half the time. I'm not good with youngsters, never was."

Henry shrugged, and gave half a smile, which was half more than she had seen on him in a long time. "I don't know, you did all right with me. Look how great I turned out." There was a thing he did, a way he shrugged and ducked his head, that broke a mother's heart but probably looked adorable to young girls. That look would get him in trouble, but then Henry had already gotten in the worst kind of trouble a boy could get into, and had it end about as badly as it possibly could. Everything on the other side of that was just survival.

"Well, you got your mind made up, and you're eighteen years old, so I can't stop you." All she could give him was her blessing, and that was the closest she could come to putting it into words.

musical interlude

RAE HOLLOWAY

I wish I was a Lord Mayor, Marquis or an Earl
Then blow me if I wouldn't marry Old Brown's girl.

I hate talking in between songs. Like it's the worst thing about a gig. I'd like to be this mysterious singer who just gets up to the mic, sings a song, and disappears into the music. But people like it when you talk. They want to have a story to go with a song—if you wrote it yourself, why you wrote it, what it's about. Like a song is about anything. If it's a cover they want to know why you picked that one, what it means to you or whatever.

I'm doing a mix tonight, some originals and some folk songs. Got away with not talking between the first two but as I finish up the last chorus of "Old Brown's Daughter" they look like they expect me to say something.

—So, um, that song always reminds me a bit of home, because I grew up over a store. Only it wasn't my father, it was my grandmother and great-grandmother who ran it.

Holloway's on Rankin Street, it's, um, it's still there. We lived upstairs over the shop....

See, this is what I hate about talking, I don't know where this is going. I have to figure out some kind of segue from Old Brown and his shop and his daughter to the next song in the set which is one I wrote, all about love and betrayal. It'd be good if I had some cute story about growing up in the shop to tell, but all that sticks in my mind is being eight or nine years old and Nanny Audrey telling me to get out, stop hanging around the shop, go outside and play. Then coming back in hours later, cold and numb-fingered. I wandered around the neighbourhood looking for adventure or kindred spirits and never found either.

That's when she'd hand down the sentence: You go upstairs now and have your bath before supper. Damn, I could write a song about that bathtub. It was huge, with steep, gleaming porcelain sides that rose up like glaciers from the narrow bottom. This long finger of rust stain spreading out from the drain hole. It filled really slowly and I never knew how long it would take to get it full enough to be comfortable, because the hot water gave out long before then.

Looking around at this crowd here tonight I bet half them are the types that buy up old downtown houses cheap and renovate them. You meet people like that everywhere these days, and boy do they love to take you on tours of their houses. And they're beautiful, no doubt about it, these old places down on Gower Street and wherever, with the high ceilings, the original tile work around the fireplace, the refinished hardwood floors. Then you get to the bathroom and there's this old claw-foot bathtub and they have to tell you the story about how they found it, how they got it all rigged up with a shower and a curtain around it. *Such a find, such a steal, you wouldn't believe.*

MOST ANYTHING YOU PLEASE

Sometimes they even tear out perfectly good built-in tubs and showers to replace them with the old fashioned tubs, and all I can think is *I bet not one of you people grew up having to take a bath in a claw-foot bathtub.*

I'd sit there in three or four inches of water, half froze, and then when I'd shivered enough I'd get out and dry off and Nanny Audrey, if she was upstairs from the shop then, would nod at me like I'd ticked an item off a list. Nanny Ellen would say, *Did you dry off good my love? You don't want to catch your death of cold, these chilly nights.*

I used to imagine if I had a mother, she'd be someone who would fill up the bath—a proper tub, like Vicky's family had—and make it warm and bubbly, with bubble bath or something, and dry me off with a big towel afterwards. Wrap my hair up in a towel like a turban, like I saw Vicky's mother do with her hair when I slept over.

All this, about the bathtub and towels and all that, is flashing through my head like a silent movie, when what's actually coming out of my mouth is some foolishness about corner stores and how they were the heart of the neighbourhood and blah-di-blah-di-blah. It's not like I'm going to tell them about getting a bath when I was nine, am I? Time to wrap this up.

—So, um, yeah, I didn't love everything about growing up over the store, but it's certainly not something you ever forget. And, um, as far as I know there was never anyone hanging around the store asking for my hand in marriage. But if there was, it probably would have ended something like this...

D minor chord, and I'm past the talking part now. On to the singing. The easy part.

TRUDY J. MORGAN-COLE

five

FORGET ME NOT

1971

AUDREY

In the dim light Audrey could barely see her watch. She squinted to make out that it was 9:45. She had told her mother she'd be back by nine for sure. Ellen was wonderful with Rachel, but not always good at getting her to go to bed on time. You couldn't expect a great-grandmother to be strict with a five year old.

Beside Audrey, Nelson Spracklin snored gently. He always booked a room for the whole night, even though Audrey couldn't spare more than an hour or two. She pulled on her slacks and blouse, slipped her feet into shoes, picked up her jacket from the chair by the door. It wasn't like some scene in a movie where he tore off her clothes as soon as they got through the door of the hotel room and she was left to pick up a sock here, a brassiere there. Nelson, she thought, would like to believe they were living out that kind of movie scene—that this was some grand passion, that he was cheating on his wife because he couldn't keep his hands off Audrey Holloway. But it wasn't that at all. He was a lonely man who didn't sleep with his wife much anymore, and Audrey was an acquaintance who was willing to go to bed with him in a room in the Kenmount Motel.

He was a nice-looking man. She wouldn't have taken the risk if he wasn't. For her it was mostly the flattery, the thought that someone would want her. It had been a long time—eighteen years since she left Harry Pickens. Over the years, she had been out on a few dates with fellows, but nothing ever turned serious. Most men weren't keen on a divorced woman, much less a single mother.

She thought about waking Nelson to say good-bye, but he was sleeping soundly. They fell into this almost by accident, one night when Valerie Gillard, who had split up with Bryce, convinced Audrey to come downtown for a girls' night. Audrey had been glad to go: it was a better night out than Bingo with Treese and her sisters. Val was mad, when the evening was over, that it was Audrey who'd managed to snag a fellow's attention. She went off and left Audrey sitting at the bar with Nelson. Thank goodness Valerie didn't know who Nelson was, didn't know he was married. The next time Audrey talked to Val she told her that there was nothing to it, the fellow from the bar wasn't her type.

The crisp evening air hit Audrey like a slap in the face after the too-warm motel room. She went to her car, wondering if anyone would recognize it, would think anything if they saw her parked here. They'd probably think she was inside having a drink at the bar. Nobody—not even Lorraine Penney or Selena Ivany, the worst gossips Audrey knew—would think she was in a motel room having relations with a married man.

Well, and what if they did? It was nobody's business. Audrey only hoped that Nelson's wife didn't find out, because she didn't want to be the cause of that kind of unhappiness for another woman. Nor did she want Nelson's wife to chuck him out and him to come running to Audrey. And she hoped her parents didn't find out, because it would break their hearts.

"At least the others are all right," Audrey sometimes told Ellen, half-teasing, when Ellen shook her head and clicked her tongue about how Audrey just needed to find a good man. "You've got all the rest of us decently married off, you must be pleased."

"But up on the mainland!" Ellen almost wailed. Except for Audrey here in the house, and Alf and Treese across town, all her children were settled in Ontario now. June had met a fellow up there whose grandmother came from Candle Cove, the same little outport Ellen was born in. Frank had gotten married up there two years ago, to a girl called Sophie Bernini. At least Marilyn and June were married to Newfoundlanders, men whose families Ellen knew. Frank's wife was a stranger with a foreign-sounding name, someone they had never clapped eyes on. "And you know she won't want to come back here to live," Ellen complained. "Marilyn and George mean to come back when they retire, and I wouldn't be surprised if June and Norm do too. But I might never have Frank home again. I've got grandchildren I've never laid eyes on, Audrey."

"Well, I've got a grandchild I never gets clear of, so take your pick," said Audrey. She loved Rachel, of course, but she wasn't reconciled to the fact that she had been forced back into mothering a small child again.

Audrey punched the radio button till she hit on a song she liked on CJON—"Help Me Make it Through the Night"—and sang along with it on the short drive from the motel to the shop, where she let herself in through the quiet, darkened store. The shop had been shut for a week now as Wes, Alf, and

Alf's crew of men worked on the renovations. Audrey had been nearly two years now convincing Ellen they had to make changes to the shop, move the counter and rearrange the floor space to make it all more convenient. The new, lit-up Pepsi sign outside cast a pool of ghostly light on the floor of the silent shop. Audrey ran her hand over the new countertop. It was all going to be so much better, everything up to date and no more smelly old barrels of salt beef or crates of potatoes and turnips going bad. Most of what they'd carry now would be tinned goods and items that could be kept in the fridge. People got all their meat and vegetables at the supermarket now and much as Ellen might dig in her heels, you had to move with the times.

The one concession they had made for Ellen was to take down the old wooden sign that had been over the door and mount it on the wall behind the counter. Holloway's Grocery and Confectionary. Alf's daughter Nancy, the artistic one, had even painted a little "Established 1936" down under the name. When the shop re-opened it would all be new and modern, but the old sign would hang there as a reminder.

She was surprised to find the upstairs silent too, only one lamp left on. When she went out after supper, her father was still working down in the shop, laying the new tile floor, though Alf and the boys had gone home. Ellen had been washing dishes and Rachel was playing in front of the TV. Now the place was empty, even Rachel's room. Audrey went back into the kitchen and saw what she hadn't noticed before: a hastily written note in the messiest version of Ellen's handwriting she had ever seen.

Gone to the Grace—meet us there. And a word crossed out. Audrey looked closer and saw the word was "Dad." Ellen had been going to write something more, something about Dad, but decided there wasn't—time, perhaps?

TRUDY J. MORGAN-COLE

In the waiting room of the Grace Hospital's emergency department she found Treese, who told her that her mother and Alf were in with Wes. "Your mother brought Rachel with her, but I sent her home with the girls—Judy'll look after her at our place. My Lord, Audrey, the shock I got when your mother called me! I can't get over it. I'm not over it yet."

It was a job, getting any kind of a story out of Treese without going down all the side-alleys of her conversation. "Mom said she heard a noise, like a thump downstairs, and of course she thought he knocked something over in the shop. But you know Alf wasn't one bit surprised when I told him, he was shocked of course, but not really surprised, because he's been saying for ages now that Dad shouldn't be working alone, he's not a young man anymore, only he never liked to admit it, did he? Mom said she came downstairs and there he was, keeled over, so of course she called the ambulance right away—Alf blames himself, he should have gone back in this evening, knowing your dad would want to get in a few more hours work, but I'm always telling Alf he got to take some time for himself or he'll end up just like his father in a few years—"

"Was it a heart attack? Is he—will he be all right?"

Treese laid a hand over her own heart, like she was about to sing "God Save the Queen." "Alf came out half an hour ago—we've been here since seven-thirty, your mother was frantic because she didn't know where you were or have a number to call you at or anything—and said it was a heart attack, a massive heart attack, but they couldn't say—I don't know, Audrey my love, Alf said the doctors couldn't tell them nothing."

"Would they let me go back there, I wonder?"

"I don't know, I suppose you could ask that nurse. She's not very nice to talk to—look at the face on her! But maybe she'll tell you more than she told me, you being his daughter and all. Oh, what a sin, what a sin."

Just at that moment a door opened and Audrey watched her brother Alf walk toward her. She didn't need Alf to say anything: she read the news on his face. He looked not at his wife but at Audrey, shaking his head, and then he came and put his arms around her, something she couldn't remember Alf ever doing in his life.

What a sin, Audrey thought, rocking in her brother's unfamiliar embrace, trying to block out his meaningless words. She couldn't erase that picture of herself, going at it in a dingy motel room with a man whose face she could barely remember, at the very moment her father was laid out on the new tile floor of the shop. The one bit of fun she had allowed herself in all these years, and it had to end like this. If that wasn't a sign from on high she didn't know what was.

ELLEN

They all came home for the funeral—Marilyn, June, even Frank, whose wife was due to have the baby any day now. All five of Ellen's children were beside her as they lowered Wes into his grave. And a good few grandchildren too—all Alf and Treese's crowd except Randy. Marilyn's oldest, Sharon, a solemn round-faced twelve year old, had come home with her mother. And Henry had flown in last night and now stood looking uneasy in a dark suit. Death brought them all together.

Ellen felt queer. That was the best way she could put it, a queer feeling. The reality of what had happened came and went. Sometimes it hit her full-force that Wes was dead, and she sank under a wave of hard sobs; at other times she forgot, and turned, expecting to see him come into the room. Still other times it seemed like his death happened a long time ago; she could hardly believe he was here with her just a couple of days before.

At the funeral home, and later after the service at church, people flowed past. They took her hand and said, "Sorry for your trouble," or "What a shame." Someone told her, "They don't make them like him anymore." An odd sentiment, as if she were planning to drop into the Arcade Stores tomorrow and see if they had any replacement husbands. But Ellen thought there was some truth to it. Alf, maybe, was a man in his father's mold, but he lacked Wes's gentleness. Frank was not that kind of man; she loved her younger son, but he wasn't half the man his father was. Alf's boys were both hard workers but she didn't see their grandfather's steadiness in them. And as for Henry—well. Best not to even talk about Henry.

She and Audrey talked about him, of course, once the funeral was over and they were back home. Rachel was in bed and Henry gone out somewhere. June, who was staying with Ellen and Audrey, made tea for the three women and put out a plate of date squares that one of the neighbours had brought over. "I can't get over how grown up your Henry is," she told Audrey.

"Well, he's twenty-two." Audrey hadn't seen her son for four years, which seemed like a long time until Ellen stopped to think that she herself hadn't seen June in eight years. June had two children, and Marilyn two younger ones, who Ellen had never laid eyes on, except for pictures. It was expensive to bring a whole family home for a holiday. Marilyn and June and Frank were always after her to come up there for a visit, but Ellen always said she couldn't leave the store. *Would Wes have liked that?* she wondered now. A trip up to the mainland to see his children and grandchildren?

"What's Henry been doing, all this time? All the time down in the States with his father's people?" June wanted to know.

Audrey shook her head. "No, no—he was down there for— what was it, Mom? Six months, maybe eight. Then Harry called

TRUDY J. MORGAN-COLE

me one day and told me they'd had a big fight and Henry was after taking off out of it. Harry and Carol were always after him, you know, to get a steady job, settle down, and you know Henry wasn't much for that at the best of times, and this wasn't the best of times."

Ellen remembered that phone call; Audrey's angry voice raised in the kitchen. She was contrary, Audrey was: how many times, when Henry was at home, had she told him to give up this foolishness about trying to be a musician and get himself a sensible job? But when it was his father and his father's wife telling him, Audrey jumped to her son's defense. "That's shocking, after what he's been through—you should have been more encouraging to him."

Then Harry's wife had come on the line, and Audrey had exchanged hard words with her and ended by slamming the phone down. "She said I was too soft on him," Audrey told Ellen afterwards, her hands still shaking with anger or something like it. "Me? After I raised that boy on my own, no help from Harry, Carol got the nerve to tell me I'm too soft on him?"

"So where did he go after that?"

"Oh, it was Nashville then—I think the idea was to hit the big time, end upon the Grand Ole Opry or something. Then after another year or two at that, he went on to New York, and he haven't hit the big time yet."

Henry phoned home—collect calls, of course—every few months to let his mother and grandparents know he was all right, and tell them about some bar he'd played in or some musician he was playing backup for. Ellen never knew who any of them were, but Audrey said it was usually somebody who had played in a band with someone who played with someone else who was famous. Ellen worried about him night and day, and she knew Audrey did too although Audrey would never admit to it. "That one will always land on his feet," she said, when Ellen raised the subject of Henry. "Nothing no good ever comes to know harm. I'm not saying Henry's no good, now, but he's a foolish know-nothing and he's the kind will always find someone to look after him." Maybe she was right; here he was home now, safe and sound.

"Is he only home for a visit, or going to stay for a while?" June asked.

Audrey shook her head. "No idea. He told me he bought a one-way ticket, but it might be that's all he could afford. He needs to spend some time here if he wants his daughter to know anything about who her father is."

"Shh. I don't know if she's asleep yet," Ellen warned.

June, Frank, Marilyn, and Sharon all went home before the week was out, but Henry stayed. "I want to be some help around the house, Nan," he told her. "And I could help out in the shop, too. I could take over Judy's shifts when she starts trade school." Alf's Judy was going in to be a hairdresser; her sister Nancy was at MUN and her brother Doug was talking about moving up to Toronto with Randy.

The renovations had been suspended for a few days after Wes's death, but Alf's men were working down there again now and the shop would soon be ready to re-open. Ellen felt bone-tired when she thought of getting up to do that early morning shift. Not that she could sleep if she stayed in bed—it was more that she wasn't ready to face people. The neighbours, the customers with their sorry faces, all still offering condolences on her loss. But it was hard to imagine Henry, who had stayed out till all hours every night since he had been home, getting up to open the shop at eight in the morning.

"It'd be good for Rachel, having you here."

Henry shrugged. That shrug—it was his most common

gesture. Hands in pockets, head down, lifting one shoulder in a gesture that said not just, "I don't know," but "How could you expect someone like me to know anything about that?" It made Ellen's eyes fill with tears. *They don't make them like Wes anymore*, she reminded herself.

The one person in the family who was like Henry was Rachel. She looked like him, although he was a handsome young man while she was a plain child. Rachel was long and stringy and brown-haired, nothing in her of the pretty Stella. She was a quiet child, most of the time, kept to herself when there was a crowd of youngsters around. And she did the same as Henry—put her head down and shrugged—when her father made awkward attempts to talk to her. Henry asked her did she like Kindergarten and Rachel shrugged. He asked her what games did she like to play; Rachel shrugged. Did she have a best friend? Still looking at the floor, Rachel shook her head.

When Henry tried to talk to Rachel she would burrow into Ellen's arms or press herself against Audrey's side. Ellen tried to explain to her that Poppy had gone to heaven to be with Jesus and the angels, though Audrey said, "Don't be at that, Mom, all that's going to do is make her scared of Jesus. She's already scared of angels from when you took her to Sunday School and they told her angels were always watching her, but she couldn't see them."

Too much change too fast for a little one like that, Ellen thought. Overnight, her great-grampa was gone, and this new man who everyone told her was her father had moved in. She and Henry were equally wary of each other.

One night, about two weeks after Wes's death, the four of them sat in the living room on a Sunday night watching Rachel's favourite show, *The Wonderful World of Disney*. Wes used to enjoy these Sunday evenings; for years he and Ellen went to the Sunday evening service at church, but these last few years he preferred to stay home, relaxing in the living room after supper, watching his great-granddaughter laugh at the television.

Henry was fidgety; Ellen thought it wouldn't be long before he got up and went out somewhere. The boy was restless, always tapping a foot or drumming with his fingers, never able to sit for long. Finally he got up, but instead of heading downstairs and out the door, he went to his room—what used to be the boys' room when the youngsters were all small—and came back with the guitar he brought home with him.

He took the guitar out with him most evenings, but this was the first time he had played it since coming home; the first time anyone had played a note of music in the house since Wes took out the accordion the Sunday before he died. Henry tuned the guitar quietly, in the background behind the noise of the Disney movie. But when he began to strum during one of the commercial breaks, Rachel's head swivelled away from the TV like Mickey Mouse had just popped up behind her. She stared at the guitar, then went to sit beside Henry on the couch.

"What's that?"

"My guitar."

"Where'd you get it?"

"Bought it from a second-hand shop in Harlem."

Another child—Ellen remembered Frank at that age, his endless strings of questions— might be diverted onto, "Where's Harlem?" but Rachel's attention didn't leave the guitar. "How did you learn to play it?"

"Um. Years ago—not when I was as small as you, but a little bit bigger—I got a friend of mine to show me a few chords, and then I sort of taught myself."

"Could I learn?"

"Sure. Someday. Right now your arms and hands aren't big enough."

"Can you get little ones?"

"Not little enough for someone your size, nope."

"Can I try, though? I might be big enough. Miss Sheppard says I'm big for my age. I'm the second-tallest girl in my class."

Another father might have commented on what a grand big girl she was, or asked more questions about school. But Henry, as focused on the guitar as his daughter was, passed it over to her and settled it on her lap.

"See?" he said as she tried to wrap her arms around it. "You got to wait till your arms get long enough to go around the body, and your hands got to be big enough to wrap around the neck of the guitar. Your fingers press down on the strings, see, to make the chords."

"It hurts."

"Yeah, it will for a while. When you're big enough I'll get you your own guitar and teach you to play."

Rachel looked up as Henry took the guitar back. She tucked up her feet on the couch. While he showed her the guitar, *The Wonderful World of Disney* ended and now *The Tommy Hunter Show* was on. Henry strummed along with the theme song.

"Will you still be here when I'm that big?"

Henry didn't answer right away. He kept on strumming along with the music on the TV, and his eyes slid over to Audrey.

"I will," he said after a moment. "Yeah, I'll still be here then."

AUDREY

"I called the lawyer today," Ellen said when Audrey came upstairs after looking over the day's renovation work down in the shop. "I made an appointment for Thursday afternoon. You, me and Alf got to go down there."

"It won't take very long, will it? I'm sure Dad's will was pretty straightforward."

"Oh, it was—he left everything to me. That's what we always planned. But I need to make out a will, now that the house and the shop is all mine—what to do when I pass away."

"I can't be thinking about that now, Mom. Dad's only just under the ground, barely two weeks. How are we supposed to make any decisions about what happens when you go too? That'll be a good many years from now, I hope."

"We can all hope, but we don't know." Ellen was chopping onions to go with the corned-beef hash she was making for supper. Handy thing, onions: a good excuse for a good cry. "Nobody knows the day nor the hour, like the Good Book says. Your father certainly didn't think when he went down to lay tile

223

that night that he'd never come back up these stairs. If something happened to me suddenly—where would you be? Who'd own the house and the shop? The bank, most likely—we owes them enough. No, it all got to be down on paper, good and legal."

"So what's it going to say, this good and legal paper we're going to sign? Who are you leaving everything to?"

"Oh. Well, I'm going to ask the lawyer for advice, I suppose. I mean, by rights the eldest son should inherit the business, but Alf got no interest in it. You been working here all these years, helping me keep it going, and this house is your home. I can't see leaving it to anyone but you. I'm sure Alf will agree to that."

"You'd better ask him about it and make sure he does, before we gets into a conversation about family business in the lawyer's office."

"What are lawyers for, if not to take your family business to?"

"I still think, talk to Alf first."

"Alf will be fine with it. Your father talked to him about it all." Ellen ladled mashed potatoes into the frying pan with corned beef and onions.

"Did he? I'm sure Dad had the best intentions. I think he meant to talk to Alf about it, but did he actually do it? And what about Frank and June and Marilyn? Do they get any say in this?"

"Oh, leave me be, Audrey. We'll talk it all out in the lawyer's office."

Audrey considered phoning Alf herself, or going over to talk to him. But awkward as it might have been for her father to bring up the question of what would happen after he died, it was going to be much harder for her to say, "Alf, Mom's making a will and she's going to leave the house and store to me. That all right with you?" There was no way to bring up the subject without sounding greedy and grasping. It just would be nice to have a bit more time to think about it all.

Audrey was by no means sure she even wanted to own Holloway's Grocery and Confectionary. It would be a ball and chain tying her to home for the rest of her life. But if she didn't own it, she might well be not only out of a job, but homeless. So she did nothing. And she had a good day and a half to think that might be the best way to go about it, until she and her mother and Alf were sat in the lawyer's office and it became clear to everyone that leaving this to discuss in front of the lawyer had been a very, very bad idea.

Ellen sat with her gloved hands clutching her purse, still wearing a black dress and coat though Audrey told her nobody went around anymore wearing mourning, even after their husband died. "Wesley left me the house and the business, of course, being his widow, and…when I'm gone…I been back and forth in my mind over what to do. But when all's said and done, I think it's best to leave the house and the business to my daughter Audrey. She's the one lives there and she does more of the work than I do, these days, running the shop. It's really her business as well as her home, and it only seems like the right thing to do."

The lawyer picked up his pen. "Well, Mrs. Holloway, if you've thought it over and—"

"Just a moment, now." Alf spoke softly—he was a big man but not a loud or blustery one. Like their father, in that way, though there was a toughness to him that Audrey never saw in Wes. "Mom, are you sure you've given this enough thought?"

"I been back and forth over it, like I said, and this is the best conclusion I can come to."

"Well, I have to say I don't think too much of it." Alf leaned forward, hands clasped in front of him. "You do know you're leaving everything to Audrey—to one child out of five, not even the eldest—and cutting the rest of us off without a cent?"

"How many cents do you think I got to leave, Alf?" Ellen turned to him, still clutching her purse. "Your father wasn't a wealthy man; he didn't have anything to speak of in the way of savings. The store brings in a little bit of income, but you know yourself it's no gold mine and we're always borrowing from the bank. That shop won't make nobody rich; all it'll do is give Audrey a steady job and a place to live. And of course you know if any of your family ever wants a job there, they can have it, same as Judy did these last few years."

"That's not the point, Mother. The point is there's no fairness to it. You said yourself there's no savings, no money put away, so the house and shop is all you'll ever have to leave. To leave it all to one child when you got five don't seem right to me." He appealed over the heads of the women to the other man in the room, the lawyer. "Mr. Power, you see a lot of this kind of dealings, I'm sure—where there's a family business and not much else to leave. You can see my point, can't you?"

The lawyer coughed. "In cases where there's not a very big estate and a large family, it's not always practical—"

Ellen interrupted. "If I divided the business five ways, there'd be nothing left, and you know it, Alf! What am I supposed to do? If I leaves it between all five of ye, and I dies tomorrow, you'll have to sell the house and the shop to some stranger. The little bit you'd get for it you'd have to divide that between five of you, and it wouldn't be enough to do anyone any good. The rest of you would all still have your houses and your jobs, and there Audrey would be with no job and no home, and not enough money to put a decent roof over her

MOST ANYTHING YOU PLEASE

head. Isn't that right, Mr. Power?"

"Mom, you make it sound like I'm a charity case!" Audrey protested, just as Alf said, "Is that what it's all about, making sure Audrey is looked after? Because you knows I don't wish you no harm, Audrey, but it don't seem fair Mom's will should be all about you."

The lawyer opened his mouth, but before he could speak, Ellen turned on Alf. "The reason Audrey got no home of her own and no other job is not that she's not capable, it's that she's the one who stayed by us all these years. She's kept the shop going, helped out your father and me now that we're getting up in years. I'm sure she'll go on doing the same for me if I last another ten years."

"Yes, but it's not like you done nothing for her all that time!" Alf shot back. "She lives there rent-free, you helped her rear up Henry and now Rachel, you and Dad did everything for Audrey and now you're telling me that the rest of us, who've all had to make our own way in the world, we get nothing out of it!"

"Now, now." The lawyer raised his hands like a teacher trying to quiet a bunch of unruly youngsters, and had just about as much luck.

"If you think this has all been a free ride for me, you got some nerve, Alf!" Audrey snapped. She could feel her temper stretching to the breaking point. In an hour she would regret the fact that they were *that* family, the ones who yelled at each other about their mother's will in the lawyer's office. But the way Alf was putting it, as if she had just had everything handed to her—well, she wouldn't stand for that.

"It's not unusual," said the lawyer, finally getting a word in, "for parents who own a family business to leave it all to the child, or children, who have had the biggest part in working in it alongside the others. Otherwise, in order to give everyone an equal share, the business would have to be sold and the profits divided."

"And there won't *be* no profits, only debts to pay off—it's only the house itself that would bring in any money!" Audrey said. At almost the same moment Ellen challenged Alf, "Is that what you want? The business I worked my whole life for to be sold off to strangers?"

"No! Of course I don't want that." Alf paused, drew a heavy sigh. "But I still don't see it fair for Audrey to get all and the rest of us to get nothing. If she's going to be the sole owner I think she should have to buy the rest of us out. Divide it five ways, give us all a share. Then when you pass away, Mother, Audrey can buy out the other four of us if she wants to go on running the shop on her own."

"Buy you out? Out of what, all the gold I got stashed away in the deep freeze?"

Again, the lawyer held up his hands. This time they actually paused and looked at him, probably less because of any authority he wielded than because they had run out of words for the moment.

"It seems to me, Mrs. Holloway, that you brought this proposal to me today without thinking it through very thoroughly—or at least consulting with the whole family. Might I suggest that you go home and take a little more time to think and talk about it—giving everyone some time to cool down, and consulting with your other children, the ones who live on the mainland? I know your intentions are good—you want to make sure that the business stays in the family and that your daughter is provided for—but it's not wise to make this decision in the heat of emotion. I know ladies often find themselves carried away with sentimental feelings, especially at a difficult time like this. I don't think any harm will be done by waiting a few weeks to make your will, after you've had more time to reflect, more time to discuss it with your sons—and your other daughters, of course."

He had as good as said that an important decision like this really should be left to the men, Audrey thought, despite the fact that she and her mother had run that shop for years and neither Wes nor Alf had had anything to do with the business. If anything, Wes had put years of his life into building up a construction business that Alf now owned, but Audrey noticed there was no talk of *that* business being divided among the whole family, of it belonging to anyone other than Alf. Of course Alf had had the good sense to get his name on the side of the truck—and, she supposed, on some legal papers—while Dad was still alive. That was only what people expected, a son to fall in his father's line of work and build it up into something bigger. *More fool me*, Audrey thought, *to trust that Alf would think the same about a daughter, when it came to the store.*

"We'll get a taxi home," Audrey said to her mother in the receptionist's office outside the lawyer's chambers. "Miss, could you call us a cab?"

"Don't be so foolish," said Alf, already striding towards the door. "I drove you down, I'll drive you back up."

"I don't want to put you out."

"Glory be, Audrey, don't go making me out to be the bad guy in this, or turning it into some kind of family feud. I don't hold no ill-will against you, you know that. I only wants to see everything done fair, everyone get an even share. Come on down to the car, I'll give you a ride home. Then, like the lawyer said, we'll take some time to think it through and talk it all over."

ELLEN

She knelt by her bed at night—arthritic old knees, varicose veins and all. She might have given up kneeling down to scrub the floors—thank the Lord for Audrey, taking over those heavy chores—but the last thing Ellen Holloway would give up was the few minutes she spent every night kneeling by her bed. Out of lifelong habit she began with the prayer she had prayed with each of her children: *Now I lay me down to sleep*.... Her usual routine was to continue through the little litany of her own petitions, laying the names of her loved ones and anyone she knew who was sick or in trouble before the Lord, and then end with the Lord's Prayer. She had been doing this since childhood and until the night came when she needed to call on Audrey to haul her back up off the floor, she intended to keep doing it.

Tonight, though, her voice—Ellen always prayed aloud—snagged on *If I should die before I wake*. Not because it reminded her of how suddenly Wes was taken from her; she was always thinking about that, how he was hard at work one minute laying the new floor and keeled off on it the next. No, what made the prayer hard to say now was that when she mouthed the words she felt such an ache of desire for them to be true. What a gift it would be, to go to sleep and wake no more in this empty bed alone. *I pray the Lord my soul to take.*

She trusted Jesus as she had always trusted Him, and believed that with her many sins forgiven she would wake up in heaven, somewhere near Wes and John (would Johnny be a baby still, or middle-aged like her other children?). She wanted it so much, and the irony was that wanting it made it untrue, for to desire her own death was, Ellen knew, a terrible sin.

She didn't linger too much on this thought; the God to whom Ellen prayed had never been overly harsh or judgemental. He was the gentle Jesus who blessed the children, and she assured herself He would understand why a lonely widow would dream of heaven. Still it was best not to dwell too much on the thought; if thinking about the peaceful sleep of death wouldn't cancel her ticket to heaven, it might unfit her for life on this earth. And this earth required a great deal of Ellen's attention right now.

The bedtime rhyme finished, she began her usual litany: *Dear Lord Jesus, please bless my children. Bless Alf and Treese, Doug, Randy, Nancy, and Judy. Bless Audrey, Henry—thank You for bringing Henry home to us—and Rachel.* Before she could get on to Marilyn's crowd she added a petition, *And blessed Jesus, prince of peace, make peace between Alf and Audrey, Lord, you know the one thing I've always prayed is that my children would never quarrel, that they would always get along.*

Well, that was a bit of a white lie there: she had also prayed that they would be healthy, that none of them would have cancer, that their children would do well in school and stay out of trouble, that their marriages would be happy, that they

TRUDY J. MORGAN-COLE

would have jobs, or husbands with jobs, and never want for anything. So it wasn't really true that peace between her children was the *only* thing she had ever asked of the Lord, but it had certainly been on the list. It was at the front of her mind now, after another big argument between Audrey and Alf down in the shop tonight, while Alf was putting in the new shelving unit. They were supposed to have the renovations finished and the place opened up again in two days. Ellen was upstairs getting Rachel ready for bed and heard the raised voices; she finally had to go down and tell them the shop was no place for that. Reprimanding the two of them like they were still in school.

"I was ashamed to have to do it, tell you the truth," she said, the words blending seamlessly into her prayer. "But you know what they're like, the both of them so stubborn. Was I wrong about leaving the shop to Audrey? I know we talked about it often enough."

She realized that she was no longer talking to Jesus but to Wes, but she couldn't stop herself; the old habit of unravelling everything with him at the end of the day, when they were alone in the bedroom, was too deeply ingrained to give up now. Wes had had little to say during the day as the business of the family swirled around him, and even when it was the two of them alone he was quieter than Ellen herself, but he would give his opinion and they'd talk things over. Without those talks at the end of the day she was like a boat drifting without anchor.

"I don't know what I should do about it, and that's the truth. And I know none of it's going to happen till I die, and it could be years, but it could be tomorrow—I could be gone as sudden as you were...."

Tears, then, and also a resolution to stop this foolishness of talking to Wes when she should be praying. What could be more of a papist superstition than that, praying to the dead? Wes was in heaven; she was even more sure of his salvation than her own, but it wasn't the kind of heaven where the dead were hovering over their loved ones, taking on God's own job of answering prayers. Wes was at peace in a place where there was no more worry and fret, which meant he couldn't be watching what was going on down here. He'd be full of worry and fret if he could see Audrey and Alf going at each other like two crackies in a dogfight. No, God must protect the dead from all that, keep them in perfect peace as the Scripture said.

Adjusting her tone to the one she used for Jesus, she finished, *Give me guidance, Lord, and show me the right path. Make peace between my children. Our Father, who art in Heaven, hallowed be thy name*....

Prayers done and theology back in order, Ellen eased herself painfully back up off her knees to sit and then lie down on the bed, little suspecting that the habit of talking out loud to her late husband before she slept was one that would stay with her for the rest of her days.

There was a tap and the door cracked open, a band of hallway light cutting across the floor. "Mom? You gone to bed already?"

"I'm in bed but I'm awake," Ellen said. Audrey took that as an invitation, came in and sat in the rocker in the corner. She wondered if Audrey would apologize for the racket with Alf down in the shop tonight.

"Is Henry home yet?"

"What, that one? He'll be out till one or two in the morning. He says he's hooked up with a bunch of fellows in a band and they're playing music somewhere. So you knows that'll be in a bar and he won't be home till all hours."

"And he'll have been drinking," Ellen said. "I don't like that, it's not good for Rachel and we've never had that kind of thing going on under this roof."

"What can I do? He's over twenty-one, a grown man," Audrey said. "I s'pose he'll move out and get his own place if he intends to stay around here."

"Would he take Rachel with him, do you think?" The thought of the child gone out of the house made Ellen feel even more bleak than she already did.

"I doubt it. I can't see him handling it all, getting her dressed and off to school every day if he's out playing guitar every night and coming home three sheets to the wind. Anyway, I never came in to talk to you about Henry and Rachel. I been on the phone to Marilyn this last hour or more."

"Oh, and what did Marilyn have to say?" Ellen knew that Alf had been on the phone to Frank because he had told her three or four times that Frank agreed with him, that it was unfair to leave everything to Audrey. And this was not the first time Audrey had called Marilyn. Ellen didn't know which of them was recruiting June to the cause—either or both, perhaps. Her children lined up in camps against each other, like warring armies. The worst nightmare.

"Well, she had a lot to say, this time around, because her and June and Frank, apparently, all got together and talked it over. And I wasn't too happy about that at first, but I heard her out and I got to say, she made a few good points. She's after changing the way I think about it all. Not that I agree with Alf entirely or I mean to give up my rights to the shop, but Marilyn made me see a few things I never thought of before."

"Is that so?" Audrey and Marilyn had always been close and if anyone in the family could make peace and suggest a compromise, it would be Marilyn, the middle child.

"She pointed it out to me, and I have to say it's been on my mind too, that if I'm whole owner of the shop when you pass on, it'll all be on me—any debt the business owes. Any money we got to borrow to keep the business going, I got to bear it all. I want to keep the store going, but I'm not sure I wants to be shackled with the whole responsibility of it myself."

Ellen had not thought of it in this light. She had always thought of the business as an asset, although in fact they were constantly borrowing money from the bank and paying it back in dribs and drabs. There were a lot of costs in running a business and although it had always made enough to pay her and whoever she had working there a modest salary, there was never much left over. They had to pay the wholesaler, the tax man, the Light and Power and all the rest. Whoever she left the store to, it would be as much a burden as a gift.

"So does that mean Marilyn's changed her mind? She wants a share of the shop?"

Audrey laughed, a short harsh sound. "Marilyn says she wouldn't take the shop if it came with a farm down south. But her idea is that if Alf wants a share of it so much, he should have a share. That way he's got to share a part of the burden and the responsibility, too."

"And how do you like that? You and Alf would be business partners."

"Right now I can't even stand the sight of him," Audrey said. "But it's not like we'd be working side by side in the store every day. It might work out in the long run. Whatever we decide, anyway, it won't take effect for a good long time. I hope we got you with us for a good many years yet."

"I been thinking, too," Ellen said, and though that part was true, she had been thinking, what she said next came as a surprise even to herself. She had been turning the problem over

TRUDY J. MORGAN-COLE

and over in her mind but until she opened her mouth she didn't know she had this idea at all. Maybe it came from Jesus (or Wes) while she was praying. "If you and Alf can come to some kind of agreement—and if all the rest of them are agreeable to it too—I don't want to just make my will. I think we should make the change now. Maybe we should have it in three shares, you, me and Alf. All three of us would have to agree to make a decision. I think—it feels like I'm too old to be the sole owner of a business. I want you to have a share in owning it—and Alf too, if he insists. But I'd be happy enough if it was just you and me."

"Holloway and Daughter," Audrey said, and her laugh sounded a little more genuine this time. "Well, I don't know what Alf will have to say about that. Or Frank or June, for that matter. There's a lot more talking it over to be done before we reaches any kind of an agreement." But for the first time since the lawyer's office, she sounded more hopeful than angry.

So they might be able to work it out after all, Ellen thought. *If I should die before I wake...*

But she would not die, not then. She would live, and sign papers in the lawyer's office dividing the business into three equal shares between herself, Audrey, and Alf. She would invite Alf and Treese over for Sunday dinner again and again till he and Audrey were almost easy in each other's presence. She would not have it, for them to be one of those families with a split down the middle and brothers and sisters who wouldn't even talk to each other. Not over a corner store, or anything else. Ellen would fight to keep the shop open and in the family, but she would fight twice as hard to keep her family together.

musical interlude

HENRY HOLLOWAY

Deep within my heart lies a memory ...

Friday night at the Strand, the band is on stage picking its way through "San Antonio Rose," and I'm playing bass. The crowd is lined up in the Mall outside waiting to get in, almost down to as far as where the fountain is—not because the band is any great shakes mind you, but because it's Friday night and the tables are pushed back and everyone's ready for a dance. And yes, I know when I say *the band* it sounds like the way Mom says *the store*, like it's the only one in the world. Which it's definitely not.

It's the Bob Eveleigh Band, and Bob's a bit of a prick who thinks he's a better singer than he is, and makes us all wear these powder-blue fringed Western shirts. The only reason I'm in at all is that my old buddy Nick Lahey's the drummer, and when their bass player moved to Toronto, Nick told Bob he should give me a shot. So here we all are, Nick beating away at the drums and me on bass, Davy Sullivan on lead guitar. Davy's the only one with any real talent but Bob won't let him have too many solos. He's jealous if anyone else is in the spotlight too much.

All the same it's a gig and I'm grateful for it. If you got to have one thing that eats up your life, better *the band* than *the store*.

I hate that place, the store I mean. When I come through it at night, coming home late after it's all shut up, the dark shelves lined off with stuff puts me in mind of urns in a—what d'you call it? One of those places they cremate people and stick them up on shelves instead of burying them. Grandma Pickens was put in a place like that while I was down South with Dad and Carol, and it gave me the heebie-jeebies. And the store at night gives me the creeps too, in a different kind of way. Like a place where everything's dead and finished.

Final notes, and Bob steps up to the mic.

—Thank you ladees and gennelmen, "Rose of San Antone." That's the song Bob Wills said took him from baloney to steak. Ain't that what we're all hoping for, folks? Goin' from baloney to steak. Well, whether you had baloney or steak for supper I hope you're all havin' a fine time here tonight, we're the Bob Eveleigh Band....

And on and on it goes. Baloney to steak. Yeah, well, maybe. I don't mind a nice bit of baloney, myself. Mom thinks I got some big dream of striking it rich in music but she don't understand, for all the time she spends listening to music she don't play it herself so she can't really know. She goes off the head at me times like today, when I turned down a chance to go out on a job with Uncle Alf because I had to come in here for sound check.

—Waste of time is what it is, trailing around after that little snot-nose Bobby Eveleigh, what call have he got to be puttin' on airs? Sure his mother was a Walsh from Mayor Avenue. Making out you're some kind of rock 'n' roll star when there's good, paying jobs to be done.

She might've said more than that but I shut the door behind me while she was still talking, got into the van with Nick and drove over here to wrestle a couple of amps out of the van. Not as many good paying jobs as she thinks, by the way. Uncle Alf calls me in now and then when there's a big job and he needs an extra pair of hands. He got two guys working full-time for him but you'll notice his own two sons are up in Toronto area where the work is steady. I went up there for a few months last year, worked alongside Doug, made a bit of money. Played a bit with a band up there, too.

Never sure why I keep ending up back home, living up over the store and having Mom bitch at me about bringing in a steady paycheque. Some sad, I know, to be going for thirty years old and still have your mother bawling you out. You don't have to tell me how pathetic it is.

—Alright folks, time to pick up the pace a little and get some of you out on the dance floor with this one… Let's go boys, a-one, two, three, four…

And then Bob growls "You ain't nothin' but a hound dog…" in a voice that's more townie tenor than southern baritone, and we follow him into the twelve-bar blues progression. Bob loves to pick out the Elvis songs, thinks he's got the right voice for it. I think he's fooling himself, but what the hell, nobody minds playing a bit of Elvis, and he's right, "Hound Dog" does get people out on the dance floor. If you're the singer and your name is on the band, you get to pick the set list too. And it's not like any song is going to show off my amazing talents on the bass. Even if I was playing lead guitar or singing, I don't have any illusions that I'd be knocking them dead. Or making millions. It's not about that, never was.

What's it about? I can't tell you, no more than I can tell you for sure why I'm back here when I could still be up in Toronto, or down in the States. Nan thinks I come home because Rachel's here, and maybe that's true, but when I'm here I don't know what to be saying to her or doing with her. Mom and Nan got all the child-raising stuff covered as far as I can see. Sometimes a whole day goes by I don't even see her, and then at night when I'm on my way out I'll look into her room. Like tonight, she was already asleep before I remembered to say good-night. Hair all tangled out on the pillow with her radio still playing CJON.

Looking at her made me think of that song, "Scarlet Ribbons"—Bob likes to throw that one into the set when everybody needs a break and a tear-jerker. Why's that such a sad song, when buddy looks in at his little girl and she got the scarlet ribbons she wanted? That's the funny thing about songs, something like "Hound Dog," all about crying and cheating, gets people out dancing, and a sweet little song like "Scarlet Ribbons" has them all crying in their beer. Something about kids, I guess, people wanting to give their youngsters stuff they can't give them. And that's not far from my mind when I look in on Rachel at nights.

She's there asleep, the radio still on, and I'm wondering if she falls asleep listening to music because she loves it like I do. Who does she like, what bands does she listen to? I should talk to her more about this stuff, but I never know how to get started.

They're all out on the dance floor now. I've been at this long enough to know all the dancers—not by name, but by type. That heavy-set woman with the dyed red perm dragging her husband out on the floor—she don't look like much but she's going to turn out to be a hell of a dancer, and sure enough, she is. And that tarted-up blonde with the make-up and the hot pants can't keep the beat at all, but then, she don't really need to, does she?

Every woman, baloney or steak, looks pretty good to me right now because it's been awhile. Not like I can take girls back to my room at Mom's place. We'll keep playing here all night, and the crowd will dance and get a little bit drunker, and a bit happier, and then a whole lot sadder. When we've packed up for the night and I'm buying a drink with the lousy bit of cash I get for this show, maybe there'll be some girl low enough down on the totem pole that even the bass player looks good to her. And maybe I'll go back to her place for a while. I'll come home tomorrow morning, walk through the store while Mom gives me a lecture and a dirty look, and I'll go upstairs and fry up a bit of baloney for my breakfast.

six

HE HAS A
LOVELY
DAUGHTER

1978–1983

RACHEL

For most of her young-adult life, when asked about her musical influences, Rachel Holloway will bring out her one-sentence zinger. "The last thing my father did before he disappeared," she will say, "was teach me to play the guitar." She will further explain, if pressed, that he taught her to play a G chord, a C chord, and a D chord. "When I knew those three chords, I guess he figured that was enough parenting, and he took off." Her listeners will not know whether they're supposed to laugh or feel sorry for her.

Reality is, as always, messier than the story. It wasn't as if Henry was there one day, a loving paternal figure helping her with her homework and teaching her basic guitar chords, and vanished without a trace the next. He had been vanishing with traces for parts of the last three or four years, heading off to Toronto for months at a time. Henry vanished bit by bit; Audrey told people he was gone up there to work. Both Alf's young fellows, Doug and Randy, had good jobs in construction outside Toronto, and it was always the busy season up there.

Henry never wrote and rarely phoned when he was away, and Rachel's life went on much as it always did, school and home, her meals cooked by Nanny Audrey or by Nanny Ellen or, increasingly as she grew from ten to eleven to twelve, by herself.

Audrey often worked through the supper hour; by the time Rachel was in Grade Six she would come home from school and pick up a box of Kraft Dinner or a couple of tins of tuna off the shelf downstairs and make macaroni and cheese or a tuna casserole for herself and Nanny Ellen. Nanny Ellen was a good cook, much better than Audrey, but her legs hurt when she stood up too long, because of a condition that Rachel, till she was ten, thought was called Very Close Veins. Nanny Ellen also got short of breath, and she was forgetful. More than once she'd let the kettle boil dry and then said to Rachel, "Now, your Nanny Audrey don't need to know about this. She'd only worry." Sometimes she would give Rachel ten dollars and send her up to Chalkers to get hot-turkey sandwiches for supper for all three of them.

When Henry did come back, his presence made little difference to that routine. Rachel would come home from school one day and he'd be down in the store, usually arguing with Nanny Audrey, the two of them gesturing at each other with their cigarettes and stubbing out butts in Audrey's green ashtray next to the cash register. Rachel's memory latches onto the last of these homecoming arguments, when he came home a week before Christmas the year she was in Grade Seven. There was nothing to distinguish that from Henry's other homecomings, except that it was the last. She suspects, later, that she's weaving together pieces of early memories, likely even putting in some pure fiction.

Still, she sees him as vividly as if it's a photograph, hears

TRUDY J. MORGAN-COLE

the ping of the door as she pushes it open and sees him leaning on the customer's side of the counter, his long thin body
wearing his uniform of faded jeans, white T-shirt, denim jacket.
Everything frayed at the cuffs and collars, looking hard-used
and second-hand, like Henry himself. She sees the look on his
face before he turns, sees the sharp etching of frown lines, hears
Nanny Audrey say, "Don't you give me none of your bull, I was
talking to Doug's wife Shelly and she said Doug haven't seen
you since the end of September. You've no more been working
on construction jobs than I have—"

The never-ending flow of her words cut off sharp as the
door opened and she nodded at Rachel. Henry swung toward
Rachel, his face changing. He reached out to hug her and she
could feel how much taller and older she was than the last time
he hugged her. How much more of a stranger he was, every
time he came back. But also how familiar the smell of him was,
how she liked hearing him say, "There's my girl, that's my girl."

"Look at you," he said when the hug was over. "You're
growing like the weed."

In later years Rachel will pick apart this phrase, *growing like
the weed*, so frequently used by both Audrey and Henry in
reference to Rachel as a child. She will even try writing a song
about it, though once you say *weed* it's hard to get away from
the marijuana references. Although Henry certainly smoked it
and Audrey certainly didn't, Rachel is one-hundred percent sure
neither of them thought of, well, weed, when they said she was
growing like a weed. They pictured dandelions or those other
spikey things with the sparse white flowers on top—yarrow, was
it called? Something unlovely and unwanted but tough and
ubiquitous, something that sprang up within a day when you
mowed it down.

She squirmed back a little from Henry's embrace and said,

"Thanks…Dad." The word *Dad* always sounded funny in her mouth, like saying *merci beaucoup* instead of thank you.

"How's school?" he said.

Rachel shrugged. "It's OK."

"You're doing good though? Good grades and all?"

"OK, I guess."

"She's doing fine in school, no thanks to you," Nanny Audrey cut in. "Doris's young one, Janet, her husband's working up in Toronto. He sends money home every two weeks, regular as a government cheque, and Janet takes it and buys new clothes and shoes for the youngsters, all three of them, new clothes every month because their father got the sense to go get a good job and send money home."

"It's not like you think it is, upalong," Henry said. "You think there's streets of gold, jobs just sitting around waiting for someone to come do 'em."

"Isn't there? Treese is always telling me how good Doug and Randy is doing, plenty of work all the time. Is there a different Toronto they're gone to, different from the one you goes up to? Yes, I s'pose now, theirs is all full of factories and construction sites and yours got nothing in it but bars and old dance halls and the like. Yours starts up when theirs is just shutting down, and there's nothing in yours but a crowd of half-assed drunks with guitars, is that right?"

"Geez, Mom." Henry tipped his head towards Rachel.

"Yes now. I got to be careful what I says, I s'pose, so your daughter don't think—"

Ping! The note that punctuated their lives cut off Audrey's words as no warning from Henry could ever do. She didn't believe in airing the family's dirty laundry in front of customers. The vast bulk of Selena Ivany filled the door along with a chilly gust of air. "My god, Audrey, what a day out, sun

TRUDY J. MORGAN-COLE

splittin' the rocks and you step outside thinkin' it's going to be half decent but then the wind is enough to cut you—oh Henry, my god, Henry, I never saw you there, is that you? You're looking some thin, b'y, you haven't been sick have you?"

On Christmas Eve, Audrey closed the shop at four. Nanny Ellen cooked fish and brewis. It was almost the only time, now, that she did cook, and she stood at the stove pushing the smelly mixture around in the pan and saying, "Oh, sweet adorable, my legs are killing me." She made raisin bread earlier in the day: Wesleyan bread, she called it. Christmas Eve supper was always fish and brewis with raisin bread, the shop closing early and the four of them around the table. This was the last Christmas Eve they would all do this, but since none of them knew it, there was no heaviness to the evening, only the mingled pleasure and annoyance of family.

The next day they went to Uncle Alf and Aunt Treese's for Christmas dinner. Treese had a turkey cooked, and everyone brought something—a cake, a casserole, a salad. The table was so crowded with food it was hard to fit in the plates. Nanny Audrey brought a bottle of wine and a box of Pot of Gold. "I don't have time to be in the kitchen," she announced, laying her offerings on Treese's coffee table.

Rachel's cousins Nancy and Judy were both there with their husbands and, in Nancy's case, her two toddlers, Melissa and Kristi. There was another cousin too—Aunt Marilyn's daughter Sharon, who came home to study at MUN a few years ago and got married in St. John's. She, like Nancy, had a pair of small loud children everybody seemed to admire. The old people were there, Aunt Susan and Uncle Marv and an even older couple from out around the bay. As always, Rachel had to go kiss the old people on their very wrinkly cheeks, which she hated.

Wedged between the boring conversations of the older relatives and the squalling of the babies, Rachel was bored. She thought back over the day, wondering did you always get worse presents when you were older, or was that just her family that did that. Tomorrow she would go over to Vicky Taylor's place; she was pretty much Vicky's best friend since Linda Ivany moved away. Rachel was willing to bet Vicky still got nice stuff for Christmas even if she was twelve. Nanny Audrey got Rachel a pair of jeans and two velour tops, and Nanny Ellen knitted her a hat and mitts. Her present from Uncle Alf and Aunt Treese was still under the tree, to be opened after supper, but she knew that Aunt Treese, like Nanny Audrey, favoured practical gifts like clothes, so she didn't get her hopes up.

Henry had handed her nothing when she opened her stocking and her few packages under the little artificial tree at home this morning, and he carried nothing with him when they came into Alf's house. But when everyone started opening gifts after supper Henry said, "Rachel, this is for you," and handed it across to her, over the heads of the small cousins.

An audible gasp of admiration went up: it wasn't as if anyone had to guess what Rachel's gift was. It was a brown guitar case, looking a little battered and worn around the edges. In the middle Henry had stuck a red bow.

"Dad!"

"It comes with lessons," Henry said. "I mean, I'll show you a few chords to get you started, anyway. I bet you'll catch on real quick."

Later, he sat beside her on Alf's couch, enclosing both her and the guitar in his arms, showing her how to stretch her fingers to make G, C, and D. The strings cut into her finger-

TRUDY J. MORGAN-COLE

tips but Rachel wouldn't admit it hurt. Henry knew, though. "It hurts a little bit at first. But your fingertips toughen up after a while. The more you play, the easier it gets."

Later, she ceded the guitar to Henry and he began to play, finger-picking gently, using not just G, C, and D but all the chords he hadn't shown Rachel yet. He stayed close to her, letting her snuggle up against his left arm as he picked. He played Christmas carols first, and Treese made a faint-hearted attempt to get a sing-song going. But the only ones interested were the parents of the littlest kids, who belted out "Rudolph the Red Nosed Reindeer" and "Santa Claus is Coming to Town" like they were trying to make their cranky children laugh. Then Henry shifted into other music, and Nancy said, "Get out the accordion, Dad."

There was a whole ritual to this, which Rachel half-remembered from other Christmases: Alf had to say no, no, a few times, until three or four people said, "Oh go on, it's not Christmas without a few tunes," and finally he went and got the little button accordion and said, "I don't say I've had this out since last Christmas." He squeezed a few mournful chords, and Sharon and Judy, who both had really nice voices, began to sing.

> She's graceful and she's charming like the lilies in the pond
> Time is flowing swiftly by, of her I am so fond
> The roses and the daisies are blooming round the spot
> Where we parted when she whispered, you'll forget me not.

Henry joined in, and a few others came in on the chorus, and then they were on to "Now I'm Sixty-Four." Aunt Susan pulled Uncle Marv to his feet and the two of them waltzed in the tiny bit of floor space that wasn't cluttered with gifts and wrapping paper and kids.

"Remember Dad with the accordion?" Nanny Audrey

said. "My, how he loved that old thing."

"He used to play it all the time," Nanny Ellen added. "There didn't have to be a crowd over or anything special on the go."

"Sundays. He played hymns all Sunday afternoon. 'Amazing Grace, how sweet the sound,' 'What a Friend We Have in Jesus,' all them old ones."

As if Audrey's voice was the string pulling Alf's accordion, he moved through a few chords from the end of "Now I'm Sixty-Four" into "Amazing Grace" like it was the one song, and Henry followed. Most of the adults were singing now. Rachel leaned into Henry's arm, wishing she could soak up how to play the guitar through his skin that way, without having to dig little grooves into her fingertips learning.

Henry left in the middle of January. By that time Rachel knew six chords, and her fingertips were starting to get calluses. One day school was closed for a snowstorm, and when Rachel got up late and stumbled into the kitchen, Henry had bacon frying in the pan while he sat at the table playing his guitar.

"What's that song?" Rachel asked.

Henry laughed: not at any joke he was going to tell her, though. Rachel knew that laugh; something funny inside his own head. "One of your nan's favourites," he said.

"Nanny Audrey or Nanny Ellen?"

"All Nanny Ellen's favourite songs are hymns. Nanny Audrey likes this one. Do you want any bacon?" He nodded toward the pan. It was nice, getting up like this and him having something cooked already, like waking up at Vicky's house on a Saturday when Rachel slept over. Vicky's mom cooked supper every night but on weekend mornings her dad took over the kitchen and made eggs, bacon, pancakes, or toutons.

251

No pancakes or anything like that here, but at least her dad had made bacon. She could hear the voices of her grandmother and great-grandmother drifting upstairs from the shop. Rachel put a slice of bread in the toaster and picked up her own guitar. "Can you teach it to me?"

"I guess so. It's only the four chords. Let me put it in C for you." His fingers shifted the key so the music sounded the same but different, which was still a little bit like magic for Rachel, but she knew she'd be able to do it sometime.

Hear…the lone…some whip…poor will
He sounds…too blue

he played, then changed the chord a little bit—from C to C7—for *to fly*. He sang slowly through the verse so Rachel could follow. It ended on a long, mournful note like a howl.

Later in the afternoon they ran through it again. "Will we play it for Nan tonight? Will she like that?" Rachel asked.

Henry rubbed his hand across his nose. "Mmm, maybe not tonight. Why don't you wait and play it for her by yourself? She'll like that better."

"But you can sing better than me, and you know all the words. Won't she like hearing you sing it?"

"No, I don't think so. Or maybe she'd like it too much." Rachel wanted to ask him what he meant, but she could tell by his face that he wouldn't answer her. "Anyway, she has it on a record. She's got them all on records. You can learn the words off that."

"Or you can teach me."

"Right, if I get the chance." And then she knew he was going to leave again. She didn't know it would be that night, after she went to bed, after an argument with Nanny Audrey, before the snowploughs had finished clearing the streets. She didn't know that he would go without saying goodbye, or that he wouldn't be there next Christmas. Rachel learned more chords and more songs, and she got good at the lonesome song, but she never played it for Nanny Audrey.

AUDREY

A tall, good-looking man came into the store twice a week to buy two packs of Export A and a package of lunch meat. They were the only two items he ever purchased. He came on Mondays and Thursdays, about five-thirty in the evening. From that and from the way he dressed, Audrey took him to be a careful, steady man of regular habits. He looked about her age—fifty, although it still shocked Audrey to think of herself as that old. He had been coming for a few weeks now, and though he looked familiar, Audrey couldn't place him, which was strange. She still knew most of her regulars by face or by name, if not both, and customers who didn't live in the neighbourhood were rare.

"Lovely day out there," he said, laying his salami on the counter. Audrey thought those words—*He laid his salami on the counter*—as if she were telling it to Doris, which she would not do, and it made her smirk because it sounded filthy.

"Something funny?"

"What? Oh, no, just what you said—smiling because we

got a bit of nice weather finally. You want your smokes?" She reached for them on the shelf.

"Just the one pack today. Trying to cut down. They tell me it's bad for me."

"Oh, if you listens to everything you hears, everything is bad for you. Salt meat and smokes and even sugar in your tea. You can't go listening to that. Give it all up and you'd be like the Seven Day Adventists, sure. You might live forever, but where'd be the fun in that?"

The man laughed. "You might be onto something there. My cousin's crowd are Seven Days and it's not only the sugar in the tea—sure they won't even drink the tea itself. You're right, girl, you can't be believing every little thing you hear about what's bad for you. You got to live a little, cause we're all going to go sometime, isn't that right?"

"So, just the one pack of Export A's, then, or two?"

He smiled. "No, I'll stick with the one—I got to go sometime, but I don't want it to be too soon, and the doctor's after giving me a tongue-lashing about my smoker's cough."

"Times are hard, running a corner shop," she said. "People cutting back on their smokes cuts into my profits, you know."

"Ah, well, throw in a bag of chips then," he said. "I'm not much for snacks, but sometimes when my sister's young ones are in the house, it's nice to have a few things around."

"Oh, your sister got a young family, have she?"

"Yes, the youngest one is eight, I think, and the oldest twelve. They drop in from time to time, they're a bit of company. Well, you know what it's like, you got a young one of your own running around the place, don't you?"

"My granddaughter," Audrey said. "She's nearly thirteen."

"Right, of course. I seen her around outside the odd time. About the same age as my niece Lisa."

"That's a dollar ninety-eight." He handed her a five-dollar bill, and she took her time giving him back his change, hoping he'd stay and chat a little longer.

He got more chatty in the weeks that followed, though he didn't deviate from his twice-weekly schedule or his routine of smokes and lunch meat. He was back to two packs in a couple of weeks. "Couldn't give it up," he told Audrey. "I 'low I'm what they calls hooked." Over the course of conversation he revealed that he got his groceries at Dominion on Wednesday so the only thing he really needed to buy at the shop was cigarettes, but he liked buying salami and baloney for his sandwiches there too. "Something about it," he said. "Buying stuff from the corner shop—just habit, I guess. I know it's cheaper at Dominion."

"Everything is. I can't afford to undercut them—I'd be in the red even more than I am."

"Ah, there'll always be a corner store. I got a lot of memories of this place from when I was a youngster— nobody wants to see places like this shut down."

This place? Audrey bit back the question that rose to her lips. That meant he was someone from the neighbourhood, then—likely someone who'd moved away and come back home. It irritated her that she couldn't place his face.

Of course it was Lorraine Penney, who knew everybody's business, who finally solved the mystery for her. A week later he was leaving the shop after the usual friendly chat when Lorraine, on her way in, passed him in the doorway. "Some shocking to see old Scabs Cadwell looking as good as that, ain't it?" she said to Audrey.

"That's Scabs Cadwell? Go away with you."

"You didn't know him? Sure I'd know a Cadwell anywhere, no matter how nice he's dressed up—something in the eyes.

They say he's done all right for himself—he was an accountant or something up on the mainland, only moved home after his wife up and left him for another man. Of course he goes by Richard now."

Richard Cadwell! Audrey wanted him to come back in so she could compare the handsome stranger with the boy who was a grade ahead of her in school—when he bothered to go to school. The next time he was in, she could see it plain as day, but she never would have made the connection on her own.

Three or four families of Cadwells still lived in the neighbourhood. The sister with the young children must be Rose or Soose: one of them lived over on Hamel Street. All the Cadwells Audrey knew of were poor, and most of the boys had been in trouble with the police. Now that Audrey thought of it, she did recall hearing there was one brother who had gone away and done well for himself, but it was a shock all the same, this nice-looking fellow with the shirt and tie turning out to be a Cadwell.

One of Butch Cadwell's grandsons, she didn't know his name, came into the shop next time Richard was there. Him and two other youngsters, younger than Rachel, skylarking around and cursing to beat the band. Audrey was about to turf them out when Richard turned to the Cadwell boy and said, in a voice quite unlike the tone he usually took in chatting with Audrey, "Vernon, you shut up with that now or I'm calling your mother as soon as I goes home and telling her what you were getting on like, here in Mrs. Holloway's shop."

The boy dropped his head, shuffled his feet for a moment, then said to Audrey, "I only wants a bag of Cheezies."

"That's twenty-five cents, now ye crowd get out of here," Audrey said, taking his quarter. She met Richard Cadwell's eyes as the boys left the shop.

TRUDY J. MORGAN-COLE

"Sorry," he said. "My nephew's young fellow. They're a bunch of hard tickets. I suppose we all were when we were that age, but some of us got a bit of sense knocked into us."

"Thanks for putting the fear of God into him. I didn't know you when you first started coming in here," she added.

"No, I could tell you didn't. Lotta water under the bridge since those days."

Those days—when the little Cadwells were all being raised by a harried mother and a father who appeared only briefly to father new ones in between his stints away or in jail. When Scabs and his brothers Butch and Flea-Bag stole gum and jawbreakers from the bins on the counter, and heaved rocks through the neighbours' windows, and were saucy to old ladies.

He kept coming into the shop, and Audrey started to give him a hard time about buying only baloney and smokes. "People like you are part of the problem," she told him. "Everyone got cars now, so everyone drives to Dominion or Sobeys and loads up on a pile of groceries, so they don't need to be dropping into the store for stuff everyday."

Richard laughed. "There's a lot a store like this can't carry. Fresh meat, fresh produce..."

"We used to carry more of that, but there's not enough call for it nowadays. People will always need canned stuff, smokes and junk food, thank God."

"Even that's going to change, though." And he told her how the construction company he was doing the books for was building a new store down where Duff's used to be on the corner of Freshwater and Empire Avenue. Another chain store—something called a Shopper's Drug Mart.

"A drugstore? Sure a pharmacy will be no competition to us," Audrey said, relieved. But Richard shook his head.

MOST ANYTHING YOU PLEASE

"This Shopper's isn't just a drugstore. They got cigarettes and candy and pop and all kinds of other gear too."

Audrey snorted. "I'm not going to worry about any old drugstore going up on Freshwater Road."

But she did worry about it, of course. She hashed it all over with her mother in the evening over tea and toast, once Rachel was off to bed. Ellen, like Audrey, said a drugstore would be no competition. "They're surely not going to be selling beans and Campbell's soup at a pharmacy?"

"No, but how many people comes in here for the groceries anymore? It's youngsters buying bars and chips and pop, smokers buying smokes, that kind of thing. And they'll be able to get most of that down at that new drugstore."

"Ah, that store's not even open yet. There's many a slip twixt cup and lip. What about Richard Cadwell, anyway? You talks about him some lot."

"Be quiet, Mother, and don't be foolish. You know I got no time for men and no interest in them."

"No? About to turn Catholic and join the convent, are you?"

Audrey laughed. She had been nearly as celibate as a nun these last few years. She certainly was never going to tell her mother about Nelson Spracklin. Any other little mistakes she might have made, whatever fun they were, hadn't lasted even as long as the thing with Nelson.

"So, do you work every night?" Richard Cadwell asked her the next Thursday evening.

"Mom does the mornings, I do the late afternoons and evenings, most of the time," she said. "But we take each other's shifts now and again if one of us needs the time. I got one young girl, Dan Taylor's girl Karen from over the road there, she works the odd shift. Mostly she does Saturday nights."

TRUDY J. MORGAN-COLE

"Oh, and what do you do on a Saturday night?"

This was sounding less and less like casual conversation. "Generally I puts me feet up and watches *Columbo*. Though the odd time Doris will have a few of us over for a game of bridge. But mostly her and Les plays with other couples, so I only goes over if she's havin' a girls' night."

"I don't mind a game of bridge myself. I'm not what you'd call a big card player but I do like a game now and then."

That was the end of discussion of Audrey's Saturday nights. When Doris was in the shop the next day Audrey recounted the conversation. "It does sound like he was hinting at something," Doris said, "but it's up to him to make a definite invitation. I mean, you're welcome to bring him along to play cards with us, but you can't be expected to ask him out, as long as he's just hinting around like that, can you?"

"I don't s'pose I can. I'll just have to wait and see."

It wasn't as if she had a lot of spare time to sit around and moon over Richard Cadwell or anyone else. She was running a business and raising a child, and more and more she was looking after her mother instead of the two of them working together like it used to be. Henry was off up in Toronto again; she hadn't heard a word out of him since he went away in January and she had no idea when he'd be back. Even if Richard was hinting around about something, Audrey would be hard pressed to make time for a man in her life. Still and all, if he were to give up smoking and stop coming in for his cigarettes, she'd miss him.

RACHEL

Rachel opened her guitar case on the bed while Vicky unbuttoned her blouse, peeled it off and pulled a T-shirt over her head, changed from her slacks to a pair of jean shorts. Their afterschool routine, most days, was to leave school and go over to Holloway's where Rachel changed, made a cup of tea for Nanny Ellen, and picked up snacks from the store and the guitar from her bedroom. Then they went on over to Vicky's house on Hennebury Place, where they hung out in Vicky's room doing homework till suppertime. Rachel tried out songs from the radio: today she was playing "Lost in Love" by Air Supply while Vicky sprawled on the floor, singing along and copying Rachel's History homework.

There was a tap at the door and Vicky's mother stuck her head into the room. "Anybody want cookies?" she said. Not Oreos from a bag; chocolate-chip cookies warm from the actual oven. Vicky's mom was like a mom on TV, like Mrs. Cunningham on *Happy Days*. She didn't have a job; she stayed home all day cooking and cleaning and had homemade treats ready when Vicky got home from school. Vicky's dad went out to work every morning and came back for supper every night. And Vicky had bunk beds in her room so Rachel could sleep over anytime.

"Are you going to stay for supper, Rachel?" Mrs. Taylor wanted to know, and when Rachel said, "Yes please," she reminded her to phone Nan. Rachel liked supper at Vicky's a lot better than supper at home. There were more people around the table, a proper family with a mother and dad and Vicky's older brother and her sister, Karen, who sometimes worked Saturdays in Holloway's shop. Also the food was usually better, like real macaroni and cheese baked in the oven instead of Kraft Dinner, or beans that were simmering in the oven all afternoon instead of coming out of a can a few minutes ago.

Rachel was just getting old enough, at fourteen, to feel a little guilty about these thoughts, about preferring Vicky's family to her own. She knew that Nanny Ellen would love to cook real meals like she used to when Rachel was little, but her legs hurt a lot and she couldn't be on her feet over the stove all day. Most of the things Rachel didn't like about home had to do with Nanny Audrey, whom she had taken to calling Nan out loud and Audrey in her head. Audrey got mad at her a lot, and nagged her about homework and brushing her hair and helping more around the house. She didn't bake cookies, or ask how Rachel's day was. Not that Rachel would tell her if she did ask.

Still, Rachel knew that if Audrey didn't work in the store all day there wouldn't be food on the table at all. Audrey often reminded her of this. So she tried really hard not to be saucy when she came in through the shop door later that evening. Audrey was listening to Mrs. Ivany from across the street.

"Shockin' is what it is, my dear, I don't know what the place is coming to, do you? Youngsters hanging around, nothing better to do than bazz rocks at people's windows—I hope you're not up to the likes of that, are you, Rachel? She's a good girl, isn't she?" Mrs. Ivany's narrow eyes darted from Rachel to Audrey.

Audrey nodded. "She don't hang around throwin' rocks at people's windows. She knows better than that."

"It's mostly that crowd from down in the apartments, they're all tough as nails," Mrs. Ivany said. "Sure the police are down there every night. We never had trouble here like that before they built them apartments. What you got there, a guitar?" she added, directing her attention back at Rachel. "You plays like your father, do you? How is he doing, upalong?"

Rachel nodded. "He's fine." Thirteen months since she'd talked to her father on the phone, not that she was keeping track or anything. She squeezed past—once Mrs. Ivany was at the counter there wasn't a lot of room between her bum and the shelves on the other side, especially where Rachel had her book bag and the guitar too.

Upstairs, *Facts of Life* was on TV and Nanny Ellen was asleep in the chair. Rachel was never sure whether she ought to wake her great-grandmother up or not; she often dozed off in front of the TV and most of the time she'd stay there till Audrey closed up the store and came upstairs. Rachel went to her own room, put away her guitar, and took *The Outsiders* from her backpack. She curled up on her bed, trying not to compare the heavy silence here to the happy noise of Vicky's house.

Later, she heard Audrey come upstairs, put the kettle on, chat to Nanny Ellen. Audrey tapped on Rachel's door. "You want a cup of tea and some toast?"

"No. Wait, yeah, ok." Rachel brought her book out to the kitchen and read while she ate her toast and drank her tea.

TRUDY J. MORGAN-COLE

Nanny Ellen was settled in her own room; Audrey poured herself a cup of tea and sat down. "Get your face out of that book," she said to Rachel. "I want to talk to you. There's going to be some changes around here sooner or later." Her teaspoon tinkled against the side of the cup, stirring in the Carnation milk. "I thought I told you to put that book down. Did you hear what I said?"

"Yeah."

Audrey sighed. Rachel wondered what changes her grandmother was talking about. Was her father coming home after all this time? No, there wouldn't be an announcement in that case; he would just show up like he always used to. Or maybe— this could be—Audrey was going to marry Mr. Cadwell, who Nanny Ellen referred to as Audrey's "man friend." It was gross to think about people their age dating, but if they got married, would she move into his house? Would she want to take Rachel with her, or leave her here with Nanny Ellen? Maybe Rachel could get the Taylors to adopt her.

"You know your Nanny Ellen is not very well these days," Audrey said. This didn't sound like any news to do with her man friend. "The one thing she always wanted was to keep working as long as she was able. But the fact of it is, she goes down them stairs every morning to open up the shop and she has a hard time getting back up. And she's getting forgetful—she's going on for eighty, after all."

"She'll be seventy-six on her birthday," Rachel said. Nanny Ellen's birthday was over the summer holidays and Audrey always got Aunt Treese to bake a cake.

"Well, that's closer to eighty than it is to seventy. She's slow making change and filling people's orders. I can't have her working down there by herself anymore."

"But Nanny Ellen loves the store!"

"I know she do, that's the problem. I can't take it away from her and I can't keep on having her do the morning shift like she's been doing. So what I'm going to do is, I'm going to start opening up the shop in the morning, and if she feels up to it, she can come down and work alongside me for a few hours, but I'll be there to keep an eye on her."

Rachel stared down at her own teacup. When she was really little, Nanny Ellen used to pour tea in the saucer and Rachel would pick up the saucer and drink it that way. She had all these little bits and pieces of memory from when she was little and Nanny Ellen was better, when she used to do the cooking and sing hymns as she cleaned the house. "I don't need anyone here in the morning when I get up," she said. "If that's what you're worried about. I get my own breakfast and everything."

"Of course you do, big girl like you. No, what I'm thinking is that if we do it that way, I'll be in the shop all day, hardly no break at all. Karen told me today she's putting in for a job over to Sobeys." Rachel had already heard this piece of news at Vicky's house, but she hadn't thought about how Karen getting a job at Sobeys would affect her grandmother or the shop. "What I'm getting at is, it's about time we started to think about you working in the store," Audrey said.

This was not going where Rachel had expected at all, certainly not any way that would end up with the Taylors adopting her. "I don't want—"

"All Alf and Treese's youngsters started when they were fourteen. For that matter, I started when I was only twelve. I s'pose I never thought of it before because you're young for your age. But come your Easter holidays, now, I'm going to take some time to get you trained in on the cash register and after that you can start doing a shift after school."

Young for your age. What did that even mean? You're as old as you are, and Rachel felt like she had lived a long time and knew a whole hell of a lot. She thought this at her grandmother: *I've lived for fourteen years and I know a whole hell of a lot of stuff, maybe more than you do.* Audrey didn't mind cursing herself but she'd give Rachel the rounds of the kitchen if she said "hell." Hypocrite.

"I'll give you some pocket money for it, don't worry about that—I'm not going to pay you minimum wage, now, like I'm shelling out for young Karen, because it's different when it's family, the food you eat and the roof over your head all comes out of our profits. But I won't see you shortchanged. You'll have a bit of pocket money for if you wants to go out with your friends or anything like that."

I don't want to go out with friends. I only want to go hang out at Vicky's. Rachel wasn't sure she even had friends, other than Vicky. But Vicky sometimes wanted to hang out with other people. Vicky was pretty; she was probably going to be popular in high school, and what would Rachel do then? If she was working in the store she could tell people she had to work Friday and Saturday nights and that could be her excuse when she didn't get invited to parties and stuff.

"I guess," she said to Audrey.

"There's no guessing about it. It's high time you were doing your share and I don't want to hear no lip about it."

MOST ANYTHING YOU PLEASE

AUDREY

"So, where do you want to go for our Sunday drive today, my dear?" Richard Cadwell said as he held the door of his car open for Audrey. When they were both inside they shared a laugh at that, although the truth was, sometimes they did go up the Southern Shore or out to Holyrood by the old road. Today was sunny, a large day in June, and she said, "Maybe we could run out as far as the Salmonier Line. If you want."

"It would be a nice day for a drive. We could go out by the highway, come back by the old road, and have supper in Holyrood." They had done this a few times; Audrey liked the view out over Conception Bay, the occasional yard sale they might stop at. But mostly it was a joke between them, this business of the Sunday drive. Sometimes Ellen would say, "Sure you and Richard are not going out on a day like this— foggy and rainy and all as it is? Have the poor man in for a cup of tea instead."

She reminded him of this as they headed off for their big Sunday drive, down Calver Avenue and over Howley Avenue

Extension to his house. Lucky Richard, all alone, no-one to make excuses to. "Mom's some good, I doubt she ever suspects a thing," Audrey said. "Now I imagine I could tell Rachel, 'Me and Richard are off to his house to have a good shag, I might not be home in time for tea,' and she probably wouldn't even bat an eyelash. The young ones these days."

Richard laughed. Audrey knew he loved the saucy version of herself she kept for when they were alone, the things that came out of her mouth. Not that she wouldn't say shagging, but she'd more likely use it as a curse word—"I can't get them shaggin little friggers out of the box," she had said just the other day, trying to unpack a box of biscuits from the wholesalers. But she wouldn't use that kind of language to talk about anyone's private business. When the women got talking in the shop, Audrey might say people were fooling around or up to no good, but she tried to say it in a way that didn't sound like she was judging too much, because people who lived in glass-fronted shops shouldn't throw stones.

Plenty of the neighbours who still thought Audrey was no better than she should be for having left her husband, and that she raised a son who got an innocent young girl in trouble and then the poor girl died in that terrible accident. So while Audrey enjoyed listening to the neighbourhood gossip as people went in and out of the shop, she rarely passed comment. She wasn't about to put herself up on any kind of a pedestal. And she would never, never say to anyone, even to Doris, her best friend in the world, that she was shagging anyone. Let alone shagging a shagging Cadwell.

But that was what it boiled down to. The Sunday drive, more often than not, was just the two of them in the big four-poster bed in Richard's bedroom, going at it like a pair of rabbits. This business with Richard had none of the bad

MOST ANYTHING YOU PLEASE

feelings she associated with Nelson Spracklin all those years ago—yes, they were sneaking around a bit, but there was no wife in the picture, they weren't hurting anyone. It was nothing but a good time, and Audrey looked forward to Sunday afternoons with the same anticipation her mother looked forward to the Sunday morning service at Gower Street. *You go to your church and I'll go to mine*, she thought.

"Do you want a cup of tea?" Richard asked when they got in the house. This was part of their ritual. The cup of tea and a smoke in his tidy kitchen, and then when the tea was done, a kiss that turned into something more pressing, and Richard's fingers exploring her body. Then he led her to his bedroom, and they took each other's clothes off. Audrey knew she should be embarrassed to have a man undress her; she was fifty-two with everything that went along with it—flabby around the middle, sagging breasts, wrinkles—but the first time they did it she was over the embarrassment as soon as Richard told her, "You're some lovely woman, Audrey Holloway." She had waited a long time—maybe always—for a man to say that, to sound so delighted and happy, so she had decided to believe him.

She had thought either it would be a quick fling, or else he'd start pestering her for something more. Wanting to get married. He did bring it up, the marriage thing, after they'd been seeing each other six months or so. When Audrey said it wasn't what she wanted, she figured he'd lose all interest.

But he hadn't. He seemed content to play bridge with her at Doris's every Wednesday night and go to bed with her every Sunday, and he didn't push her for more than that. She told him this was all she had time for, what with the store and looking after Rachel and her mother. Someone to make up a couple in a card game, a good shag once a week, and no obligations. It had been going on over a year now and Richard still had that same look of delight, that catch in his voice, when they were in bed together, like he couldn't believe how he ever got so lucky.

He didn't even want her to cook for him. On Sunday nights, when all was said and done, they usually went out for a meal. Once in a blue moon Richard would grill a steak or something. He didn't have to be a very good cook to be better than Audrey.

This time, it being such a nice day, they did go for that Sunday drive to Holyrood afterwards. There was still plenty of time, with the clocks gone ahead, to drive out that far. These last couple of years, Audrey had gotten into the habit of spending Sunday afternoons with Richard, while Rachel and Ellen when to Alf and Treese's for Sunday dinner. Rachel usually heated up leftovers for Ellen's supper, so Audrey had the day to herself. Herself and Richard.

"I s'pose sooner or later Mom'll have to go in a home, once she can't manage the steps anymore," Audrey said to Richard over her cod au gratin at the Beach Cottage. "Alf and Marilyn both thinks I should have her name down at St. Luke's, but going in a home would kill her, I think."

"Everyone says that, but it happens to plenty of people, in the end, and most of them survive. Sure look at my Aunt Claire, over to Escasoni." Richard's own parents had both died young, more or less as you might expect from the Cadwells. His Aunt Claire, who had pitched in to help raise some of the younger ones, had been in a home ever since she broke her hip three years ago. "She swore she'd get someone to shoot her before she went into a home, and there she is down in the lounge every day playing cards with four or five other ladies, happy as a pig in shit, pardon my French."

"I s'pose Mom would manage if she had to go, but I'd like to put it off as long as we can. If I had a nice little bungalow like Alf and Treese got, now—and of course they made the offer, for Mom to come live with them, I can't say they never. But she don't want to leave her own home. Them stairs up and down to the shop will be the death of her, I'm sure."

"At least you got Rachel home to give you a hand."

"Yes, she's all right," Audrey admitted. "She can be hard to get along with, but I was myself at that age so I knows what it's like. She loves her Nanny Ellen, anyway, so she don't complain when I asks her to do something for Mom. I got it pretty good, I know, I can't complain much myself. If I only had one wish, I s'pose…"

"Yes?" Richard leaned toward her a little, and Audrey was startled by the hope in his voice. Was she a fool, to think that just because he never asked for anything more, he was content with the little she could give him? But she couldn't give him false hope, couldn't tell him anything more than the bare truth.

"I wish I was easy in my mind about Henry. I tries not to think about it too much, but it's always there, at the back of my mind—wondering how he is. Rachel don't talk about him much, but I know it bothers her. He called on her birthday when she was thirteen and that's the last call I had from him." Rachel's fourteenth birthday, and the Christmas in between, had gone by without a word. The phone number Audrey had for Henry had been out of service for ages, and the last letter she sent had been returned to sender.

She had tried to find out where he was, mad as she was at him for cutting off contact. There were more of the family up in Toronto area now than there was back home, and all of them—Marilyn, June, Frank, Alf's boys Doug and Randy and their wives—had had a go at trying to dig up news of Henry. They called people who knew him, asked around that network of Newfoundlanders that seemed to be strung all across

TRUDY J. MORGAN-COLE

Ontario. Someone told Frank that Henry had gone west, out to Vancouver. That was the last news Audrey had heard, nearly a year ago. Little enough to go on, but she clung to the belief that if the worst had happened, word would get back to her.

"Maybe he's all right," Richard suggested. "Maybe he's met someone, settled down."

"If he did that, he'd get in touch. He knows I worries about him. No, the only way Henry is away this long and out of contact is because he knows whatever is going on with him would only make me worry more." Audrey lit up a smoke and pulled the ashtray closer. She tried so hard not to think about it. Most of the day she could block it out of her thoughts, but late at night she lay awake and imagined every bad thing that might have happened. That last time Henry called, he had sounded drunk, and he wouldn't answer any of her questions about what he was doing. He didn't ask her to send money or anything; that was never Henry's way. So damn determined to sink or swim on his own, and she was sure that he was sinking.

"I'm sorry, girl, I knows it's a hard thing to go through," said Richard, whose family had had its share of missing relatives, people who lost touch for years on end. He called the waitress over and ordered coffee and a piece of cherry pie; apple pie for Audrey.

"No more about that now," she said. "What can't be cured must be endured, like they say."

"True enough." Richard said. He passed her a cigarette and lit it for her, then took one himself, and they smoked, drank their coffee and ate pie as they watched the sunset over Conception Bay.

AUDREY

They brought Ellen to St. Luke's on a pouring-rain April day. Audrey had pictured it in her head so many times this last couple of years, as her mother had grown more and more frail. Ellen had given up doing her few hours alongside Audrey in the shop, even given up going to church. Audrey had imagined that when the day came, she and Alf would be there to guide their mother out of her home for the last time. They would stand on the sidewalk in the sunshine and look back at the house and the shop she had moved into almost fifty years ago. "You had some good times here, you and Dad," Audrey imagined herself saying, and she thought it might give Ellen some measure of peace. Sometimes she imagined Marilyn and June and Frank were home for it too, to make it more of a big day.

What really happened was that she had put her mother's name down for St. Luke's after Ellen had stopped managing the stairs, but when they called from the home to say there was a room, Audrey had said she could manage, that her mother wasn't ready to go yet. She had never told Alf and Treese about that phone call, though she told both Marilyn and Richard and neither of them blamed her. About three months later, Ellen slipped in the bathroom and broke her wrist. That day, Audrey and Rachel had managed to get her down over the steps and into the car to the Grace. As they walked her through the shop Audrey thought, *I wonder if Mom will ever set foot in this house again?*

An ambulance, now, took her from the hospital to the nursing home, the social worker having decreed she could not go back to a house where Audrey was working down in the shop all day and Rachel was out at school. "Your mother needs twenty-four-hour care, Miss Holloway." So Audrey and Alf were back at the house taking two suitcases full of Ellen's clothes and things to bring over to St. Luke's, to get the room ready for her arrival. Treese was minding the shop till Rachel got off of school.

Ellen was cranky when the orderlies brought her into the lobby at St. Luke's. She'd had a bad infection and had been feverish and disoriented much of the time she was in hospital. Audrey had tried to explain about moving to St. Luke's, why it was necessary. There were times when she thought Ellen had accepted it and other times she was sure her mother didn't understand at all.

Now Ellen looked around at the institutional-looking lounge furniture, the drab walls. "It's pouring out," she said. "I don't know why you had to do this to me on such a miserable old day."

"The room was ready today, Mom. They got to move people in when a room is ready." *When someone dies*, Audrey did not add.

"I told you I wanted to go back home."

Audrey sighed. Alf said, "You can't manage at home, Mom. You fell down in the bathroom, and most of the day there's no one around to help you to the bathroom or get things for you...."

"Don't even bother, Alf. We been through this all before," Audrey said. "She knows, she just don't want to know."

"You thinks you knows it all," Ellen says. "You both thinks you knows what's best for me, but I'm not helpless. I can shift for myself if neither one of you wants the burden of looking after me."

"Now, Mother, that's not fair—" Alf didn't know when to quit, Audrey thought. He was right: he and Treese had offered, several times over the years, to take Ellen in. She always said she wanted to stay in her own house, she didn't want to streel all the way out to Mount Pearl, where their new house was, and she wouldn't want to be a burden on Treese. They got the doctor to sit down with her and explain that going back to the rooms over the shop wasn't an option. That day, she had seemed to understand that if she wouldn't go with Alf and Treese, she would have to go into a home.

But the reality was another thing. Audrey tried to be patient with her mother as they went up to the room and met the woman she would be sharing it with. They spread an afghan that Ellen had knitted herself out over the bed, and put up the framed pictures of all her grandchildren and great-grandchildren on the dresser. Ellen sat in the wheelchair and looked around at it all and sniffed.

Her mood changed when a nurse took her around to see the other rooms on the hallway. She stopped complaining, spoke sweetly to the nurse and, eventually, even to her room-mate, Mrs. Mackenzie, although she had refused even to make eye contact with the woman at first. "Mom seemed to settle down a bit when we got her in there. I think she'll be all right," Alf said as he drove Audrey home later.

"More fool you. The only reason she changed her tune is she was too polite to complain in front of the nurse. She's always had lovely manners, that's not going to change, but mark my words she wasn't one bit happier about it than when she got there. I don't like to think of her sitting in that cafeteria trying to eat her dinner with a crowd of strangers. I should have stayed."

"Well, you never liked to think of Mom sitting all by herself upstairs while you were working, either, so I'd say you're as hard to please as she is. Far as I'm concerned, she's in a good place with company her own age and qualified staff to look after her. I'm a lot more easy in my mind about her now that she's in there."

And when were you ever not easy in your mind? Audrey wondered. It wasn't as if Alf spent much of his time on worry or fret. He wasn't the kind. As long as Mom's bodily needs were taken care of in St. Luke's he wouldn't lie awake wondering if she was happy or lonely or what.

Rachel was perched on the stool behind the store counter reading a book. "How was everything?" Audrey asked.

"All right. Aunt Treese left as soon as I came, she had to go pick Melissa and Kristi up from school. Vicky was here with me for a while but she had to go home for supper. There was a bunch of kids in buying stuff after school, oh, and Mrs. Parsons wanted to tell you she came in and to ring her later, tell her how it went with Nanny. How did it go?"

Audrey peeled off her coat and laid her purse on the counter. She squinted at Rachel, hunched over her book. "You should sit up straight, you don't want to get a hump on your back. Your Nan is not too bad," she added. "I'm not going

MOST ANYTHING YOU PLEASE

to say she's pleased with the situation, because she's not, but she's always one to put the best face on things so I imagine when you go in to see her she'll be smiling and telling you how nice it is."

"Oh—when do you want me to go in? Can Vicky come too?"

"Why not? Vicky's some cheerful little thing, Mom loves her. She must get that from her mother's people; young Karen's a Taylor through and through, a real sad sack." Mention of the Taylors stirred something in the back of Audrey's mind: what had she heard, now, about that crowd? Oh, that there was trouble between the mister and missus ever since Dan Taylor got laid off from the dockyard. But likely Rachel would already know all about that from Vicky. Anyway, a visit from the two young girls would cheer Mom up, Audrey thought.

They'd have to sort it out between the family, who would go to visit when, and space it out so Ellen didn't have everybody in there on a Sunday afternoon and nobody all the rest of the week. If Alf and Treese went in Sundays, that would be best for Audrey. She'd just as soon not give up her Sunday drives with Richard.

"I'll bring you in there some evening the week, if I can get someone to watch the shop for an hour," she told Rachel. "I'm going to need you to work supper-hour tomorrow, because I'm going to go in and have supper with her, try to get her used to taking her meals there."

"I don't really like old folks' homes and hospitals and stuff."

"Nobody likes them places. Bad enough you got to go visit someone there, just pray it's a long time before you ever got to be in one yourself." She wasn't thinking of Rachel, of course, barely hatched like a baby chick. She was thinking: *I'm past fifty*.

More than half a hundred.

Audrey shook herself. A day like she'd just been through would have anyone thinking morbid thoughts. "I'm going upstairs to put on the kettle," she told Rachel. "You'll have to work till close tonight, I needs to put my feet up."

ELLEN

Mrs. Mackenzie would not shut up. Natter, natter, natter all day long, whether she had anything to say or not. After years of living with Audrey, who had plenty to say when she wanted but also knew how to shut up, and Rachel who had grown from a quiet child into a quieter teenager, Ellen felt like her head was going to burst with the nonstop gabbing from her new roommate.

Roommate. What a word, what an idea. What the young ones called it when they went off to college or something, like when Marilyn's young one, Sharon, had to share a room in the residence at university with some girl from Rushoon. And that was all right when you were eighteen or nineteen. When you'd lived for years with your husband and then got used to living without him, and you'd worked out a way of getting along with your grown-up daughter—well, it was a sin to have to get used to sharing a space this small with another person.

It wasn't just Mrs. Mac, it was the whole lot of them,

nurses as well as patients, always going on at her, and when everyone was in the dining room the wave of noise that hit her was like a wall of water breaking over the landwash. She felt soaked in it.

"You'd hate it here, Wes," she whispered in bed at night. "You're some lucky, to die right quick like that and never have to go through all this. Never have to get old."

She hadn't been able to kneel down by the bed for four or five years now. But she kept up the habit of prayers, lying in bed before sleep. First the old bedtime prayer, then the blessings and requests for her family, then the Lord's Prayer, and then her conversation with Wes, which finally trailed off into her falling asleep. It was better this way, in fact; sometimes she went right into dreaming that Wes was alive and they were sitting down to dinner or doing some little job about the house, just the two of them. Those quiet retirement years they never got to enjoy together, sometimes she had them now in her dreams. It was lovely until she woke up, and had to remember.

RACHEL

They walked home together from Booth Memorial, Rachel and Vicky, happy that they could finally leave off jackets and sweatshirts, let the sun pour down on their shoulders and their arms, bare in short-sleeved blouses. Vicky had a blouse with a ruffle down the front, that whole Princess Diana thing all the girls were into this year. Rachel knew she couldn't pull that off, though she did try her best with feathering her hair. With her dark hair and pale skin she'd really rock the headbanger look, but she felt weird around the metalheads, didn't like the music and didn't know any of them well enough to start dressing like they did. Plus, it's not like Nan would actually let her out of the house wearing a leather jacket, a spiked collar, and black eyeliner.

The usual route home was over Merrymeeting Road, where they walked with a whole crowd of people past Mary Brown's until their classmates stopped at the bus stop. Rachel and Vicky continued on, turning down before they got to Chalker's. This whole strip of Merrymeeting Road, from Mary Brown's to Chalker's, smelled of chip fat. If they had pocket money, sometimes the girls would go over and get chips at lunchtime, joining the crowd from Booth and Bishops and a handful of the weird kids from the Seventh-day Adventist school, all converging on their lunch breaks and jostling for places at the counter. After school, a bunch of kids dropped into Coady's store for Cokes and bars and ice cream, but Vicky and Rachel went on past, because they could get stuff for free when they got to Rachel's place.

There were still lots of kids on the street after the girls passed the bus stop, but none of them were friends with Rachel and Vicky, and some were actively unfriendly. A crowd of guys, Shagger Cadwell and Reggie Walsh and that crowd, hung out on the corner by Chalker's. If both the girls were together they would call out stuff like, "Hey, blondie! You and your friend wanna come over and check out what I got in my pocket? Hey! Hey you! Can I get two for the price of one?" If Rachel was by herself they'd yell something like, "Hey loser!" or "Who smacked you in the face, ya weirdo?" She couldn't decide which was worse but it was interesting, she thought, that they called different things depending who was there. It wasn't like the things they yelled at Vicky were compliments. Guys like that, maybe it was better if they did think you were a loser and a weirdo.

Today the girls were together and one boy shouted, "You make me cream in my jeans!" Vicky said to Rachel, "Ignore them." It wasn't like she needed to, because Rachel had never said anything back, not once. But Vicky often did stuff like that, gave Rachel sort of basic life advice that didn't need to be said.

Rachel was well aware her life would be much worse if Vicky hadn't become her friend in Grade Five. Vicky had stayed loyal even after it became obvious that Rachel was a bad choice as a friend, and that dragging her around would prevent Vicky from getting access to any really popular groups. Kind of like how a dog with one of those big cone collars on couldn't get through a hole in the fence. Rachel was Vicky's big cone collar. She kept thinking the magic spell would end sometime, that Vicky would wake up and look around and think, *I'm blonde and pretty and more or less normal. I don't have to be friends with this loser*. But it hadn't happened yet.

At the corner of Rankin and Calver they stopped into the store. Some days, Rachel had to work; if she didn't they just dropped in and picked up snacks. Vicky's Aunt Carolann was in there today, talking to Audrey. "I don't know what to be sayin' to her, she's off the head with worry over him," she was saying as the door opened. When she saw the girls, she shut that conversation off and said, "Look at the two of you! My Lord, Rachel, it's been some long time since I seen you, you're grown right up. Same as our Vicky here, what a pair of lovely young girls." She looked at Audrey. "Next thing you know they'll be going around with fellows, what? How time flies, hey?"

"I hope Rachel got more sense than that," Nanny Audrey said.

Vicky went over to the cooler and got a Coke for herself and a Pineapple Crush for Rachel, while Rachel got two bags of chips—salt and vinegar for Vicky, ketchup for herself. They leaned on the glass-topped counter to open their drinks and chip bags. Nanny Audrey asked if Rachel had any homework. She never checked to see if any of it got done, but she felt like she had to ask, especially if anyone was in the store.

"She's the spit of Henry though, isn't she?" Carolann said, sizing up Rachel.

"She got his eyes and mouth," Audrey agreed.

"Who do you think she takes after? Poor Stella? She got no Nolan in her that I can see."

"No, no, none of the Nolans. She got the Holloway nose, though—Henry never had it, he was like his father that way, but Rachel got it," Audrey said. She was quick to dismiss any suggestion that Rachel took after her mother in any way, and everyone skirted the topic of Poor Stella. Rachel met a couple of the Nolan kids—they went to Catholic school of course, but they were around the neighbourhood, and it was weird to think they were her cousins, that she had this whole other set of grandparents and aunts and uncles she didn't even know. Like anyone needed more relatives; the Holloways were more than enough. Audrey alone was more than enough, most days.

Rachel rolled her eyes at Vicky, and Vicky grinned in a way that took the sting out of the older women sizing up Rachel's face and body like cuts of beef. "Mom says I looks like her grandmother born again," Vicky offered, and both the older women nodded.

"Oh yeah, I can see that, old Mrs. Hynes, with her fair colouring—she was some looker in her day," Aunt Carolann said. "Long before our time, of course, but you could see it even when she was an older woman—good bones, you know. You got good bones, Vicky, you're one of the lucky ones. Hair goes grey, you gets wrinkles, you puts on a bit of weight—but good bones lasts forever."

"Get some Lune Moons to take over to my place," Vicky said, and Rachel reached for the Vachon box. They were really called Half Moons, each one a cakey semicircle the size of her palm with a sweet cream filling sandwiched in the middle. When one of the girls was little—Rachel couldn't remember anymore if it was herself or Vicky—she misread the bilingual box label and they had been calling them Lune Moons ever since.

The door pinged and Vern Cadwell, Shagger's little brother, poked his head inside. Audrey broke off midsentence. "You get out of here you little tartar! I told you last week I don't want to see your face in here no more! That's it, get out, and tell that crowd out on the step they can't come in either, not one of them!" As Vern made his hasty exit, she said to Carolann, "I caught him with two bars in his pocket last week—it don't seem like no time since I was chasing his father out of the store for the same thing."

"Them Cadwells," said Carolann, shaking her head. "Of course they're not all bad," she added quickly. Most people in the neighbourhood knew Audrey had some kind of an understanding with Richard Cadwell. What did you call it, anyway, when people were that old? Rachel wondered. Surely not *dating*. Nanny Audrey and Richard Cadwell were not exactly *dating*, but all the same, people made a point of mentioning that the Cadwells weren't all bad when they were talking to Audrey.

Rachel and Vicky took advantage of the Cadwell interruption to leave the store. If Rachel didn't have to work, Vicky's house was where they liked to hang out; it would always be warmer and more welcoming than her own home, Rachel thought.

In fact, this was not true. After today, the store and the rooms above it would seem like a haven compared to Vicky's house. Rachel did not tell the story of this day to anyone for a very long time, and then only to one person. By the time she told it she wondered which of the details she had made up, or stitched together from other afternoons. They had walked from the school, to the shop, to Vicky's house so many times.

The routine was well-worn and smooth as a beach rock, and little things like Vicky's Aunt Carolann being in the shop might have happened on any one of a dozen days. Rachel remembered the conversation Carolann and Audrey had been having before the girls came in and other conversations like it, the little hints of something wrong that teenagers would never have noticed. Later, maybe, she pieced them into the narrative of that afternoon.

From the end of the street they could see the car, a beaten-down Olds 88, in the driveway. "Dad's home," said Vicky.

Growing up, Rachel used to think Vicky had the perfect family. Now that they were older, she couldn't decide whether Vicky's family was falling apart a little bit or whether she was just better able to see the cracks in the perfect surface. Barry and Karen had moved out, so it was just Vicky at home now, although Karen moved back in whenever she had a fight with her boyfriend. Vicky's dad got laid off a couple of years ago and while he kept getting new jobs they never seemed to last for long. Vicky's mom got a job at Woolco in the Mall; she worked odd hours and wasn't always home to cook, and meals at Vicky's house were now almost as unpredictable as meals at Rachel's. But Rachel figured life at Vicky's house was still a lot better than living over a store with a cranky old nan, a dead mother, and a father who had disappeared up in Toronto.

"Hey Dad," Vicky called out as she opened the screen door. She kicked off her shoes. "He's probably out in the shed," she said, dropping her bookbag next to the shoes. The girls trailed through the house, threw their pop bottles in the garbage, headed upstairs. Vicky had to go to the bathroom, so Rachel went straight to Vicky's room and had just laid her stuff down on the bed when she heard Vicky scream.

That was Tuesday. On Thursday, Nan took Rachel to the funeral home "where they're waking poor Dan Taylor," she told Aunt Treese, who came in to cover the shop.

"That's right," Treese said, "Rachel's right good friends with the little one, Karen, is it?"

"Vicky," Rachel said. She hadn't seen Vicky since the afternoon it happened. She had stayed with her, Vicky screaming and incoherent, till Rachel finally thought to go get Mrs. Kelly from next door, who called the police. When the house was full of neighbours and police and family, she had said to Vicky, "Do you want me to stay?" and Vicky had shaken her head, looking at Rachel like she wasn't even seeing her.

"Anyway, we got to pay our respects," Nan said to Treese. "I'll be back in an hour."

"I might want to stay," Rachel said. "With Vicky. She might need me."

"If she needs you that bad, one of her crowd can give you a run home. Come on now."

"Shouldn't I have something black on?"

"Go 'way, that's foolishness. It's old-fashioned, nobody expects youngsters to be wearin' black to funerals nowadays. And this is not a funeral, it's only the wake."

Rachel had heard the word "wake" because Nan and Nanny Ellen had been going out to them as long as she could remember. When she was really small, five or six, she had asked what a wake was and Nan told her it was where you went to see dead people. Rachel worried about this for a long time, especially after she got up late one night and couldn't get back to sleep and her father let her watch *Night of the Living Dead* on the late late show with him.

Eventually she got old enough to figure out that her grand-mother and great-grandmother were not going to Barrett's or

Carnell's (or, occasionally, Caul's for Catholic neighbours) to watch reanimated corpses stagger around and moan. It was Vicky's mother, when Rachel's Aunt Susan died, who explained a wake was something that happened at a funeral home for a few days before the actual funeral, when the dead person was laid out in the coffin for people to look at and "pay their respects," and you could bring flowers and comfort the bereaved. "It's in funeral homes now, but people used to have the wake at their house," Mrs. Taylor had added.

"In their *house*? People had a coffin with a dead body in it lying *in the house*?" Vicky had echoed.

"Oh yes, seems strange now, don't it? But at the time nobody thought it was odd at all. I remember when my grand-mother died, the wake was in the living room and they lifted me up to the coffin to make me kiss her on the cheek, and I didn't want to. It was cold as a stone. Thank God nobody makes children do that anymore."

Mrs. Taylor had seemed so sensible, so calm and all-knowing then, sitting down at the table to explain things to children instead of dropping cryptic comments here and there, leaving a child to piece things together, which had been Nan's way of teaching Rachel about the world. Now Mrs. Taylor was what Nan called "a basket case," sitting in a chair at the funeral home surrounded by her sisters and sisters-in-law, red-faced and bawling. Vicky's sister Karen was on the couch crying into her boyfriend's shoulder. Lesser relatives, various aunts, and cousins circled around the room shaking hands and talking to people. Despite what she'd feared, Rachel noticed with relief that there was no dead body to look at, only the long, shiny wooden box covered in flowers. She had seen Mr. Taylor's dead body swaying from the rope in the bathroom, his face unrecognizable. She had no desire to see it again.

"Closed casket," Nan said. "Makes sense, under the circumstances. Carolann, my love, how are you holding up? Some shocking thing, isn't it?" She sailed toward Carolann, and Rachel went to look for Vicky.

"She's outside," a cousin said, and Rachel stepped out into the cool air of the parking lot. There was a little patch of grass at the far end, and Rachel saw three or four people there, leaning on the hood of someone's car. She heard Vicky's voice, a sharp harsh note of laughter. She had imagined she was coming here because Vicky needed her, because she couldn't go through this awful thing without her best friend. For the first time in years of friendship, Rachel felt she had something to offer Vicky, and she had come here tonight ready to give it.

Instead, Vicky was out here in the parking lot with, Rachel now saw, her brother Barry and his girlfriend Angela, and Angela's younger brother who was in their class but who Rachel had never spoken to. All four of them talking and laughing like it was a party instead of a funeral, Vicky's blonde head bent next to theirs as they all looked down at something in their hands, making a little circle that looked so complete that Rachel stopped walking halfway across the parking lot.

But Vicky had seen her already, and waved her over, though she didn't raise her voice to call. When she got in close Rachel saw that Barry was rolling a smoke, like Aunt Treese's roll-your-owns, except the smell was different, and then she realized he was rolling a joint. Hard to believe she hadn't watched anyone do this before, but Rachel had lived a careful life so far. Nan, who chain-smoked like a factory chimney, says she would beat the living daylights out of Rachel if she caught her smoking or drinking, never mind doing *the weed*, as Nan called it. Vicky didn't smoke—not anything at all, as far as Rachel knew up till this moment—and the girls' experiments with beer had been few and cautious. Both their fathers drank too much; maybe that's why they were careful.

Now the joint was getting passed around, and Vicky took it like she knew what she was doing, but when she hesitated Barry showed her how. What a great big brother, teaching his sister how to smoke a draw outside their father's wake, Rachel thought. Vicky coughed and sputtered, then passed it on to Rachel. Rachel took it and felt like something was broken, like the window of the shop when Nan had finished laying stuff out in it and writing the specials up on the glass. Making it look nice, but somebody came along with a baseball bat and shattered the window.

All those years going to Vicky's house, borrowing Vicky's perfect family, fitting herself into the edges of it. Her own family came pre-broken. Rachel, too, coughed when she inhaled, and didn't feel anything but sick, but she smiled. There was something right about it. This was who she was after all, not a part of Vicky's family but her own Holloway thing, daughter of Henry and Stella, both doomed and damned. Granddaughter of Audrey, who would kill her if she got in the car reeking of the weed.

musical interlude

HENRY HOLLOWAY

Mama tried to raise me better, but her pleading I denied ...

Merle Haggard's "Mama Tried" is not a hard song, but I'm giving it all I got, lacing into the guitar like if I play it hard enough I can grab them by the throat, make them all listen. But the friggers never listen. Not in a place like this. They love the country music though, keep it coming, that's the stuff they come out to hear. Might as well just be playing a tape over the sound system for all the attention they're giving it, bunch of truckers, two or three guys in suits on business trips, and a few middle-aged couples out for the evening. A down-at-heels crowd because nobody would consider The Dewdrop Inn on Highway 2 much of a place for a night out.

What a laugh. If Audrey heard me sing this song, she'd probably say every word of it's true, except the part about turning twenty-one in prison. Mama tried. Hell yeah she did.

Fingers slip on the last chord, it gets away from me. Play a G chord instead of a D and then slide back to the right one. Not like anyone here is going to notice. Most of them are more drunk than I am, and that's saying something.

After Merle Haggard it's—where the hell is that set list? I wrote something down, back of a store receipt or something, where is it? Noodle around on the strings for a minute while I try to figure out what to do next. The bartender—stern looking woman, what's her name? Georgina, Geraldine, something like that. Her and her husband own the place, the motel and the bar. She's tough as nails, that one. Giving me a look from the bar, face on her like a pig's arse.

"Now I gotta song here I bet some of ya know...." I shouldn't be at this, trying to talk between songs. Words get away from me, singing's easier than talking. And nobody listens anyway. They're all talking and the only time they look up is if there's feedback on the mic.

I remember what I was going to do next—"El Paso." Marty Robbins. Crowd-pleaser at these kinds of places. All that shooting and heartbreak and the Mexican girl, Fellina, dancing around. Fellina. Hell of a name.

Not the best song for a night like this. Too many words. Started the verse about Fellina's eyes, blacker than night, in the wrong place. Already sang that verse. Can't skip ahead or it won't make sense. Georgina or Geraldine at the bar is eyeing me again, and a couple at a table near the front looks up. Dammit, they noticed. Somebody was listening after all. What the hell, it's just background music to their night out at the saddest bar in the West. All these fools with their cowboy hats, looking like something out of a B western, who the hell do they think they are?

Woke up this morning in a boarding house in Calgary with

no clue how to pay this week's rent. Then I remembered this gig. Davy Sullivan's a decent fellow, always looking out for Newfoundlanders up here, he lined it up for me, even got me a ride out.

—They don't want nothing fancy. Country music and maybe a few old rock 'n' roll classics. Do the job and they'll have you back. They just want reliable.

Not like I got anything fancy to offer.

Shit, I just missed a whole verse. What the hell am I gonna do with five mounted cowboys now, halfway through the song? Oh who gives a shit? I gotta make it to Rosa's back door, and to the end of this set. I'm going to be sick any minute now.

Made it to the end – Fellina, goodbye! – with a bunch of the words still intact. Some guy yells something.

—What? Wha'd you say there? Is that…a request?

A little laugh from the couple up front. They're on my side, aren't they? The missus is, anyway.

—I said siddown, you're half-cut!

—Every musician you ever saw was half-cut!

—Are you a Newfie? Genevieve said you were a Newfie!

Genevieve. That's her behind the bar, the owner, the manager, missus with that look on her face. Words tumble out before I can stop them.

—I haven't been back there in years…you know there's more Newfoundlanders up here in Alberta than there is Newfoundland? That's the truth, I'm tellin' you. Everybody says they wanna go back home but nobody ever goes.

—Sing us a Newfie song!

He is not, no way, a Newfoundlander, nothing of home in his accent. He wants a Newfie song and dance, now, something I'm not giving this crowd, no way.

—I don't do no Newfie songs.

Try to lean forward into the mic and slip off the stool a little, stumbling. Guitar crashes to the floor and somebody else yells something. What can I sing, what am I going to sing to get this crowd back? Like I ever had them in the first place.

The bartender, Georgina or—what was it? She's there now, standing by the stage. She comes up, grabs the mic before I can get back to it.

—Ladies and gentlemen, that's Henry Holloway, big round of applause please.

She takes my arm, drags me more than leads me off the stage to no applause at all. When we're out of the spotlight and she's got canned music on the speakers again she gets right up in my face. She's the one with the accent—why didn't I hear it before? Pure bayman, though she's probably been up here thirty years.

—I only took you on as a favour to Dave Sullivan, and I'll be tellin' Davy not to send me no more drunks and losers. I hope you knows I'm not paying you for this. I'm going to pay your cab fare home and that's it, and you can tell Davy he won't be sending you back to the Dewdrop Inn.

—Missus, you don't have to be a bitch about it.

—I'm not. Believe me, this is not me being a bitch.

She keeps her voice low but I guess I don't. People who weren't looking at me when I sang are looking over here now. A young guy, big, with huge muscles, stands up and moves quietly nearer.

—It's assholes like you that killed Hank Williams, you know that! They fired him from the Grand Ole Opry, did you know that? Greatest country singer of all time, and they kicked him out of the Grand Ole Opry.

Geraldine stands there with her arms crossed, pink glossy lips all pursed up.

—I did know that as a matter of fact. They fired him for going on stage drunk. I would have done the same, and you, my love, are no Hank Williams. Now I'm calling you a cab, and you're going home out of it.

—If you don't pay me...I gotta pay my rent tonight. If you don't...

—I'm running a motel and bar, not a homeless shelter.

Over the speakers, a song echoes my set list, the original artist mocking me with his talent, his success. Old Merle leaving only me to blame, cause my mama sure as hell tried.

seven

I PRAY
YOU
LEND AN
EAR

1985–1989

RACHEL

"And what is it she's doing at university again?"

"Forklore. Some old foolishness. I don't see how she's going to get a job at that."

"It's *folklore*, Nan!" Rachel had corrected Audrey a dozen times and now figured she had to be doing it on purpose.

"You must be some proud of her, though. Goin' to university," said Mrs. Penney.

"I don't know what she's at that for. Woulda been better off going to trade school, she coulda done a secretarial course or something useful." The women's voices continued to drift up the stairs behind her as Rachel headed upstairs.

"Valerie's young one did that secretarial course and she've been two year now looking for a job in it. She's still workin' part-time at the K-Mart."

"Well, see? If a girl with a secretarial course can't find a job, what chance do she have with a degree in Forklore?"

Finally, the door closed behind her and cut off their voices. Sometimes Rachel felt like a character in a story in which

Audrey was the narrator. Audrey had been commenting on and explaining Rachel's life to everyone who walked into the store for as long as Rachel could remember. Maybe she was an omniscient narrator: she might know more than Rachel did herself.

Audrey knew, for example, that Folklore was a useless choice of a major, nothing that would ever get Rachel a job. Based on the people Rachel knew, the whole idea of having a "job" at some point seemed as remote as riding a unicorn anyway. Everyone she went to high school with was either drifting through university like she was, or unemployed, or gone away to the mainland. University, whatever the degree, at least postponed the future for four years.

Saturday afternoons, and a couple of evenings a week in the shop: that was Rachel's version of having a job, and she knew she was lucky to have it. Her shift started in half an hour; she had come in late last night, slept till nearly noon, and then gone down to the shop to get a loaf of bread. A slice of toast, a cup of coffee, and she'd be ready to face an afternoon behind the counter. She could have picked up a package of bacon—they still kept a small selection of meat products in the cooler—but Rachel didn't want a big breakfast.

Audrey glanced at her watch as Rachel came back downstairs after her coffee. She always did that, even if Rachel was early for her shift. "Don't keep me waiting now, I got to stop into the Giant Mart before I goes out to visit Mom, and then I got to go all the way out to Treese's. She got some soup made she wants me to bring out to Mom, though I don't know why she couldn't have brought it out herself. She takes advantage of me having the car, is what it is."

Rachel propped a library book up on the cash register and leafed through it; she had a paper due Monday and hadn't

TRUDY J. MORGAN-COLE

started yet, although she had a few rough notes on index cards. She should have brought those down. She could still run up and get them; it wasn't like the store was going to be that busy this time of day. Even the neighbourhood kids wouldn't be in looking for candy till the afternoon; they were most likely still sprawled out in front of their Saturday morning cartoons. Rachel thought fondly for a moment of Huckleberry Hound, Heckle and Jeckle, Scooby-Doo. What were the youngsters watching now, she wondered? Someday you'd be able to get a Folklore paper out of this, Saturday morning television.

She turned the idea over in her mind as she turned pages of her book, and tried it out on Larry Kennedy when he came in at half-past two to buy a pack of Export A. After paying for the smokes he offered her one and they leaned on the counter together, smoke drifting in wreaths over their heads.

"It's not folk art, though, is it?" Larry said. "I mean, not really—it's mass-produced by the broadcasting networks, it's just there to sell advertising, like everything else on TV."

"Maybe. But I mean, somebody's still writing the stories, it's still storytelling—I'm not sure it's any less valid than, like, this fairy lore stuff I'm researching."

Larry was already grinding out his first smoke and reaching for a second; he was a fast, fierce smoker, especially when he was hungover. "But the fairy lore is real folk culture—oral tradition, stuff people pass down. *A woman's story at a winter's fire, authorized by her granddam.* That's from *Macbeth*," he added. He was the biggest show-off and also definitely the smartest person Rachel knew, and certainly the only person who would have this conversation with her, half hungover, on Saturday afternoon in the store. "Folk culture is about passing on legends, not selling candy bars."

"Don't knock selling candy bars, that's how my family

MOST ANYTHING YOU PLEASE

built our vast commercial empire." Rachel waved a hand around at the shelves. "Anyway, I'm not sure we can say it's not folk culture if somebody's making money off it. Haven't people always made money off culture? Didn't the Brothers Grimm have to make a living?"

"Sure, but the people they got the stories *from*, the real old storytellers, you know, they were legitimate, they were genuine. There's a purity to it, you're not going to get that from Scooby-Doo and Shaggy."

Rachel shrugged. "Yeah, I guess. I'd still like to write a paper about cartoons though. Where were you at last night? I thought you were coming by Brenda's place?"

"I was going to, but I went downtown. This Irish guy was playing the bodhran at Erin's Pub. You should have been there. It was amazing. A bunch of us ended up going out with him after. It's true what they say about the Irish, how they can drink, you know. He even showed up the Newfoundlanders. You should've been there."

"What, to try to drink some Irish guy under the table?" She wished she had been there; it wasn't until she was here actually with Larry that Rachel could admit to herself that she had spent the whole time at Brenda's last night half-watching the door, waiting for him to come in.

"No, for the music. There's great stuff happening over there in Ireland, and some of it's happening here too. Screw studying fairy stories: the music's the real thing. That's where our culture—whatever bit of it is left—that's where it is. In the music."

"You keep thinking I care about music more than I do."

"You keep thinking you care about music less than you do."

This was their oldest argument. It began the day Larry had dropped by the house with Rachel to get something and saw her guitar. She rarely played it these days. Picking up the guitar stirred too many memories. Henry teaching her those first few chords. Playing pop songs after school with Vicky singing along. Everyone Rachel had ever played or sung with had disappeared, and if she sat down to play with Larry, as he kept nagging at her to do, he might vanish too, wispy as one of the smoke trails above their heads.

And yet. She did play, alone in her room. Not Top 40 songs anymore. She bought a lot of albums, listened to all kinds of things, and then she dug through Nan's country records and listened to some Hank Williams. One night she sang "I'm So Lonesome I Could Cry" and when she looked up, Nan was standing in the doorway. "I heard him sing that live," Audrey said.

"My father was a musician when I was a kid," Rachel told Larry. "As much as he was anything useful. There's nothing pure or authentic about Newfoundland music. I mean look at people a lot more successful than my father was—people like Joan Morrissey or Dick Nolan or whoever. What were they singing except tunes and rhythms ripped off of American country music and dressed up with Newfoundland words? This place has nothing of its own anymore. I'm sure it did one day, but those days are gone."

"No they're not, that's where you're wrong! Look, you've heard Figgy Duff—"

"They're an oddity, swimming upstream against the tide. And don't say Ryan's Fancy either because they're not Newfoundlanders, they're Irish, so how is that any different?"

"It's different because—look, there's no point in me explaining. Come with me to Twillingate next week. I'm going on the weekend, you won't even need to skip class."

The door pinged and a swarm of little snotty-nosed Husseys and Cadwells moved in to the store. The Husseys all looked exactly like Loretta and Claude, who were both in Rachel's class at various times. Surely the Husseys she went to school with couldn't be having kids of their own already, but could Lorraine's mother still be producing kids? It seemed there was a never-ending supply of Husseys, though no corresponding demand.

"Missus! Give us a bag a jawbreakers!" shouted one of them. Nan would have had these little buggers whipped into shape the minute they were through the door and they'd be asking for stuff properly, probably even saying please, but it was all Rachel could do to keep an eye on them and make sure they weren't stealing stuff.

"Just think about it," Larry said over the swarm of tangled heads. "Twillingate. Next Saturday. Bring your guitar."

RACHEL

There was tea in the cups, smoldering butts in the ashtray, and Purity Jam-Jams and Lemon Creams on a plate in the middle of the table. Effie Mifflin gave them tea and biscuits and apologized that she had nothing homemade; she had made a fruitcake but her grandsons had just polished it off yesterday before they went up in the woods. The chit chat and pleasantries went on for an hour before, almost hesitantly, Larry pushed the red Record button on his portable cassette player. "Now Mrs. Mifflin, you promised you'd sing for me, remember?"

"Oh, you don't want to hear me sing."

"No I do, I really do." Never mind that he and Rachel had driven four hours from town and booked a room for the night in the Albatross motel in Gander, just to spend Saturday afternoon listening to this seventy-eight-year-old woman sing folk songs.

"I can't carry a tune like I used to. Now my sister, Rose, she got a lovely voice. Just like a nightingale, Rose is. And she got some memory for songs. I gets halfway through and I forgets the words, like. But Rose, she knows these old songs, twenty and thirty verses to 'em, and she can go on for hours."

Larry glanced at Rachel. How far away did Rose live, she could see him wondering, and was a trip possible? "And where is Rose now?" Rachel asked.

Mrs. Mifflin touched a hand to her chest. "Oh, Rose have been gone this twelve year now. A cancer of the breast, it was. Poor Rose. I likes to imagine I can hear her singing, sometimes, when I'm going around the house, doing my work. What a lovely voice."

The cassette spun, recording all the old lady's protestations, her arguments that it would have been far better if they could have recorded her dead sister singing. Finally, Larry coaxed a song out of her. "Now this is an old one, my grandmother taught it to me and Rose. Rose could have made a better job of it…."

Twas in the merry month of June
When the rosebuds all were swellin'
Young Jamie on his deathbed lay
For love of Mary Ellen…

Her voice was lovely, if a bit worn by age and cigarettes. It had a clear, sweet quality, and as she sang Rachel understood a little bit of why Larry loved to do this, why he wanted to go to tiny coves and bays and record old people singing songs before they died. There really was something pure about it—not that this woman didn't have a TV or radio, but the song reached back to something older and more isolated than that, to a time when songs and stories were handed down, grandmother to granddaughter, father to son. If this woman's grandsons only stopped by to get a piece of fruitcake before heading into the woods, something would be lost.

The song—which had many, many verses, and the singer didn't stumble over a word once—was clearly a version of "Barb'ry Allen." A song sung in England at least three hundred years ago, and collected in different versions all over the world since.

"It's got to be pure oral tradition—where else would she have learned it, or her grandmother?" Larry said as they drove away from Mrs. Mifflin's house, cassette tapes full of songs, bellies full of the fishcakes she insisted on giving them for supper. "That means that song probably came over from England with the first people who settled this cove, and people have been singing it, learning it, changing or mis-remembering the words ever since. I'll check in the archives when I get back—I know other people have recorded versions of it here in Newfoundland, but I don't think anyone has got this exact version."

"Which is good, right? It means it's more—authentic, or whatever."

"Yeah." Larry's fingers tapped and drummed on the steering wheel; he was full of energy, in constant motion. Recording songs was like doing a line of coke or something for Larry. Not that he actually did coke, as far as Rachel knew—in fact she didn't know anyone who did, all her university friends were into copious amounts of beer and weed and nothing stronger—but she couldn't imagine any drug would get him much more charged up than three hours of listening to an old woman sing folk songs.

"Those other ones, the local ones—those are important too though, right?" Mrs. Mifflin had sung a song about her great-grandfather who was lost out on the ice at the seal hunt. "Rose used to sing this, it was lovely," she had said before launching into it.

"Hell yes. Those are even more important. She's probably the only person alive who knows them. Before we had this, before people could go around and record songs, these things would just be lost. Gone forever, if none of the younger generation wanted to learn them. And they didn't, mostly, because our generation is crap, and all we care about is the Top 40 and MTV and whatever other crap comes up out of the US on cable. By the time we have kids it'll all be gone. Everything, a whole culture, washed away." The jittering hadn't stopped, but he had gone from excited to agitated in the time it took to turn back onto the main road.

"Right. And that's why you do this."

Larry shook his head. "No, it's not enough. I mean it's important, it's got to be done, but what good is it, if recordings of old songs sit in the archives at the university? Sure, someone can dig them up in a hundred years—if they can still play cassette tapes—and hear Mrs. Mifflin singing a song her grandmother taught her, but it's just—it'll be like, I don't know, reading some Greek or Latin shit. Caesar's *Gallic Wars* or something. It'll be dead, on tape or on a page. If people aren't singing it, it's not alive."

Rachel saw that this genuinely upset Larry, and later, in the hotel room, she understood why he had asked her to bring her guitar, why he brought his own. He wasn't interested in this just as an archivist; this was more than Forklore to him. He didn't want old songs pressed like dead roses between the pages of dusty books. He wanted to sing them. And he wanted Rachel to sing them too.

Larry played the tape, guitar cradled in his arms, trying to pick out the tune as Effie Mifflin sang about her great-grandfather dying on the ice. "It's got a lovely little thing going on there, that minor-key thing," he said. "But she's all over the place with the timing. Hard to tell how it was meant to go. In some parts it's almost like a three-four time."

"Rose would have done it better," said Rachel.

She took her own guitar out of the case, because Larry wasn't badgering her to play. He didn't even seem to notice as she tuned, until they were playing together and Rachel said, "What if the whole thing was like that? Like in the three-four time, but faster? Way faster, and with percussion."

"A bodhran, maybe."

"You're obsessed with the bodhran."

"It'd be a totally different song if we did it fast."

"But isn't that the—you know. The whole point of it?" Rachel suggested. "Like it's this really sad thing, and she sings it like that so it's what you expect. But speed it up, put in a drum, like it's some kind of dance tune you'd sing at an Irish wake when everyone's half-cut, and then—bam. You know. He's dead there on the ice, and his eyelids are frozen together, and it just hits you. The contrast. Or whatever."

Adding "or whatever" to pull back her words, make them less definite, was a trick she had learned arguing with guys in class. But she didn't need it with Larry; he was nodding, his fingers speeding up on the strings as he played. "Right, right, right...how does the next verse go? Dammit, play the tape again."

An hour later they had it, the verses—the four best ones, leaving out the other seventeen—ingrained in both their memories, the haunting tune with its new, faster tempo. Rachel played lead guitar and Larry strummed along, thumping his guitar with the heel of his hand to simulate the beat of the bodhran. They sang it together, alternating lead vocals as they alternated the verses about the sealer dying on the ice and the wife waiting at home for him, seeing his token come to stand

MOST ANYTHING YOU PLEASE

by her kitchen stove at the same moment he closed his eyes and let them freeze shut.

"It needs a chorus," Larry said. "None of these old songs ever have a chorus."

"She's got lines she repeats over and over, though. Like the way it says, *he never will come back no more*. Or when it's one of his verses, it's *I never will come back no more*. You could build a chorus out of that." And that was enough to set Larry off, fingers flying over the strings, blending the words into the melody they already had.

That morning, on the highway out, Larry had said, "I, um, I booked a room in the motel out here. I would've booked two but I couldn't afford it. But it's got two beds. I asked for that. Just so you—you know, I didn't want you to think. You know."

"Oh right. Of course. Of course not. Uh, thanks."

It was the most awkward conversation they had ever had. But what else could you say? *Come on this trip with me, we've never even kissed or gone on a date but should we sleep together?* You had to say something out loud, to get it off the table.

Rachel had gone through kind of a slutty phase, where she lost her virginity in the bandstand at Bannerman Park with Roger Ivany and then slept with a few other guys, but that was really only the summer after Grade Twelve and the first semester of university. She had gone through all of junior high and high school tied to Vicky's coattails or apron strings or whatever, and had assumed she'd cruise into university the same way. Then Vicky kind of fell apart after the whole thing with her father. Her house wasn't a great place to be anymore and she stopped asking Rachel over after school.

Rachel had thought that the fact that Vicky's father killed himself might create an added bond between them; Rachel's mother had died in an accident that, from the little she could

TRUDY J. MORGAN-COLE

figure out, might have been suicide, and her father had gone away and might be dead too. But it didn't work that way. Instead of growing closer, Vicky pulled away from Rachel, then dropped out of school halfway through Grade 12. She moved to the mainland to stay with some aunt or cousin or something. People went away; that was the main thing Rachel had learned.

So the summer after Grade 12 Rachel got drunk and high a lot and slept with a couple of guys, and her whole first semester at MUN was kind of like that. But when she flunked a course and got put on academic probation she had to smarten up, pull things together. And even though sex, unlike drinking, didn't actually take up that much time or affect her studies, it kind of fell by the wayside too. She hadn't had a serious boyfriend yet, and it was only on the drive up here that Rachel had admitted to herself that she wouldn't really mind at all if the motel room she shared with Larry only had the one bed.

Now they were both lacing into the guitars, singing and playing together. They had taken words and music from eighty years ago and made this new thing out of it. As Larry's voice soared on the last "Never will come back no more," Rachel found the harmony and their voices twisted and twined together, and when it was done they looked at each other and smiled. Larry laid aside his guitar and crossed the room from his bed to hers, and before Rachel could put her own guitar down he took her face in both his hands and bent down to kiss her, and there was no need for the second bed, after all.

RACHEL

The stage at the Ship Inn was a tiny triangle, like a corner dog-eared on a page. Rachel picked up her guitar as she followed Larry up the single step onto the little space. There wasn't a big crowd here tonight. A few of their friends, a few Ship regulars. It was early—9:30—and there would be more people here later, and bigger acts on stage. It wasn't like the *Evening Telegram* was going to send out a reporter to cover the fact that Larry Kennedy and Rae Holloway were performing live for the first time.

Rae. She had decided to go with Rae. That was how they had introduced her tonight and that's what she had asked Larry to call her, if he had to say her name onstage. Truncating her name, making it into a stage name, gave her at least the illusion that there was some separation between Rae and Rachel. Not that she expected that a six-song set at the Ship would bring them instant notoriety and have the paparazzi pounding at the door. The need to hide, to be a different person onstage, was something she couldn't explain even to Larry.

"We could come up with a name," he had said when she finally told him about the Rae thing. "I mean, not a name for you. A name for us. Like, as a duo."

"Like Figgy Duff." Only she couldn't think of any name for the two of them that wouldn't sound—well, pretentious. After she laughed at the first few names Larry suggested, he started pitching names just to make her laugh. Moonglow. Stormswept. The November Gales. "Save that one," she said. "Some band will come along where they're both named Gail, and those chicks will be *all over that*."

"Fish and Brewis?"

"No, because I feel like I'd be Brewis."

They told the guy at the Ship just to announce them as Larry Kennedy and Rae Holloway.

"Just Larry and Rae, maybe?" he had suggested.

"Like Corey and Trina? Hmm, I'm not sure," Rachel said.

"Last chance," Larry had said as they walked into the Ship tonight. "Gut-Foundered. I'm just saying. Great band name."

But no. She was just Rae Holloway, "Forklore" student, on stage for the first time with her musical partner, her boyfriend, her lover, Larry Kennedy. As she shifted up onto the stool she had a quick memory of Henry, dressed up to go out for a show, in a blue cowboy shirt with long ridiculous fringes. She had never seen him play with the band, being much too young to go to gigs, but once or twice he had brought her along to a sound check and she remembered seeing all four of the men in those shirts, some parody of—what? American bands, maybe, back in the 50s and 60s. At least nowadays you could get up on stage wearing your own clothes.

Larry introduced their first song, a lively and toe-tapping "I'se the B'y." Then he shifted the mood, changed keys with a little finger-picking. How sexy was that, a man finger-picking on the guitar? Rachel could be over at Larry's place working on a paper for school or whatever, and as soon as he started idly picking away at the guitar, it was as hot as if he had come up behind her and kissed her on the back of the neck, and she couldn't keep her mind on anything anymore. Now, though, all that energy had to go into her own guitar, her own voice, as she harmonized with him on "She's Like the Swallow." It was Larry's favourite folk song, so haunting and eerie, and Larry wanted her to take the lead vocal because he said it was made for a woman's voice.

As she sang, she could feel how the song gathered the attention of the room, even of the little clutch of people talking by the door. Get their attention with "I'se the B'y," hold it in the palm of your hand with "Swallow," then give them something new. It was going to work, she was sure, yet even as she sang the final notes...*and love is no more*, she felt a nervous flutter in her chest.

"Hi, um." It was the first time she had ever spoken onstage, and what an opening. People would be talking for years, no doubt, about Rae Holloway's brilliant debut at the Ship. "So, um, Larry and I collected—" that was the right word, the folklorist's word—was there a different word that musicians would use?—"this song, from an old lady named, um, Effie Mifflin, last fall up near Twillingate. We've been working on it for awhile, trying to take something—something that was a family tragedy for this one old lady's great-grandfather, and turn it into something that everyone could hear, could—relate to, I guess." Worse and worse. Shut up shut up shut up, Rachel, let Rae take over and start singing. "Anyway, hope you like it, this is 'Never Come Back No More.'"

She shifted her weight on the stool again, leaned back a little from the mic, and sang the first line acapella.

TRUDY J. MORGAN-COLE

My man is gone off at the swilin…

Then she hit the chord and she was on her way, the woman's lament unrolling out of her throat as if she had herself stood in an outport kitchen boiling the kettle on the woodstove and waiting for her love to come back. Larry took the second verse and she didn't even have to look down at the audience to know they were listening, and nodding, and loving it.

From there they did another familiar one, then the song they wrote based on the old woman's version of "Barb'ry Allen," and finally, for a big rousing finish, "The Ryans and the Pittmans." Feet were stomped, hands slapped on tabletops, everyone ranted and roared on the chorus, and there was a big round of applause for Larry and Rae. Afterwards, their friends and even a few people they didn't know came up to say what a great set that was, bought them drinks. Opportunities for a couple more gigs. It was everything you could hope for in a first performance.

Much later in the evening, two or three bands later, Rachel was at the bar next to an older guy—well, forty-something, anyway—whose name she couldn't remember, although she should. A drummer, maybe, with some band she had seen a few times. They were both a little drunk when he said, "I knows who you are now. I couldn't place you before. Holloway…Holloway. You anything to Henry Holloway?"

It was like everything in the room went into slow motion and Rachel shook her head automatically, denying it before he had even finished saying it. But though her head was shaking now, the words, sounding slowed-down like draggy tape, came out of her mouth. "That's my father."

"Go on, you don't say. I knew it though, you got something of him in you. Where is he to these days, your old man? Up on the mainland, last I heard?"

"I…I'm not really sure. We're not…not in touch." She counted back in her head. He called to say Happy Birthday when she was thirteen. Six years, nearly seven.

The long-haired man shook his head now, sighed into his beer. "Sorry, sorry 'bout that. Musicians, nobody ever said they made good husbands and fathers. Well, that's a damned shame, but you know, Henry was…I mean, he was pretty decent. On the guitar," he added after a moment, as if to clarify that he didn't mean to imply Henry was decent as a person.

"That's going to happen again," she said to Larry as they wove their way home, hand in hand, through the dark streets up to Larry's apartment on Cochrane Street, each with a guitar in their free hand. "Again and again, if I keep playing around here. I mean…it's not like my dad was a big star or anything. And he's been away for years. But people knew him."

"Is that so bad?" Larry formed the words slowly, like he was trying to remember the right ones. "If people's…if they have good memories of him."

"Yeah. I just. Don't like it when people…I don't know." She stumbled a little, instinctively gripped the guitar tighter, but Larry tightened his hold on her other hand.

"You OK? Careful." They were only a few houses away from his place now. Rachel had told Nan she'd be out late, and, not for the first time, it looked like late meant all night.

"Don't mind me, I'm just being stupid."

"No, you're not." At the door, Larry laid down his guitar, fumbled for his keys in the pocket of his jeans. "You just…you don't like to be reminded of him. At all."

"I don't know. Maybe that's it." Rachel followed him into the dark hall and up the long narrow flight of steps to his place on the third floor.

AUDREY

"All right now, I know you got this big thing on the go tonight, but I got to drop up to Contessa to get my colour done and then I got to go see Mom. I won't be no later than three o'clock getting back, but I got to spend some time with Mom, because you know she's going to take this hard."

Rachel, settled behind the counter, nodded. "Just so you know. I've really, really got to go by three. If you're not back by then I'll have to call Rhonda and see can she come in. We've got sound check at four and this is, like, a really really big deal."

"You don't have to tell me again." It was a really, really big deal every time, as far as Rachel was concerned. Some kind of outdoor concert down in Bannerman Park didn't seem like that big of a deal to Audrey, but Rachel's idea of an important event did not always line up with hers. The girl had been off with her boyfriend half the summer, taking off every weekend to every little Buckety Bay and Tickle-Me-Arse folk festival, playing and singing, leaving Audrey to run the shop with the help of young Rhonda Hiscock from down the road, who was that spaced-out Audrey sometimes wondered if she was all there. But no matter. Rachel was here till two o'clock today. Audrey would be back by then, and in the meantime she had other fish to fry, like getting her hair touched up and then breaking the news to her mother about Frank's phone call last night.

Really, Audrey thought as she left the beauty salon after her appointment, there was no reason the news should upset to her mother. The death of a woman she barely knew, a woman she had only met once, who had been fighting cancer with varying degrees of success for four years—in itself, it wouldn't be devastating. But the woman was Frank's wife, Sophie, and they were all thinking of Frank and young Frankie, whose life these last years had been so bound up in Sophie's cancer that there had hardly been time for anything else.

"Oh my word, poor Frank," said Ellen when Audrey told her. "What is he going to do now, at all?" After a moment's pause she added, "At least she's out of her misery, poor thing."

They hardly knew Sophie, but they knew a lot about her misery. She and Frank had been married for twenty years and had a seventeen-year-old son. ("Only the one," Ellen would say, "I wonder if she couldn't have no more? You don't like to ask, of course.") Frank had brought his family to Newfoundland for a vacation when Frankie Junior was twelve. It wasn't long after that Sophie had gotten her first bad report.

So many people Audrey knew had had cancer by now that she knew the routine like the steps of a dance. The Bad Report, then the First Biopsy, then the First Chemo followed by the First Surgery ("They think they got it all"). Then the refrain: She's in Remission, Thank God. Sophie had a break of a year that time, and Frank took her on a trip to Italy. Nobody Audrey knew had ever gone to Italy, but Sophie's grandparents came from there, and she'd always wanted to go. And then, not long after Italy, the second and third verses: It Came Back, and Where Did It Spread?

Some people went quickly, but for most it was a long, hard slog. Audrey's old school friend, Valerie, had been at it for six years before the cancer that started in her breast and moved to her bones finally took her last year. For Sophie it had been four years, and these last months Frank was on the phone to his sister and his mother two and three times a week. His voice sounded strained, stretched thin. June, who visited Sophie in the hospital often, had told Audrey, "He's good as gold, Frank is. You wouldn't think it—I never pictured Frank as the kind who'd be good in a crisis. But he's been like the rock for her all through this, and when she goes I wouldn't be surprised if he breaks down altogether."

"What about poor Frankie Junior?" Ellen wondered. "How is he taking it?"

"I don't know, Frank never said, but you know he's got to be taking it hard. He's a handful, anyway, from what June says—this last year, with his mother in hospital so much, he's been giving Frank a lot of worry."

They were sitting in the lounge at the end of the hall in St. Luke's, Ellen in the wheelchair which she was now confined to. Audrey was convinced that if the staff would have encouraged her mother to walk more, to use her limbs, she wouldn't be wheelchair-bound, but it was easier for them if she simply sat in the chair and got pushed around. Ellen always wanted to go down to the lounge when her family visited and Audrey was much of her mind; the shared room was tiny and the other woman, Mrs. Gregory—in seven years Ellen had outlived

MOST ANYTHING YOU PLEASE

two roommates—always had her TV on full blast, which made it hard to have a conversation.

"He should come home, the both of them should," Ellen said. "There's always a place for any of the family here at home, and when something like this happens, you wants to be around your own people." She spoke, Audrey thought, as if she still lived in her own home, with a spare room she could offer up to any family member who wanted to return.

"I suppose he could if he wanted to, I got two—I got an empty room there now." She had two empty rooms, and was about to say so, but she couldn't tell Ellen that Rachel had moved out and was living with her boyfriend. "But I don't say Frank would come home. I mean, he got a job and a house up there, his whole life is up there. What's there for him if he comes back here? There's no jobs here, the young ones are always saying. Look at Rachel, university degree and she's still only working part-time."

"With the crippled children though, I'm sure she's good at that," Ellen said. Her face was always bathed in smiles when she talked about Rachel. She adored all the grandchildren and now the new generation of great-grandchildren—Judy's girls, Melissa and Kristi, and Nancy's three little boys, as well as the ones away that she rarely saw. But Rachel was her first great-grandchild, the one she had helped raise, the one closest to Ellen's heart.

Rachel came in to visit once every month or so, usually with her young man, Larry. They brought their guitars and sang folk songs and hymns with her down in the lounge. An admiring circle of old folks and nurses would gather around and listen and sing, and Ellen lapped it right up. Those visits with Rachel, Larry, and the guitars brought Ellen far more pleasure than Audrey's dutiful twice-weekly visits ever did.

319

Rachel had a part-time job at Exon House with the handicapped children, who probably enjoyed her singing and playing the guitar as much as the old folks did, though she had a lot of less pleasant work to do to, wiping dirty backsides and lifting them in and out of their wheelchairs and all that. "I'm sure she's good at it, but she didn't have to go to university for four years to get that job," Audrey said, "and there's no signs of it turning into full-time, she still needs her hours at the shop to get by."

"And there's still no talks of her and Larry getting married? He's such a nice young fellow."

"No talks of it that I've ever heard." They seemed happy to live in sin, as people used to say. Ellen would surely think of it that way. Now mind, she'd changed her tune about some things over the years—forty years ago when Alf and Treese got married it was a shocking thing that her son had married a Catholic girl and it caused a big dust-up between the two families. But now Ellen looked at Larry Kennedy from the Southern Shore, as Irish as they made them, and only saw a nice young fellow. So maybe she wouldn't be so shocked if the youngsters shacked up together.

Maybe she wouldn't even be shocked if Audrey said, "Mom, Richard's still after me to move into his place with him, and I think I just might do that." Audrey still had no interest in getting married, but after so many years of keeping company she occasionally thought about giving in to Richard's suggestion that they move in together. Two of her three excuses for not moving—caring for Rachel and her mother—were gone. But she still enjoyed the convenience of living right over the shop, not to mention having the house to herself and everything to her liking.

"I don't say Rachel and Larry would have enough money

between them to get married," she said now, returning to the conversation she was actually having with her mother rather than the one in her head. "He's a nice enough young fellow and all, but being a musician is hardly a steady job. They're always darting around like a pair of blue-arsed flies, playing a show here and a show there—he teaches music lessons and the like but you got to have something more steady than that if you wants to start a life together."

"It's harder now than it used to be, for the young folks," Ellen said. "Harder than it was in our day."

This didn't seem likely to Audrey—hadn't her parents built a house and opened up a shop in the middle of the Great Depression? But Ellen never spoke of any hard times in the past; her memory seemed to cast a rosy glow over everything, and Audrey sometimes wished she had that kind of memory herself. Maybe when she was older, she would look back on the past as fondly as her mother did.

But not likely. Her own past, after all, contained Harry Pickens and the godforsaken farm in Louisiana, and the hard years of raising Henry alone, and poor Stella's death. Then the aching loss that echoed like a door slammed in an empty house: Henry's disappearance. Any good memory she might have, of Henry as a baby or a child or a young man, was too sore to linger on. She wondered if Frank felt that way too now, if every happy memory he had of his life with Sophie would always be blighted by the thoughts of these months in the hospital.

Don't look back, Audrey told herself. Lot's wife was turned to a pillar of salt for looking back—she remembered that much from Sunday School—and she herself might be all salt tears if she thought too much about the past. Far better, even at sixty, to live in the present and look to the future.

TRUDY J. MORGAN-COLE

When she called Frank that night she said, "Mom thinks you should come home. For awhile, anyway. I told her you'd probably want to stay where you are but you know there's always a room for you here if you want it."

She only meant to let him know she was willing to have him, more like a nice thought than anything. But after a long pause, Frank said, "Tell you the truth, Audrey, I might end up doing that. I mean, I'll see where I'm to after the funeral and everything, but…I think so much about home, these days. And Frankie Junior, well, this is hard on him. He got a lot of bad influences up here, it's not like home at all, you know. A fresh start might be good for both of us."

Audrey felt a little rush of panic. Frank *and* Frankie Junior? Here, in her quiet house?

"Well, you'll need to take some time to think about it, won't you?" she said. "They always say, don't make no sudden decisions right after a big loss. But you know you always got a place here."

RACHEL

The phone call from Des Grant came just as she was leaving the shop to go do the sound check at Bannerman Park. Definitely some metaphoric resonance in that. Or whatever. Rachel listened more than she spoke, and ended the call by saying, "I need a day to think this over—you know I'm excited, but it's a big step—yes, yes—I'll call you tomorrow with a final answer. I will. Thanks." As she spoke, the shop door pinged, which she was pretty sure would be either Nan come back from visiting Nanny Ellen, or Larry coming to drive her to Bannerman Park.

It was Larry. "What are you going to give a final answer about tomorrow?"

"Lots of things. Everything. I'll tell you about it later—it's no big deal. Right now I can't focus on anything except this show."

This was the biggest gig they had ever had, on the main stage at the Folk Festival. It was a big step up from playing on the side stages for the last two summers. And here was Rachel, putting a whole other plan into action without discussing it with Larry.

Larry did nothing, as far as she could tell, without talking it over with her. Since they had both graduated last year he had been completely focused on music, but for him it was a shared enterprise, something they were both equally involved in. "When is that one going to get a proper job?" Nan asked too often. "You mark my words, girl, you don't want to go through life tangled up with someone who's not going to be a good provider. Now, I'm not old-fashioned, I believe a woman got to be able to earn her own living, if I didn't believe that I wouldn't have sent you to university, though the Lord alone knows what good it did you. But you don't want to be supporting a man either."

Larry made enough, teaching and working a few afternoons a week at Hutton's music store, to cover his share of the rent. But his real job was writing, performing, and recording music, some of it solo but mostly with Rachel. Despite the skepticism of the older generation (Larry's parents, as well as Nan), Larry & Rae, as a duo, had gathered a following. People came to their shows, invited them to open for bigger artists. They had been all over the island this summer, playing at a bunch of festivals, and they had released an EP, six songs, that was selling all right down at Fred's. This gig at the Folk Festival was the climax of everything they'd been working toward.

She pushed everything else, the phone call with Des Grant and the decision to be made, out of her mind as they got to the park. Something inside her shifted into Show Mode; she dropped Rachel Holloway like shrugging off an old sweater and became Rae. Rachel might be confused and conflicted, but Rae could step on stage with only Larry and a guitar and be perfect, clear, whole.

It was a warm August night and their set was right around sunset, so they began with a blaze of orange light flooding over the audience picnicking on the grass, and they ended, eight songs later, when the sky was a soft indigo and you could just see the first two stars. That would make a good song title, Rachel thought as she waved to the crowd one last time and followed Larry offstage. "The First Two Stars." Already there was a thread of melody in her head. Then they were off stage surrounded by friends and fellow musicians, and there were hugs and kisses on the cheek. Anita Best and Sandy Morris both stopped her to say what a great set that was, really fantastic.

The tide of energy buoyed her up till midnight, when she and Larry and all the other performers gathered on stage to sing "The Ode to Newfoundland." For this one night it all felt so complete, this whole "St. John's music scene" people talked about. It was easy to forget how many of these people came home for these few summer weeks around the folk festival and then went back to other lives, other jobs, other hardscrabble attempts to make it big, usually on the mainland. Her euphoria had begun to ebb by the time she and Larry were reeling back to his place, half-drunk, at three in the morning. Rachel was starting to replace Rae, practical Rachel whose voice in her head sounded a little like Nan's. *A proper job.*

She waited till morning, real morning, to tell Larry. Woke on the mattress on his floor to find him already up, no sign of a hangover or even sleepiness, scrambling eggs on the hot plate, brewing coffee.

He was two steps ahead of her, as he almost always was. "What was the thing? From yesterday afternoon, before the festival? When you were on the phone."

Rachel realized Larry had been thinking about this too,

325

TRUDY J. MORGAN-COLE

and had put it aside, waiting till now to ask. He knew it was big; why else would she be on the phone telling someone she'd give them an answer to a question she had never even told him about?

She rolled over so her face was almost buried in the pillow. "It's about a job."

"Oh yeah? Which job is this?"

"It's—I should've told you about it. I'm sorry. I don't know why I didn't."

There was silence, then she could hear Larry moving around. *If I take this job*, she thought, *and if he doesn't want to come with me, then I have to break up with him twice. I have to break up as his girlfriend, and then I have to break up the duo. Larry & Rae. I wonder which will be worse for him? Or for me?*

"Rachel?" His voice was much closer now and Rachel turned her head to see him sitting cross-legged on the floor near her head, a plate of scrambled eggs on his lap. "There's more eggs over there if you want."

"No." All through her childhood she had dreamed of having a mom or dad who would make pancakes or waffles on a weekend morning for breakfast, only to find out, as an adult, that she didn't want anything except coffee before about 2 pm.

"So, what's this job? Are you going to tell me about it now?"

Rachel rolled over enough to look up at him with one eye. "It's a really good job. Working with kids, like disabled kids, like the ones I'm working with now, you know, but teaching music. Kind of using music like therapy, I guess. It's sort of experimental but they've got a grant and…it's just something I'd really like to try."

"That sounds awesome. And it's…here? This is at Exon House?"

"It's in…Halifax. If I take it, I'll have to move up there."

Her face was buried in her pillow again. She could see Larry's knees in her peripheral vision. His eggs sat on his lap, getting cold.

"So…are you going to take it?"

"I don't know." A lie. The answer was yes. It had been yes since she had seen the ad, since she sent off the application. It had always been yes. She had always been going away, ever since the first time she and Larry kissed in the Albatross Motel. "I think yeah, probably. I really want a full-time job. I want a paycheque. And this is something that's, you know, music *and* working with kids. I'm never going to get that kind of job offer here."

"Why didn't you…"

"Tell you. I don't know. I should have. We should have talked about it. I wanted to ask you, would you ever consider moving away? It's only Nova Scotia."

Larry picked up his coffee cup and only then did she see, in the slice of him she allowed herself to look at, that there was another mug on the floor beside him. The coffee he made for her.

The things Rachel wanted to say weren't in words, just feelings and pictures. If they were words, they might sound something like *I am twenty-two years old and I've been in love with you since I was eighteen. There's a story where two people meet and fall in love and marry and have kids and make music together forever, but it's not my story. My story is about people going away.*

"I just…I can't see myself leaving here," Larry said. "I know so many people feel they have to move away, but you know I've always been committed to us staying here, trying to make something that just grows out of—I don't know. I guess

I just assumed that this was—that it was something we were both committed to. Equally."

"Right. You assumed." Something hard crept into her voice, something that felt as real as buckling on a bulletproof vest. Even if her words weren't completely true, what mattered was they would protect her. "You always assumed. You made the plans. Larry & Rae is your dream, not mine, and no matter how much we discuss things it's always been clear that in the end, we're going to do what *you* want."

"That is not true! That's totally unfair!" Good, now he was getting angry too and they would have a fight. A fight was something real. Not like this weird feeling that she just had to get away, to run as far as she could from a man she loved and from the music she loved. Rachel sat up on the mattress and hurled accusations at Larry like she was flicking shoes at his head—he was controlling, he was domineering, he was a male chauvinist pig, he didn't respect her as a person, he was too ambitious, he wasn't ambitious enough. Soon they were both yelling and crying and it was easy to grab her clothes and her guitar and stomp out. Back home to Nan and the store and the room that was still hers, where she could close the door behind her and play sad angry music all day and all night.

musical interlude

RACHEL HOLLOWAY

—No, I told you, I don't play anymore. Haven't played in ages except for work.

At work I lead little sing-along circles with the hospital kids, and at the school for the disabled kids I help them make up little songs of their own, encourage them to pound on the piano or beat the drums. They don't have the fine motor skills for the guitar and anyway it's hard on kids' fingers. Henry told me I'd build up calluses on my fingertips and that was the one piece of good parental advice he ever gave me. Anyway. I used to think when I moved up here I'd keep making my own music, look for chances to perform, but instead I've stayed as far away from the music scene as possible.

—Come on now, don't be like that, I know you can play. Give us a song.

Sharla leans over a tangle of long-legged bodies on the floor, pushes a guitar into my hands. A dozen or so of us are sprawled around Evan and Leah's apartment, a little drunk, a little high, talking and laughing. A long relaxed Friday night.

It was hard getting to know people, making friends in a new city. But I met Sharla at work, she's a nurse, and after awhile I started hanging around with her crowd. I still think of them as Sharla's friends, not mine, but I'm comfortable coming over here with her and spending the evening. Not so comfortable picking up the guitar, even though there's been one making the rounds most of the evening. Halifax is like home this way. Every other person seems to be a musician. None of this crowd are professionals, or trying to be, though. Just people with day jobs who play and sing a little on the side. Normal people.

—I'm not talented, I just do music therapy. I play and sing enough to make sick kids smile, that's all.

The guitar lies in my lap where Sharla put it. I refuse to curl my fingers around the neck.

—So modest! Do you want to see what I found? What secrets I've dug up on you?

—What?

Suddenly alert, like someone's walked into a dark alley with me at night, like I'm in danger. The only danger here is the past, but that's enough. Why am I so scared? Why do I get that sinking feeling in my gut when Sharla pulls out the cassette with the embarrassing hand-drawn cover art? How the hell did she get hold of that, or even connect me with Rae from the not-so-distant past?

—Ooh, is this you?

—Who's Larry?

—Rachel, I had no idea!

Voices crisscross over each other, the cassette passed from hand to hand. It's Logan MacTavish who says—Come on, Rachel, give us a Newfie song.

A Newfie song. *I hates that old Newfie music*, Audrey used to say. But Henry liked it, though he mostly played country and rock standards. Sometimes he'd play an old song he learned from Grampa Wes. He would probably have liked some of the stuff on that tape, the stuff I played with Larry. If he'd been around to hear it. Two voices on that tape I can't stand to hear: my own younger voice, Rae, full of hope and yearning, and Larry's voice that I've tried so hard to bury in the back of my memory. I shift the guitar in my lap, start finger picking. Anything's better than letting them put the tape in the cassette player.

—Give me the tape and I'll play you a Newfoundland song. One my great-grandfather used to play on the accordion on Sunday afternoon. You can't get more authentic than that, can you? Only you've got to give me the tape.

It's tossed from hand to hand, Logan to Leah to Sharla to Rachel. I shove it in my bag and move my hands back to the guitar. Truth is I barely remember those Sunday afternoons with Grampa Wes; I was so little. Hymns and then folksongs. Uncle Alf would play now and then in later years, and people would say it reminded them of Grampa Wes. Henry would say—Here's a song your grandfather used to sing. Meaning my great-grandfather, but that wasn't a distinction we bothered with much. Years of listening and learning folk music with Larry built on that foundation, but underneath it all are those old tunes I heard first.

> Ye ladies and ye gentlemen I pray you lend an ear
> While I relate the residence of a lovely charmer dear
> The curling of her yellow locks first stole my heart away
> And her place of habitation was down in Logy Bay

—Any chance that youngster had for a normal childhood went off the cliffs in Logy Bay with Nick Lahey's old Dodge Dart.

TRUDY J. MORGAN-COLE

Audrey's voice in my head, as it nearly always is, talking to Treese in the kitchen when I was supposed to be asleep in bed. I guess that's why this song is so tangled into childhood memories. Grampa Wes would already have been dead a few years when I heard her say that, but "The Star of Logy Bay" and the car that went off the cliffs in Logy Bay all got knotted together in my mind, and that was even before I learned that the name *Stella* means *Star*. She had the yellow locks too. Nanny Ellen kept the picture in a little frame on her dresser with the others, Henry and Stella young and beautiful, their arms around each other, in Bannerman Park in the sunshine.

Oh Venus was no fairer, nor the lovely month of May
May Heaven above shower down its love on the Star of
*   Logy Bay.*

Henry taught me a few guitar chords, a few country classics, one or two folk songs. He didn't tell me anything about Stella. If he'd stuck around, could I have asked? I picked up the story in dribs and drabs: they were married as teenagers, and my mother died in a car accident that might not have been an accident. She left me behind and drove into the night, right off the cliffs at Logy Bay. Just like Henry went away years later, looking for God knows what. Steady work, Audrey used to pretend.

Oh now I'll go a-roaming, I can no longer stay
I'll search the wide world over in every count-er-ie
I'll search in vain through France and Spain, likewise
*   Ameri-kay*
Till I do sight my heart's delight, the star of Logy Bay.

A little silence in the room after the last note lingers.

—Well, that was worth waiting for. What a voice—you've been keeping that a secret, haven't you? says Logan MacTavish.

—It's such a haunting song. Sharla, sounding dreamy.

Logan is staring at me, and he's never paid me any real attention before but I know I could slip away with him tonight, sleep with him no trouble at all. It's not me, it's the song. Music does that, to men as well as to women. I might do it too. It's been awhile and I'm lonely. But if I slept with him, then I'd have to slip out of his life and lose this whole group of friends, this circle where he's at the hub and I'm just circling the outer rim.

I don't want to lose these people, but if I stay, they're going to want me to sing again, ask about the cassette, about Larry, about my quote-unquote music career. Maybe it would be better to have one night with Logan and then disappear. Alone again. *Now I'll go a-roaming, I can no longer stay.*

eight

COME AGAIN
THEY
NEVER WILL

1992 – 1993

AUDREY

"What it comes down to is, the place is losing money and you can't afford to keep going on like this."

"What it comes down to is, Mom and I got two shares in it, Alf only got one, and you got neither one. So it's not your problem and it's not your decision."

They were sat on the four sides of Audrey's kitchen table: Audrey, Alf, Frank, and young Frankie, and it was her against the three of them. Not for the first time, Audrey wished there was one person in the world whose full-time job was to be on her side.

"It's a bad time, that's all," she added now.

"You been saying that for nearly ten years, since Mom went in the home," Alf said.

"It's not just a bad time, it's the end of time for shops like this one," Frank added. "Look around you, girl. You got a Shopper's not half a mile away from here, and every gas station got a little shop in it. Those shops belong to big chains, Needs and the like, they can weather out storms. And who used to be around you? Brewer's, Coady's, Butler's, Tulk's…all closed down. Holloway's can't stand against the storm."

"Somebody has to. There'll always be corner stores."

"Sure, there'll always be some kind of a chain store," Alf said. "Stores like this? I'm not so sure. You said yourself there's three shares in this business: you, me, and Mom. And we all know Mom's getting more forgetful and confused every year."

"She's pretty sharp for eighty-seven."

"Yes, she's sharp for talking to visitors and remembering the names of her nurses, but she's not running-a-business sharp and she haven't been for years. When she passes on, her share gets split, and the business is fifty-fifty between us. But for now, you basically got her vote and yours, because she goes along with whatever you say."

"Since I'm the one lives here and does all the work of running the store, it only makes sense I should have more say than you."

"My name is on them papers too," Alf pointed out. "And now you're going looking for another loan, and none of us thinks it makes sense."

"And I guarantee you the bank is not going to think that either," put in Frank. Frank, who had no share in the store, who had been working plumbing jobs for Alf's contracting business ever since he moved home three years ago. What say did Frank have in it? They had cooked something up between them, the men, and sat her down to tell her about it.

Audrey looked from one of her brothers to the other. "So, what, after fifty-five years you think we should just—we should close up shop, is that it? Or do you want me to try to sell it?" She was surprised by how difficult the words were to say. Tried to imagine sitting by her mother in St. Luke's Home, telling her, "Mom, we're selling the shop."

"None of us is getting any younger, Audrey," said Frank. "And times are changing."

"We been talking it over," said Frankie Junior, and Audrey looked at him as if the stove had spoken. If it was a mystery why Frank was here, young Frankie's presence was a complete enigma. Frankie Junior worked in the store, it was true, but he was an annoying little prick and he hung around with a hard crowd. Audrey was always afraid Frankie's buddies were stealing stuff, though she'd never caught one of them at it.

"Young Frankie got a good idea there," Alf said, and it took a good ten minutes of the men nodding their heads and repeating themselves before they finally came out with what it was.

"Pizza? You wants to turn the store into a pizza parlour?" Audrey said, when she had finally grasped the concept.

"We got to do something," said Alf. "Stuff like pizza shops, fast food, video stores, you know—now there's a growing market. People don't want to pick up groceries at the corner store on their way home and make supper anymore, they wants to pick up a pizza and bring it home."

"It would still be a shop too," said Frank. "We'd open up that storage space in back, put the pizza ovens and stuff in there. You'd have the counter up front for the cash, and you could still carry pop and chips, smokes and beer and lottery tickets. People will want to pick up something to take home with their pizza."

"The way things are now, you got to be willing to move with the times or lose the business," Alf said. "Look around— what do you see where all the corner stores used to be?"

Audrey wouldn't have admitted out loud that Alf was right about anything at this point, but she knew it was true. There was a Chinese take-out a few blocks over where Tulk's used to be, and Mrs. Bennett's old shop on Freshwater Road had been a hairdresser's this ten years. And the video rentals, of course. "What if we rented videos?" Surely that would be less upheaval than pizza.

"Everybody's renting videos," Frankie Junior said. "A couple of racks of videos is not going to save the business when people can go over to Jumbo and choose from all the videos in the world."

"You've all given this a lot of thought," Audrey said. "Been talking it over behind my back, I can see."

"We're not working against you, Audrey." Alf sounded like someone trying to explain things to a cranky youngster. "Frank wants to come into the business too, to buy out Mom's share. We think we can put it to the bank to get a loan for the renovations, with the business plan for the pizza shop. You can keep on managing the convenience store side of it, and Frankie Junior will manage the pizza shop."

Audrey had to stop the meeting at that point. Told them all she'd have to take time to think about it, and then let off steam to Richard later when he came over for a game of cards. "What do young Frankie know about making pizza, much less about managing a business?" she said. "I'd be surprised if that one knew how to put butter on a slice of bread. And do I want to be living over a pizza shop, with the smell of it, and people coming and going all hours?"

"You don't have to live here," Richard reminded her.

He had been making the offer a long time now, even more since Rachel moved up to Halifax. Audrey could come live with him—get married or don't get married, he wasn't particular either way—and rent out the rooms over the shop. Audrey always said she'd think about it. She needed more time. And Richard, to give him credit, never pointed out how much time she'd already taken. They were none of them, as Frank said, getting any younger. Like that maudlin old song Alf played on the accordion: *Oh how I long for those bright days to come again once more, but come again they never will, for now I'm sixty-four*. Audrey didn't like those old songs anyway but she liked that one even less now that she would be sixty-four her next birthday.

The next person she went over it with was Marilyn, on the phone that night. "None of it sounds like a bad idea to me," Marilyn said. "Let Frank and Alf go to the bank, get their names on the loan, and let Frankie manage the pizza. You could take it easy, maybe even retire. And for what it's worth I don't think you moving in with Richard is the worst idea in the world. He's a good man, and his house is all on the one level."

Marilyn certainly didn't mind change: her George had a year to go till he got his full pension up in Toronto, and they already had a piece of land bought down in Torbay where they were going to build their retirement home. And here was Audrey moaning about having a pizza shop downstairs and the possibility of moving in with a man who lived a few blocks away. "I s'pose it all makes sense," she told Marilyn, "but I likes things the way they are. Richard and I are set in our ways. And as for the shop, Frankie Junior don't know his arse from his elbow, how is he supposed to manage anything?"

In the background the television flickered. Newfoundland was on the Canadian news again tonight. More complaints about the fishery. The cod were disappearing, the quotas were too low, the French and the Spanish were catching too much, the arse was going to fall out of the whole industry. Maybe Alf was right, Audrey thought, maybe this was something more than just a bad time. Maybe it was the end.

RACHEL

The *Joseph and Clara Smallwood* pushed through the grey water, more like a snowplough going through a pile of slush than like a ship at sea. The water looked frigid and the ship itself lacked any beauty or grace; it was basically a floating second-rate motel with an engine. A utilitarian way to get Rachel and her Honda Civic back onto the Rock so she could face a ten-hour drive home.

She had been back only once since she moved to Halifax. Her second Christmas away, she went home. Nan was alone in the house; the store was struggling and the shelves were increasingly bare. Nanny Ellen was in St. Luke's, trundled out in the car for the Christmas dinner at Uncle Alf and Aunt Treese's, then taken back again as night fell, like a Christmas sweater folded and put back in the drawer. Alf and Treese's crowd seemed like a real family, arguing and laughing, the grandchildren getting married and having babies, not necessarily in that order. Life seemed to tumble around her at their place, like clothes in a dryer, matched sets of everything.

Nan and Rachel were the two odd socks, going home at the end of the day to the rooms over the store, guaranteed to have one big fight before the holiday was over and Rachel beat a retreat to Halifax.

Other than family, what was there at home for Rachel? She didn't really have old friends, just old acquaintances. Apart from Audrey and Nanny Ellen there were really only two people in St. John's that she had ever loved, Vicky Taylor and Larry Kennedy, and she hadn't spoken to either of them in years. They were both gone, too—Vicky to Toronto, years ago, and Larry to Ireland to study with some musician there. That's what a Newfoundland trumpet player in a Halifax bar had told Rachel late one night, when she got up the nerve to ask if Larry was still playing around town.

So he had moved away after all, after telling Rachel he could never leave St. John's. Made her out to be the bad one by leaving. If he had been willing to move to Nova Scotia three years ago, would he and Rachel still be together? Probably not. She had cared too much about Larry. If she ever did settle down, get married or whatever, it would have to be with someone she liked but didn't love. Someone she could live without, if he ever decided to leave.

She met Jake that night on the boat. He played bass in the band that provided live entertainment in the lounge; he and Rachel got talking and ended up having a beer after his set. He was a Hibbard from Bonavista but lived in St. John's, though he went up to Toronto to work in construction every spring. "Just long enough to get my stamps so I can come home and play in bands the rest of the year." He was coming home earlier than usual this year because his friend's band lined up this gig playing on the ferry.

"What about you? You play at all these days—up there in

MOST ANYTHING YOU PLEASE

Halifax?" he asked. She had already admitted to having been half of a duo called Larry and Rae a few years ago and he nodded as though he had heard of them.

She shook her head. "No, not at all. I didn't really know many musicians up there, wasn't into the music scene. I guess with teaching kids music, the music therapy thing, you know, all day long, I didn't really want to go play in some smoky bar all night. Or I just didn't know where to break into the scene. I think you've got to have drive, more than anything, and I don't really have that."

"Ambition," Jake said.

Rachel nodded, although she didn't think that was it, exactly. You wouldn't say Larry was ambitious, exactly, but he certainly was driven. She eyed Jake Hibbard, trying to gauge how driven he was, what drove him.

"You'll play a bit when you gets back home though, won't you?" Jake asked her.

"No plans to. I mean, I've been away for years, I don't really know anyone there anymore."

"Well, you knows me now, and I knows everybody. And it's a good time—lotta stuff going on in folk music at home now. Have you heard Rawlins Cross?"

"I haven't really been following Newfoundland music that much."

"Oh, you gotta listen to some of this stuff. I got a few tapes here I'll loan you. You can look me up when we gets back in town and give 'em back whenever, I'm not in no hurry."

"Thanks. I guess I should…you know." Rachel shrugged. "I should know what people are playing, anyway."

"Yeah, it's great, real happening time in Newfoundland music. It's like while everything else is dying, the music scene is just waking up, you know? This moratorium, eh? It's going to change everything. People out home are moving up to the mainland in droves."

She had heard the news stories on CBC radio yesterday as she drove to North Sydney to get on the ferry. A two-year moratorium on fishing the northern cod stocks. Crosbie, the minister of fisheries, making the announcement in that dry, nasally St. John's accent of his, and crowds of angry baymen yelling at him. Crosbie losing his cool, yelling that he didn't take the fish out of the goddamn water.

It all felt distant, remote to Rachel. She had never set foot on a fishing boat, after all, didn't know a soul who worked in the fishery, though in high school she knew a girl who used to go out to Petty Harbour or someplace like that every summer and make a ton of money working in the fish plant. "It's a weird time to be moving back home, I guess, when everyone's moving away."

"So why are you doing it?"

Rachel shrugged. "I had this job offer back home. Same kinda thing I was doing in Halifax and…I don't know. I just thought it was time to come home." She had picked up a few psych courses and done some workshops over her years in Nova Scotia and now she actually had the qualifications to go for a better job, and there happened to be one back home. Of course there were probably jobs in other places, places in Canada where thirty thousand people hadn't suddenly been put out of work, but she hadn't thought of looking in any of those places. She was like the spawning salmon, drawn back home to a place she wasn't even sure she wanted to be. "Anyway what I do is kind of therapy, for, like, disabled kids but also kids who are messed-up, you know, mentally ill. And maybe any kind of therapy will be a growth industry in Newfoundland now."

"You're probably right about that."

Jake Hibbard gave her five cassette tapes and his phone number. Rachel thought she'd probably see him again, after she returned his tapes. He was a good bass player, easy to talk to, and not hard to look at. He seemed like someone who'd be easy to like and easy to leave.

AUDREY

When the renovations started downstairs, Rachel moved out. She had only been home a couple of months, since the beginning of July, and Audrey had been pleased to have company in the house again. Rachel seemed older, more responsible, after three years on the mainland, and of course the fact that she was coming home to a full-time job made all the difference in the world, even though everyone said it was a queer time to be moving home, with so many packing up and moving away.

"Somebody got to have some confidence in this place, in the future," Audrey had told Rachel after Treese spent half an hour moaning about Judy and Rod and their crowd moving to Calgary, and how soon all the young folks would be gone.

"I'd say Frankie Junior's got enough confidence for all of us," Rachel said.

While his father and uncle Alf and a couple of Alf's men were tearing up the shop downstairs, Frankie was running around town meeting with people and making big plans. He had a sign-painter in to do a new sign for the pizza shop and someone else making up flyers—all buddies of his, of course. Audrey thought it was a lot of flash with very little to show for it. "Oh yes, that one, running around busy as a fiddler's bitch at a flea circus, but he haven't made a single pizza pie yet, only a friggin big mess where my shop used to be."

The bank loan had come through and the shop closed for renovations at the beginning of September, which meant a lot of money going out and none coming in, and nothing for Audrey to be at all day. It seemed like a lot more tear-up than when they'd renovated the shop twenty years ago, but of course it would be more work, what with bringing in the pizza ovens and all the new electrical and plumbing that had to be run through for it. Back when they did the last renovations, Audrey and Alf had been full of new ideas and energy while Ellen had been cautious and worried. Audrey knew she herself was now the cantankerous old woman who didn't want change.

"This is a hell of a mess," Rachel told her. "I might stay with Jake for awhile. He's got a nice place down on King's Bridge Road—an old house somebody renovated, and he's renting the top floor."

"There's a lot of people buying up them old dumps downtown, people with more money than sense if you ask me," Audrey said. "But I don't blame you if you goes and stays with him, or even if you wants to move in there. I'd move out myself for awhile if I had any place to go."

Rachel, washing dishes at the kitchen sink, looked back over her shoulder at her grandmother. "Don't you? Hasn't Richard been after you to move into his place for ten years?"

"It's not that long," Audrey said, although it probably had been. "Anyway, it's different for you. Nobody minds young folks living together nowadays, not like when I was young. And at least you're getting a bit of nooky out of it."

TRUDY J. MORGAN-COLE

"Nan!"

"What, did I embarrass you?"

"Nobody else's grandmother says things like that. And also, nobody calls it *nooky* anymore."

"Well, whatever you calls it, there's nothing wrong with it. I know there's still people my age goes on like it's something shocking, young people living together before marriage. Or instead of marriage. I mean, not everyone goes on to get married. You and Jake might not. And I think that's fine. No, it is," she added, although Rachel hadn't contradicted her. Maybe she was arguing with the voice of Ellen in her head. "Not everyone who falls in love, or falls into bed together, is meant to be married. Me and Harry Pickens should have never got married. If we could have just lived together for awhile, had a good roll in the hay—is that better than saying nooky?—we would have realized it wasn't meant to be. And then how much trouble would we have been spared?"

"Well, I'm glad you're not shocked. Grandmothers aren't as easy to shock as they used to be," said Rachel. "And I think you should go stay at Richard's till this is all over. Or maybe for good." She hung the dishtowel back on its hook and picked up her knapsack. She had a proper full-time job now but she still went around carrying a knapsack like a teenager, and wearing jeans and T-shirts all the time. And that choppy short new cut she had made her hair look like a birch broom in the fits. But Audrey bit her tongue when she got the urge to tell Rachel how she should dress or wear her hair. She had missed the girl more than she'd want to admit during those years she was away.

"Are you going on now?"

"In a few minutes. Jake's got a gig tonight and I'm going down to hear him."

"Do you sing with him like you used to do with Larry?"

"He's after me to, but I don't think so, no."

"You got a lovely voice." Funny how Rachel used to be so into the music when she was with Larry Kennedy, like singing and playing the guitar was the only thing that mattered, the same way her father used to be. Now she was working at the hospital, doing music with sick youngsters. Music therapy, she called it, and she was taking courses too to get a degree in it all the while she was working. It was all a bit complicated and sometimes when Audrey thought it was too much trouble to explain to people she just told them Rachel worked at the hospital. Half the neighbours assumed she was a nurse, but what harm in that?

"Well, I don't know, I might start singing again. I never missed it when I was up in Halifax but back here…I guess because I used to play and sing so much when I lived here before, I find I do miss it now sometimes," said Rachel.

"Nothing wrong with it, as long as you got a day job to put food on the table." In the little silence that followed Audrey's words, the evening news from the TV seeped into the edges of their day. Someone in a suit said that the TAGS program was failing people in rural Newfoundland, retraining them for jobs that didn't exist.

"They say there's some place on the Southern Shore where twenty-five women that used to work in the fish plant went and got their TAGS money and got trained to be hairdressers," Audrey says. "And the town only ever had the one hairdresser, and even she don't have enough work to keep going with so many people moving away, so what's the good of twenty-five trained hairdressers? You tell me. The government got this whole business arsed up if you ask me."

"Hard to see what's going to happen to places like that," Rachel said. "Or like this, for that matter."

TRUDY J. MORGAN-COLE

Audrey drained her teacup and looked down. Doris used to claim she could read tea leaves; right now, Audrey almost wished she could read them too, although as she always used teabags there wasn't much chance of that. "Well, this one is going to turn into a pizza parlour, so it seems."

"*Pizza parlour* is like *nooky*, Nan—nobody calls it that anymore."

After Rachel left, picking her way out through the chaos of the shop downstairs and locking the door behind her, Audrey put her feet up and watched the end of *The National*. There wasn't much good news on the go, but it was always better to stay on top of it.

The phone rang just as Peter Mansbridge was saying goodnight on the television. Audrey expected it to be Marilyn, who phoned once or twice a week at about this time of the night—her rates went down after nine. Audrey, picked up the receiver, ready to pitch into her litany of complaints about Frank, Frankie Junior, and the mess downstairs.

A man's rough voice, familiar and unfamiliar, crackling with long-distance. "Hello…is this Audrey Holloway?"

It was like the floor had dropped out from under her feet. No amount of time and change could prevent her from recognizing the voice, even before he added, "Mom?"

"Henry."

"Yeah, it's me."

"My God, Henry, the turn you gave me."

Weak laughter down the line. "Had me given up for dead, I s'pose, did you?"

"As good as. Sure it's been—how long?"

Silence on the other end, then, "Must be ten years, isn't it?"

Twelve years and seven months since the last phone call. "All of that and more," she said. "Are you…you're all right?"

"I'm all right now. Good enough, anyway."

"Is there...do you need anything?"

Another silence, this one longer. Audrey's heart pounded in her chest and she thought of her father Wes: heart attacks ran in the family.

"No, Mom," Henry said at last. "I didn't want to call just because I needed anything. I s'pose it's the other way round—I was waiting to call till I didn't need help. I didn't want to come home till—well, the time just wasn't right before, that's all."

"Come home? Where are you—are you in town now?"

"No, no, I'm up in Toronto. I—the thing is, I wasn't sure I was going to come home, or even get in touch, or anything. It's hard to know—where to pick up, I guess. But the other day I was on the GO Train and I saw this fella looking at me, staring really, and then I realized it was Randy. He made me come back to his place for supper with him, wouldn't take no for an answer, and I was all evening talking to him and Denise, and then—well, I told them I'd call you. Denise would have picked up the phone right then and told you, but I said I needed a day or so, and I promised her I'd call."

"Well, God love Denise. You're OK, though. That's the main thing. You're all right."

"I'm all right. I've been worse and I've been better, but I'm all right. But Mom...how is Rachel? Is she OK?"

"She's all right. She was just here, she's doing fine." All the while thinking, *How the hell am I going to tell Rachel?*

RACHEL

Rachel and Jake were recording an album. Well, Jake's band, Muscles in the Corner, was recording an album, and Rachel was doing backup vocals. Jake was right, there was a lot going on in the St. John's music scene now, as if the slump in the economy had stirred up the musical action. Maybe there was a correlation: more people with time on their hands led to more people trying to make a career in the arts. Or maybe it was something to do with people being angry about the moratorium, like poking a stick into a wasp's nest.

Not that Muscles in the Corner was playing anything particularly angry or political. The band did a mix of covers of traditional tunes and 70s rock classics. No original music, because nobody in the band wrote lyrics, although Jake told Rachel she should try her hand at writing something for some of the tunes his lead guitarist, Roddy, came up with.

"I'm not a songwriter," Rachel said, and Jake accepted that. Not like Larry would have done, poking and prodding at her (the hornet's nest again), telling her she really *was* a songwriter, a soloist, whatever he believed she could be. It was restful to be with someone who accepted her own assessment of her limitations. Mostly restful.

So the band thing was going OK; and she liked her job; she was taking courses towards a master's degree. Even living with Jake was going OK, though the relationship had been accelerated by her need to get away from the construction at Nan's place.

Nan was drove nuts without the store. Or without the store as it used to be, the hub of the neighbourhood, the place that gave a shape to her days. When Rachel dropped into the store now it didn't look anything like the place she grew up in. The renovations were finished and Holloway's Grocery and Confectionary had become Pizza Presto! Most of the shelves were gone; new tile was laid down and a fresh yellow paint job covered the walls. The old wooden sign that once hung outside and then got moved inside had disappeared altogether.

One end of the room was the pizza take-out counter, with the oven in back where the storage room used to be. Another wall had glass-fronted coolers filled with two-litres of pop and two-fours of beer. One shelf held a few cartons of milk, the only nod to anything you might consider groceries. Frankie Junior worked the pizza ovens, and by the front door Frankie's girlfriend, Lisa, slouched behind a shrunken, half-sized counter with cigarettes shelved behind it and chocolate bars and chips in the front. People got their pizza, grabbed a dozen beer or a two-litre of Coke, picked up smokes and chips and lotto tickets at the cash, and paid. That was all that was left of Nan's store, the store that used to supply three blocks of families with everything they needed for dinners and suppers, seven days a week.

Rachel didn't come over to see Nan as much as she

probably should. Nan was not the kind of grandmother you felt guilty about; even with her hours cut back at the shop, Rachel didn't imagine Audrey sitting alone in the house waiting for Rachel to drop over. But she went there tonight for supper—canned pork and beans, a stack of white Wonder bread on the plate in the middle of the table, tub of Eversweet margarine. Audrey was no more dedicated a cook than she had ever been.

A week had passed since Audrey had called to tell her about Henry's phone call, to tell her that he was alive and reasonably well. That he'd asked for Rachel's phone number, but Audrey had said she would talk to Rachel first. "I didn't want to go ahead and give it to him without letting you know."

That had been the right thing to do. Rachel told her grandmother she needed to think about it. Now, over supper, she told Audrey that the next time Henry called, she could give him Rachel's number.

"It gave me a turn to hear his voice on the phone, I don't mind saying," Audrey admitted.

"It would have given me a turn too. I'm glad you told me first."

"Are you mad at him? Seems to me like you'd have every right to be."

Rachel pushed beans around on her plate, took a piece of bread to sop up the sauce. "I'm a little mad, I guess. I don't really know. You said he's talking about coming home?"

"Well, he mentioned it. I don't know why. There's not much on the go back here. Of course if Henry's anything like he used to be, he don't even know what kind of work he's out of, so that might not make much difference to him."

"I can't think about him here in St. John's. I mean, I can't even picture it."

"What did Jake have to say about it?"

Rachel looked up, blinking a little. "I didn't…tell him, yet. I mean, I never thought about it. It's kind of a private thing."

"And who do you talk about private things with? He's your boyfriend, isn't he?"

"*Boyfriend* sounds like we're teenagers."

"Well, I don't know what else to call it. What do they say now, do they say partner or is that only for the gays?"

The Gays. Rachel pictured them as Audrey named them, a glitzy army of Liberace lookalikes, arms hooked over each other's shoulders, sashaying down Merrymeeting Road kicking up their legs can-can style. Here Come The Gays.

"Anyway," she said aloud, "Jake's going back up to Alberta for work soon."

"Are you staying in his place or moving back in here?"

"Not sure yet…can I move back in, if I can't afford the rent on his place? It might be better for him to sublet."

"You always got a home here, you know that, girl."

Always a home here, but home was always changing. The shop downstairs more often filled with Frankie Junior's crew of friends than with the familiar neighbourhood shoppers, but at least Frankie didn't live over the store; he and his father had a place on Freshwater Road. If Henry came home, surely he would expect to move back here. Would the three of them, three generations of Holloways, be under the one roof? Rachel finished the last bit of bread, thinking of all the things she had chased around these Corningware plates on this table, sauces she had sopped up with bits of bread. Ketchup, egg yolks, gravy. In the background, on what might be the last functioning vinyl record player in St. John's, George Jones sang "He Stopped Loving Her Today." The comfortable predictability of meals at Audrey's table, country music in the background, the ping of the shop door downstairs punctuating it all.

TRUDY J. MORGAN-COLE

After supper they turned on the TV and watched *Wheel of Fortune*, which Audrey was good at, and *Jeopardy*, which Rachel was good at. Loud voices drifted up from the street below as people came and went, ordering pizza by the box or by the slice.

On her way out, Rachel stopped to buy smokes for Jake at the counter downstairs—she had quit smoking, herself, back in Nova Scotia, figuring it was bad for her voice. Though living with Jake it was hard not to take it up again. Lisa rang her in and Frankie said, "How's it hangin', Rae?"

"What's up, Frankie? How's business?"

"Lookin' good, lookin' good. Aunt Audrey's going to have to admit when she sees the numbers at the end of the month, this is the best decision she ever made."

"Yeah. Well, I don't think she's thinking that way right now." Rachel moved from the checkout counter to the pizza counter, looking around again at the shelves of chips and cheezies, the coolers of beer and pop. "It just takes some getting used to, I guess. I pretty much grew up in this shop. It's hard not to compare to how it used to be."

"Nothing is like it used to be no more, that's just life. This is what people want."

"Smokes and junk food and lottery tickets," Rachel said. "People used to get their groceries here, I remember the neighbours dropping in for bologna and eggs and loaves of bread, all that stuff."

Frankie Junior stared at her for a second, then said, "Well, don't blame me." In a nearly pitch-perfect nasally John Crosbie imitation he added, "I never took the baloney outta the goddam cooler!"

The joke took Rachel by surprise, her laugh almost a whooping sound. Frankie laughed too; they were both cracking up, sharing a rare moment of camaraderie. Even Lisa, whose face

Rachel had assumed to be incapable of registering complex emotions, laughed, and in the glow of that warm moment the door pinged and a guy covered in tattoos came up to the counter to order pizza.

Rachel tried to hold to that laugher on the way home, to think that Frankie Junior was really all right and things would be OK with the store and with Nan. But Frankie's joke was like that one warm day in April in St. John's when it was still stony hard winter underneath. Underneath the joke was the reality, more insightful than she would have given Frankie credit for: it was all the same thing. The fish outta the goddam water and the baloney outta the goddam cooler; the moratorium and the death of the corner store. People were leaving on every ferry and every plane out of Torbay airport, and only Rachel was crazy enough to come back. At least she wasn't as crazy as Frankie, trying to forestall the Decline and Fall of the Rabbittown Empire with pepperoni pizza by the slice. She didn't know what would be sadder, Frankie failing or Frankie succeeding.

But the saddest thing of all, maybe, was knowing that Henry was alive up in Toronto, riding alone on a Go Train, recognized only by chance by a cousin, dreaming of coming home to his mother and his daughter and a world that no longer existed. If it ever had.

musical interlude

HENRY AND RACHEL
(NOT A DUET)

The Stetson. Never been up on this stage before, I'm not even sure this place was here when I lived home. And for obvious reasons I haven't been to a lot of bars since I came back. Step up onto the stage, grip the neck of the guitar a little tighter to keep my hands from shaking.

Blinking in the lights. That's been awhile too. At least there's not many people here yet. Four acts on tonight and I'm the first, and hardly anyone in the place except what you might call my entourage. Rachel and a couple of her friends, Mom and her—boyfriend? or something?— Richard. Mom's friend Doris. Aunt Treese with Nancy and her husband. God love 'em for coming. The whole ragged-arsed family, gathering round. Not exactly the prodigal son, no fatted calves killed, but a Sunday dinner at Alf and Treese's, steaks on the barbecue another evening over at Richard's place. A room ready in the house I grew up in, and all the pizza I can eat downstairs. Oh yeah, sketchy little Frankie Junior and his girlfriend are here too somewhere. More than half the people in the bar are my family. Hell of a lot more than I deserve.

—Good evening ladies and gentlemen, thanks for coming out. It's good to be back home. Long time since I played in St. John's.

And never played here like this, never as a solo artist. Always backing up someone else, in someone's band. Only reason I'm here tonight is because Bob Eveleigh somehow, against all odds, turned out to be kind of A Big Deal after he went to Nashville and recorded an album that made it into the Top Ten on the Canadian country charts. He's the headliner tonight; in a couple of hours the place will be wall-to-wall with people coming out to hear him. It was all his idea, adding me into the lineup for tonight.

—Just a couple of songs at the beginning, he said. Get you warmed up.

—Nah…what am I warming up for? If I do start playing again it'll just be doing backup for someone.

—No way! You did a lotta solo stuff up there in Toronto, I know, I heard all about that.

—Yeah but that was years ago.

—You gotta jump back in, it's like riding a horse or a bike or whatever the hell they say. Come on. This is a great time to be back home, well, not if you want a job, but if you want to perform, it's a great time.

People change. Bob used to be a self-absorbed blowhard, and maybe he still is, but he's decent too. He wanted me to do this tonight and here I am. The rest of it—the family showing up, making a night of it—well, that was all Audrey. I don't think she ever came out to hear me play when I lived here before, but she said she wouldn't miss tonight.

—Anyway, since I'm here, back home after so many years away, seemed like it would be kinda appropriate to cover a song from here, a song everyone knows. About doing what I did, going away. What we've all done, maybe.

Strum the first chord, settle onto the stool a bit more, lean into the mic, as I sing those familiar words about living on a farm, in that wide open space. Sure enough, they're all singing along by the second line.

~

—Well you're not gonna go wrong, are you, doing a Ron Hynes song in front of a crowd like this, says Nick Lahey.

I'm at the bar talking to Nick, this seedy old drummer I've known forever who used to know Henry. He's playing with some band that's on later tonight. We're listening to Henry's voice, rough-edged but not unpleasant, belt out the song that might just be the unofficial anthem of Newfoundland.

—Yeah, it's a good choice.

—Must be something for you, eh? Seeing your old man perform again.

—It's not really again. I mean, I never saw him perform before.

—No?

—Well, no, I mean I was, like, twelve when he moved away for good, so I wasn't going out to bars to hear him or anything, back then.

—And you never heard him play up in Toronto or nothing? All those years.

I didn't even know he was alive. I don't say that out loud.

—No, I never heard him up there.

—I heard him, when was it, 82, 83, something like that? My God, was it that long ago? Could've been even longer, I s'pose.

Nick is Henry's age and has that beaten look you see in a lot of older musicians. Makes me wonder why I even want to make it in a business that makes you look like that after twenty years.

—Definitely in the early 80s, he says. He was playing in this, hell, this scuzzy little place out on the highway, not even in Toronto, it was about halfway to Oshawa. Me and Mike Davidge, it was, we were up there working construction, and we borrowed Mike's sister's car and drove out there.

—So it wasn't just by chance? I mean, you actually knew he was going to be playing, you drove out there to see my...to see Henry?

—Oh yeah, yeah. Mike knew someone who told him Henry was playing, you know how it is with musicians. And Newfoundlanders.

Early 80s. So all that time I was growing up thinking I was an orphan, all that time Audrey believed her only son might be dead, there were musicians from home who knew where to find him, knew through the friend of a friend that he would be playing in some motel bar off the 401 halfway to Oshawa.

—Was it...was he good? What was it like?

—Oh, you know, it was one of those places, where, you know....

—Everybody's drunk and nobody's listening?

—Yeah. You know. But he did a good set, nice set. You know what?

—What?

He nods toward Henry on the stage. The old folks, Nan and Aunt Treese and Doris, are singing along.

—You talk about that song, a Ron Hynes song—you heard that new one of Ron's, that one about the Man of a Thousand Songs?

—Yeah, yeah, of course.

—Right, and everyone's like, that's Ron, you know, he's writing about his own life, he's the man of a thousand songs, you know? But he's not. I mean, he is but he's not, you know? He's writing about guys like your dad, you know. Ron Hynes was like that once, maybe. But now, back here at home, he's a local hero. He's like a rock star, well, not a rock star, but you know what I mean, right? But guys like your dad, geez, there must be a million of 'em. Guys going around singing in bars, in little dives no one's ever heard of, no fans, no fame, no glory. Just like—doing it. For the sake of the music, that's all.

On stage, Henry moves into Randy Travis's "Forever and Ever, Amen."

—Guys like Henry, he's the real man of a thousand songs, you know? Nick says.

—I guess. Peeling at the label on the beer bottle with my thumb. —I guess, yeah, maybe.

$\sim$

One local standard, one country pop favourite. Time to get a little more rock 'n' roll now. Not too rock 'n' roll, this is The Stetson after all. But the Eagles should be OK. Bob said four songs, so I start into "Take it Easy." A few more people have drifted in, probably here early to hear Bob. Rachel's at the bar talking to that old sleazebag Nick Lahey. Does Rachel know that Nick knew her mother? That it was Nick's car she took off in? Not likely. I accused Stella of sleeping with Nick, might even have been the night she died. What does Rachel know about Stella, I wonder?

It's been harder with her than with Audrey, or Nan, or any of the rest of them. I imagined some big scene with Audrey and Nan, tears and accusations, explanations and apologies. Instead I come home to find Nan is in St. Luke's, happy just to see me whenever I visit. Sometimes I bring the guitar and sing hymns, she loves that. As for Audrey, she never asks questions about the time I was away, says nothing about those years.

We eat supper together at her kitchen table, most nights. I'm learning to cook because nobody's going to survive long on Audrey's cooking, although apparently it's worked out OK for her all these years. We eat supper and she complains about Frankie Junior and the crowd that hangs around the shop, about the smell of garlic and pizza sauce. Then she goes out with Richard, or over to Doris's for a game of cards. I stay home and play the guitar, or I go out and walk the streets of St. John's, looking at what's changed and what stays the same.

But Rachel, she's been skittish, and who can blame her? We live under the same roof but she's rarely there for our supper-times, though she does say she prefers my cooking to Audrey's. Rachel is out most of the time: work, her own friends, her own music. She's got a lovely voice. I went to hear her one night at the Carriage Works, but she didn't talk to me after the show.

She'll never know how much nerve it took me, to ask her if she'd do a song with me here tonight. Flat-out refused, she did. Wouldn't even think about it. And she was right. It would only be, what, sentimental. Like we were going for some big reunion scene, me with the daughter I never really knew. I didn't try to talk her into it.

Last chord: now for the last song.

—This one's for the woman who never gave up on me. I know it's kind of an old cliché to dedicate a song to your mom but she deserves it, and old Hank was her favourite singer, so...

TRUDY J. MORGAN-COLE

Everyone's right into it, the old folks and the young ones, as Henry rocks out "I Saw the Light." It's his best performance of the night so far, raw and open and showing me something I've never seen in him before, not that I've had occasion to see all that much.

There's a lot of Jesus in this song, isn't there? What with the intro about his dear old mother folks probably have the impression that his mother gave him a good churchy upbringing and prayed him safely back home. And that's a misrepresentation, to say the least. Nanny Ellen, maybe, but certainly not Audrey. But I guess "I Saw the Light" is kind of like "Amazing Grace." Nobody wants to pick apart the theology. They use those churchy old words to sing about a different kind of redemption. Seeing whatever kind of light leads you forward, getting lost and found and carried home on three aching chords. Maybe old Hank himself meant it that way, or maybe he actually meant he'd let the dear Saviour in. Bit hard to tell at this point.

Henry finishes to a big round of applause, ducks his head and waves as he gets off stage, heads straight over to Audrey's table and gives her a kiss on the cheek. It's a bit stagey but what the hell.

I'm done being mad at him, I think. We've got this far. He's been home six months, we've talked, we've lived in the house together, now I've listened to him sing. And life goes on. Turns out it wasn't that big a deal after all.

He comes over, gives me a hug, and I try not to be stiff and weird and pull away from him. Can you believe he actually asked if I'd get up and do a song with him tonight? I told him no way, wasn't going to happen. Maybe I'm over being angry, but saying no to him feels really good.

When Jake went back to Alberta the last time, Muscles in

the Corner broke up, and so did Jake and I, although we didn't realize that at first. I haven't been in a band since then; I've been doing solo gigs, writing a lot. After spending a year telling Jake I wasn't a songwriter. My day job got cut to part-time, and now I spend a lot of afternoons over a cup of coffee at Hava Java with my notebook, writing and writing, then going home with a guitar to see if the music in my head can be picked out on strings. I lock myself in my room with the guitar and a cassette recorder and that notebook full of scrawled pages, looking to see if there's one good song or even one good line in the reams of crap.

Someone else is on stage now, and I'm back at the family table, wedged in with them all telling Henry what a good job he did.

—Buy you a beer, Henry? says Frankie Junior.

—I'll take a Coke, thanks, says Henry, which confirms my suspicions that he spent at least some of his lost years hitting bottom and drying out. I haven't seen him take a drink since he's been home, not that we've been hanging out together a whole lot, but I would have noticed. Well, more power to him, if that's the case.

Nan and the other old folks head home before Bob Eveleigh, the headliner, gets up on stage. Nancy and her husband stick around with Henry. Frankie and Lisa peel off to meet up with some people at some other club. I end up hanging out with the guys from Muscles in the Corner, one of whom is now in a punk band that's playing at Bar None later. I trail along after them, and later, when the band (Pease Pudding Cold) turns out to be not as good as their name, I go to another bar with some other people.

It turns into one of those downtown nights, getting drunk, walking arm in arm with people I don't know that well, listening to one band after another. At one point I see Frankie Junior with his crowd but I don't see Henry again, which is good. I hope he's back home safe and sober in bed. Which is a weird and sad thing to wish about your father, but when it comes to Henry, what's not weird and sad?

Two in the morning, Erin's Pub. Pretty drunk now, and I barely know the people I'm with. This one girl, Sarah…plays the violin. And her boyfriend, I can't remember his name. Another guy and girl, but not a couple because the guy is One of The Gays, as Nan would say. And they're at this table drinking Guinness, and up front there's a guy singing acapella with just a bodhran, singing something in Gaelic in a voice so haunting and pure it gives me the chills.

Then he looks up. How, even late at night, even drunk, even years later, could I have mistaken his voice for anyone else's? No other voice, no one else, anywhere in the world. Even when, for all I know, he's been in Ireland so long he's been kidnapped by leprechauns. It's Larry Kennedy singing Irish songs in the middle of the night in downtown St. John's, and it seems my father's not the only ghost who can walk through the door.

nine

TILL I DO
SIGHT MY
HEART'S
DELIGHT

1994 – 1995

AUDREY

The only shift Audrey did behind the counter now was two to five on weekdays. They got a little crowd in the shop when the youngsters got off school and came in to buy pizza slices, pop, bars, and chips. She had to give Frankie Junior credit: he was in the shop every day from eleven in the morning till after midnight. He had an annoying habit of running out at odd times for ten or fifteen minutes, but he did put in long hours, and apart from Audrey's daily shift he seldom took a real break. Nearly two years now since the old Holloway's sign came down and the Pizza Presto! sign went up, and he was making a go of it.

"I could go back to doing Saturdays if you wants a full day off," she offered once.

"You're supposed to retire at sixty-five, aren't you?" Frankie said.

"I'm offering to do you a favour."

"Are you? Or do you just want more hours so you'll have something to do?" The mouth on that one, no respect for his elders.

"Come back and talk to me about it when you're sixty-five and see if you're so glad to be put out to pasture," Audrey said.

"How old will you be when I'm sixty-five?"

"A hundred and something, smart-ass."

"When I'm sixty-five I'm not gonna be flipping pizza dough in this place, I can tell you that. I'm gonna be relaxing on my yacht in the Mediterranean."

"You think so? You better have some kinda business on the side, because I been working this shop since I was half your age and let me tell you, pizza or no pizza, running a corner shop in Rabbittown never made anyone rich."

"Well, I got bigger plans," Frankie said. "I mean, I figure I'm doing all right, twenty-three years old and running my own business, right?"

Audrey gave him a long look. He was a stringy little thing, Frankie Junior, with a stringy little mustache, and just because he turned out to be a decent worker didn't mean she couldn't take him down a peg or two. She folded her *Evening Telegram* and laid it down on the counter. "Yes now, I s'pose you're doing all right for yourself, twenty-three and running your own business. Only because you walked into a shop that your grandfather built with his bare hands sixty years ago and your grandmother and me ran ever since. You just waltzed into what other people built, is all you did."

"Yes, but I saved it. This place wouldn't be running now if it wasn't for the pizza."

"Saved it?" *What's saved?* Audrey wondered, looking around the yellow room. Not the business she ran for all those years, not the place that used to be the centre of the neighbourhood. Only the legal entity, that the Holloway family still owned a business on this location, and if anyone saved that it was the Bank of Montreal. "I don't know about savin' anything."

TRUDY J. MORGAN-COLE

"Well all I'm saying is, I got friends my age unemployed, and I got friends up in Alberta working, and I'm pretty happy with how things are going for me down here. And I don't mean this to be the end of it, this is just the start."

Why did she still want to work in the shop every day? Audrey wondered about it herself sometimes. It wasn't for the money. The bit of income she got out of the shop was little enough on top of her old-age pension, but it would come whether or not she worked. Something to do, mostly. She couldn't sit looking at the four walls every day, even with Henry living there for a bit of company. She had bridge once a week, a scattered trip to the mall with Doris, occasionally Bingo with Treese. Sunday dinner, either at Alf and Treese's or with Marilyn and George all the way out in Torbay. She still had her Sunday afternoon drives with Richard—these days they mostly did go driving, which probably meant they were getting old. Twice a week she and Marilyn went together to St. Luke's to visit Mom. It wasn't like she had nothing at all to do, but still and all she'd miss work if she didn't have it.

As she watched Frankie mix pizza dough, Audrey thought that maybe the whole point of work was to look forward to getting off work. When her shift was over she'd go upstairs, take off her shoes, put her feet up and watch *The Price is Right*. Heat up some tinned spaghetti for supper, most likely, unless Henry was in and wanted to cook, as he sometimes did. If she didn't have the job she could have her feet up watching TV all day, but then it would feel like a waste of time instead of a reward. Work gave a shape to the day. She didn't know what people did after they retired, although most of her family and friends were retired now and they seemed to get by all right. Marilyn and George went on a cruise last year and they were after Audrey to go with them, but she couldn't picture herself at the likes of that, never mind the cost of it all.

Ping. Finally, a customer. Audrey figured it was a bunch of youngsters from Booth, pipping off early to get a slice of pizza before the rest of the school crowd got there. But no. Billy Walsh and Vern Cadwell slouched into the store. Those two were bad enough when they were little friggers trying to steal Fudgesicles out of the freezer. Now they were grown men hanging around the shop like teenage boys, neither of them with a proper job, sponging off Frankie.

"Whaddya at, b'ys?" Frankie greeted them. "What's on the go?"

"Starved, buddy, gotta slice for me?"

"I s'pose, b'y. Wait till I gets this one out of the oven."

They lounged against the counter, lighting up smokes, talking about nothing. "Ronnie around?" Frankie asked.

"Nah, Ronnie's gone up to Alberta. Sure he's makin' twenty dollars an hour up in Fort Mac. He got nothing to spend it on either except booze and blow, he's wasted twenty-four-seven."

"Sounds all right, I'm surprised you never went up with him."

"He wanted me to. I wouldn't be makin' that kind of money though. Ronnie got a trade—got his journeyman electrician."

"Yeah but up there, even unskilled labour, you could be makin' ten bucks an hour. Fifteen, maybe," Billy pointed out.

"They got it knocked up there in Alberta," Vern said.

"How come you're not up there, then?"

"Nah, can't be at that. I'd only be up there wantin' to come home out of it."

One of the fellows leaned over the counter and said something to Frankie that Audrey couldn't hear. Frankie said, "Yeah, alright, I got this done now. Aunt Audrey, can you keep an eye on things? I gotta run out for five minutes."

"I was keeping an eye on this store before you were born."

The phone rang while he was out, and it was another one of those friggers wanting to know if Frankie was in and hanging up when she said he was out. No pizza order, no message, no manners.

Audrey wished she could put her finger on what was wrong with the young people. Lazy, was that it? But she had always known people who were lazy. Look at the Walshes: three generations of lazy. And dishonest. She felt like she had been chasing snot-nosed Walshes and Cadwells out of the store forever. Richard was the only Cadwell who ever made anything of himself, and she couldn't think of a single Walsh who wasn't on welfare. So laziness was nothing new.

The young folks, Rachel's and Frankie's age, were always drifting around complaining and doing nothing at all. Did any of her crowd ever complain that much? She didn't think so. Although maybe they did complain when they were young and she just didn't remember. At her age, most of her time with friends was spent talking about the old days, and people's memories didn't often line up with the way Audrey remembered them.

Take Doris, for example. Doris loved to tell the story of how she came over on a boat during the war, thousands of miles from home, knowing nobody. She said she came with the other war brides while Les (Poor Les, as she called him now that he'd passed away) was still on a naval ship at sea. Doris told everyone how she had cried and cried those first weeks, how afraid she was that Les would be killed and she'd be stuck here forever in this godforsaken place. She even gave an interview to some missus from the CBC that was doing a piece for the TV about war brides. As Audrey remembered it, Doris didn't get to St. John's till well after the war, when her and Les came back together, but Doris was right into her version of the story.

"I stuck it out," Doris liked to say, "I did, settled down and did my bit, and when the war was over Les came home and we got our own little place, it wasn't much but it was ours. Two rooms, no running water, but it was our very own little place, and a year later Laura was born…."

She told the story that same night over a cup of tea at Audrey's table—to Rachel, who had heard it before, and to Rachel's young man, Larry, who hadn't. Larry was face and eyes into everything Doris was saying, and although he didn't have a notebook and pen in front of him, Audrey knew he was filing away every detail, picking out bits and pieces that would probably end up in a song somewhere. She had clipped out the *Newfoundland Herald* article that called Larry Kennedy "one of the brightest lights in this generation of songwriters," though the reason she cut it out and kept it was for the pictures of him and Rachel and the part about "Rae Holloway's haunting, soaring voice."

Anyway, if Larry could get a song out of Doris's war-bride story, why not? It wasn't like the thing was made up of whole cloth. Doris did marry a Newfoundlander, and come over here as a war bride, and no doubt she had her hard times. If she had shifted the story around a bit over the years to make the hard times sound harder and herself a little braver, what harm in that?

Doris made noises about calling a taxi around nine-thirty, and Larry said no, him and Rachel would give her a ride. Henry said he wasn't going out anywhere tonight; he sat in what used to be Wes's old chair in the living room, playing his guitar. "I'll call you tomorrow or Monday," Larry said to Henry as they went out the door, "about that gig with Dave at the Ship. Thanks for the tea and cake, Audrey."

"Good night, Nan, good night, Henry," Rachel called, blowing Audrey a kiss as she went to the door. She seemed so much happier, Audrey thought, since Larry came back and she got back together with him again. More easy, more relaxed. Henry said it was wonderful to see but what the hell did Henry know? Audrey knew Rachel and Larry went back a long time, and she had never seen Rachel look at Jake Hibbard or any other fellow the way she looked at Larry. If the girl ever did settle down, it would be with Larry Kennedy. But that meant if she was going to get her heart good and broke, that would be by Larry too.

When they had gone out through the shop, which was still open for the late-night pizza orders, Audrey picked up the mail from the table where she had dropped it earlier. "Nobody writes letters anymore. Bills, bills, bills. A letter from June."

"You said nobody wrote letters," said Henry, contrary as always.

"June don't count. She'd rather make a long-distance phone call than pick up the pen."

"But she did write you."

"It'll only be four lines on a card. Who's this from?"

"Hard to tell when you've got it in your hand and I can't see it."

"Don't be saucy. It's got an American stamp, but it's not from Louise, or Marilyn's Tina—who else do I know in the States?"

"What's the return address?"

Audrey squinted at the tight, tiny handwriting. "Shreveport," she said. Her stomach tightened, and she looked up at Henry. This wasn't Harry Pickens's hand-writing. "When was the last time you heard anything from your father or Carol?"

Henry shook his head. "Years ago. I was out of touch with Dad longer than I was with you. So I guess...what? 76 or 77? God, it's been nearly twenty years."

"I've heard from him since then," Audrey said. "I called him when I heard from you again, when I knew you were all right. We didn't keep in touch much, over the years, but I did tell him that. But that was, what, nearly two years ago."

"Open the letter, Mom."

It was from Harry and Carol's son. Henry's half-brother. A man she had never met. She scanned the lines quickly.

"Lung cancer," she said. "Last Thursday. Well. I suppose it makes sense...he smoked like the tilt."

"You're one to talk. Anyway, you don't even know—he might have given it up years ago. You don't know a thing about him. No more than I do."

Audrey sat down across from Henry, still holding the letter. Neither of them really knew the man. But his son had known they would have to be informed of his death. More Henry's business than hers, really: whatever else, Harry was still his father. But Audrey's was the address Harry's son would have had.

"Well, there you go." Audrey read the few lines over. *I know Dad would have wanted you and Henry to know of his passing. He was pretty much at peace in his last hours. Not a lot of pain. He was a good man and I hope you all have some good memories of him.*

There wasn't much else to say, was there? Good memories? Audrey found she had hardly any memories left at all of Harry. Dances at the Caribou Club, Harry in uniform. When it all seemed so grown-up and glamorous, going out with an American soldier.

What kind of memories did Harry have of her? Maybe it

375

was like Doris and her stories; if Harry were to tell the story of him and Audrey, he'd remember it all different. But she would never know now. Harry was gone and all his memories with him. And someday they all would be—Audrey, Doris, Henry, everyone. So what difference did it all make if the stories were true or lies?

RACHEL

"How's your Nan these days?" Larry asked Rachel.

"She's all right, I s'pose. Oh, she called and asked if we wanted to come over for supper Saturday night. Hopefully Henry's cooking, unless you want Kraft Dinner and Vienna Sausages."

Larry was fond of Audrey, and of Henry too for that matter. He liked going over to Nan's place, playing 120s with Nan, Richard, and Doris; sometimes they'd do that on a Saturday evening. Rachel and Henry, neither of them big card-players, would do a little father-daughter bonding, play a few songs while the others played cards. Larry dragged her off up the Shore to see his own people, his parents and grandparents, and they played cards and played music down there too. Larry genuinely liked older folks. But even for him, just asking about Nan out of the blue was odd. "Why?"

"Just wondering. How are things going at the store?"

"Same as usual as far as I know, why?"

"I don't know. It's probably nothing…something somebody said, is all."

"Who said what?"

"I don't know…like I said, it's no big deal."

She left it there. Lots of women wouldn't, but Rachel didn't care to play games. If Larry wanted to tell her what he did or didn't hear about Pizza Presto!, he'd tell her. If it really was nothing, why pester him about it?

Anyway, Rachel had a lot on her mind. She and Larry were working on another album, and they had a huge gig coming up, opening for Blue Rodeo when they came to St. John's. Rachel was also teaching voice lessons to a dozen students, which was great, because on top of arts grants, teaching was the one thing that brought in some actual money. They couldn't count on something like the Blue Rodeo show coming up on a regular basis.

They had been living together a year now, managing to make their rent and buy groceries. Rachel's Honda Civic was still running, barely, so they even had a car when they needed it. Not bad, Rachel figured, for two musicians who were making a full-time gig out of the music business. Her last contract doing music therapy didn't get renewed: another government funding cut. Playing music with sick kids was all well and good but you couldn't prove, on paper, that it made money or saved money. Therefore, in the St. John's economy of the 1990s, you might as well forget about it.

For Larry, being a full-time musician included working a couple of shifts a week at Fred's Records and doing the sound for a lot of other people's shows. Larry and Rae—they had gone back to the old duo name—got a fair few bookings, but even so, the music business was never going to be easy. Rachel could imagine dizzying heights of success: what if they were as

MOST ANYTHING YOU PLEASE

popular as Great Big Sea or the Irish Descendants? She knew damn well how hard those guys worked, how much they toured, and how little spare cash they had. Even "making it" in Newfoundland—with "making it" being defined as "people who aren't other musicians recognizing your name,"—didn't always add up to a living wage.

They had a nice place—the first two floors of a Gower Street house, not one of the ones that had been renovated but one that was in its original rundown state after years as a boarding house. Someone else rented the top floor, and Larry and Rachel rented out a room in their apartment to Larry's friend Mikey Fitzgerald. Mikey was a stand-up comedian, one of the few professions with a less rosy outlook than musician. His day job was stocking shelves at Sobeys.

She had been scared, moving out of the security of Nan's house into an apartment with Larry, and then losing her contract so soon afterwards. Rachel knew herself well enough to know the fear was only partly about money. She had fallen, so fast and so hard, back in love with Larry Kennedy after all these years. The day after she first saw him back in St. John's she could have moved in with him, even married him; she was that sure of her feelings. Could a feeling so strong really be trusted?

Late that night—the same night he asked, out of nowhere, how Nan and the shop were doing—Larry came home from running the sound for a gig at Junctions, and slipped into bed beside Rachel, who had already been asleep for a couple of hours. She loved this: him getting into bed, her half-waking, drowsy, to say hello, remembering that he belonged here, that they were finally together.

"You know what I think?" Larry said.

"Mmmmm. Your feet're cold. Mmmmm."

"I think…we should have a baby."

TRUDY J. MORGAN-COLE

"You're crazy. You're an actual crazy person. Go to sleep."

"I can't. I'm wide awake. And I want us to have a baby."

Rachel rolled over, half-opened her eyes. "Where is this coming from?" It was the second thing he had said today that was out of the blue, no context. Generally speaking, Rachel was not a huge fan of surprises without context.

"Terry had his baby with him."

"He took a baby to Junctions?"

"Not for the show. He dropped by earlier to bring in his amps and stuff, and the baby was with him."

"So what, you saw a baby and now you want one? They're not puppies, you know. Actually even puppies are not—I mean, you can't just say you want one and then get one. They're a lot of work."

"What, puppies or babies?"

"Both."

"People do have babies though. All the time."

"Yeah…other people."

"Not us? Not ever?"

"Not now." This was the sort of thing you were supposed to talk about before you got married, which was one good reason for getting married, Rachel supposed: it gave you kind of a deadline for talking about this stuff. Whereas if you had known each other forever, and you got back together after years apart and then moved in together, maybe the topic of having babies never quite came up until you were lying in bed at two in the morning and your boyfriend was wide awake and had just seen his friend's cute baby.

"It's just. You know. We're nearly thirty. This is, kind of, the time of life when people think about this."

"People who have two jobs and a mortgage. Not our kind of people."

"So our kind shouldn't reproduce? That sounds a little… Nazi."

Rachel laughed. "Look, I don't hate kids or anything. I just—you know, we barely make rent as it is. And that's with Mikey here. If we had a baby, Mikey would have to go, and the baby wouldn't be able to get a job at Sobeys to help with the rent. Babies don't make money, they cost money."

"But we'd have an exceptionally beautiful baby, and it could be a baby model, and make money from being in commercials and stuff."

"So we don't even have this baby yet and already you're exploiting it. What a great dad you turned out to be."

Now it was Larry's turn to laugh, and Rachel hoped he would drop the subject like he dropped the other thing. Because she didn't want to untangle it all, to put into words the fear that if they had a baby, someone would have to give up music. Someone would have to get a full-time job and the someone would probably be Rachel. She had a degree in Folklore—useless—and half a Masters in Psychology. She might have to finish the degree, work in a school as a psychologist or something. Ten years would go by, and she'd keep saying she would get back to making music, but there would never be time. Talking about a baby felt like standing in a long hallway and, all around, doors were slamming shut. Slam, slam, slam till you ended up standing in the hall looking at a bunch of closed doors.

AUDREY

"All right, all right, hold your horses, I'm comin' down," Audrey called out, the second time Frankie bawled up over the stairs at her. She kicked off her slippers and pushed her feet into her comfortable shoes. The heels were a bit trod down but that was better than bending down to put them on properly. Much as she hated to admit it, she was getting to that age where she had to stop and think every time she bent over: "Is this really worth it? How much trouble is it going to be to get back up?"

Climbing up and down this steep set of stairs several times a day was not her idea of fun. That was what had forced her mother into St. Luke's, in the end—living in a house where she couldn't get around with her bad legs. Marilyn and George were in a bungalow; so were Alf and Treese and so was Richard, and Audrey had to admit she could see the value in it. She'd be glad if she didn't have to come down over the stairs all the time, especially in response to Frankie Junior hollering at her.

It was only quarter to twelve and she wasn't supposed to work till two, but Frankie had asked could she run down and watch the counter for a few minutes. Audrey almost told him it would have been better to flip the sign to CLOSED for that amount of time. But she had given him a tongue-lashing a few weeks ago for doing that very thing—told him that customers counted on the shop being open regular hours, and you couldn't go shutting it whenever you had to run out to do some message or whatnot. Frankie's recent habit of calling her down every time he went out was his way of punishing her for that lecture, she was sure.

"Fine, I'm here, you can go on and do whatever it is you're doing," Audrey said when she got down to the counter. "But don't be no more than twenty minutes now, I wants to get up and get some dinner before I comes down to work."

"Back in fifteen, I swear," Frankie said, and ducked out the door.

Not a soul came in the shop in the twenty minutes he was out, which proved he was probably right about putting up the CLOSED sign. It made Audrey contrary, so when Frankie came back and told her she could go on, she said, "I'll go when I'm damn well good and ready, this is still my shop." It was one-third her shop, which made Frankie Junior her employee, whether he called himself manager or not. "I might just stay down here now till my shift, it's only an hour anyway."

"I thought you wanted to get your dinner."

"Maybe I'll have pizza."

"Ha! That'll be the day." Audrey was no fan of the store's product. It wasn't just Frankie's pizza—she'd never really taken to pizza anyway. An awful lot of flavours all in together, and eating it with your hands felt untidy.

All the same she stayed down in the shop and had a bag of chips for her lunch, which was why she was there at quarter to two when the door opened and two policemen walked in. Audrey assumed they were there for pizza, or maybe to buy a pack of smokes or something. She glanced at Frankie and only when she saw the look on his face—pure terror—did it occur to her to worry. She'd never thought anything bad about the police being in the place. There were certainly people in the neighbourhood who had good reason to worry when a cop car pulled onto the street, but the Holloways had never had any kind of trouble. If anything, it made her feel more safe, like the store was less likely to be robbed, if she saw a cop around.

It was pretty clear Frankie didn't think of the police the way she did, although after the first moment of shock he smoothed out his face and put on a different expression. He didn't say a word as they walked straight towards the pizza counter. It was left to Audrey to say, "Good day, officers, can we help you with anything?"

"We're looking for Francis Holloway," said one.

The "Francis" should have tipped her off. Even so, Audrey was about to be helpful and tell him that Frank wasn't there, he was at his own place over on Freshwater Road, when the cop added, "Junior."

"That's him over there," she said, when Frankie still didn't say anything.

"Francis Wesley Holloway Junior?" the cop said.

"What? I never done nothing!"

The cop put his hand on Frankie's shoulder. "Francis Wesley Holloway Junior, you are under arrest for the possession of marijuana for the purposes of trafficking, and possession of hashish for the purposes of trafficking. Please put your hands behind your back." Audrey watched, fascinated, as Frankie turned around and the cop put handcuffs on him. The other cop turned to her. "We have a warrant to search these premises," the officer said.

"You can't search my shop!" Frankie said.

"Please be quiet and come with us, Mr. Holloway," said the cop, at the same moment as Audrey said, "You won't find nothing in this shop, we got nothing to hide!"

Frankie, escorted by the two officers toward the door, shot her a glance, and Audrey wished she could bite back the words. She never went over onto the pizza side of the shop. What did she know about what he had hidden away over there? She thought of all his useless friends coming into the shop, all the times he darted out for a few minutes for no reason, the phone calls from people who only wanted to talk to Frankie. *I've been a damn fool*, she realized.

At that moment the door pinged again.

Audrey hoped it would be some snot-nosed school kid. Instead, it was Selena Ivany, the last person she wanted to see. The mouth on that one, she'd have it all over Rabbittown by suppertime that the cops were at Holloway's and young Frankie was being arrested.

"My Lord, Audrey, what's on the go in here? Have ye had a break-in?"

That certainly would have been the best thing for Selena to think, but it wasn't like she could miss the fact that the officers had Frankie by the arm and were leading him towards the police car. As they led him out the door Audrey could hear the cop telling Frankie he had a right to legal counsel. "Ma'am, could you please leave the shop for now," another policeman said, and Selena's mouth got round till she looked like a fish just pulled up on the wharf and gasping for water.

As Selena backed out of the shop, still agape, there were footsteps on the stairs. Henry, who had been out playing at some bar till three in the morning, was just now getting up and coming downstairs. He paused in the entrance to the

TRUDY J. MORGAN-COLE

shop, taking it all in. "You all right, Mom?"

Audrey nodded at the cops who were just leaving the store with Frankie. "The police are in here. They're after arresting Frankie."

"Sweet Lord. What for, drugs?"

He certainly didn't sound surprised, Audrey thought. "He says they got to search the place."

"They're probably going to want to talk to both of us, too," Henry said.

One of the police officers came back in. "You'll need to close the shop while we carry out our search," he said. "Both of you stay here, please; we'll need to ask you some questions."

Audrey flipped the sign in the window to CLOSED.

RACHEL

"You should have told me," Rachel said to Larry as soon as she hung up the phone from talking to Nan.

"Told you what."

"About Frankie. Selling weed out of the pizza shop. You knew, didn't you?"

"I…ah, I heard stuff. I didn't know if there was anything to it."

"Tell me right now, exactly, what you heard." Rachel was reaching for her jacket, getting her shoes on.

"It was…who was it? Oh, Brian Wells and a few of the b'ys from Skeet Patrol. We were talking, I don't even remember about what, and somebody said, *Is Rae any relation to Frankie Holloway.* And someone else laughed and said, *Frankie Holloway, d'you want pepperoni, pineapple, or pot on that?* Then another fellow said he was amazed the cops hadn't busted that place by now."

"So everyone knew. Nan says Henry wasn't surprised either.

But I guess he's got a lot of experience knowing where people are selling stuff."

"Brian was talking like it was a well-known fact, like everyone knew the pizza shop wasn't where Frankie was making his real money. I guess there's not that much money in selling crappy pizza by the slice."

"It's not like Frankie's going around driving a BMW and taking vacations in the south of France," Rachel pointed out.

"No, but he's doing all right at a time when hardly anyone else is, and I guess that's enough to make people suspicious."

When she got to Audrey's place, Rachel let herself in through the closed shop with her key. It was three o'clock in the afternoon; Audrey had called her as soon as the police left. "I came as quick as I could," Rachel told her grandmother.

Audrey was sitting at the kitchen table with a cup of tea, a cigarette burning down in the ashtray. The TV was showing the weather channel with the sound turned off.

"So the police talked to you to?" Rachel asked.

"They talked to me, and your father, and they said they might need to talk to us again tomorrow or the next day, and they'll probably want to talk to anyone in the family who had anything to do with the business. I think they're looking for Deb now, wanting to have a word with her. You knows she had to be in on the whole thing." Deb was Frankie's latest girlfriend.

"Where's Henry?"

"Gone over to Frank's to tell him. He said Frank shouldn't hear about it over the phone."

When Rachel told her what Larry had said, Audrey said, "It's like all the men knew what was going on and all of us women didn't have a clue."

"I doubt Uncle Alf knew. He would have said something. Or Uncle Frank either."

"I'm sure Alf didn't know but I wouldn't be so sure about Frank. He'd protect Frankie no matter what. You know they found the weed stashed away in pizza boxes in the back room? Nobody ever went in there except Frankie and Deb. All that crowd used to come in here, and the people who would call and hang up if Frankie wasn't there—they all knew. He had regular customers, like."

"Did the police say you had to keep the shop closed?"

"For today, while they were investigating. I can open it tomorrow if I want, but I don't know if I can. If people come in they'll only be coming in to gawk and ask questions."

"I could come in and work, I don't mind."

"What for? Sure all anyone comes in for anymore is the pizza and I'm not going at that." Audrey stubbed out her cigarette, shook another out of the pack and lit it. "We never closed the shop. Not for anything. We closed Christmas Day, that was it, and Good Friday. And Sundays, of course, till they brought in the Sunday shopping. Mom wasn't best pleased about that, she thought it was flying in the face of God to have the shop open Sundays. But you couldn't stay closed when everyone else was opening up. We were closed for renovations when Dad died. Oh, and St— we closed for your poor mother's funeral. That's the only times I can remember the shop ever bein' closed. This is going to break Mom's heart."

"You don't have to tell her about it, do you?"

"It'll be on the news," Audrey said. "Oh my, Rachel, I got to get over there. You know she watches *Here and Now* every night. If she sees young Frankie arrested—"

"She won't see anything, there wasn't any TV camera there, was there?"

"No, but they could say the name. There was four or five cops down there, I think this is a big deal."

Rachel crossed to the window and looked down at the street. "There's somebody down there now," she said. "With a camera. Not a TV camera, but a big camera. Like maybe from the *Telegram* or something."

"Oh, that's the start of it. They'll all be here soon, swarming around like flies round a carcass. I got to get out and go see Mom—is some reporter going to stick a microphone in my face as soon as I puts my foot over the door, I wonder?"

Rachel and Audrey got out the door unmolested by reporters. The man with the camera had gone away and nobody else appeared as they got into the car to drive to St. Luke's. Perhaps, Rachel thought, it wasn't that big a deal after all.

Ellen's hearing was starting to go and she forgot things, but she didn't have what Audrey called Old-Timer's Disease; as long as she could hear what you were saying she made as much sense as she had ever done. She listened as Audrey explained that young Frankie had been arrested.

"What, Frankie? Not my Frank…?"

"No, his son, young Frankie. Your grandson." Audrey pitched her voice to Ellen-level, torn between her desire to be heard and her desire not to have everyone know their business.

"Young Frankie…arrested? For stealing?"

"No, for selling drugs."

"What kind of drugs?"

Rachel and Audrey exchanged glances. Did Nanny Ellen even know what marijuana was? Rachel wondered.

"Illegal drugs. Stuff he shouldn't have been at," Audrey said, and Ellen shook her head.

"Well, that's shocking," she said. "I thought Frank brought him up better than that. Of course, it wasn't easy, rearing him up without a mother those last few years. And even when she was alive, his mother—well, we never knew anything about her people. You never know, with foreigners, do you? There's a terrible lot of crime up in Toronto."

Did she think young Frankie was still up in Toronto? That might be for the best, unless Holloway's storefront did show up on the evening news or in the paper. But Ellen surprised them by leaping to the conclusion they had avoided. "He wasn't at that in the shop, was he? In my shop? Didn't young Frankie work in the shop?"

Audrey nodded. "He worked in the shop. He was selling pizza, remember?"

"Pizza," Ellen said, with great disdain. That, too, was foreign—Italian, like Frankie's late mother. All these foreign things—pizza, drugs, Frankie's mother and thus half of Frankie. "Well. It's shocking, that's what it is. I can't believe anyone in our family would do such a thing."

They ended up visiting through the news hour and not watching *Here and Now*, which was good because Treese called later, when they were all back at Audrey's, and said it was on the news, they said Frankie's name and they showed a picture of the front of the store. Larry had come up to join Rachel by that time, and Henry was back as well.

Audrey hung up the phone after listening to Treese and sat back down on the couch next to Rachel. "Treese says she can't hold her head up in public. What do she got to be ashamed of, I wonder? It's not like she've been the one standing behind the counter of that store day in and day out for forty years. When people think about the store, they don't think about Treese or Alf. Most of them don't even think about young Frankie, the little frigger. People in this neighbourhood think about me when they thinks of that store. If there's anyone can't hold their head up, it'll be me."

"You got nothing to be ashamed of, Mom," said Henry.

The phone rang again. Rachel moved toward it but Audrey got up with a sigh, waving her away. "That'll be Marilyn. I might as well answer it. I wonder if she've called June to tell her yet?"

"What did Frank say?" Larry asked Henry.

"About what we expected—he won't admit Frankie could have been dealing in any kind of a big way, just says he must have been smoking a bit of it and had it on hand for himself and his buddies."

"The amount of weed they found down there? For himself and his buddies? Frank's cracked."

"He believes what he wants to believe," Henry said.

"Could he have been using the business as, like, a front or whatever? I don't know, laundering money or something?" Rachel had no idea how any of this worked; it was all stuff she'd seen on American cop shows, except there it was usually cocaine or something. She and Larry smoked the occasional joint when they were out with friends or had someone over, and it never seemed to be a big deal to buy a bit of it off someone, though Larry always took care of it. The cops storming into the store, searching pizza boxes, arresting Frankie—that seemed like a much more serious business. "Could he have been connected to, like, organized crime?"

Audrey sniffed. "*Disorganized* crime is more like it."

"There's no gangs, no organized crime in Newfoundland, not like up in Toronto," Henry said.

"And if there was, Frankie wouldn't be smart enough to work for them," Audrey added.

"But you knew he was at it?" Rachel asked her father.

"I was suspicious. I never knew nothing for sure."

"But wouldn't that make it—hard, for you? Knowing it was going on just downstairs, in the same house?" Rachel had always trod cautiously around the edges of this conversation, her father's history of addiction. It was one of a thousand things they didn't talk about. Rachel and Henry talked about how Audrey was doing, what kind of help she might need but not admit to. Mostly they talked about music, and that was usually the three of them, her and Henry and Larry. Between the music, and Rachel and Henry conspiring to do things like getting Audrey to the eye doctor to upgrade her ancient glasses prescription, they had carved out a kind of relationship that seemed to work.

But the list of things Rachel and Henry didn't discuss was a long one. They didn't talk about Stella, ever. Rachel wanted to ask him about her, told herself that someday she would. They didn't talk about him going away, leaving her to be raised by Audrey and Nanny Ellen, or about the places he went or the things he did when he was away. The closest they ever got was once when Henry told Rachel he was going to be out because he had a meeting. It wasn't like Henry was on a lot of committees or anything so she was pretty sure what kind of a meeting that had to be.

Now Henry just shrugged. "If you used to be into that shit and you're trying to stay off it, it don't matter that much if it's downstairs, across the street or on the other side of town. You know where it is and you know how to get it. Even if I wanted to be at that again, I wouldn't have bought off Frankie. You don't want to go getting mixed up in the family business."

Audrey sniffed. "The family business! What am I supposed to do tomorrow, go into that shop and open up? First person through the door is going to be some reporter and the next one is going to be Lorraine Penney or Selena Ivany wanting to know all the dirt. It's been on the news, it'll be in tomorrow's paper. Should I go down there and face up to all that for the sake of the few skeets who wants to buy a pack of smokes or a lottery ticket?"

Rachel wanted to give her grandmother a hug but they had never been the hugging kind of family. In all her life this was something she had never heard: Audrey saying she couldn't face the neighbours. Audrey giving up.

"I can come in and work if you want," Rachel offered again. "It might not be so bad anyway. I mean, the people on the street are our neighbours. They'll understand."

"That might have been true twenty years ago," Audrey said. "It's a different crowd around here now, not many of the old ones left and so many new people." She stood up and looked around at her own living room as if she'd never seen the place before. "I'm getting out of here," she said. "Henry, you're all right here if I goes on over to Richard's for the night, aren't you? I'm going to stay there till this all blows over. If it ever does."

AUDREY

It was a funny feeling, moving into someone else's house. The only other time she ever did it, she was twenty and so many things were different: new husband, new country, new life. Leaving her parents' home for the first time to move in with Harry and his parents in Louisiana had been a huge change, but she could hardly remember being the girl who made that journey. Now she made this shorter journey: three blocks from her house to Richard's.

"That man has the patience of Job," Ellen used to say about Richard Cadwell. "It's not like I got a gun to his head," was Audrey's usual response. Privately she had to admit her mother was right. A good-looking divorced man with a house of his own and a nice little pension; he wouldn't have had a hard time finding someone to marry him if another wife was what he was looking for. But when Audrey turned him down, over and over, he kept coming around.

"I know you're used to having your own space," he said over a late supper. Audrey had shown up on his doorstep at nine o'clock the night of Frankie's arrest carrying a single overnight bag, and told him she hadn't even eaten yet. He heated up the leftovers of his own supper and opened a bottle of wine. "You can keep your things in the spare bedroom if you want, but you're more than welcome in my room. Just because you're staying here, don't worry, there'll be no talk of weddings or anything like that."

"I think we're both past all that now," Audrey said. She hung up the few clothes she had brought in the spare-room closet when supper was over, and then sat down with Richard to watch *The National*. At least with that there was no fear of them covering a story about a drug bust in a St. John's corner store. The national news had bigger fish to fry.

Bedtime, then, and she wasn't sure what to do. Richard got up and took Audrey's hand to help her to her feet. He held it a minute longer. "Come on, girl. Come in my room for the night. Unless you can't stand hearing me snore."

"If it gets too loud I can always go back in the spare room," Audrey said.

Richard went with her went back to the house the next day to pack more of her clothes. She took her case of CDs as well—Henry and Rachel and Larry had finally got her to switch over to CDs, although she'd kept all the old records too. But there was only a CD player at Richard's place and if she was settling in she'd have to have her music with her. Two suitcases full of clothes, some CDs, a few framed pictures of the family—it didn't take long to pack up her life.

Going back to her own place wasn't as bad as she thought it would be; this was St. John's after all. It wasn't as if there were news teams camped outside the shop shoving microphones in her face as soon as she went in or out. Henry and Rachel had already said "No comment" to reporters from both the CBC and NTV, and after that they seemed to have lost interest. There were the neighbours to think about, of course. Audrey came downstairs to find Lorraine Penney banging on the door of the shop. "Oh, you're not opening up today are you? When do you think you'll be open again?"

"I got no idea," Audrey told her, standing in the doorway, jingling the keys in her hand. Richard waited behind her with her suitcases.

"Are the police still in there?"

"If they were, I'd hardly tell the whole street, would I? Anyway, I got no thoughts of opening up anytime soon, so you can go on buying your smokes at Shopper's where you been buying them this five years."

"No, there's no need to get saucy with an old friend, Audrey."

Audrey wanted to push her old friend right off the step but instead she said, "I'm sure you can imagine this is a bit of shock, Lorraine. All any of us wants is to be left in peace."

Lorraine left then, and Henry followed them downstairs, carrying a few bags of his mother's odds and ends. "You don't mind staying here alone?" she asked him as he put the bags in the trunk of her car.

"Hell no, I've slept in worse places," Henry laughed. "Anyway somebody got to be here. You can't have the place standing empty. The windows would be beat out of it."

Audrey looked at her son, standing under that big stupid Pizza Presto! sign. "What would you do if I sold the place?" It was the first time she had said the words out loud like they were a real possibility.

"Oh, don't you worry about me. I'd land on my feet. I got a gift for that."

Audrey had never seen a scrap of evidence to suggest

Henry had that gift. But she was sixty-six years old and her son was forty-five. It made no sense at this point to be lying awake nights wondering how her youngster was going to make out.

When Henry dropped over the next day he brought Audrey and Richard up to date on the latest news about Frankie. He had been charged, but it would be months before his trial. The police had decided nobody but Frankie would be charged, and the lawyer said if Frankie had the sense to plead guilty he would avoid a trial and probably have to serve less than a year in jail. "And I hope he does have the sense to take it, because if he does, none of us are going to have to go through testifying. But if there's a trial, who knows who they might call?"

"Frank must be heartbroke over this," Richard said. "It's no easy thing, to see your son up on charges like that—I know our Butch was tore right up when Nicky got sent up to Dorchester for five years." And the Holloways weren't used to it like the Cadwells were, he didn't bother to add.

"It's no easy thing, for sure. Frank haven't shown his face since it all happened, and Uncle Alf never seen him either. You heard anything from him, Mom?"

"Not hide nor hair of him," said Audrey. "I'm not surprised. Frank got to know me and Alf are pissed off at Frankie, and we got every right to be."

Later, when Audrey looked back on those weeks after Frankie's arrest, it seemed like her life was nothing but one meeting after another. Giving statements to the police. Meeting the lawyer. Long, awkward conversations with Alf and Frank—Frank couldn't avoid his family forever—about what was going to happen to the business. All the while, young Frankie cooled his heels, laying about at his father's place, waiting for his court date. Audrey stayed at Richard's, and

Henry stayed on alone in the rooms over the closed-up shop.

She talked with Richard, with Marilyn, with Henry about what to do about the house and the shop, which was still closed. Finally she talked to Rachel, who looked thoughtful and said she would go home and talk it over with Larry.

"The house is fully paid off," Audrey reminded her. "That place you're in on Gower Street wouldn't be paid off for twenty-five years even if you bought it tomorrow."

"We couldn't afford to buy a house," Rachel said. "We're both musicians. We'll never be able to own a house."

"Unless I makes my house over to you," Audrey said.

"Then you get nothing out of it."

"I wouldn't get all that much if I sold it," Audrey replied, "not in this market." Houses in the centre of St. John's were sitting on the market for months, their prices knocked down over and over again.

"Is she thinking about taking the house, do you think?" Richard asked Audrey after Rachel left that evening.

"She might be. It's the best deal she'll ever get. And I don't know that I'll ever want to live there again."

"You don't have to."

Audrey looked up at him. "Are you sure? You're not sick of having me here yet?" All these years she had thought it was better that she and Richard lived apart, that they were two old people so set in their ways they'd never be able to manage under the one roof. She'd been at his place six weeks now and the strangest part was she wasn't thinking of it as his place anymore. It felt like her place. She caught herself asking Marilyn to drive her home, and meaning Richard's house.

"Not sick of you yet, girl," he said. "Why don't I borrow Eddie's van and we'll move the rest of your stuff over here on Saturday?"

TRUDY J. MORGAN-COLE

RACHEL

Rachel walked down Rankin Street in the rain, her hood up and boots splashing in the puddles. It was a warm rain, the kind that came too rarely in St. John's. She stopped on the corner of Calver Avenue, at the big window where she and Larry had hung up brown paper, at the door with the permanent CLOSED sign. The sign over the door that said Pizza Presto! She remembered the old sign, Pepsi logos on either end, that said HOLLOWAY'S GROCERY AND CONFECTIONARY. It used to light up at night; she remembered switching on the sign as it got dark. She stood on the sidewalk in front of the store and remembered everything: running in with Vicky to get Lune Moons and bottles of pop. Coming in crying after Loretta Hussey pushed her down on the sidewalk and tore holes in the knees of her tights. She even remembered things she might be too young to remember: playing with a doll or teddy bear in the crib in the room behind the counter. Audrey had told her that she used to play there while either Audrey or Ellen was working in the shop, if the other one had to go out and couldn't watch her. "And the younger ones in my family," Audrey said, "they all had their turn in that crib—June and Frank and poor Johnny, when they were babies, that was where they spent their days while Mom was working."

Rachel imagined her great-grandmother, a young mother with five children, standing behind that counter. Then Audrey, the war bride come home, taking her turn in the shop. Only Henry had gotten away without ever doing more than the odd shift there. They grew up and grew older there, all the Holloways, and the neighbourhood changed around them. Rachel couldn't find, in the streets of Rabbittown, one single corner store that was still just a corner store. If it wasn't gone or changed to something else it had been bought out by a chain like Needs, and the family name was no longer over the door. Frankie and his pizza had saved the family business, and then he had to screw it all up for them.

Rachel had the keys. She went inside, stood in the empty shop. Now that she was inside, she no longer saw the past. Instead she tried to see a future. The pizza ovens all gone and cleared out, the shelves and racks and coolers, even the front counter itself, maybe, gone. Though they'd need some kind of counter, wouldn't they?

She tried to imagine tasteful wooden shelves and hooks all over, musical instruments and CDs and sheet music, the back of the shop converted into little studios. "It's what you've always wanted," she had told Larry. "A studio space, room to give lessons, a little shop—a music shop, to bring in a little money. They'd sell us the business for next to nothing, and Nan says the house is mine already as far as she's concerned."

They'd stayed up till all hours, her and Larry, spinning dreams about the Corner Music Store—that was what Larry

401

wanted to call it—and what it might contain. A space for students and fellow musicians and music-loving customers. A place like the old corner store, where people could gather, except instead of people from the streets around, it could be anyone who loved traditional music and wanted to play and buy and learn. If they ever did have kids of their own—something Rachel could more easily imagine here than anywhere else—this would be the place they'd grow up, living in an apartment above the shop like Rachel herself did as a child. A shop full of the sound of the bodhran and accordion and guitar instead of the ring of the cash register and the chatter of neighbours buying chips and pop.

Larry was as caught up in the fantasy as she was, but he was also practical: "OK, so we get the premises for next to nothing, but what have we got then? An apartment to live in, a building to pay taxes on, and no money for renovations." Any assets left in the business would go to pay off the debts and if there was anything left over it would be divided between Audrey and Alf. Frank, shamefaced about his son's crime, had agreed to be cut out of any profits from the sale of the pizza ovens and other machinery. "I can see it all, just like you describe it," Larry said, "but how would we ever make it happen? Renovating the shop, starting the business—that would take money we don't have."

Rachel didn't have any good answer for this, except that she had faith it could happen. She pictured fellow musicians coming in to paint the walls and refinish the floors; imagined friends offering to trade graphic design hours for music lessons. She couldn't imagine anyone offering them actual stock to sell for free, but if they could get far enough to own the place and renovate it, surely anything could happen?

She walked from the old shop over to Richard's place,

MOST ANYTHING YOU PLEASE

which, she thought, she should now start calling Audrey's place too, since her grandmother seemed to have settled in there. Over a cup of tea she tried to sketch out a picture of the dream to her grandmother. As was often the case, when dreams were laid out in front of Audrey they suddenly looked flat and simple, like a picture in a child's colouring book instead of the priceless work of art you thought you had.

"So you wants to open a music store?" Audrey said.

"Well. A store, I mean, there'd be a small store, selling music books and some CDs, and we'd be offering lessons. And we'd have studio space for musicians to rent, too. For practice and things like that."

"That's going to make a lot of racket; you'll get complaints from the neighbours."

"Not, like, rock bands and stuff. Just folk music."

"Don't O'Brien's do that already? Selling music stuff? How many music stores do people need? Hutton's have been at it for years and they're closing down. It don't seem like much of a time to be opening up music stores."

"It's not mainly about the store," Rachel said. "It's—I mean, Larry's already giving lessons, he could take on more students, and we could get other teachers in to give lessons, if we had the space."

"Yes, but is that the best space? There on the corner in the middle of Rabbittown? There's no parking lot or anything, and the kind of parents who puts their youngsters in music lessons generally wants a place to park the car too. I mean, I'm not saying it won't work, I'm just saying it's a long shot. A music store, music lessons and all that, in our corner shop?"

"I just thought...," Rachel stopped. What did she think? Why did it mean so much, when she and Larry were talking about it last night? *You got carried away*, Audrey used to say when Rachel was little and she got excited about an idea. "I just thought it would be nice," she said, "to have something still there, where the family business used to be. Maybe we could even keep the name. Call it Holloway's Music Centre or something. Like it would be paying tribute, somehow, to Nanny Ellen and Poppy Wes, to what they did there."

Audrey sighed. "What they did was build a house, start a business, raise their youngsters. I know they wanted to pass it down in the family—that's what everyone expected, in those days—but they must have known it wouldn't last forever. Nothing does. Seems to me, if you was thinking of opening a studio or a store or whatnot, your best bet would be talk to someone who knows a bit about business, one of your smart university friends, and see what the best spot is for something like that. Not go moving into a place just because your great-grandparents owned it a long time ago."

"So—what? You wouldn't give me the house like you said, if we wanted to use it for that?"

"Don't be so foolish, Rachel, and don't look like I just pulled the tail on your kitten," Audrey said. "My offer stands, no strings attached. You and Larry wants the house, I'll go to the lawyer and sign the papers and it's yours, move in tomorrow. It'll be off my mind and off your father's. Neither of us wants it. And whatever you wants to do with the downstairs—a music studio, or an apartment you can rent out to make a bit of money. Open up a bawdy house down there for all I care—that's your own business. Say the word and it's yours. I'm only saying, don't go getting all carried away with an idea just because you're attached to the house and the shop. Sometimes you got to let things go."

Rachel was embarrassed to feel tears stinging behind her eyes. Why did either idea—the thought of moving into the house and transforming it, or the thought of walking away from it all—make her cry?

"One thing you should know while you're thinking about it," Audrey added, "Jim Maher with Century 21, he called me the other day, asked if I was putting it on the market. Says he got a client wants to buy the building right out. If he can get what he says his client is willing to pay, we can sell off the stuff in the shop to a buyer Alf knows, pay down the line of credit on the business, and clear nearly a hundred thousand. That's good money for a house in this part of town, I don't mind telling you."

"It is," Rachel said, blinking away tears.

"If I were to sell it, I got no intention of sitting on the money till I'm dead and gone. Whatever we gets from the assets of the shop, after the debts are paid, I got to split with Alf. And whatever I got for the house itself I'd split three ways—a third of it to see me through my own retirement years, another bit for your father, and the rest for you. You could take the money and put a good down-payment on the house you're in now, or open a music store, if that's what you want, in some neighbourhood where you could really make a go of it. It's no odds to me either way—you take the place, or I sell it and we'll split the money. It's up to you."

Rachel saw the flaw in this at once—if she took the house as her grandmother offered, she would essentially be taking thousands of dollars out of the pockets of both her grand-mother and her father, both of whom could use it. In return for—what? An idea, a dream, of keeping the Holloway name over the door of a corner shop. "I'll talk to Larry," she said. But what was there to say, in the face of a solid offer on the building?

She meant to walk by the shop again on her way home, to see if enough of the dream still lingered around to outweigh the

TRUDY J. MORGAN-COLE

hard cash a buyer could put into their hands. But in the end, it was getting dark and she wanted to start supper. Rather than doubling back to Rabbittown she walked home the more direct way, past Rawlins Cross and down over Prescott Street as the evening fog rolled in from the harbour and covered the city.

RACHEL

Rachel sat next to Nanny Ellen while the racket of *Wheel of Fortune* blared out of Mrs. Stevens's TV. Ellen had never liked to eat meals with the TV on; when she lived at home she used to badger Audrey, who was fond of supper on a TV tray in front of the news, to sit at the table and eat properly, having a conversation. For many years now Nanny Ellen had eaten her meals in the dining room here at St. Luke's, but just in this last year she had complained of being too tired to go down the hall for supper.

Tonight Ellen had her dinner brought in on a tray and ate it in her wheelchair, and Rachel sat with her, chatting as well as they could with the TV on so loud. There was no shortage of family news to bring her up to date on: cousin Kristi was having a baby; Aunt June and Uncle Norm would be home in August for a visit and they were planning a celebration for Ellen's ninetieth birthday. And Rachel and Larry were planning a wedding, but only a simple one, she assured everybody, no big deal.

"Frank said young Frankie will be out of…that place… soon," Ellen told Rachel. She hadn't said the word *jail* since they told her Frankie had gone in there. His case had taken months to come to trial, and when it finally did he got six months.

"Yes, that's what Nan tells me," Rachel said.

"Frank calls me every Friday night at eight. You can set your clock by Frank."

"It's good that he's so reliable," Rachel said. Relations between Frank and the rest of the family were still a little strained; a few months ago he had moved back up to Toronto, and apparently the plan was for Frankie to join him there after his release. Best place for Frankie, Rachel thought. She wondered if her great-grandmother cherished some image of the whole family united, all gathered under the one roof. They would do the best they could with her birthday party when June was home, but real families were not like TV specials. There would always be some Holloway or another missing.

"I hope he's all right in that place," Ellen said, not explaining whether she meant Frank in Toronto or young Frankie in the Pen. Her eyes drifted towards Mrs. Stevens's screen; she was at once annoyed and fascinated by the large screen and the blaring noise of *Wheel of Fortune*. "What have she got on?" she said as Vanna streeled across the screen in one of her glittery ball gowns. "Sure the whole back of it is wide open, she'd catch her death of cold going out like that."

Rachel laughed out loud at the image of Vanna White going out the door into a windy St. John's night and Nanny Ellen telling her to put on a jacket or she'd freeze. Ellen smiled too; she forgot a lot these days but she was still pretty sharp.

"What is it like at the shop, are you busy these days?" Ellen asked. In the little silence she looked at Rachel and her own face fell when she saw her great-granddaughter's

MOST ANYTHING YOU PLEASE

confusion. "Oh, you don't work in the shop, do you?"

Rachel seized gratefully on this, which had the advantage of being true. "No, I don't work in the shop," she said. "Remember, I'm a music teacher?"

"That's right, a music teacher." In fact Rachel had gotten back into doing some of the music therapy stuff on a contract basis this year, but "music teacher" was easier to explain to Ellen so that was what she had settled on. She and Larry had a new album coming out; Ellen liked Rachel's music and cherished the CDs. She listened to them if someone helped her put them in the CD player, and she would often say, "Your grandpa Wes would have liked this."

But Ellen liked to have a proper name to give to someone's job, and whenever anyone said that Rachel was a singer, Ellen said, "Yes, but she teaches music to children as well." Sometimes Ellen would add, "Her father is a singer," although Henry was far less popular and well-known than Larry & Rae. Rachel thought that for her great-grandmother, identifying Henry as a singer was a way of acknowledging that he had failed at normal life, while there was hope for Rachel yet.

Anyway it had gotten them off the subject of the shop. Sometimes Ellen remembered they had sold the shop and the house; other times she talked as if it was still there, Audrey still behind the counter. It was hard to know what to say at those times. Aunt Treese was a great believer in just playing along; if Ellen mentioned the store as if it was still a going concern, Treese was likely to say yes, she just dropped in there the other day and picked up a bag of potatoes. Audrey and Aunt Marilyn, on the other hand, argued that Ellen didn't have dementia, she was only forgetful and it was better to keep her anchored in the real world as much as possible. Audrey would say, "No, remember, Mom, we sold the shop. I'm retired now

TRUDY J. MORGAN-COLE

and I must say it's grand, no worries about opening that place up every morning. The fellow who bought it got the downstairs turned into another apartment and he got them both, upstairs and downstairs, rented out to students from the University. I'm glad to be out of it I don't mind telling you."

You never knew where Ellen's mind was going to go. One time, after they'd been talking for a good half hour about things completely unrelated to the store or young Frankie—Ellen had, in fact, been telling her about a visit she had from Melissa and how Melissa's little girl was cute but very spoiled—she had stared off into space for a few moments and then said, loudly and clearly, "That was a shocking thing, what he did. A terrible thing."

Rachel was sure Ellen was thinking of young Frankie and what he did to the store, and to the family name. "Thank the Lord your father never lived to see it," she added, and Rachel understood this, too. Though her father, Henry, was alive and more or less well, she knew that Ellen was likely to say "your father" to any of her grandchildren or great-grandchildren as well as her own children. It was understood that she meant Wes, the father of them all.

"You'll never guess who I saw the other day," Ellen said. Again, this could go in a number of directions. She was still, as Rachel told everyone, pretty sharp, and often the person she had seen was indeed someone who had been in to visit. But she had been known to confuse TV with real life and once spent most of a visit trying to explain to Rachel how Isaac Hynes, who used to work in the butcher's shop, came in the room every night before she went to bed. The mystery wasn't solved until Audrey and Rachel were both watching *The National* together one night at Audrey and Richard's place, and Audrey realized the striking similarity between Peter

Mansbridge on *The National* and the late Mr. Hynes. So now Rachel just said "Who?" without any idea what to expect.

"That little one you used to go around with. That one Taylor, you know? Haven't laid eyes on her for years, but she was in here the other day."

Oh, another misplaced memory. Rachel still felt a little jab below the breastbone when she thought of Vicky Taylor. Everyone grew away from their high-school friends and it was likely that if there hadn't been any sharp break between them, she and Vicky might not be friends anymore anyway. Still she missed Vicky, regretted how it had all ended. "Poor Dan Taylor," Ellen said aloud, echoing Rachel's thoughts. "I don't suppose his wife and youngsters ever got over that. But of course I said nothing about that to the little one when she was in."

"What was she in for? Just to say hello?" Rachel wanted to play along, to imagine a world where Vicky Taylor might walk through the door and they might renew their friendship.

"She's with one of the churches," Ellen said. "Church of England, I think. Did you know they got lady ministers now?"

This was so unexpected, so unlike anything Ellen might come up with to account for an imaginary visit from a long-vanished neighbour, that it gave Rachel a moment's pause. She asked one of the RNs if there was a list anywhere of the chaplains from the different churches who visited the nursing home. It took some time to dig up the list, but the nurse found it at last, a typewritten, many-times-folded piece of paper in a drawer. Under "Anglican" three names were listed, one of which was the Reverend Victoria Mills. Mills could be a married name, or Victoria could be a sheer coincidence, of course.

It was not, in fact, a coincidence, though it took Rachel a while to track her down. "I'm half afraid," she admitted to Larry. "It's been years. But I've always wondered what happened to her. An Anglican minister is the last thing I would have guessed. I'd have thought of topless dancer or corporate CEO before I'd have come up with that one."

"Well, you don't know for sure it's her," Larry said.

Finally Rachel dropped by the chaplaincy office on one of her visits and saw that each of the visiting chaplains had a little pigeonhole there, and she dropped in a note for the Reverend Victoria Mills to ask if she used to be Vicky Taylor from Hennebury Place. They met by accident, in the hallway outside someone else's room when Rachel had gone to get her great-grandmother an ice cream bar from the freezer near the nurse's station.

"Rachel," said the ash-blonde woman. They were the same age, of course, but Vicky looked more adult, like a proper grown-up in a nice blouse and skirt and heels. The clerical collar was very discreet, peeking out at the neck of her navy blue blouse. "I got your note, I've been meaning to call," Vicky said, which Rachel guessed was a polite lie.

"Nanny said you'd been in to see her. I mean she said it was you, but she gets confused sometimes, and I—you know, I hadn't heard anything about you in years so I didn't think...and the name..."

"Mills was my married name," Vicky said. "I'm not married anymore. I only moved back here just over a year ago. You're doing well though—my sister Karen told me she saw you perform at the Folk Festival. She sent me one of your CDs."

"Yeah, it's been...um, you know, music is a hard business, kind of, but my...Larry's very talented, and very focused on getting our stuff out there, so I guess I've been lucky that way. How about you, how did you...?" Rachel waved her hand vaguely towards the clerical collar, and Vicky put a hand to her throat and laughed.

"Oh, that's a long story. I know it's not what you'd expect, but...well, we should go have a drink sometime and I'll tell you all about it. No, really, we should. I'd like to catch up. I feel bad about the way we drifted apart, but, you know, it was a really rough time. I wasn't thinking all that much about other people."

If they'd met in the mall or something, that might have been it—the way you say you're going to catch up, and exchange phone numbers, and then never see each other again. But because Vicky did have a regular visiting schedule at St. Luke's, their paths crossed often enough that it eventually made sense for them just to meet up and have that drink. Sometimes, Rachel knew, re-connecting with an old friend gave you just enough material for one evening over drinks: that had been the way when she met up with Sharla on a trip to Halifax. But it wasn't like that with Vicky. Something of what made them click together all those years ago was still there, and one drink turned into an occasional evening out together.

"So it works out kind of nice that you have a friend who's an actual priest," Larry said. "I mean, Anglican, but still."

Rachel was at the sink washing their supper dishes. They owned the Gower Street house now, more or less—she used the money Audrey gave her from the sale of the house to put a solid down payment so that the mortgage was no more than what their rent used to be. They rented out the top floor, and someday, if they ever had money, they planned to do the place up properly. A room on the first floor that used to be a parlour was now a studio suitable for their own practice and their students' lessons. They had talked over all the possibilities when they got the money, but without the connection to the old store in Rabbittown, Rachel found she wasn't actually that interested in owning a business. What she really wanted was a home.

"Why, you think I need a good influence in my life or something?" she asked.

"No, I think we need someone to marry us. I mean sure, Paddy offered to do it, he claims he's some kind of minister but I'm pretty sure this is something he wrote away for, had to send in six box tops." Paddy was Larry's younger brother. "My mother's going to be crying anyway if it's not a proper mass with a real priest, but maybe an Anglican minister will be better than nothing."

"You think I should ask Vicky to marry us?" It wasn't a bad idea, but it also wasn't what was on Rachel's mind at the moment. When she thought about reconnecting with Vicky, picking up those loose threads and weaving them into the pattern of her adult life, she thought about other loose ends. "I'm going over to see Henry tonight," she told Larry.

"Cool, I've got some CD's I want to bring over."

"I'll take them for you. I mean, if it's OK—I just kind of want to talk to him alone."

"Sure." Rachel had always been glad that Larry got on so well with her father, mainly because it meant she rarely had to be alone with Henry. But Larry didn't seem surprised that, out of the blue, she wanted to go visit Henry on her own.

After the dishes were cleared away she walked up to his place, which was only a couple of blocks from the old store, a basement apartment on Salisbury Street which Rachel thought was the dingiest place on earth. It seemed to suit Henry, though. On the step outside his apartment door she paused, wondering if she should have asked him to meet her down at Hava Java for a coffee or something. But no. She'd been putting off this conversation—they both had—ever since he came home. Nearly three years. But it was time to talk.

Rachel knocked on her father's door.

AUDREY

"You look lovely," said Richard. "For all the worrying you did about it."

In the end, Audrey went to the Model Shop and said, "Grandmother of the bride, but the bride's not wearing white, she got some kind of long hippie skirt on, and the wedding is in Bannerman Park." And the woman at the Model Shop had exactly the right dress for that. Richard looked lovely in a gray suit with a nice dark red tie. If Rachel and Larry and all their musician friends wanted to show up looking like a bunch of hobos, that was their business. If they wanted to get married in Bannerman Park when there was rain in the forecast, that was their worry. Audrey had a lovely dress and a handsome man by her side, and that was all she needed to bring to the party.

Despite the forecast, it didn't rain. They pulled into the parking lot at one-thirty to find a crowd of Rachel and Larry's friends putting up folding chairs, and a girl playing the violin up in the bandstand. It was overcast and windy, but there were a few slivers of blue in the sky. Maybe Rachel would be the bride the sun shone on after all. Audrey and Richard sat in the front row, their chairs marked out by ribbons. The rest of the family arrived: Alf and Treese in the van with Ellen and her wheelchair; Marilyn and George; June and Norm; the various cousins. A whole rowdy bunch of Larry's relatives with one elderly lady who raised her cranky voice saying, "What kind of a wedding is this, why didn't they have it at St. Patrick's?" Hearing the old cat complain made Audrey stubbornly determined to have a good time, no matter how queer a wedding it was.

There was a bunch more of Rachel and Larry's friends, and young Vicky Taylor in one of them Anglican priest's robes. Neither Audrey nor Ellen was completely sure that Vicky could be a real minister, but Rachel insisted she was going to marry them, and like the outdoor venue and everything else, she was determined to have her way.

Henry, who had refused to put on a suit but was wearing a decent, black button-down shirt with clean jeans, came and sat next to Audrey and Richard. Everybody was settled now, the violin girl joined by a couple of more players as the music built up a bit louder. And here they came down the path, Rachel and Larry hand in hand. She wouldn't have her father walk her down the aisle; that was foolishness, she told Henry. "I'm a grown woman. Nobody's giving me away. Larry and I are coming together to get married, that's the only way it makes sense." Rachel looked down at them as she passed and Audrey remembered that she had also added, "If I was going to have anyone give me away it'd be Nan—you know that."

Well. That was as it should be, Audrey thought. She'd feel foolish actually walking her down the aisle, or the path or whatever, but Rachel said it was her place to do it, and that was good enough.

musical interlude

HENRY HOLLOWAY

—Now, this is a song my grandfather, Wes Holloway, used to sing, and I imagine Rachel might have heard it when she was so little she didn't even know it was getting tucked away in her memory. But it's the song she asked me to sing today, and it's a pleasure to sing it for two young people who finally managed to sight their heart's delight.

I worked over that intro a bit, let me tell you. There's a lot I'd like to say, and a lot I can't say, about the song and the reason she chose it, about me and Rachel and all that water under the bridge. But she's here now, hand in hand with Larry, vows said and everyone watching us. And this is the one thing she wanted me to do at her wedding.

Play the first chord, lean in to the mic.

Ye ladies and ye gentlemen, I pray you lend an ear
While I locate the residence of a lovely charmer dear ...

It's no lie. This was one of Pop's old songs, and maybe that's where Rachel first heard it. As for the other reason she wanted it, well, that's between the two of us. What it took for her to finally break down and ask about Stella! And what did I have to tell her, after all these years? That she was pretty, and clever, and I loved her once, and she kind of fell apart after having a baby at sixteen. Like anyone might.

How can you be so cruel to part me from my love?
Her tender heart beats in her breast as constant as the dove.

—She loved you.
That's what I told Rachel, and I'm almost sure it's true.
She told me about the song, how it was like a charm for her. I never let on that Audrey got it wrong, that it was Outer Cove and not Logy Bay, a few miles further down the road, where Stella drove the car off the cliffs. She's Rachel's Star of Logy Bay, and if a girl can't have even one memory of her mother, she might as well have a song.

And if she can't have a father with enough sense and guts to stick around and rear her up, well, she had something better. She had a grandmother, a whole family, who stepped in and did the job instead. I might not be much of a father or much of a singer, if it comes to that, but if it's what she wants, I'll sing that old song for her today, for two people who are far better musicians than I could ever have dreamed of being. In the end, I never had that much to give, but this is what she asked me for.

May the heavens above shine down their love
On the Star of Logy Bay.

coda

SOMEONE WILL ENTER
THE PEARLY GATES

RACHEL AND ELLEN

Someone will enter the pearly gates
By and by, by and by

I've been singing to her, though I don't know if she hears me.
In the last few days her face has changed. It's as if a switch has
been turned off, though the switch that keeps breath going into
and out of her lungs is still on. Until Wednesday, I could still
see a light in her eyes, a smile when I walked into the room.
Now I sit by, press the button to adjust the height of the bed
to where I can comfortably lean on it and take her hand, and
Nanny Ellen doesn't stir or mumble or open her eyes. A nurse
looks into the room, smiles.

    —No change since yesterday. We gave her a little shot of
morphine for the pain, when we were washing and changing
her this morning, she seemed a little uncomfortable.

Something for the pain. Does it even matter who comes to visit? Can she hear, or sense, anyone nearby? Audrey left an hour ago; Aunt Marilyn is coming in later. Between us all, Nanny Ellen hasn't been alone since the stroke on Monday that left her unable to speak clearly or swallow.

I pull my chair in closer to the bed, take her thin hand. Such a cliché, to say that an old woman's scrawny hand is claw-like, but that's how it feels, all bone. Everything stripped bare. She's like that all over, such a tiny little woman, even the white hair covering her scalp looking superfluous now. It's all bone underneath, really, and the closer she comes to death the more clearly you can see that.

I only sing to her if no-one else is here. Weird. It's not like I'm embarrassed; singing is what I do for a living, after all. But there's a strange intimacy to it that makes it completely different from singing on a stage in front of a few hundred people.

I dig back deep in memory for the songs she sang when I was little. Nanny Audrey used to have the radio or records on most of the time, but in the spaces between, Nanny Ellen would sing hymns. Those were my lullabies, hymns from hymnbooks so old even the churches don't use them anymore.

> *Someone will enter the pearly gates*
> *By and by, by and by,*
> *Taste of the glories that there await,*
> *Shall you? Shall I?*
> *Shall you? Shall I?*

If you'd asked me at gunpoint, I don't think I would have been able to recall the words of that hymn, but now, as I'm singing, one line follows the other.

A haunting tune and old, old words. As old as Nanny Ellen, probably. She is ninety-five, dying on the cusp of a new century, having lived through almost every year of the old one.

Now that I'm singing them over and over, the words of this hymn are actually kind of weird. Such confidence in the existence of heaven, pearly gates, streets of gold, and whatever. But so unsure about who's going to end up there. *Shall you?* OK, well, you might not be certain about whether anyone else will make it to heaven. Where will *you* spend eternity, and all that. But why the *Shall I?* Shouldn't you *know*, if you're among the faithful, that those pearly gates will swing open for you?

Someone will gladly his cross lay down
By and by, by and by
Faithful approved shall receive a crown…

Lay this down, now. It's getting heavy, carting it around all day.

The cart has *Holloway's* painted on the side. Pulling it up Rankin Street, full of potato sacks. It's heavy, after so long, and it must be nearly tea-time.

Johnny rides on top of the bags. He'll be big enough to pull it someday. Will he? I want to lay it down now. He's getting heavy. It's getting heavy. Go inside and put my feet up. I've been all day behind this counter.

They brought Johnny to me the other day. He was small again, I could hold him in my lap like I used to. All wrapped in a blanket. I kissed the top of his little head. Another redhead, like my Wes when he was young.

Singing hymns in Sunday night meeting. *Someone will*

TRUDY J. MORGAN-COLE

enter the pearly gates. Over the edge of the hymnbook I see that redheaded boy, Wes Holloway, looking back at me, brazen as brass. Mother says don't encourage him. He waits after church to walk me home.

~

The round skull so clearly visible beneath Nanny's white wisps of hair, under the shining fragile skin. All bone underneath, and after this…what? Pearly gates? What would she say if I could ask her now—Shall you enter the pearly gates? Shall I?

—I shall, but I'm not so sure about you, Rachel.

But no, she wouldn't say that. It wasn't her way to be harsh in her judgement. She prayed and worried over all her wandering children, but she never condemned.

Ellen's breaths are shallow, dry and fast. She could die any minute now. I ought to call one of the grown-ups: Audrey, or Aunt Treese. I'm thirty-four years old, I'm a mother myself now, and there's still some little part of me looking for a grown-up to take care of things. Will it always be this way?

Each breath so light, it's hard to guess when the last one might be. I switch to a different tune, another half-remembered hymn. Still leaning in to try to get close enough to Ellen's ear, though there's no hint that she can hear.

One thing to be grateful for: I brought John Henry in a few weeks ago, when she was still well enough to see him and smile. I held him in her lap, and she put her lips against his little head, his little wisps of ginger hair. He was a month old.

It was Larry's idea to call him John Henry. His father's name, my father's name, and a song title to boot. It was perfect. I told Nanny Ellen the name and she repeated it with an approving nod.

—John. Johnny. She said it over and over, sounded so happy.

—She likes it because it's a good, old-fashioned name, I told Larry. Melissa's children are called Braedyn and Maddyson. She loves them but she never knew what to make of the names.

That moment, her kissing the baby's head, comes back again as I kiss her wispy white hair. I see how alike they are: skin light as onion-skin paper over the bone beneath, though John Henry's skin is like smooth silk and Nanny Ellen's is creased with a thousand wrinkles.

They're the same because neither of them can talk, each is full of experience, past or future, that they can't put into words. I hold John Henry and I think, *All of life, folded up inside that little head, waiting to unfold.* Everything he'll ever do—first argument, first day at school, first kiss, first heartbreak.

And it's the same here, the same and the opposite. All her life lived already. Love and marriage, children born and dying, a corner shop, a day's work, prayers and tears. Folded away, tucked back inside where she can never speak about it again. All of life, folded up and put away so small.

TRUDY J. MORGAN-COLE

ACKNOWLEDGEMENTS

John Newton, "Amazing Grace" (1779). Hank Williams, "I'm So Lonesome I Could Cry" (MGM, 1949). Willie Nelson, "Crazy" (1961) performed by Patsy Cline on *Showcase* (Decca, 1961). G.W. Hunt, "Old Brown's Daughter" (circa 1878). Bob Willis and His Playboys, "New San Antonio Rose" (Okeh, 1940). Jerry Leiber and Mark Stoller, "Hound Dog" (1952) performed by Elvis Presley (RCA, 1956). Bobby Newcomb, "Sweet Forget Me Not" (1877). Merle Haggard, "Mama Tried," from *Mama Tried* (Capitol, 1968). Marty Robbins, "El Paso" from *Gunfighter Ballads and Trail Songs* (Columbia, 1959). Mark Walker, "The Star of Logy Bay" (circa 1900). James McGranahan, "Shall You? Shall I?" (1887).

Every effort has been made to trace copyright holders and to obtain their permission for the use of copyright material. The publisher apologizes for any errors or omissions in the above list and would be grateful if notified of any corrections that should be incorporated in future reprints or editions of this book.

AUTHOR'S NOTE

I grew up in, and still live in, Rabbittown, the network of rabbit-warren-like streets in the centre of St. John's where this novel takes place (yes, I've heard all three of the explanations Audrey gives Doris for the name of the neighbourhood, and I believe all three are equally likely to be correct). Over the years, I've discussed with many friends the fact that, when we were growing up in the 1970s, there was a family-owned convenience store on every corner, most of which have since disappeared. *Most Anything You Please* is the novel that grew out of those memories and conversations.

The Holloway family in this book is engaged in two pursuits I've never followed, but have been an enthusiastic consumer of: running a corner shop and making music. Many thanks to all the friends and readers who shared with me their memories of owning, working in, or shopping at corner stores, both in St. John's and in other places. Thanks also to Chris Dreidzic and Paul Kinsman for answering some questions and checking details about the local music scene and the business of performing. For answering my questions about Frankie Junior's contribution to the family business, I am grateful to Inspector Paul Woodruff and Superintendent Marlene Jesso of the Royal Newfoundland Constabulary.

If you're as obsessive a fan of Hank Williams, Senior, as Audrey is, you'll note that Audrey hears Hank performing "I'm So Lonesome I Could Cry" at the Hayride in August 1948, more than a year before he released the song. I allowed myself this small historical inaccuracy on the grounds that it's possible a musician might choose to perform a song live before recording it, though there's no record that Hank did perform this song at that time, and I think it's unlikely he did. I hope readers will allow me a little leeway with history here. And while I'm talking about Hank Williams, I'd like to take a moment to thank the person who uploaded the entire audio recording of his funeral to YouTube. The Internet age is truly a wonderful time to be writing historical fiction.

As always, I have nothing but gratitude to my family—Jason, Chris, and Emma—for their love and support. To my dad, Don Morgan, and my aunt, Bernice Morgan, not only for the love and support but for reading an early version of the manuscript and sharing memories of St. John's in the 1940s and 1950s. To Tina Chaulk and Jennifer Morgan for reading and offering critiques, and to them and the rest of the Strident women— Nat, Lori, and Christine—for always being there, making me laugh, and providing my real-life and online growlery.

One final note: sad as I am about the decline of corner stores, I am equally happy that this era has seen the rise of the neighbourhood coffee shop. (We still need one in Rabbittown). A hearty thanks to the staff of all the coffee shops in which I have written pieces of this book. Your service to the arts community has not gone unnoticed; we salute you.

ALSO BY
TRUDY J. MORGAN-COLE

*By the
Rivers of Brooklyn*

That Forgetful Shore

A Sudden Sun

TRUDY J. MORGAN-COLE is a writer and teacher who lives in St. John's, Newfoundland. Her previous books include *By the Rivers of Brooklyn* (2009), *That Forgetful Shore* (2011), and *A Sudden Sun* (2014).